INTERSECT

ALMOST A CHRISTMAS STORY

COPYRIGHT © 2021 JB WALL

All rights reserved. Without limiting the rights under copyright, no part of this publication may be reproduced, stored in or introduced into a retrieval system, or transmitted in any form or by any means (electronic, mechanical, photocopying, recording or otherwise) without the prior written permission of both the copyright owner and the publisher of this book.

Cover photograph by RT Wall

Intersect: Almost a Christmas Story is a work of fiction. Names, characters, places and incidents are either the product of the author's imagination or are used fictitiously and any resemblance to actual persons, living or dead, events, businesses, companies, or locales is purely coincidental.

ISBN: 9798488767546

JB WALL

TO RON

Chapter 1

The touch of skin was on Lynn's mind, as they walked past the shops and numerous small diners on Denman Street. With Toque she strolled, feeling quite euphoric with their arms around each other's waists. But Lynn was wanting more. And then there was Joe trailing behind. Lynn could not resist trying to cop a more intimate feel so slid her hand under the back waistband on Toque's slacks, resting her full hand on Toque's bare butt. Meanwhile, Joe increased his grumbling, though before his tone reached full volume, Toque removed her arm from around Lynn's waist and wriggled herself free and moved a half-step ahead.

Toque felt a little out-of-sorts, much like the time of year. Although it was barely past Remembrance Day, and just couple of weeks past Halloween, shop decorations were changing to those for Christmas. It didn't seem right that pumpkins still sat in doorways and the poppies hadn't even been tossed when every third or fourth shop was already displaying blinking white or multi-coloured Christmas lights. Some businesses even had windows painted with cartoonish holly, bobbled trees, candy-canes, reindeers, and Santa Clauses.

And then there was her issues: very personal issues.

Up ahead, at the lights on Georgia, a man and his dog on a lead were approaching.

"Hey Brock," yelled Toque, as she waved a little too vehemently, stepping further forward to distance herself from her all-too-friendly cliff-climbing mates. Yet as she waved, she tried to dodge her not-so subliminal attraction to this man down the street.

Rex strained on his lead, anxious to have new hands to lick.

Brock had seen the three of them before he heard Toque's call and sensed the stirring inside that he tried to rein in more times than he'd care to admit.

He regarded the three approaching. Toque was wearing her trademark piece of clothing: a toque, dark brown for the day, along with her navy-blue climbing pants and pastel-blue long-sleeved T-shirt topped with a greenish-blue fleece vest.

Her companion, Lynn, was wearing beige khakis with a red plaid shirt over a white T-shirt while the other friend, Joe, wore similar pants and shirt, though his was blue plaid over black.

At first, recognizing his work partner, Brock first locked down the emotions that were way too close to the surface, and put on his usual smile for Toque: that of a gender-neutral buddy. But in no time, the frown of wariness visited his features when he noticed the proximity of Lynn and Joe as they moved in on Toque.

"Hey," Brock called back, trying to act casual, "What are you doing in this neck of the woods?"

As Brock hurried his pace, so did Joe, who soon stood by Toque's side while he draped his arm over her shoulders, so that his hand and fingers rested suggestively just above one of her perfectly-proportioned breasts.

Toque flushed. "We were just getting over the crazy amount of snow that shut down today's climb up the Grind."

Joe attempted to pull Toque a little closer and she wriggled in the opposite direction.

Lynn, unimpressed, from the other side, re-engaged her arm around Toque's midriff, again tucking the fingers of one hand under Toque's waist-band.

Toque turned redder – in fact, crimson might best describe her complexion.

Rex happily wagged his tail and licked Toque's hand that had fallen forward as she nudged away from her too-amorous friends.

"Yeah, we've just finished having a couple of beers and a late lunch," explained Toque as she squirmed to release herself.

Both Lynn and Joe increased their grip.

"But I was thinking about dropping by ..."

"What, without me?" cried Lynn.

"Or me?" tuned in Joe.

"Well, yes, sorry, but I need to see Brock in relation to work ... I'll see you two in a few days at the next climb, weather permitting," stammered Toque as she unsuccessfully tried to break free of their grips.

Lynn and Joe held their ground.

Brock understood immediately that something was going on with Toque as he grimaced and then with an ironic tone remarked, "Hey you got to realize that the best friends of all, are those who support each other, listen to one another, and in your cases, climb with each other, but most important, when a friend needs some space – you flock off – like a round of robins when the wind changes direction."

Joe reddened. "That's no analogy!"

Lynn's face showed angry agreement.

Brock paused. "Okay. A better analogy? How about once the switch plate has been re-set, the other trains move onto another track."

"Aren't you the poet," grumbled Joe.

Toque managed a relieved smile as she petted Rex and said, "Don't worry about it, guys. It's just a little brevity. After all, Brock's nick-name is Getzlaff. But Brock, and I just need to talk."

"On your day off?" questioned Lynn.

Brock looked serious as he said, "Sometimes it's really important that we do."

Lynn was suspicious, glanced at Joe with his hands hanging empty and muttered, "Well, I might as well be off to the Christian Climbers Elemental Assemblage."

Joe, though still disappointed, spoke to Lynn, "I saw your car when I parked. As we're on the same block, we might as well head off together."

"Okay, let's go," agreed Lynn.

But before Lynn and Joe left, each had one last attempt at eyeing up Toque, undressing her with their eyes, as if she were a prize to be won. Then after a rather indecent ogle, the two climbing friends left, side by side. They were less than a few feet away when with a giggle, Lynn pushed her hand down the back of Joe's pants and pinched a cheek.

Joe straightened with surprise. "What the hell!" But then his face took on the appearance of understanding and he laughed and added, "Why not try the front? Use both hands if you want."

And the two of them hee-hawed as they headed off together.

With that, Brock and Toque both seemed a little relieved as they turned to the opposite direction – and moved off along Denman.

Once they were out of earshot, Brock asked, "So what in the non-
activity of our recent shifts was it you were wanting to work out?"

But without even a word, Brock could see that Toque had suddenly become less harried. Her face showed just a glimmer of a smile as she rolled her eyes in a gesture of a mutual understanding. Nothing to discuss. They just couldn't. She knew it. He knew it.

Then both of their faces took on an almost visible positive expression.

Chapter 2

Brock, Toque and Rex crossed the eight lanes of traffic at the light at Georgia and Denman, and reached the corner adjacent to the marina, when they heard their names being called. Through the snow that was starting to fall, they scanned around, soon seeing the Vasiliev family at the bus stop nearest Stanley Park, just a couple of hundred feet west of them.

The friendly waves of the family could not be ignored.

They're the best of New Canadians, thought Brock, *But it's hard to get over her brother; he was a real piece of work.*

But Rex, sans any form of inhibition, strained at his lead, knowing that there was the potential of more friendly hands that could pet him.

But before they could move another step, the cacophonous roar of the horn of a metro bus blared continuously, and was so deafening that it could have awakened the whole city. The bus tore through its lane alongside the busy traffic. Then, in a doomed effort at pulling into the bus zone, jumped the curb, and could have easily killed Brock and Toque.

As the bus reached a standstill on the sidewalk and boulevard, resting at a perpendicular angle to the traffic, front and back doors flew open. The first to exit was the bus driver. He looked like the actor who played Captain Picard and as if he discovered that the entire cast had been bingeing on pork and beans. The driver yanked off his uniform jacket, threw it onto the ground, and yelled, "That's it! I quit!" as he stormed off towards the intersection through which Toque and Brock had just passed.

"I'd better contact the transit police," volunteered Toque.

"Good call. I can't see that anyone could be hurt but transit will have to deal with this bus."

Next out of the bus was a business man wearing a black suit, clearly on his way home from a management-type job. But he was swearing, as he followed in the direction of the bus driver. As he passed Brock and Toque, a frog jumped from his brief case and onto the snowy pavement. Then half a dozen frogs bounded from the back door of the waylaid bus.

Next came a mother with two small boys, one in each hand. Each boy dragged his feet, exclaiming, "I want to go back! I want a pet frog!" The mother strained to rein them in.

Next, five frogs leaped out, almost getting trod upon by the next three ex-passengers: three teenage girls, with face expressions discordant with their well-tuned sense of fashion.

"Oh gross! One touched my hand! It was slimy!"

"One landed on my shoulder!"

"One landed on my knee! Ugh!"

A hippie-looking man next exited, with numerous frogs jumping alongside, though one was clinging to the back of his packsack. And yet another peered out from a well-used bed-roll. But this man cared only about the bus passage, asking, "Where's the driver? I need to get to the shelter in time to put in my name."

Then exited even more frogs along with a woman in an unbuttoned coat, tugging at her loose blouse as some random shape bounced around underneath. She screamed as she tore the blouse open, and a much more frightened amphibian planted his rubbery little toes on the ample bosom and took flight.

"What the hell!" cursed Brock as another passenger exited: a youth of about fourteen with a sketchbook and a large box. Toque hurried to block the teen from getting any further away, and introduced themselves, "We're both cops. What's going on?"

"I was out drawing trains. It's my theme for my art class: see my sketchbook."

Brock and Toque looked at the book as the teen flipped through about forty pages of train drawings. Then, with his voice trembling with the fear that he'd been caught red-handed, the teen continued, "And I found this box."

"And?"

Before the teen answered, one last passenger exited, an unwashed ne'er-do-well, with long oily hair, a stringy grey beard and saggy clothing long past its prime. In his hands he coddled a small frog. The ne'er-do-well soon spied the discarded jacket, tossed his own relic to the side, pulled on bus driver's former apparel, and with a raspy voice called out, "All aboard!" as he dropped the frog into a side pocket and hurtled off.

Brock and Toque watched and did nothing, knowing that the uniform jacket had just passed its best-before date.

They refocussed on the teen who continued his explanation, "I opened it, removed some packing and stuff, and saw the frogs in little plastic containers. I thought they were unconscious but might come to life if I gave them some air and then brought them home. So, I dumped them from the containers and back into the box."

"And they got out in the bus because …" asked Brock.

"Well," the teen continued, then embarrassed, "I thought I'd have a look once the bus was going. But as soon as I opened the box, they started jumping all over the place. I…I…I…"

By this time, the Vasilievs were there. With a noticeable accent, the mother cried, "These frog will die in the snow: we must tries to catch them!"

Brock and Toque's faces showed agreement and in no time the two Vasiliev adults and their two pre-schoolers, who were screaming with joy, rushed about, catching escaped frogs.

While this was going on, Brock tried to calm the clearly anxious teen. "This is probably just a shipment misplaced. But give me all your contact information – just in case."

As one, then another, then another frog was captured, the Vasiliev boy asked, "Are they ours?"

The mother smiled, but shook her head. "No, dear. I keep them in this zipper carry bag till we get them to the aquariums. They will be warm and safes inside."

Then, as Toque and Brock concluded their talk with the teen, Yana, the mother of the family, made a surprising, though possibly irrelevant, connection. "Constables Brock and Burden, I couldn't believe it: first a robbery of all the insect sample at University and this – now!"

"Good to see you too! I'm not sure what you're talking about, though. But you think the frogs are related to another crime?"

Yana paused. "Yes, then maybe, the insects were to be a food for the frogs. Maybe the thief didn't know what frogs eat, and some of the stolen samples would be the food. But the also, yes, glad to see you, too."

"I don't know about a robbery at any university," mused Toque.

"Nor I," added Brock, "And Yana, how do you know about all this?"

Alik, the father of the family, clarified, "Yana now has a job in a university science lab that was recently robbed."

"Strange coincidence, perhaps," remarked Toque as Brock's face expressed agreement.

Alik continued, "But other than the robbery issue, she loves the role. It's just part time but it works great for us."

"Awesome," praised Toque, "We'll have to hear more about the robbery before we go but I've got to say that I'm really happy to see the four of you. It's been awhile!"

Alik smiled and extended his hand. "But what a crazy incident! Frogs on a bus! Who would believe it? But Constables Burdon and Brock, like Yana, I have to say that it is so good to see you. How have you been?"

Brock also reached out and smiled back. "I've been well, thanks."

Toque too, smiled. "Yeah, I'm so happy to see you four looking so well! But ..." Toque's smile turned to confusion as she glanced at Yana's stomach.

Yana smiled with a glow. "Yes, everything's are good. You can see from this stomach that we will have the new family member pretty soon now."

"Congratulations! But, forgive me for asking, but weren't you pregnant last time we saw you a little over a year ago?"

Alik's hand reached for his wife in a gesture of profound sadness coupled with sympathy.

Yana's head hung as her pained voice spoke, "I was. Unfortunately, a babe is lost. God saw fit that he takes that unborn before it has to face this life we live."

"Oh, I am so sorry for your loss," empathized Toque, as she touched Yana's shoulder, in sympathy.

Brock's eyes paused on Toque's hand, her hand on Yana's shoulder. For a fleeting second, he wished that hand on his shoulder ... but only for a moment.

"It was really rough," explained Yana, "The doctor said that I won't conceives again."

"Yet here we have another on its way. It is a miracle! The Lord has come to our aide! We are so thankful that we may yet have a third child."

"Yes, that is the blessing, I am sure," agreed Yana.

Then after a silence of what seemed like an hour, but was, in fact, just a minute or so, Toque tried to be supportive of their lives by asking, "What brings your family to this area of town, anyway?"

Alik smiled as he began to disclose the details of their leisure time. "Now, in every way, our lives are better. Today was like so many other volunteer experiences. It was like a gift to us!"

"Oh, what were you up to?"

"We've been volunteers at the Vancouver Aquarium for a number of months now. Today was the day to help handicapped children get around and enjoy the aquarium. We were matched up with another family and it seems that by helping, we have each gained a new friend!"

"That's fantastic," applauded Brock.

Alik beamed. "Yes, the volunteer work has been a positive force in our lives."

"That is really impressive," praised Toque, and then continued, looking at Yana, "Especially because I know you were having trouble with learning the English language."

"Well, believe it. Yes, I was and still are taking English class Saturday morning. But I gains more than I expect from a class. The professor and the researcher in my field is husband of my teacher. She connected me."

"What, a professor at one of the local universities?"

"Yes: Capilano University. They got the big grant from the government for the very special project and they needs evening staff."

"Yes, it works great because I can look after little Matvey and Vanna in the evenings," added Alik.

Toque grinned. "I don't know how you do it. Both of you. You've got to be tired – alternating child-minding with working, to say nothing of – in Yana's case, expecting a new one."

"Yeah, I must say, it is tiring – but Alik mainly puts the kids to bed and, as for me, Matvey and Vanna go to daycare three afternoons the week so I do get the little bit of the break," explained Yana.

In the distance they could hear the siren of an approaching emergency vehicle. Probably the transit police and VPD, thought Brock at the same time that Toque also recognized the summoned law enforcers.

But continuing with the conversation, Toque asked, "In Edgemont Village?"

"Exactly. All the worker there are really good but we're especially happy with the woman named Petra because she is also from our homeland and seem to really understand our value and traditions." Yana paused, then continued, "But you'll never guess who also in the day care?"

Brock's eyes clouded over as he remembered Angela, his own infant in arms: smiling, laughing and then, overwhelming his mind, the terrible end.

Brock tried to get a grip on himself and join into the exchange as Toque asked, "Oh who?"

"Do you remember the Lacy White that was in the news two or three years ago? The famous bridge disaster?"

Brock and Toque, almost simultaneously, said, "Of course."

"Her little child, Danielle Klee Wyck, is to the same daycare."

Toque smiled. "I'm glad to hear she's doing well. We were there at her birth."

"What, on the ... Lions Gate?" asked Yana.

Toque looked at Brock and remembered holding him, holding him tighter than she ever thought possible, holding him because their very lives depended on it.

"One and the same," replied Brock.

He flinched, trying to not think of the night he'd almost died: with one failing hand, he'd been hanging over an abyss to black nothingness: his hand-hold was weakening; his limbs and wounds aching and the illness was taking over.

It was Toque who came to help him. It was Toque who saved his life.

But forcing himself to return to the world of now, Brock asked Yana, "So how are you enjoying the work at the university?"

"I cannot believe my luck. I know my English are not perfect but I have science training from back home."

"Yeah, she was a bit of a prodigy before we married. Actually, her whole family has a real talent in sciences, and in commerce."

Brock grimaced. "Yeah, unfortunately, we know about Yana's brother, Borya, and his commerce brilliances."

Yana looked uncomfortable, then tried to maintain her composure as her feelings of great sadness cascaded onto her facial expression, as she quietly said, "The truly great mind on a wrong side."

Alik agreed, "Yes, but he is not here anymore."

Brock grimaced. "Borya might be in hiding, but someone will find him. He's wanted in too many countries to never be caught."

Yana hung her head and Alik turned away, embarrassed at the reminder of their family member who was on the most-wanted lists held by international police forces.

After an uncomfortable pause, Alik tried to re-introduce the topic of his wife's background. "But with Yana, after her science degree, we got married – but back in our home town it was expected that she should then become a home-maker."

Brock nodded, understanding but tempted to not accept the cultural difference, so continued, "So, Yana, what do you do at the university, then?"

"Well, the last day or so, I try to help with cleaning up the mess."

"From the robbery that you mentioned?" asked Brock.

"Yes, we already report to a RCMP!"

Toque interjected, "Oh? I guess it wasn't on our beat – perhaps it was a different time of day."

"It is, er… was very late at night – early morning, actually. We work with the experimental DNA modifications."

"You've got you got to be kidding! Not the with the human brain, I hope!" exclaimed Brock.

Yana managed a patronizing grimace. "You know that would not happening in a university here. We work entirely with the insects."

Brock laughed. "I'm not sure how you could improve on the insect world."

17

"You never know. The lab have some amazing success with combining the DNA of lice and blow flies."

"Don't tell me you've invented lice that flies!" joked Brock.

Yana smiled, then explained, "Not at all. But through the mutation, we have now lice that is larger and with fluorescents colour so they are easiest to see and also to catch."

Toque's eyebrows raised. "Might be an improvement. Not sure, though."

"Yes, I know your point. There are divided opinions about the good or bad of this mutations. But it is the starting point, perhaps to making some change for the better."

Brock sighed. "Sometimes one has to wonder about scientific inquiry."

Yana saw Brock's point and responded, "Of course we have to be careful to not disturbing nature's interrelating cycles."

Toque smiled. "I agree entirely! Judging from the crazy weather caused by global warming, we need to be so careful of our impact on the earth and its resources."

Yana took note of Toque's words, but was clearly anxious about the robbery but at the same time, proud of what the local university had become, as she praised her place of employment, "You would be amazed at the high-tech Capilano University. We are approaching the stage of the world in terms of researches!"

Brock regained his professional demeanor, asking, "Exactly what was stolen?"

"As I say, we reported to a RCMP already. Aquariums, samples, lab stuffs."

"What in blazes could the thieves want with those items?"

"Probably – what you call them – um – planksters."

Toque raised an eyebrow. "Oh, you mean pranksters?"

"Ah, yes, that is it. My English still has the way to go."

Brock shook his head. "Insects and aquariums. I imagine anything living won't be around long if they're left in a truck if the weather stays cold."

Toque agreed, saying, "Hopefully."

"But speaking of that, we'd better go back to the aquariums to drop off these frog," mused Yana.

At that point, a transit police vehicle and a VPD cruiser pulled up. A total of four law enforcement officers joined them. But before anyone spoke, they all looked at Yana's insulated carry-bag decorated with a copy of an Emily Carr forest scene. No one could ignore that the bag had a strange and very noticeable movement bouncing around inside its zippered chamber.

CHAPTER 3

About an hour later, not far from the abandoned bus, and just beyond the line of vision from Brock's boat, Toque paused, thinking to herself, while she gazed at the life-size sculpture of a woman seated on a bench. The bronze figure's handbag was on her lap and open and someone had placed purple winter pansies in it. Absently, Toque reached over and touched the softness of a pansy's petal and then felt all the more alone in the presence of these flowered faces that shared a soul-mate-like companionship never enjoyed by Toque. She glanced down at Brock's boat, took a few dozen steps in the direction of the marina's gate but as soon as she got there, an expression of troubled sadness visited her more-than-attractive features, and she forced herself to walk eastward, into the chilling wind beneath the pale, cold sun.

I should go back to my condo: my empty condo, she thought, and increased her pace. In no time she was in what was like a valley in the dark shadows of the high-rises. Drivers glanced at her while their passengers stared as Toque sauntered onwards, her long legs moving her with such grace that it was as if she was born to illustrate that movement perfected. In the distance she could hear the faint cry of a passing train.

Brock heard the same wail as he sat alone in his vessel's cockpit with his silent cell phone on the seat beside him. But in contrast to Toque, Brock had the companionship of Rex who was curled up at his feet but was already asleep. Brock reached for the rope where he'd tied a bowline knot and examined the knot's perfection as he felt the smoothness of the rounded-off white rope.

It seemed as though just seconds had passed since he'd boarded the *Angel* when he looked up, surprised when he heard a woman's voice, seductively cooing, "Hey handsome, how about teaching me something naughty? That bowline is really sweet!"

Brock looked up and saw a buxom young woman, grinning as she leaned flirtatiously on the teak tow-rail of the *Angel*. He was dumfounded as he acknowledged the presence of this tanned (or was it brown–skinned, he asked himself) dark eyed, red lipped, platinum blond woman who was shaped as if she worked out every day, and almost every minute of every hour.

After a stunned pause, he asked, "You want to learn to tie a knot?"

"Sure! Let's start with that," laughed the woman as she hoisted her jean-clad tight ass onto his deck and sat beside Brock, so close that he could not help inhaling the aura of her cologne – Always Amorous – which was like the scent of an evening in the tropics wherein the plants emit dense perfumes so erotic that the combined fragrances were considered by most to be the embodiment of foreplay more extraordinary than could be imagined.

"I'm Delila – I'm living on that Golden Hind over on the next pier."

"I'm Brock. So … you want to learn how to tie a bowline?"

Delila moved closer so that her thigh was right up against Brock's. His leg immediately warmed, though his mental bewilderment was mixed with an acute anxiety from the past.

He remembered his deceased wife, April, their budding romance, their wedding vows: the most amazing woman that could ever exist. A woman and marriage that was too good for this world. If he struggled, he could mentally revive the beyond-our-mortal-contact marriage with his soul-mate who, in the world beyond the physical, would share their love forever in the post-earthly halls of flawless, unblemished relationships: the only place pure enough that unabridged devotion could last eternally. That marriage would never really end: instead it would live on as perfection – never marred by time's cruel hand.

But on this day Brock had to fight with palpable reality. He desperately wanted to insert some distance between his leg and that of Delila but the male ego, the testosterone, and the biting mortal aloneness held him at bay. Sometimes Rex just couldn't fill the empty gap of human isolation.

"Let's see that knot," murmured Delila as she put both hands on top of Brock's and let her thumbs under long red fingernails caress the bowline that had joined the innocent and sexless rope ends. In spite of the cool weather, her purple leather jacket was open and, her ample breasts were not at all hidden under a white skin-tight T-shirt. Her breasts spilled out and pressed up against Brock's arm. There was no doubt. These breasts were the real thing: not implants.

"That's really something," purred Delila, and as she reached her hand onto his thigh just near the growing bulge in his pants, asked, "Do you have something else you'd like to show me?"

"Do you want a beer?" asked Brock almost stammering.

Delila threw her head back with a laugh and said, "Sure, bring two – and then bring what-ever you'd like."

Brock stumbled into the galley, his motion impaired by arousal, opened his fridge, downed a beer just as Delila glanced at Brock's phone and tossed it to him adding, "And while you're at it, let's have a little privacy."

Brock turned off his phone and placed it on the galley counter just before grabbing a couple of beer and a bag of Cheesesnacks. But before seconds passed and just as he was about to climb back into the cock-pit, Delila began the decent into the *Angel*'s cabin.

CHAPTER 4

Just days before, it was a dazzling sunny November morning and as a backdrop to the shinning skyscrapers of Vancouver, British Columbia, the mountains were topped with a frosting of brilliant white snow. Beneath those massive and magnificent dark blue geological forms, and adjacent to Stanley Park, the halyards on the sailboats at Coal Harbor Marina gently knocked against the masts, creating a cheery and animated chatter. There, on board a white and blue-trimmed thirty-eight-foot ketch, made unique by its wooden masts, Brock stood on a seat in his cockpit, tying a bowline on a cord that he'd wrapped around a furled sail. At the base of the cockpit's seat was his faithful friend, Rex, who curiously eyed a spider running towards a drain in the corner. Brock rubbed his hands together to work away the chill, then looked up as he was approached by a neighbor live-aboard, known in the marina community as a "boatie": she was a stout, aging resident. Over her shoulder was slung a mesh bag filled with half a dozen library books.

Brock glanced up at the approaching woman. "Hey, how are you?"

The boatie looked at her feet, a little embarrassed to approach another soul. "Oh, I'm good. I'm sorry, but I think I need thank you for when you saved my life when I was drowning."

"What?" questioned Brock, scratching his head, "I don't think so."

"I'm mortified to tell you how long ago it was and how long it's taken me to approach you. It was over a couple of years ago: it was probably in 2035." She uncomfortably shifted her sac of books, trying to support it on one of her ample hips.

Brock widened his eyes in surprise. "What? Several years ago?"

"Embarrassingly, it was. I would have found it easier to approach you when you first moved here – before you cleaned yourself up and before I was forced into the water. But for quite a while now you've been dressed in clean and ironed clothing: a look that makes you seem much like a professional golfer. You're just not the kind of person who would be my soul-mate, if you know what I mean."

"Oh, come on. A golfer? I can tell you that Rex here would be pretty annoyed if for putting practice I used these cockpit drain holes that are the homes of his friends, the spiders. Plus, the ocean's a little wet for doing any driving, to say nothing of the fact that after one swing, it's always a lost ball."

"Ha! Very funny! But whatever, you did save my life and I must thank you for it. I can't believe that you don't remember it!"

"A few years ago? Maybe it was when there was a real crisis on the force."

"Then you do remember?"

Brock smiled, knowing full well that the event was not going to fade in his memory banks. He feigned a distant recall, saying, "Oh, that! Ah, forget about it; there's nothing for which to thank me."

She looked at him in the eyes: eyes that were the colour of a deep but warm blue ocean under eyebrows that were full and well-formed and felt as if she could almost smile, except for the painful memory of almost drowning and the resulting fight between Brock and the two who assaulted her. "Don't under-rate yourself. You put in a huge effort dealing with those thugs who pushed me into the water."

"It was nothing. Forget it. But by the way, as we're neighbours, we might as well at least know each other's name. I'm Brock."

A smile almost touched the corners of her mouth. "Oh, I'm Rita, and I really am glad to know you. But there is something else …" Rita seemed afraid to speak. She focused on distant waters.

"Yeah? Go ahead," encouraged Brock.

"I kind of hate to bother you with it but …" Rita let the fingers of one hand run along an uneven frayed hem on her army green canvas jacket while she held onto the shoulder strap of the book bag with her other hand. The cover-up didn't meet at the front and hung over her multi-layered mis-matched patterned garments that flowed over her generous form. Her baggy plaid purple skirt hung down to the deck of the dock, almost hiding the orange socks and budget black and white running shoes, which peered out – though mainly when she walked.

"Hey, you're not a bother. What's on your mind?"

"Well, did you know that there was a guy down here asking for you the other day?"

Rex lay down and closed his eyes. Relaxed, he stretched so that one leg touched one end of the cockpit while the other bent as it reached the other side.

"Oh? Did he leave his name? Did he resemble a mannequin?"

"Oh, that guy! No, I haven't seen him for at least a year. Longer, probably. Maybe two years. The person who came by the other day asked that I not mention that he was here."

Brock grimaced and then tried to show no concern while he questioned further, with a feigned casual tone, "Oh? Did he say what he wanted?"

"Not a word."

Brock frowned. "Can you remember what he looked like?"

"Well, he was fair-haired – kind of tall. I can't remember a lot but I think that he might have been easy on the eyes. Oh yeah, he had a light complexion – now that I think about it."

"Do you feel that you might have seen him before?"

"He looked kind of familiar but I can't say for sure. But I think that he had an accent. Yes – I think that he did. In fact, that's probably what triggered the memory of those two thugs that knocked me into the water. The accents sounded similar. Maybe. Not sure. But remembering those two is probably what made me think that I still had to thank you for saving me."

"Possibly. Where do you think his accent originated?"

"Like I said, I just don't know. Possibly eastern Europe? Russia? But honestly, I can't say for sure."

"Was he polite?"

Rita leaned onto the side of the *Angel*, her hand appreciating the smooth varnish on the teak tow-rail as she gently taunted, "Aren't *you* interested in everything!"

"Well, was he?"

"Ah – not really, he treated me like an underling and was really demanding: all in all, he wasn't in the least bit pleasant. It was not a friendly visit."

"How was he built?"

"Well, let me see. I'm pretty sure that he was just over six feet tall."

"Anything else?"

"He was kind of scary – although I wonder if it is just me remembering those other two hoods. But as for this guy, it was just something about his mannerisms that set me off. I remember later thinking that I should have felt more at ease – after all, he was carrying a book-marked Bible ... or maybe it was the Old Testament."

Brock raised an eyebrow. "A bit odd, I guess."

"I thought so." As she spoke, her face colour bleached to that of grey and her voice trembled.

Brock bent towards her, kindly touched her hand, and in a voice as gentle as he could muster, asked, "What *are* you most concerned about?"

Rita's eyes watered and she floundered with her bag. "I hate to seem like I'm over-reacting but he really gave me the creeps. Although he didn't make a specific threat, something about him was both evil and threatening. It felt like he would happily inflict some kind of horror that would be worse than anything I could imagine. In fact, I'd rather drop right here on the pier than have to again face him!"

Anger mixed with concern in Brock's mind though he hid his feelings and offered assurance, "Don't worry. You'll be fine, I'll see to it."

Rita smiled, unsure of his ability to protect, but turned, and lumbered her way along the pier towards her own vessel, carrying her weighty book bag with both hands.

As Brock saw her clamber into her cockpit, he pulled out his cell and said, "Phone Toque." Then, as the phone was just about to dial the last digit of Toque's number, Brock interrupted with, "Cancel call."

CHAPTER 5

Delila flung herself onto what had been the settee in the galley.

Because it had been cold the previous night, Brock had made the seating area near the galley stove into a bunk and upon it lay the rolled up sleeping bag in which he had slept. Delila leaned back, with one arm on the back of the seat, the other on the upright sleeping bag so that her breasts were spread out like sunflowers. One leg was extended midway on the bunk while the other was leaning on the side of what had been a seat so that her thighs were apart ... just enough to be obvious about her unhindered intentions.

Brock leaned forward, handing one of the beers to Delila. "Here you go. As the table's not up, if you want, I'll get you another when you're ready."

"Not a problem," she smiled as she raised the beer to her full lips and slowly licked the rim as she languished on the bunk.

Still standing, Brock paused, trying not to stare.

"Oh, come-on, lean on me," laughed Delila, pulling Brock towards her so that he was soon sitting between her legs.

As he went to have a gulp of his second beer a strange screeching could be heard from outside.

Rex, dozing in the cockpit, rallied himself from his sleep and scanned around, searching for the perpetrator of the screaming. He saw someone and starting barking.

"What the ..." cursed Brock, his arousal fading like that of pansy in the rain.

"Ignore it. Let's have some fun. Close the hatch. Your dog will be fine."

"I can't have Rex barking continuously."

"Let him in then. We can lock him up while we enjoy each other."

Brock frowned as he spoke, "Come here, boy. What's wrong, Rex? Why are you holding back? Dam it, I'll have to go get him myself."

As Brock climbed up the galley's ladder, impaired by an almost-erection, and onto the deck he heard more screeching, only this time he could easily make out the words being screamed.

"Brock! We need to go to the detachment hall! Now!"

Brock looked over at the banks beside the marina and there stood his work partner, still wearing the toque that was dark brown, and frantically waving her arms and calling for his attention.

Almost instantly, Delila's head appeared through the cockpit's hatch and Toque's mouth opened in surprise, not incorrectly guessing at what had been transpiring.

In minutes, Brock and Toque were in his rusty 2019 beat-up bleached-out red four-by-four – a white elephant of a vehicle – being a stick shift with a V8, one black fender and a blue hood over the engine.

"So, what is going on?"

"Dispatch just phoned. They tried you first but your phone was turned off." Toque looked accusingly at Brock.

"Hey, we all have our lives to live."

"I thought that you'd sworn off women!"

"And you – men – *and* women for that matter," added Brock, thinking about Toque's climbing partners.

"Let's just forget it … and deal with the fact that detachment wants us in early."

"Because?"

"Something about a school covered with some sort of red liquid."

"What the hell?"

"I'm telling you now, I don't even want to think about it."

Chapter 6

Three men were adjacent to the Sea Bus arrival zone where they stood under a sheltered drop-off or pick-up waiting area as the premature slush-like-rain filled the air and one of the hundreds of icy puddles on the sidewalk had risen like the tide, and formed an ice-thickened stream working its way onto the concrete floor of the shelter, moving towards Egor and Ras's already soaked canvas sneakers. On the other side of the traffic turn-around three cabbies waited in the designated area in their steamed-up vehicles, anticipating passengers arriving via the Sea Bus. No private vehicles were arriving at this time; the Sea Bus had just left; its passengers dispersed and there would not be another for half an hour.

"A lot of time has passed since we worked together," recalled Ras, pausing as a sense of awkwardness ensued.

"Not long enough, as far as I'm concerned," sneered Borya.

Ras and Egor both frowned. "Still pissed?"

"How could I not be?"

"So why did you bother contacting us again?"

"There are opportunities just passing us by but …"

"But what?"

"Just wondering – how is it that you're not in prison when you both got 'life'?" questioned Borya.

"We have day passes so that we can work."

"I can't believe that this week-kneed prison system has allowed you a second of freedom after you both were given a full sentence."

Egor and Ras continued their explanation, "Yeah, this country is a joke: their excuse is that the city is desperate for workers."

"Because no one can afford to live here. They're desperate for anyone to fill positions."

"What total idiots their governments have been! They managed their real estate assets so poorly that all the workers have left."

"Exactly. And subsequent governments conveniently forget election promises to address the increased housing need."

"Unbelievable! Not only did they not anticipate a problem

from allowing a massive number of residential properties to be sold to people from out of the country, they encouraged the aged to stay at home, taking up valuable space – often homes suited to whole families. Even without encouragement, after the big pandemic, everyone living here wants a single-family home."

"And adding to the lack of availability, is that there was no anticipation that others in Canada want to live here."

"Right! And to add insult to injury, the governments also allowed a massive number to come into the country, money laundering in the real estate market or just using land acquisition as a portfolio item. What it has added up to, is that anyone who goes through the school system here eventually has to move away because the residential areas are already filled. The result is that the city is now full of seniors who have lived here forever or have come here from the rest of Canada and the masses of people from abroad who often don't work or even speak the language, so they can't take jobs even if they want to."

"Lucky for you two that they are so inept. So, we can start working together again?" asked Borya.

"Limited chances – but possible. We have to return to lockup right after work, although there is some room for us to get away – they love their coffee breaks here."

"Plus, they do give us quite a bit of time to come and go – because they are always trying to compensate for one thing or another. And leaving work now and then doesn't seem like much of a problem, either."

Borya questioned further, "Still, I can't believe they're letting you out at all. Are you sure you didn't grease some palms or …?"

"No way. They were totally fooled by our make-believe good behavior."

"Yeah, what a laugh! To make them think that we'd made amends, we went to their Chapel every Sunday, and we even held Bible classes," smirked Egor.

Borya's eyes widened, as if an idea occurred to him. "Any potential workers for us?"

"Possibly. There are a number of people who'd be glad to have their hands on a lucrative project!" said Egor as he laughed and made an obscene gesture as he rubbed his groin.

Borya smiled. "Who'd think there'd be a bonus to being in prison?"

"But anyway, seeing that we have book-keeping experience, we are temporarily working at the headquarters of a huge car insurance company not far from here," explained Egor, gesturing in the direction of just up the roadway.

Looking interested, Borya continued questioning, "How far away?'

"Less than five minutes."

"Is there any likelihood we might be able access their systems?"

"Could be. But what for?"

Borya managed the glimmer of a smile. "Maybe we could find addresses for any potential new drivers who failed the test. That type of person might be marketable … you know … after we've worked them a bit. After all, a flunky is already feeling inept. They'll be vulnerable. And there might be other potential types … but before we get into that, we need to plan how the three of us can get together as a team again."

"But even if there are opportunities, as you say, it is hard to believe that you want Egor and me as part of your crew. You were really intense about being done with us!"

"I was. After all, you are such losers to have gotten caught!" retaliated Borya.

"We had no way of knowing that the Canadian would find our hide-out."

"I did tell you to change locations after one or two uses!"

"We were almost ready to move! But we were having trouble unloading the ugly older one! And who would guess that the intelligence guy would be so fast in figuring it out!"

"Whatever. But what has to happen now is that we form another acquisition team as soon as possible."

Egor and Ras smiled.

Then Egor spoke, "But how? They are slack here, but we do have to make sure that we don't arouse suspicions while we're making the most of the time loop-holes!"

"Of course. But I'm sure we can figure it out. So, you're in?"

32

"In? Just the three of us? We've never been the main designers of the acquisitions (ha ha) and the later deployment."

Borya looked at Egor and Ras as if they were lesser beings, then quickly changed his expression to that of a car salesman about to make a deal. "Don't underestimate yourselves. Plus, children are pretty easy. And, I do plan to have others join our team."

CHAPTER 7

In a white lab with narrow window slots at the top of the walls that showed the darkness outside, Yana stood at a sink washing petri dishes. The air seemed lifeless under the stark white brilliant florescent bulbs built into the institutional drop ceiling.

Her mentor, Professor Ralph Blanchard, entered the lab. Huge dark circles under his eyes spoke of many sleepless nights. Blanchard iterated his bewilderment, "Yana, I cannot understand why someone has stolen all of those eggs and larvae. What could the thieves be thinking?"

"I could understand the theft of bees, if we had them. There are so many problems now with pollination. But the theft of the egg and larvae of other insects? Confusing!"

"I know – the initial stages of insects! What could anyone possibly plan to do with those?"

Yana finished the pile of petri dishes, and regarded the kind, rounded face of the quiet academic scientist, his appearance pristine as usual: his dark bald head shining over a close-cropped and fuzzy fringe of grey hair and his rounded belly showing beneath his lab coat. Yana continued, "I cannot understand some of a thing that happen in this society."

Blanchard acknowledged her thoughts but was skeptical. "My bet is that it isn't only Westerners who do crazy things."

Yana agreed: "That is true. Unfortunately, I know it is all too well."

Blanchard briefly looked curious, then rubbed his temples sadly, as he continued with his concerns. "I just don't know where we're going to go from here. We have lost so much from this robbery and we will have to wait weeks before we can get replacement eggs. Only then can we again start our research and recreation of the larvae."

"We are set back so far. I understand why you have upset. Is there something more I can do with help?"

"We just have to keep the lab in the best order we can."

"That I can do. But you worry about more?"

"Yes, but you don't know the half of it. With this delay, we will have to apply for additional funding for the extra time we will need."

"Surely we will gets back on our feet. Now that you got a funding once, you can have it again."

Blanchard took off his wire-framed glasses and rubbed his dark eyes with his hands. "Maybe. But I fear what I do not know. And I fear what might become of the larvae and eggs."

"Surely no bad will come of them?"

"I truly worry about it. Considerable mischief is possible."

"I hope not terrorisms."

"I pray not."

"May the Lord help us."

"And likewise, may God help us."

CHAPTER 8

In their cruiser, Brock and Toque drove along Morven Drive in West Vancouver, then entered the driveway to the private school named Rockwater Christian Secondary, past an entranceway flanked by healthy large trees landscaped into bedded areas in the midst of grassy lawns; though at this time, were covered by the unseasonable early snow. Entering the grounds of Rockwater, they passed the parking lot and pulled up behind a couple of West Vancouver police vehicles parked directly in front of the entranceway. Standing alongside were four officers, gaping at the sight in front of them.

There, laid out like a set in a horror show, was a scene worse than the atrocities committed in the name of urban graffiti. It was the vilest school vandalism that had ever been considered by school-age pranksters or whatever sort of saboteur that had been involved. And it was certainly the foulest defacement Brock had ever witnessed at a school site.

The building was about fifty years old, but looked so ghastly that Brock couldn't remember what the school previously looked like. In front of Brock and Toque was a long two-story building underneath cascades of red that was dripping from windows and the brick facing where it stuck, then froze. The substance on the clock tower had turned to disgusting frozen droplets that oozed from the tower's eaves and from the overhang above the once-elegant front doorways. The front steps that had been designed to give a feeling of spaciousness with a grandiose quality, was likewise covered with the red substance. The liquid of defacement had collected into puddles of gel and in many cases, had turned purple or a rust colour where it stained the surrounding snow.

"What kind of perverted sick prank is this?"

"If it is blood, or even part blood, it is too horrible to be at prank. Let's hope that it is tomato sauce."

"I know those kids get carried away but this is beyond anything I've ever seen – or anything I've imagined in my nightmares."

Just as Brock and Toque were opening the doors to exit the cruiser, the four West Vancouver officers approached.

The first officer, a woman who was narrowly built but tall for her Chinese heritage, extended her hand. "I'm Lily Sun." She then gestured to her partner, a woman of African descent, who was just under six-feet, was also of a lean build, and had noticeably large watchful dark eyes, and a generous load of black hair braided tightly to her head. Officer Sun did the introduction, "And this is my partner, Nat Boucher, who recently joined us from the Toronto police force."

The other two West Vancouver officers also extended their hands. The smaller built one reached out, and with a French-Canadian accent, introduced the two of them, "I'm Marcel Trembley and this is Erv Karima. He's one of your home grown – born and bred in North Vancouver. But in spite him being born across the river – on your side, our dispatch thought that you guys should pitch in because after all, a number of students here are from your district. And will be suspects. We're hoping to work with you on this one."

"Glad to be here. Call me Brock."

"And likewise, call me Toque."

"Good to meet you," said the West Vancouver team.

"Do you know anything so far?" asked Toque.

Sun responded first, "This looks like real blood. But you never know. Let hope it's not. The entire exterior of the building has been covered with it."

"How was it applied?" asked Brock as they moved closer to the police tape encircling the building.

Boucher was first to point out, "If you take a look, there's a ton of broken balloons at the bottom of the walls, on the ground. It seems that somehow they managed to fill balloons with the red liquid."

Brock shook his head. "Unbelievable. Why would someone want to do that?"

"Well, unfortunately for the PR of the school, as we just indicated, the students are going to be the first line of questioning," remarked Sun, while shaking her head.

Brock grimaced but couldn't resist a joke in bad taste, asking, "You don't think it might be the teachers?"

Trembley grimaced and responded in a similar ironic tone, "Not on a school night. They'd be too busy with lessons and marking."

Boucher seemed to agree, though was clearly unsettled by the sight, saying, "I haven't seen anything like this, back in Toronto."

Karimi added, "Or in wilds of North Vancouver."

Toque, thoughtful, added, "Joking can't cover up the possibly grotesque nature of this. So, this red stuff has to be sent in for analysis, I suppose?"

"We're hoping your team will take samples to your lab. Our dispatch doesn't have the facility of the RCMP."

"Not a problem. We have an amazing forensic team, with an extremely experienced scientist, Marol Carrier, who will be on this in no time."

CHAPTER 9

While at the school covered with the repulsive red substance, Toque paled and she nervously moved her hand up the nape of her neck to make sure that her hair – a beautiful array of multi-toned auburns, stayed tucked beneath her RCMP hat. But no gesture could hide the beautifully orchestrated pattern of curls that no hairdresser could ever match. No one could miss her classical beauty: her body and facial features so well proportioned; her skin so smooth, and clear of blemishes; her blue-grey eyes softly emphasized by dark eyelashes. Trembley and Karimi stared at her, momentarily stunned. Even Boucher, with her mind almost always on her much-loved wife and their son-to-be-born child, could not dispute Toque's unabridged beauty.

While Brock winced when he saw Trembley and Karimi mesmerized by Toque's appearance, he paid no heed to Boucher's much more subtle reaction. Lily Sun, out in left field, was unaffected and was already mentally absorbed by the task at hand. She suggested, "Why don't we pair off and search the exterior of the property?"

Trembley, not to miss a chance, said, "How about mixing forces? Toque and I can look around the back of the property if …"

Trembley, before getting too far, was interrupted by Karimi who said, "Why not really mix it up? I can go with Toque: after all, I grew up in North Vancouver and that knowledge might become useful when we investigate."

Brock rolled his eyes, saying, "Where you grew up will have no more influence on our effectiveness than the colour of the boxers I chose this morning."

Sun managed a smile in response, while Boucher almost suppressed her most immediate reaction which was a deep-throated chortle.

"In any case," added Brock, "I'm sure that the RCMP would like to keep our portion of the investigation in the hands of their own."

"Of course," added Sun, "We can pool ideas and observations and that way, hopefully get ahead faster."

Trembley and Karimi had the look of two high-stakes players who had just lost the lottery but begrudgingly agreed.

Toque managed a smile as she and Brock, at a good arm length's distance from one another, walked towards the back of the school, searching for clues. Sun and Boucher examined the snow-covered school grounds at the front of the building while Trembley and Karimi, giving the kind of knocks known to be common between young bucks in the wild, shouldered each other as they headed off to the far end of the school.

In front of the building, in amongst the shrubs and snow groundcover, were hundreds of shredded multi-coloured balloons, spread out like a child's party gone horribly wrong, with red pooled on their torn forms and frozen as it oozed from the rolled lips. On the surfaces of the smashed balloons, the red liquid had turned into ice puddles. The smell was particularly unpleasant.

As with the front of the school, at the back there were the remnants of torn balloons that had once been filled with a red substance. Gradually, all were extracted from the stems and leaves of shrubs, the snowy ground, and every living thing on the borders of the building.

Carefully, and painstakingly, as suspicion of something foul settled in their subconscious minds, the officers started breathing through their mouths and with noses internally pinched,
as they moved each balloon into an evidence bag, as the gel ice puddles stained the blue gloves of the law enforcers.

Then the search of the property began. Sun and Boucher walked through the parking lot, bagging any debris, of which there was little. The lot was pristinely clean, already plowed, as would be expected, considering that it was a private school and that appearances and safety were foremost in the minds of those in sales trying to rope in more fee-paying students. Furthermore, the affluent parents would demand the best of every aspect of the school, including that of maintenance. As the student drivers always arrived in high-end cars, and even the most wanting had, at the very least, a new non-economy car, the student lot had no markings of car leakage of oil or whatever other bodily fluids existed in vehicles. There were only the markings of tire rubber as the hormone-charged youth tore from the confines of the school and its parking lot. The delivery area and the staff lot were somewhat different – those areas were stained here and there – oil, antifreeze, grease, and the rubber of tires left behind as the aides, teachers or administrators exited, with their back seats full of marking, administrivia, or a large mesh bag holding a load of basket or volleyballs for one of the school's athletic teams that had a game scheduled for that evening.

In the treed snowy areas left partially vacant for summer flower beds, Sun and Boucher found a half-buried foil wrapper from a cigarette package. A number of meters away there was an almost empty energy drink can, also half buried in the snow, with no summertime ants feasting on the contents. Further searching led to the discovery of one gum wrapper, and a semi-snow covered and torn instant noodle wrapper that had become lodged in an inner branch of one of the cedar shrubs.

In the search of the treed areas on either side of the school, where snow had made it through the huge and sheltering branches, Trembley and Karimi also found a few items: a v-shaped plastic storage container with a pizza slice half eaten, three cigarette butts, a torn wrapping from an energy bar, and an almost entirely buried chap stick. Everything was bagged as potential clues to the perpetrators of the messy crime.

At the back of the school, Brock and Toque commenced with their search. Unlike the West Vancouver cops, rather than having one of them hold the evidence bag while the other deposited in it an item found, they worked independently, each with their own pack of bags. Once they had gathered the balloon debris, they moved over to the Baden Powell Trail that backed upon the school where there was just the occasional trace of snow – snow that managed to get though the canopy of the giant trees.

They then found more items: some which would be best not mentioned. In one clump of trees, Toque found some crumpled papers that looked like cheat notes for a history test, two candy wrappers in different locations, a used condom and the butt end of a reefer. Brock had less fun: search as he would, he found several mounds of dog poop and, believe it or not, a used tampon, which he picked up as if it carried the Bubonic Plague itself. Wanting to match Toque's findings, Brock eyed the trees and was just about to turn around when he saw a glimmer of red on a tree branch far above.

"Wait a minute, Toque, what's that up there?"

"A bag of some sort. Looks like it could be new. Perhaps it got caught in the wind and got lodged there."

"I'd better grab it."

"Grab it! It's got to be sixty feet high!"

"About four stories! Not a problem for Brock Edwards, aka Dudley Do-Right."

"Forget it! Wait till we get some staff in with proper equipment!"

"If it is a clue, we should get it – now."

With that, Brock scrambled up the tree, in an improvised lumberjack style, sliding back down a few feet, here and there, skidding more than once, but managing to make his way to the branch that seemed to be miles above ground level. Looking down at Brock, an eagle soared overhead. This bird seemed to be a threat, with a giant wingspan, large keen eyes that, though a muted yellow, were fierce under the overshadowing layer of feathers. He was on full alert, as if Brock was a demented seagull about to prey on helpless eaglets, even though any such offspring had long ago matured and happily cleared off. But keeping his focus on the human interloper, the eagle continued his guard, his bright yellow beak and long sharp talons – nasty weapons – that were always ready, should anyone or anything be viewed as a threat.

As the eagle soared even closer, Brock, at almost fifty-five feet in the air, with one arm around the tree trunk, and the other reaching towards the plastic bag that fluttered in the wind, Brock found that it was just a little beyond the extent of his grasp.

"For heaven's sake, Brock, give it up!" screamed Toque from the ground, as she squinted up into the sunlight, straining to see her partner just millimeters from throwing himself off his precarious grip.

"I can get it," yelled Brock, as the eagle passed within a couple of feet, so close that Brock could feel the air gusting as a result of the movement of the massive wings.

Brock stretched for all he was worth but as he strained, the arm around the tree trunk became less and less secure. A draught of wind caused the plastic bag to flutter some more, as if taunting the human who was so out of his natural stance on the ground.

The eagle again soared closer, moving his wings gracefully. As this great bird passed, the wind currents from his huge wings caused the plastic bag to again flutter, but this time it waved in the right direction, and was just enough closer to Brock that he was able to grasp it in the brief instant it passed within his reach.

"Got it!"

"For crying out loud, come on down before you fall!" urged Toque.

Brock skittered down the tree trunk, gingerly feeling for handholds and footing on the generous boughs of the cedar. A little less than a meter above the ground, the branch on which Brock rested his weight – snapped, and he hurtled down, landing on his butt. The patronizing eagle gracefully came to rest on the tallest branch that would support its cumbersome form, and let out a piercing cry, as if trying to draw attention to his smooth landing and superior elevation.

"Are you alright?" asked a concerned Toque.

"Of course."

Toque studied Brock still sitting on the ground and bit her lip, trying to hold back a giggle. "Well, I hope that this was worth you risking your life," she remarked, trying to keep the mood serious, "And your hands are blue from the cold! It's lucky you didn't lose your grip!"

"Ah, you're making too much of it," responded Brock in a tone that suggested he'd done no more than pick up yet one more piece of garbage from the trail alongside, "But look, this *is* a balloon bag and it has a partial label on it."

Toque's eyes widened. "Good on you, then. I hope that our team can figure out exactly where the balloons were bought."

Just then, Karimi called, "Hey!" as he, Sun, Trembley, and Boucher rounded the corner of the school.

Toque waved back and when the West Van team were within speaking distance, Karimi disclosed their progress, "We've pretty much finished up the front and sides. How are you doing with the back?"

"I think we're also done ... for now."

"Any problems?"

"Nah," dismissed Brock, as if he fell out of trees on a daily basis, and continued with the reporting back, "We can carry all the evidence bags to our detachment building. As we'll all be using the same forensics lab, we might as well drop off the lot."

"Yeah, that's what we were thinking," said Trembley as he again looked at Toque as if she were a birthday present.

She flushed and turned away, but not before Karimi met her eyes and said, "I hope we'll be working together again."

In Toque's mind, they were just too interested.

Brock tried to re-arrange his face from his immediate unchecked reaction of irritation to that of indifference but his voice showed his feelings as it was at least an octave lower, caused by his suppressed aggravation. "Maybe. Possibly. If more has to be done ... here."

Sun added, "It may be that we'll have to interview students, teachers, custodians and anyone else who is connected to the school. For that, a combined North and West Van effort would be a good thing."

Brock's face showed agreement, though he was soon walking ahead of them and towards the cruisers, with Toque not too far behind, and Karimi and Trembley hurrying behind her. Toque sped up.

Boucher let out a little laugh while Sun furrowed her brow in an effort to maintain a professional demeanor as the two of them pulled up the rear.

Once in their cruiser and on the road, Brock and Toque sat in silence, mulling over their experience at Rockwater. For Brock, he mentally paged over the assaulted school, putting to the back of his mind Toque's over-zealous pursuers, Karimi and Trembley. But for Toque, something quite different was triggered: childhood nightmare memories.

Her head filled with the images of that man from her past: her mother's brother, Uncle Kane – with his sand-paper rough chin, his nauseating and almost suffocating breath, and then the thing that happened.

Beginning when she was a small child of six: her reactionary screaming, her crying, her kicking – though none of this behavior slowed him in the least. The chaos of nightmare images kaleidoscoped into a sickening mosaic, though one day, in particular, stayed as clear as polished glass in her memory banks. It was when she was almost twelve when she defied him with an intensity beyond her previous protestations: she stalled, she dragged her feet and screamed, "No! I am going to tell my parents!"

"Like I said, many times before, they will never believe you!"

Later, she did as she'd sworn to, she told her parents. But in reaction, both looked at her in disbelief. Toque persevered in her attempt to tell the story of her real-life nightmare. Her parents, who loved their daughter entirely, could not believe that the care-giver they'd relied on, was the worst choice of a child minder. They couldn't believe that a blood relative could possibly … plus, they had never heard of such a thing. As they blinded themselves to the error of their choice, they likewise told themselves that Toque's complaints must have come from something that was wrong with her – perhaps a tumble on the rocks at the beach … it had to be anything other … than what she said.

Kane laughed. "Oh, you guys! You got to see that your daughter lives in a fantasy world: she looks like an angel and lives an imaginary existence. You'd better lock her up before the boys come calling. Look at that hair – the prettiest on the planet."

Toque's parents were speechless and paralysed by Toque's shocking allegations and Kane's suggestion of what life might be like when her male peers took notice. And her parents just couldn't accept that they'd left their child with someone who wasn't a decent care-giver, nor could they believe that their beloved brother was anything other an all-round, great guy, like every one said.

Toque's father could not admit the simple truth. In the anger of denial, he gave Toque a backhand, while tears formed in his eyes as he spewed, "We treat you like a princess and now you thank us by lying about your uncle!"

Her mother's eyes watered. "I can't believe this! Go to your room. Now! And don't come out. Ever. And if you do, tie back your hair! You need to learn modesty!"

Since then, the girl named Carol wore toques, every day of her waking life, and soon became known as Toque.

CHAPTER 10

Next door to the furnace in the basement of the dispatch building was a large room often used for informal gatherings. There, where the heat was more than ample, and set in a linear manner, were a number of folding tables. Upon some of the them were a few piles of neatly folded and stacked blankets. Also, strewn all about the room were piles of even more blankets that had been dropped off at the dispatch hall or at various collection points around the district.

Brock stood at one of the tables, picking up a blanket – one at a time, sniffing it, then folding it, and then placing it upon the table. Four other male officers were also there. Three of them, like Brock, were still in uniform pants but had stripped down to undershirts while the fourth cop was in a civilian T-shirt and jeans.

Brock paused, after folding a double-bed sized old Hudson's Bay blanket that still had many years in it, reached into his jacket pocket and extracted his excuse of a meal, loudly rustling the bag, then crunching conspicuously on a portion of the contents: a Cheesesnack. Beside him was a coffee cup from the favorite RCMP hang-out, Muriel's Coffee.

One fellow recruit, Constable Scott said, "Hey Brock, hope you don't get any of that Cheesesnack fake powder on the blankets."

Brock smiled and said, "You under-rate my dietary choices. If you read the label, you will see that these little gems have real cheese on them! If you dined on the same thing, you might be able to put some meat on that massive height of yours."

"Ha, with your height you should be trying to eat something to encourage growth. I don't know how you can justify eating that processed garbage."

Brock then feigned being a self-assured expert in the field of self-care and fine cuisine. "I beg your pardon. I'll have you know that I am almost six feet. And again, read the package. These little delectables are also made out of the finest corn."

Scott scratched the side of his face where traces of acne could be seen as a cause for the irritation and added, "I wonder when this room last had any real air."

Another cop, Constable Brown, who was sinewy from his bicycle beat, said, "Yeah, it's hard to believe that I'd prefer ploughing through the slush outside, but at least the air is good."

Brock peeled off his shirt. "Man, not only is it stuffy in here but it must be at least a hundred degrees."

A third officer, Constable Singh, threw his shirt to the side and added, "H-m-m-m. Not a bad idea. We don't want to sweat up the blankets for the shelter. With the threat of serious snow, they are going to really need them."

At that moment, Toque entered the room and glanced at the five men who'd suddenly become motionless when she appeared. She glanced at the fully clothed men, then at the decent shape of Singh but then she regarded Brock.

Brock was built like a stallion of a human. His shoulders and chest broad, his biceps bulging even without lifting, and his entire torso so toned that it could have been a model for Michelangelo, should he have wanted to create a sculpture of a Greek god. Any woman on the planet would have taken a second look, or more likely, never been able to take her eyes from him.

Toque blanched, her heart beat aloud, and her breathing altered with an instinct so base she did not want to accept it. She tried in vain to glance anywhere but at Brock but could not
keep her eyes from this magnificent form. Though there was a swath of a scar from a major burn on his chest, it did not detract from his over-all sexually; in fact, it somehow contributed to the masculinity of his aura. Finally, Toque got a grip on herself and asked, "What's going on in here?"

Brown explained, "You know what a do-gooder Grant is?"

"Of course. It's unbelievable how many charities he's been involved in."

"Well, the latest is that he volunteered our detachment to join in the Adopt A Shelter Program and has personally already put in a ton of time and cash."

Scott added, "So we've been doing a drive for blankets."

Toque struggled to accept the explanation but found herself preoccupied with fighting off the emotion stirred by Brock's naked torso. She tried to focus on Scott's remark, though to begin with, her voice was out of kilter and seemed as if she was half moaning. "Darn! I must have been asleep! I would have brought some in! Why don't I know about this?"

Brown suggested a possible reason, "It was organized about a week and a half ago when you had a couple of extra days off."

Brock added, "I think that you went climbing."

Toque flushed again as if the climbing venture had been an illicit affair.

Brock eyed her flush and in reaction, his face became quizzically thoughtful.

"So, we're..." Toque glanced up and again saw Brock's naked chest and lost all train of thought.

Brock grabbed his shirt, pulled it on, explaining, "We're getting these blankets ready for a drop-off."

"Exactly, a contractor with a truck is coming to pick up the bulk of them, just to help out," said Scott.

Brock continued, "Yeah, and Toque, we know him. It's Alik Vasiliev."

Toque now looked at Brock, relieved that he had pulled on his shirt, and felt ready for a normal exchange, as she remembered, "He does a lot for the community, doesn't he?"

Brock smiled, saying, "I wish that more were like him."

Chapter 11

Mrs. Bean, with a ball of white hair, dressed in a flowered purple dress and matching flat purple shoes, entered Commanding Officer Grant's office.

Grant, a man who was like a kind and balding uncle, glanced up at his assistant and said, "Hey Mrs. Bean, what's up?"

"The West Vancouver Chief is on the phone. Perhaps I should mention that she seems very agitated."

"Is it about the school?"

"I think so. I'll put the call through immediately."

Then seconds after she exited the room, Mrs. Bean's boss picked up the phone with, "Grant here; what's up?"

"It's Abraham, you know that disgusting mess up at Rockwater?"

"Yeah, our lab is on it. Checking out the fluid samples. There are hundreds of balloons, though, and they all need to be fingerprinted. But at a first go, it looks like the perps wore gloves."

"Shit. Even if we get prints, I can't see that we can finger-print the population of the whole school. Plus, it's just as likely that it is students from a rival school. What are we going to do? Finger-print every student on the North Shore? The parents will be livid!"

"No kidding. But who knows, maybe something will turn up if we run it through the database. We can always hope that the vandals will be in our system."

"I wish. Just so we're on the same page, how about we send a team to talk to the principal?"

"Worth a try, for sure."

"But what prompted this call seems potentially really serious," forewarned Abraham.

"Yeah?"

"A note was sent to my station's contact email that claims to be from those that vandalized the school."

"And it says?"

"That there will be more torment unless certain criminals in Scheveningen are freed."

"You've got to be kidding me! The Scheveningen detentions unit in the Hague?"

"I'm guessing likely. Maybe."

"I can't believe that we are dealing with some people with connections to the United Nations detention unit! It must be a practical joke!"

"That's why I phoned, to see what you think."

"I suppose you tried to find the sender of the email?"

"Yeah, we have a really strong tech lab, as you know, but even then, it didn't take much for us to figure out that the message was sent from a burner and an email account from a free provider."

"Shit. So, we'll have to wait and see."

"Yeah. I don't like it, but we can hardly contact the big guns when it might be clump of high-school pranksters. And on that track of mischief-makers, the email might not even be from the people who tossed the balloon bombs."

"But you think local pranksters?"

"Could be. But the dam story of the mess was covered on the local news. Anyone could have pretended to have done it."

"Crap. And the emailer didn't say anything about the balloon contents?"

"No. But for sure, that is most worrisome."

"Let's hope it's some sort of finger-paint. But in any case, let's keep each other on the speed dial."

"Agreed."

Chapter 12

Brock walked along the ramp towards the *Angel,* named after his child Angela, who had been so cruelly taken from him. The snow was lightly falling, making the surrounding harbour a variety of shades of grey and blue.

As he approached the vessel, Rex woke from his nap in the cockpit, instinctively knowing that his master was nearby. Happily, Rex dove from the boat and onto the pier, running towards his best friend.

In seconds, he was nuzzling his nose into Brock's hand and with a smile Brock scratched Rex under the chin.

"Let's get that ball and play some catch," Brock suggested as Rex jumped into the cockpit, retrieved a chewed orange ball from the corner, that was momentarily jiggling over the drain hole, then leaped back by Brock's side, dropping the ball at his feet.

Brock picked it up and threw it the to the end of the pier where it bounced into the water. Rex jubilant, and not caring less about the cold temperatures, dove in after the ball, then happily swam back to the pier. Brock kneeled down to get the ball out of the swimming dog's mouth and threw the ball again. Off Rex went, swimming happily as he reached the ball and brought it back. Again, Brock reached down, got the ball and tossed it.

As Rex swam, Delila sashayed down the pier, wearing open-toed black stilettos and a generously proportioned three-quarter-length red down coat that wasn't zipped, though it more or less met at the front.

"Hey," she murmured, "You woke me up. How about bringing in doggy and giving me a little drink. That might help me get back to sleep."

Brock looked at Delila, took note of her bare legs – and then, saw almost up to her thigh when she placed one foot ahead of the other. He had the distinct impression that there was nothing under the coat except Delila and reddened in anticipation of what he might see if that coat opened just a little bit more.

"But I'm glad to see you boys are getting a nice warm-up to the real exercise that we can have later!" As she spoke, she laughed at her little joke as she put her hand on Brock's shoulder and moved up against him so that her one of her breasts, though covered with the coat, was tight against his arm. The rich tropical scent of Always Amorous enveloped the two of them.

Brock stammered. Rex returned and was swimming happily, waiting for his master to again toss the ball.

Delila tugged at the zipper on Brock's jacket. "Come-on, let's get doggy out of the water and get to know each other while we have a drink. Do you have any of those Cheesesnacks? They'd be great with a glass of champagne!"

Brock was bewildered and asked, "Champagne? How about a beer?"

"I thought you'd never ask."

With that, they both hoisted Rex from the water. As Delila bent forward to help with lifting Rex, Brock could see what Delila intended: he had an unobstructed view of what was inside her opened coat: a scanty black negligee was the only garment. As Delilah was bending forward, the front of the flimsy garment fell forward, softly skimming the shiny lining of the coat, revealing her full, firm breasts just above her toned and flat stomach. For a moment, he thought that he could see further, to her naked groin, though that was only his imagination at work.

Brock felt his knees weaken; his pants tighten.

In no time, Delila had helped Brock unlock the hatch to the *Angel*, had thrown her coat to the side, and was unbuttoning his shirt under the already undone RCMP bomber jacket. Delila smiled, licked her lips slightly, as she ran her fingers across his chest, moving her hands to his shoulders so that his jacket and shirt fell from his torso.

Her negligee was soon off; she lowered herself onto the galley bunk. Brock couldn't help but notice that she had a Brazilian: smooth skin ... everywhere.

Rex growled and clambered into the cockpit.

Brock paused before he lay down beside Delila. But then a memory. A nightmare. First, the cynical face of a man dressed entirely in black, saying, "Because of what you have done to us, you fucking plant, you will regret being born. And those important to you will suffer – all because of you. What happens will be all your fault."

And then the flames. His wife, April, screaming. Their infant child, Angela, screaming.

The words *all your fault* repeated in his mind. Flames roared in his tormented memory banks.

"What's with you, anyway?" interrupted Delila as she reached for her negligee and pulled it on. Then her coat.

Brock's eyes widened, as if he had just awoken. He looked a little surprized at seeing Delila there, but then, was uncertain as to how to proceed, realizing he had zoned out of reality, so apologized, "Oh, sorry. But ..."

"Forget it." Delila glanced at the groin of his pants, no longer tight but hanging loose on his narrow hips. Hips that were so attractive and that chest ... she felt she should touch him, should stroke ... but his face ... it was so handsome, and yet so tormented ... Then Delila looked a little pained herself, and said, "Maybe another time, eh?"

Brock blanched, embarrassed, yet knew that this gift of a moment with Delila was gone.

As much as she attracted ... anyone, Brock could not find it in himself to proceed with any form of encouragement. He stared out the port-hole and mumbled, "Sure."

Delila vanished up the stairs, stepped over the confused Rex, and walked with some deliberation, back to her own vessel.

Chapter 13

Brock and Toque pulled up behind the West Vancouver cruiser parked in the loading zone in front of Rockwater. As it was Saturday, there was only one vehicle parked in the lot: plugged into a charging station was a five-year-old silver EV with a scuffed left fender and worn tires. Brock guessed that it belonged to the principal with whom they had an appointment.

They climbed the wide concrete stairs with Brock keeping a good arm's distance from Toque. That being the case, she forged ahead as he reported, "Principal Bothe said he'd leave the far-right door unlocked but that the school would be alarmed everywhere except the lobby and the adjacent offices."

Toque pulled the door open and in front of them were pinkish tiled floors, teal trimmed walls, a couple of windowed classrooms on the left, what looked like a resource center on the right, and a wall of glass windows in front of them that separated the foyer from the receptionist pool. Through the glass they could see the backs of two West Vancouver officers also waiting.

Above the glass windows was a painting of a huge awe-inspiring jagged dark grey rock, in which rested several puddles of water that reflected the brilliant blue of the sky above. And from the remarkable rock flowed a stream of crystal-clear water that seemed rejuvenating by the fact of its very existence. The stream cascaded downwards, forming a million brilliant white bubbles, like that on breaking ocean waves in a pristine and isolated location. On the side of the rock opposite the pure blue waters that here and there became a frothing stream, a lone walking stick rested, as if a passer-by had somehow been revitalized by the very existence of so pure a stream and as a result, continued on without a need for the walking aide.

When they reached the windowed wall of the reception area, Toque was a couple of yards in front of Brock. As she pulled open the door, officers Trembley and Karimi leapt to their feet at the sight of Toque, and lost no time invading her space.

"Hey, Toque, looks like we're working on this one again," remarked Trembley as he lifted his regulation cap, and smoothed back his mousey brown hair, his features delicate but his brown eyes large, as he reached for Toque's arm to help her move towards one of the chairs in the waiting area.

But before he could make contact, Toque took a step back, leaving Trembley's hand dangling, just as Karimi slipped by and positioned himself so close to Toque that Brock could barely get into the office. At first unaware of crowding the doorway, Karimi was entirely happy to be simply alongside the gorgeous constable: he was so enrapt in her aura that he simply stood in the reception area with an oversized smile on his brown face, under his black curly hair.

"Hey, good to see you guys," said Brock, and the West Vancouver officers, realizing their magnetic attraction to Toque had stalled Brock's entrance, backed off, moving towards the visitor chairs.

"Yeah, likewise," said Trembley, extending his right arm for a handshake.

Karimi followed suit with shaking Brock's hand and then the three of them, awkwardly faced Toque. For Brock, it would have been silly to shake Toque's hand but for the other two, it felt as if they would be shaking the hand of the most desirable woman they'd ever seen: a woman they would be entirely interested in dating on anything but the platonic level. Perhaps a two-handed shake, with palm against palm and a second hand on top of hers, with a little caress for special effect, might have been more the order of the day as far as their feelings were concerned.

As the awkward silence began to settle, a tall man in a rugby shirt entered the reception area from a side hall and with long strides, joined the four officers, and with a commanding voice greeted them, "Glad to see that you all made it here. I'm David Bothe, the principal. Would you care to join me in my office?"

Without pause, he cut though the reception area of four work stations that were on the outside of a glassed-in conference room overlooking the city. They followed Bothe down a hall leading past offices on either side until they got to one at the end: its door, like all the others for administrative staff, had glassed-in windows with privacy blinds.

For anyone entering, at least those who didn't have view property, the most striking thing about Bothe's office was the wall of windows that overlooked the city. But in second place was an impressive huge mahogany desk and when he saw it, Brock wondered what expense account might have paid for such an extravagant piece of furniture. Dryly, he thought, probably the account intended for props to impress the fee-paying parents. Along two of the walls of the office, under three pictures of rugby teams, as if set up for this meeting, were four chairs, with padded seats the same colour as the teal trim that acted as an accent to the colour scheme of the entire school. Bothe's desk was devoid of any paper and shone as if it had been just polished.

The only object on the desk was a brass name plate that read, "D. Bothe, Principal." On the walls behind him were two framed certificates: a BPEC from a local college that offered undergraduate degrees and a MA from a correspondence program.

Bothe forced a smile. "What can I do for you people?"

"We just have a few questions about the vandalism," explained Toque.

Bothe sighed. "Now that we've cleaned it up, we'd just like to put it behind us."

"But there is a possibility of a repeat incident," pointed out Toque.

"I certainly hope not. Why would you suggest that?" asked Bothe.

"If we don't know the motive, what's next could be worse," warned Brock.

Bothe frowned. "I'm sure it's just some misdirected person who got it out of his or her system."

"As we still don't know what the red liquid is, we have to proceed with caution as it could have some kind of toxicity and could make students ill ... or worse!" worried Toque.

Bothe maintained his stance. "That won't happen. No student was allowed in the vicinity until it was entirely cleaned up."

"What if you missed an area that a student or group of students find and get infected with something?" asked Karimi.

Bothe insisted, "That is very unlikely. You people are just too worried about dubious scenarios. The students here just want to get on with their studies."

"But what if a student does become ill? What if there are viruses in the liquid that became air born?" asked Trembley.

Bothe rubbed his chin as he thought. "Well then, what do you suggest? Or are you hinting at something? Have you found out anything I should know about?"

Trembley, sitting beside Toque, could not help his repeated sideway glances at her amazing form and struggled with focussing.

Karimi, on the other side of Trembley explained, "Our concern is that we now have a threat of a something more!"

"And you think this is aimed at Rockwater?"

With some effort at interior restraint, Trembley managed to move his focus from that of Toque, and answered, "We just don't know – but want to look into any possible clues or leads."

Bothe grimaced. "Then what can we do here?"

Brock cleared his throat, shuffled slightly in his chair so that he was a millimetre further away from Toque. Bothe's eyebrows raised in surprise but soon returned to their furrowed, worried position.

Toque began, "As soon as we came, we figured out that the school had been vandalized with hundreds of liquid-filled balloon bombs."

Bothe's frown lines deepened, then after a hesitation, said, "Yes, and this takes us where?"

Brock continued the explanation, "As yet, we don't know exactly what the liquid is. It seems like blood but we haven't got word yet. We have just found out from the forensic team that the balloons are all identical – made by the same manufacturer, although that's not much of a clue. However, if we search lockers, we may find a store carry bag, or more balloons, or some sign of involvement of a specific perpetrator."

Bothe protested, "Search the lockers? That is impossible. That is a breach of student privacy!"

Karimi looked worried. "You will have police officers and RCMP constables doing the searching. With your permission ..."

Bothe again paused, then informed the four cops of his position, "I first need to consult the school's legal expert and also the parent council."

"So, we leave, then come back? When? A week? Two weeks?" grumbled Brock.

Bothe affirmed, "Well yes, it might take some time."

Karimi reminded Bothe of what they did know. "Let us not forget that there is the threat of more."

Toque was worried. "We do not want to put students at risk. Until we have more information, we need to find the perpetrators."

Bothe seemed almost defeated. "Fine. But I insist that you work two in a team so that no one can say that something was taken."

"We do, anyway," remarked Trembley.

"And," demanded Bothe, "I would like to see one constable and one officer form each team. That will also add some legitimacy to any argument that you have conspired against some parent or student who feels that their privacy has been deliberately breached."

"Sounds like a plan!" agreed Trembley, glancing at Toque.

"And I will form the teams," deliberated Bothe, "Officer Karimi will be with Constable Burdon, and Officer Trembley will be with Constable Brock."

In response to the team formations, Toque seemed unsettled, Brock relieved, Trembley as if he'd just lost the lottery, while Karimi's smile went ear to ear and his chest pumped up.

Bothe noticed the reaction of the officers and momentarily was undecisive. He glanced at Toque and paused … just a little longer than usual. He saw her face, her form. But he soon returned to the pressing issue at hand. "I will circulate and be with all of you on-and-off through-out this unfortunate … need for a search."

Bothe scowled, then went on, "Now that we have – uh – er … teams assigned, I must ask you to wait in the reception area while I turn off the alarm system and lock the front door. There was little threat of intruders when most of the school was alarmed, but once the entire system is turned off, it will be too easy for others to enter."

Toque's face showed understanding, but then thinking forward asked, "Do we get a list of locker combinations?"

"Oh, not at all. You'll get pin codes. Rockwater is much more to up-to-date than those schools still using archaic combination locks. What a chore they were: every first day of school the junior students were always frustrated and there was often a few that were crying because they couldn't figure out the three times right, digit, left one full turn, second digit, then direct to the third digit. Considering a lot of those lock-resistant students were babysitting, it frightens the hell out of me to think that a child's life might be in their hands."

Brock looked amused. "But they did figure out the locks after the first day?"

"Yes, unfortunately – but all too well. Various students would tell friends their combinations, then they'd have a spat with the friend and then the ex-friend would blab the locker combination or worse, steal something from the ex-friend's locker," related Bothe.

Trembley laughed. "I've heard of worse than that. Some students would peer over shoulders to get combinations, then victimize the locker holder by breaking in or passing around the code numbers."

Bothe agreed. "How well I know. Stupid practical jokes but worse, things stolen: books, electronics, wallets, clothing, and probably even dope, though that specifically is never reported, of course. The digital locks we installed are much better. If the combination gets out, in seconds we can change it – from any of the office computers. As a result, there's been no incidents – well – except for one."

For a moment, Karimi took his eyes off Toque. "Oh? You mean the time last year when we had to investigate that kid called Peanut?"

Bothe inwardly cringed. "Exactly, although the mother was furious that we'd called in the West Vancouver Police."

Toque became more interested, saying, "Do tell."

Bothe shook his head, then maintained, "It couldn't possibly be relevant to the red stuff on the building."

"Let's hear about it. You never know – fresh perspective, and all that," suggested Brock.

"Very well." In his mind, Bothe remembered the distasteful episode of the mealworms.

It was a sunny morning, almost a year ago. With only the occasional teacher entering the staffroom; the office, classrooms, and halls were mostly vacant and were a-glow with light from glass-walled rooms that shared the sun which was flowing through the windows. Though the teachers' desks were covered with computers, books, and the work of the day, the student desks, like the halls, shone as if just waxed. The lockers were without a mark, shining brightly, still in pristine condition.

Then, as usual, at 7:45, the first bus arrived and was shortly thereafter followed by ten more yellow-orange buses, all labelled with Rockwater. High-end cars were arriving in the student parking lot where the senior students paused to chat with friends. As if the floodgates had been opened, soon the halls were filled with masses of bodies, ranging in height and size from about four feet to that of over six. Some students were covered with the blight of acne; the more fortunate had the skin of babes. The occasional senior male student had a full beard and what looked like a beer-belly. In the throngs in the hall, the younger and smaller students gawked at the members of the football team as they entered the main hallway, with a gaggle of girls attached.

The captain of the football team, Todd, passed with his private entourage as if a float in a parade and the younger students parted like the Sea of Galilee. Todd did not acknowledge the falling away minions as he perceived them as being of no significance at all, so proceeded to his locker with two girls on each arm that moved beside him, as if attached.

Todd eyed one girl, then the other, as he said, "That was a great after-party last night."

One of the dreamy-eyed girls smiled, saying, "Thanks for helping me out in the garden, if you know what I mean."

Another girl looked concerned, but then boosted her spirits, by saying, "It was fun sharing that bottle of vodka."

"Been there, done that," smiled a third.

"What party?" asked the fourth.

"Hey girls, you're all great. You're all number one with me." Then, with two girls in each arm, he squeezed, enjoying one of many not-so-innocent group hugs.

Standing at his open locker, a child-sized grade eight student across that hall dropped his jaw in envy.

The fourth girl, to gain ground on the others, half-whispered, "I can get something from my parent's liquor cabinet for after tomorrow's game."

Todd gave her an extra squeeze. "Sounds good. But let's keep this talk under wraps. The coach will be super pissed if he finds out I've been drinking."

Todd opened his locker door and out spilled a paper cup that had been filled with squirming mealworms and a small residue of their food, oatmeal. Also, several black beetles hopped out, one onto Todd's sweater and one onto the closest female companion who screamed as if covered with tarantulas. The cup had been positioned in such a way, balanced on a pile of books, so that it would fall forward, dumping the mealworms onto those dumbfounded and horrified standing in front of the locker.

In no time, all the students were carefully opening locker doors so as to not knock over the booby-trapped cups of mealworms, but to no avail. Soon the halls were filled with screaming, running students shrieking as if they were infected with some deadly disease, even though it was only harmless, though wriggling, larva. Several students got knocked about as the masses exited, and three students were trampled and had to be sent to the hospital.

Within an hour, the students were calmed down and in their classrooms, while an unfortunate custodian had to clean up the mess of trampled mealworms, racing beetles, and the squirming little oatmeal-coloured bodies. While he worked, parents lost no time in calling the principal to complain.

And five students from three separate families were pulled from the school. What hurt the most was that one of the families was known for frequent and extremely generous donations.

Bothe cringed at the memory.

"Were all the lockers done?" questioned Brock, puzzled at the scale of the vandalism.

Bothe shook his head. "Thank goodness, no. It was senior students that were targeted – mainly those belonging to grade twelve males, but there were a few grade elevens – but again, only those used by males."

Brock raised his eyebrows in disbelief. "How could that have happened?"

Karimi related the findings of their investigation. "The kid nick-named Peanut figured out that there is an administrative access code to the lockers."

"You're kidding! One of those super kids?" asked Toque.

Bothe wore the smile of disenchantment as he revealed the named student's abilities: "Yeah, one can never forget that some students can walk circles around the average adult mind. Peanut's a super-exceptional kid in all the courses. In fact, his parents have set up the bucks to send him to any ivy league school, although my bet is that scholarships will pay his way to any institution he wishes to attend. Trust Peanut to figure out the access code. But on the positive side, he was an immediate potential suspect as there's no one else smart enough to hack into the system."

"One kid – alone planted mealworms in all those lockers?" asked Brock, in a tone of being impressed mixed with surprize.

Karimi shook his head. "Probably not. He most likely had help. Peanut was and is a member of a group called, Society To Advance Global Species (STAGS). Although we suspected the whole group was part of the mealworm business, we couldn't find any evidence leading directly to them."

"How did you prove the involvement of this Peanut character?"

Karimi answered, "We found bins and bins used for breeding purposes in the heated garage of his home."

Toque raised an eyebrow, and asked, "The parents didn't notice? Or worse, sanctioned it?"

Trembley replied, "Believe it or not, they were away on an extended holiday, thinking that their kids would be fine on their own."

"There's a sibling?"

"Yeah, if I remember correctly, Peanut has an older brother at Capilano University, but the brother is entirely absorbed with basketball and his own social life so is never around to see what's happening at home."

Brock understood, but questioned further, "So Peanut used the administrative access code to open the lockers."

Trembley further explained, "Yeah, with the code, Peanut could target individuals because he also managed to hack into the school files of locker assignments."

"So other than his proven brilliance, was there something more that made you suspect that the perpetrator was Peanut?" asked Brock.

Karimi explained, "There was. It was a bit of luck and a bit of stupidity on the part of his friends: two of the STAGS members, though not Peanut, were laughing their heads off while the other students were either horrified or just plain unimpressed. That aroused our suspicions so we checked into their whereabouts the night of the planting of the mealworms. Everyone in the group had an alibi except for Peanut. When we couldn't reach his parents, we went to their home for a look."

Trembley added, "And what do you know: a mealworm farm right in one of the best neighbourhoods!"

Brock took off his regulation hat and scratched his head pensively. "Why don't we all have a look at Peanut's locker?"

Toque added, "And how about all of the other members of STAGS?"

Bearing that suggestion in mind, as Bothe moved towards his office, he replied, "Sure, although I don't think all four of you need to check the same lockers. Groups of two will be faster. I'll split the locker numbers into two lists, although I doubt the searches will get us anywhere."

Brock then asked, "So why wasn't he kicked out?"

As he exited, Bothe was bleak, as if guilty of corruption. "Let's just say that some parents who are high profile contributors to high stake politics and various causes and who are also major benefactors to the school, have quite a bit more room to manoeuvre than the parents in a public school. And Peanut's parents' contributions are significant and ongoing. For those reasons, from the very start of our investigations into the incident, Peanut wasn't the least bit worried about any real discipline or getting expelled. It was just a game to him."

Toque glanced at Brock as they both thought, *Nice for those that have the bucks.*

"A waste of time, investigating his part in the incident," surmised Karimi.

Trembley added, "To add to his feelings of invincibility, is that there is a new wing planned that will bear their surname."

Brock rolled his eyes.

Minutes later, Bothe returned, holding two pieces of paper in his hands. "Here is the access code and the locker numbers: there are nine students involved. Constable Burdon, you're with Officer Trembley and Constable Brock, you're with Officer Karimi. The shorter list has Peanut's locker. It might need the most thorough search."

"But …" stammered Karimi, wondering why he wasn't still partnered with Toque, as Bothe had suggested.

But before he could speak, a much too happy Trembley took the shorter list and almost instantly said, "Right! We'll first take a look at Peanut's locker. Come on Toque! Let's do it."

Karimi curled a lip, took the second list from Bothe, then acknowledged Brock as his new locker search partner, and succumbed. "Let's meet back here in as soon as we're done!"

"Good, I'll circulate," said Bothe.

Twenty minutes later, they were back in the waiting area of the school's office.

"Anything?" asked Bothe, concerned about the invasion of privacy but also the plight of his students.

Brock spoke first, "Nada. But these kids should get awards for tidiness."

Bothe agreed. "A lot of the studious kids are like that."

"We didn't find much, either," reported Trembley.

"But was there something?" asked Brock.

"Just this," said Toque, holding up a store receipt. "As you can see, it's the type from a cash-register that doesn't show the vendor's name or the specific articles purchased. But it does list the prices of fifty-three items, all at two bucks and ninety-eight cents. Could it have been bags of balloons?"

"Might," agreed Brock.

"We'll talk to the kid who had the receipt in his locker," volunteered Trembley.

CHAPTER 14

Not visible from the street, in the back of Alik and Yana's four thousand square foot retro-Victorian home was the kitchen. There, just beyond a small entry lobby where coats hung, were five sets of shoes: three adult pairs, and two pairs belonging to small children. In the kitchen, there was white wooden cabinetry, some with glass doors, which displayed white dinner wear inside, dishes that shone like the white gloss crown moulding in the room. Stainless steel appliances complimented the colour scheme, or one might say, lack of colour scheme: the room was entirely white, save the table and chairs and the polished concrete flooring.

In that room, sat the lady of the house with her brother, Borya, both of whom were seated under a chandelier of spiraling miniature white lights, at a modern-yet rustic table built from solid planks of white oak timbers and supported by two contemporary-looking wide stainless-steel supports at either end. Two small children happily played on the kitchen floor with a toy plastic barn set which included an assemble-yourself fence, numerous farm animals, a tractor, a truck, and a woman, a man, and two children.

"I am happy you are alive but I don't know how long you can keep hiding from the polices."

"Why can't Unkabora come and live in the house with us?" asked the fair-haired pre-schooler with hazel-brown eyes identical to those of his uncle.

"Not this times, sweet one," responded Yana. The child momentarily pouted but then went back to playing with his younger sister. Yana continued, "Like I said, I am very anxious about you staying anywheres around here."

"Don't worry about it. As your brother, I know what is best."

"Borya, forgive me, but I must say that I, like you, have the respected university degree. I have proven that I am no half-wit who cannot makes reasonable choice."

"That's a bad joke. We both know that I am the real brains in the family. Your science degree means nothing: your male instructors were directed by their penises or were brain-washed

66

and/or paid off by those gender-equal lobbyists who are trying to cheat all men of what should be exclusively ours. Every minute of the day the gender-equals are licking the asses of the equal opportunity idiots. Your degree was a gift, not a measure of what you achieved. It is as good as a fake! My degrees are the real thing! You must respect that I am the absolute authority in our family!"

"That is a thinking of only a few of our ancestors, and thank the Lord it is gone now. But even if I agree with that old way, I have a husband now and if he finds out, he would also have concern about your uses of our garage."

"Don't make me laugh! He doesn't have the strength to pull off a strip of painter's tape! He has sissy degrees! Engineering and architecture! Hah! Those degrees are merely instruments of candy-ass city planners and self-absorbed land-owners!"

"You have too much hate, Borya. Most Canadians are kind and honourable, as Alik and I are and will continues to be. And for that matter, the whole Russian community here in Canada."

"Honour? Hah! The people of whom you speak are traitors. Your woman's mind is warped by hormones!"

"My family and I have chosen to live within and cherish a peaceful traditions of this country! We pray and strive to be good people. This is the right way!"

"You are not right in your choices. You and Alik are dupes! That is why real men must make the decisions! I'm sorry, but as a condition of your birth, you are not capable. And as for Alik, he should rejoin the real world of men who are willing to work as citizens of our homeland."

"How can you insults my husband? He is the father of my children: and an unborn here in my belly."

"Don't insult me with the fact that you can spread your legs. Any animal can do that."

"My gosh, Borya, what have you turned into? You are reducing my life of the honourable family to trash!"

"As you are. You shouldn't have the right to reproduce our genes. You are a traitor to the Russian cause and an insult to our genetic heritage."

"Borya, I think that I have had enough. Last time we met you seemed genuinely interested in my life and the careers I am establishing at the lab. You asked many questions. It seemed we were really connecting!"

"Yes, I remember that – I did find some of your experiments interesting but …"

"Well, you wouldn't now. Did you know that the labs were broken into and all of the egg and larvaes were stolen?"

Borya paused and looked away from Yana. A glimmer of a smile touched his features, as his voice changed to one that showed some empathy. "What? I'm sorry. That is rough. But surely you can restock?"

"I suppose so, but it will take the time. A lot of time. But Borya, as I said, I am very worried about you getting caught as you are the wanted man in this country. Being around here is putting all of us at some risk."

"As I have been trying to say, I have everything under control."

"But must you use the garage? It cannot be good if you insists that Alik and I not even go near our own garage!"

"I just don't want you involved. No matter what our differences are with regard to who is the legitimate head of the family, you have to agree that I am right in saying the less you know, the better."

"But why our garage?"

"It's in a safe neighbourhood. I can leave my stuff here. It's a bonus that the garage is heated. I can crash here whenever I want."

"Yeah, and track dirts into the house when you use the toilet. But that is of no concern in a faces of the big issue: please tell me that you are not doing somethings that will harm others!"

"Look, I just want you to be removed from what I am doing!"

"I am sure even Alik would agrees with that. But you should not be at a very location, this house, where they know you have family. The police have checked here before and will likely come again. It seem obvious that you may come here."

"Matters of the law here are not much better than children playing hide and seek. Once they've checked a location, they're not too likely to return. I think I'm fine … for quite a while. Plus, a lot of time has passed since I disappeared. The cops may have even forgotten about me."

"Not so. I know the constable who, just the other day, spoke of you. I don't know how you can be so sure of yourself."

"I have a plan but just need to be able to use your garage to work on a very short-term project. I'll be gone before the authorities decide to retrace their steps. And only if they decide."

"I wish that they have forgotten you but know they haven't."

"Ah, don't worry about them; after all, they are imbeciles in every sense."

"I fear you are short-changing the police forces. Two constables I know are not to be discount. I have to say that they are not at all dense, as you think. Borya, I feel that you must leave here and find other place. I have a very bad feeling about you being here!"

"But I want Unkabora to come for a sleep-over!" interrupted the older child.

"Not right now, Matvey."

"Oh, please?"

"Other time, maybe."

Borya looked insulted, then asked, "And what would Alik think?"

"He would agree with me."

Borya snarled, then mocking, "The man agrees with his wife! Does he hide under your skirt as well? Well, let the Chernobyl fall-out gather on you then! And your mutant family! I will leave your garage soon enough and you won't ever again have to worry about me or your ..."

Borya's last words blurred into the ether as he threw on his coat and stomped off, through the back mudroom, and out the adjacent door.

ER 15

the much-publicized North American All-Star Basketball Challenge at Capilano University's brand-new Squamish Nation Gym. It attracted as much attention as the 2010 Winter Olympics. Young athletes from every post-secondary institution all over North America wanted to be at this event: as it was relatively near the beginning of the season, this was where fresh impressions could be made; teams could be feared or discounted, and, equally important, visual recordings of the teams would be analyzed for any strength or weakness that would need to be considered in subsequent games. Talent scouts for the NBA would be there.

And, as if this wasn't a big enough pressure cooker, the challenge was taking place at almost the same time as two large political events that were slated for the city: the premier's conference and the election of a new federal leader for the party in power. Consequently, security was more than apparent at major events, with secret service personal in place for every attending premier or politician hoping to replace the Prime Minister of Canada.

Because of the many who were already in the city for one or the other of the political events and because of the hype for the basketball challenge, the media were there en masse: there was a ton of radio stations and all the major North America-based television and internet networks. Outside there were lighting trucks, cables all over the place, and media security personal that acted as if they were the most important people at the event.

Inside, the gym was a glorious tribute to modern architecture. The floor was a mosaic of Canadian hardwoods made into a First Nation's design of stylized human faces, fish, ravens, bears, and eagles formed from inlaid wood. The roof of the gym was mainly chrome and mirrors over an elaborate maize of wiring and lights. The place was suitable for almost any event, including music concerts. Rather than using the blue colour of the Cap U teams, the designers decided to go for a multi-national colour scheme.

To that end, the lowest seats were a liberal red, the midrange were a conservative blue, and the top three rows of seats were coloured with white alternating with yellow, green, orange, and purple: the mix symbolizing all other political leanings.

The surface of the walls was a cream-coloured tile that looked like a warm terra cotta stone but was actually a man-made material made to look both soft and approachable. On the seats of the audience chairs was a new type of covering which was as plush as a leather sofa but was totally water resistant. Every seat had arm rests that were high-tech – with imbedded fold-up screens so that the spectators could replay any portion of the game, learn about individual players, or review any information no longer posted on the score board.

A special area by the floor was roped off for the dignitaries and behind that section, were a dozen secret service men and paid guards, all armed.

The event was sold out. At least fifty people waited outside the doors, hoping against all odds that they might get entry because of a seat or two opening up.

A lone singer stepped onto the stage and a floor opened up to reveal a full orchestra beneath. Down from the roof, a puzzle-like mass of mirror-like plates moved down on robotic arms to form huge screens. When national anthems belonging to Mexico, the United States, and Canada were sung, beautiful scenes of that country, interspersed with shots of winning athletes in a variety of sports, flashed across the massive screens. The singing of the American anthem was joined in by well over one third of the audience, almost as many as there were Canadians singing when it was their anthem's turn. The Mexican fans, through fewer in number, were just as proud to sing and revel in the glory of their homeland. Not even the smallest iota of national pride was diminished.

Two teams of basketball players entered the gym. They had been selected through a draw. The first teams to play were McGill and the University of South Dakota. Players were in position on the floor; basketball hoops hung temptingly. The team members not on the floor were seated in a bench area inset from the rest of the bleachers. The athletes' bench was spread out with individual plush cushions in a row, with water dispensaries at the ready – just knee high – in front of the players.

Also, the arm-rests had a fan mechanism similar to that in planes, but in this case, the player could access cooler or warmer air, depending on their needs. Also, as with the audience seating, each arm rest had a small screen on which the seated player could view any data he or she wanted to see, such as the strengths or weaknesses of the opposition. Or, if needed, the coach could send individual or group messages.

Just before the tip-off, the audience became a little quieter, and music piped in: it was the singing of *God Save the King,* perhaps chosen to give the American players a flavour of Canadian sentiments.

Nevertheless, most of the audience was watching the gym floor, waiting for the start. Then, just as the tip-off ball was tossed by the referee, a small shaped loped across the floor.

One politician leaned over to her husband, asking, "What *is* that?"

"It seems like a frog!" exclaimed the husband.

"How could it – but look! Another one!"

A buxom young woman in the stands with white racing stipes running up the outer sides of her leggings and a colour-matching low-cut top which resembled a sports bra, screamed the loudest.

Several frogs had dropped from the screen directly above her, and one landed on her cleavage before romping away, the sticky little toes of both back feet having pushed from her breasts for momentum, then landed onto another screaming guest.

A top-end business man with salt-and-pepper hair that was cut in what had to be a costly salon, sat in a perfectly fitted navy-blue suit in the front row. He looked up, to ascertain the origin of the bounding amphibians, and possibly determine which staff member should be fired for the creation of this despicable outbreak.

However, before he'd decided on a deserving scapegoat, he was rudely assaulted with several slaps to the face as one gangly frog landed on him, one slimy foot, then the others, and then the confused creature clambered across the gentleman's facial features before lift-off and jumping sideways, onto another bellowing guest.

Just a few seats over, a woman, perfectly made-up with high quality streaks to what was probably greying hair, was totally colour-coordinated in an ankle-length casual olive-green ultra-suede skirt, matching vest, ivory silk blouse, and a bulbous strand of amber beads, some with preserved insects. But rather than sitting like a queen at a benefit, this woman who reeked of class, suddenly stood and screamed, though briefly, because in seconds her scream turned into a continuous hysterical wail when one precarious frog jumped up and under the woman's skirt.

Also, frantic, the frog tried to escape but could not find an exit, leaving the woman to feel the slippery creature hopping to-and-fro under what had been a slime-free skirt. As the frog jumped about in the skirt, one could see a bulge form here, then there, as the feared beast jumped against various parts of the skirt's inner sanctum.

A security guard hurried over to another, frantically asking, "What do we do about this?"

"Damned if I know. Can't Taser them."

"What the hell!" Yelled one of the security people as numerous huge nets intended for balloons lowered down from the ceiling and hundreds of frogs were released. Those that landed on the players or the fans lived; most of those that landed on the floor didn't.

People rose, screaming as if they were in the midst of a plague that could cause death. Frogs were on their shoulders, up the legs of their pants, and occasionally perched on one of the audience's heads.

Audience members rushed from their seats and crowded the isle. Several frogs got squished as the panicked crowd attempted to exit. One player grabbed control of the ball and headed for the opponent's net but as he moved, he slipped on a frog and crashed his long limbs to the floor. Another player got the ball but it was then that the umpire declared a time-out. Most players just stood, watching the frogs leap in every imaginable direction.

One player from the South Dakota team looked at a McGill player and asked, "Say, where do you honkeys keep your biology specimens?"

The Canadian player, unused to the term *honkey,* pulled a punch, just as another American student called out, "Frogs. Ha, ha. This is hilarious. Now we can say without doubt that Canada's overloaded in the frog department!"

Five other Canadian players who were French Canadian, didn't know what to make of this remark but did know what to do with their fists and joined the fight and within seconds both teams were duking it out, with frogs bounding every which way.

With the fight on the floor, the guests were clamouring to leave, and started pushing each other: some lost their balance and fell between the seats or in the aisles while others were being trampled.

***

The chaos caused by the frogs was well underway when Toque and Brock arrived.

Their cruiser pulled up while the panicked guests were fighting their way from the building and were spilling onto the plaza staircase that staged the gym's main entrance.

Still in the cruiser, Brock glanced out the window and cursed. "What the ... is going on here? It looks like the guards are trying to hold back people while they usher ... "

Both Brock and Toque immediately sensed the urgency as the audience members, desperate to exit, tried to overwhelm security. Numerous frogs were also in the process of departing, though without a plan, bounding willy-nilly, many vanishing into the darkened snowy campus grounds.

Toque's eyes rounded as she tried to make sense of the pandemonium unfolding, asking, "Brock, what's going on? Frogs? Again? In November?"

"I know global warming is bad but I didn't think ... my gosh, we'd better move!"

They jumped to exit the cruiser, and Brock tore past a patch of fresh oil that had formed a shiny black circle on the irregular skiff of hardened snow left behind by the last snow plow.

Toque looked beyond the bounding frogs and eyed the faces of the exiting masses, and said, "Oh, – there is the Saskatchewan premier – and – I think the man behind her is the premier of Newfoundland-Labrador!"

"No kidding!"

Toque further perused the panicked faces, then added, "And there is our premier and hey, even the North West Territories is here!"

Brock's face momentarily showed silent acknowledgement, but at almost the same instant, he skidded to a halt, thinking that he should take another look at the oil patch he'd just charged past. In spite of the fact that his partner was already in the midst of the obvious emergency, Brock snatched two sterilized gloves and a kit, and within seconds took a sample of the oil. Then feeling the harried anxiety that accompanies a major crisis, he rushed to join Toque and the security personal that were not doing well with the bedlam of under-staffed crowd control.

CHAPTER 16

Entering Commanding Officer Grant's office, Mrs. Bean with her ball of white hair, wore brown pumps with scraped toes, and a rust-brown floral dress that had a pattern similar to that used on vintage sofas.

More tired than usual, Grant rubbed his eyes as he said, "Another problem, Mrs. Bean?"

"I think so. The West Vancouver Chief is on the phone again. She still seems really agitated."

"About the school? Or is she wanting to follow up on the crazy amount of press coverage for the fiasco at the basketball challenge?"

"I'm not sure, but I'll put the call through immediately."

In seconds, the CO picked up, saying, "Hey, Captain Abraham, Grant here. What's up?"

"Another note on our contact system!"

"And?"

Abraham left no pause as she dug into the issue. "The note-writer is taking credit for the frogs at Cap U as well as the liquid at the private school! They claim that it is blood."

"Blood? Frogs? Are these people crazy?"

"Likely."

"I'm guessing these frogs are somehow connected to some that were recently released on a Vancouver bus. I'll contact VPD to see if they've got anywhere with it. But what are the emailers wanting now?"

Abraham moaned. "As with the alleged blood, they're saying that they will continue with assaults, until certain criminals in Scheveningen are freed."

"Shit."

"Yeah, more atrocities for us to face."

Grant sighed. "Still transmitted on an untraceable phone?"

"Unfortunately, yes. Anything known about the school yet?"

"I wish, but our lab is still on it. No fingerprints yet. I'll let them know about the claim of it being blood."

"It's looking less and less like it was students at the school."

Only in part Grant agreed, saying, "Probably not, but the school *is* one of the feeder schools for the University. So, there could be a link."

"Right, there could be a common animosity."

"Yeah, who knows: we'll just have to keep on it. Have you talked to the principal?"

Abraham sighed. "Yeah, he's nervous as shit about bad publicity. Plus, the parents' group is pissed, claiming that they paid big money to have their children experience the sanctum of ivy-league learning while at the same time removed from the sordid world of public education."

"Money for nothing: the sordid came after them, nevertheless."

"I guess. But, what do you think should be our response?"

Grant moaned, almost inaudibly. "We have to do the Canadian thing and say we don't play ball with blackmailers, kidnappers, or trash out there trying to dictate conditions."

"I anticipated your response. Do you think that we should contact any higher authorities?"

"Until we get some facts, no. Not unless things get a lot worse."

"I agree. I'll respond then, with our answer: no dice to blackmail. But in the meantime, fingers crossed that it is just students and that they'll go no further."

"Yeah, and we'll be diligent with our investigations. I'll let you know when the lab report comes in."

"And let's keep each other on speed dial."

"As before."

Chapter 17

The new Centennial Theatre had been open only a few years, although the plan had been to rebuild it in 2020. But local politicians who wanted to have their say and argue this way or that way, just for the sake of self-importance, then again to the original way if they thought that that might give them a chance of being re-elected, postponed the rebuild of this theater that had been a mainstay for North Vancouver culture for many years.

Then, in 2035, heralded by a great yawn from the dispirited general public, the new theatre opened and was glorious except for the fact that it was reduced in size from its original plan by sixty percent by provincial and city planners that felt the smaller venue was just as good as a larger one and certainly more affordable from the dollar and cents point-of-view. So, it was a mini-theatre of sorts, a cottage theatre so to speak, but it turned out to be particularly perfect for school concerts wherein presentations had very small audiences as they were attended only by the performers' parents, grandparents, occasionally a devoted aunt or uncle, and a handful of misdirected seniors confused but attracted by the free admission. But the new venue was less than adequate for a group of performers who had a fan base larger than immediate family.

But one group outside the school crowd, was the city's elite, and they found the venue most appropriate for a fund-raiser in which only the high-rollers were invited by virtue of the fact that the price of the entrance ticket for the evening was in excess of the average citizen's yearly income.

As exclusive as this might seem, this one particular benefit was a very good thing as it was to raise dollars for safe and clean housing for the poor: the unfortunate souls whose numbers had only increased, and never seemed to abate since the early 2000's.

The fund-raiser was to be a gala affair: first, there was hors d'oeuvres and beverages in the lobby for an hour before the show. And then a glorious performance executed gratuitously by the VSO and the Royal Winnipeg Ballet.

And at the end of the entertainment, all would be treated to specialty coffees prepared by Muriel's Coffee Shop that had a flavour cherished by all income groups. And there was to be desserts, that, like the hors d'oeuvres, were supplied by the top caterer in Vancouver: Jacquet's Culinary Cuisine.

The attendees were not going to miss out on the chance to show off their wares. Women were dressed in elegant long gowns: diamonds, precious gems, and gold adored their appearances. The dress at the annual movie awards paled in comparison. Regardless of age, all women had the appearance of youth, their hair a shining blond, brunette, or red: anything but grey or white. The men wore tuxedos and over two thirds of them had gray hair and noticeable signs of aging. But that didn't matter: everyone was sharp, elegant, and on the top of the world. Anyone who had seen them arrive, would have stopped to look at the unparalleled number of high-end cars parked in the lot usually filled by a much lower class of folk, groveling for a chance at the electric plug-ins. The teens hanging around the icy adjacent skate board park stared at the cars, the ice leaving them with nothing to do but wonder what mischief they might manage with regard to these private means of transportation: these vehicles that the kids considered to be like gods.

It was almost time for the performance. The pleasant one-note prompt and the diming of the lights in the lobby indicated that all audience members must make their way to their seats. A bustling of long gowns followed. The ladies' arms on the men's arms, leading their way down the aisle, as if princes and princesses, perhaps even kings and queens.

The venue was lovely: twenty huge floor-to-ceiling arcs made of golden-stained BC cedar crossed over the spans of ceiling above the entire seating area, forming an inner sanctum-like feeling, as if the arcs were like giant hands about to hold the stage and the orchestra area. It was clearly designed with Manhattan's Radio City Music Hall in mind, in combination with the feeling one gets in an old growth forest wherein huge, graceful boughs on towering trees, act as shelter to all earth-bound creatures, so far beneath. Between the great arcs of cedar, the walls were covered with sea shells painstakingly applied, making a textured white pattern, then covered with a matt epoxy-like substance so that these shells could never be damaged by visitors.

All in all, the shells formed a wall covering derived from the very sea by which lay the District of North Vancouver. The seats were upholstered with the plushest leather-brown cushions and arm rests were set within a high-tech plastic chair frame. But the highlight of the entire theatre was the floor: the floor was an enormous aquarium, supported at regular intervals by generous and strong concrete columns.

Once all were seated, the theatre lights dimmed. The stage glowed with light while the orchestra pit was quietly luminescent. Beneath the feet of the audience in an almost impossible-to-see dark blue aura, the population of salmon swam carelessly here and there, their quiet absolute.

The orchestra finished preparing their instruments and silence reigned. Audience anticipation peaked, and a handful of the ballet dancers moved onto the stage with a grace that showed both talent and the experienced knowledge of live performance.

But in the audience, a flick of a hand on the shoulder.

A scratch of the head beside.

A brushing of the skirt, a hand on the sleeve, trying to sweep away what was there.

Then the strangest sound, almost like the less-than-a-whisper noise of someone opening a dry mouth: fsst, fsst.

Another scratch of the head ... then another... and another; then almost everyone was tearing at their heads.

Metallic blue, green and black insects of about half an inch, or twelve millimeters in length were burrowing into all the patrons' heads, looking for the first meal they were to have in hours.

As the mutant lice descended onto the scalps, almost every woman started screaming and the men began to bellow. Though the bald men, less so.

The dancers on stage and the orchestra members brushed themselves continuously, and scratched their heads, as if a horrible blight of fallout was upon them.

Millions of small shapes continued falling from the giant arches above and members of the audience fought to gain access to the exit aisles to remove themselves from this nightmare of a venue.

All lights were immediately ablaze and one could see the millions of bugs-from-hell fall all over the theatre.

Hungry fish under the transparent floor rose to the level of the glass and open and closed their mouths, hoping for a morsel, not understanding the invisible glass barrier that separated them from their prey.

In a matter of minutes, Centennial Theatre was empty. Members of the orchestra had fled to the lower-end cars in the lot, except for a violinist and sax player that had run to the nearest bus stop. The ballerinas were cowering, crying in the school bus that had brought them to this nightmare evening.

In the parking lot, elegant women cried, shuddered, and shook. Most had then become carriers of the metallic-coloured lice. A few heads with thinner hair – three men and one woman, must have got mother-loads as they were positively glowing from the brightly coloured lice scurrying about between the hairs, like some horrid alien life-form.

Smartly dressed men were on their phones, some to their lawyers, others attempting to find some politician or authority who could seek appropriate revenge.

CHAPTER 18

By the time the RCMP arrived, the fire department already had looked at the bug infested venue, had subsequently happily exited, and then met in a clump in front of the theatre, not far from their fire engines with flashing lights still blazing.

It was almost blizzard conditions when Toque and Brock parked behind the crime scene forensics van, just in front of one of the many piles of snow that were here and there on road sides, because the snow banks on either side of the road had reached their maximum height of four-to-five feet. Toque and Brock emerged from their cruiser and as Brock then moved towards the street in front of the theatre, he scanned the snowy ground he was crossing. On the plowed road lit by the street light he noticed wet oil that had dissolved in a circular shape in the freshly fallen snow that had blanketed the road just moments before. He quickly pulled an evidence bag from his pocket and took a sample.

They then both hurried towards a fireman and Brock spoke first. "So, what is going on?"

The fireman looked appalled, and explained, "In the theatre there are millions of live insects all over the place."

Toque cringed. "From where?"

"They were falling from the ceiling."

Brock was quite interested, as if the fireman was describing an unusual weather pattern, and questioned, "Do you know how?"

The fireman tried to express himself in a tone of professionality, though his voice cracked as he spoke, "We don't know yet, but I can tell you from dealing with the homeless and from going on school meet-the-fireman visits, that the insects look a lot like lice – only these ones are larger, and in colour – fluorescent metallic!"

Toque closed her eyes, groaning. "Yuk! Do I get a hazmat suit?"

Brock looked at her like a parent telling his child she must go to school. "Of course; let's get suited up and check it out."

At the forensic van, Brock and Toque found Marol Carrier, the assistant manager of the laboratory technicians. From work, they knew Marol well, especially from a previous investigation involving terrorists that challenged even the strongest of hearts.

Brock smiled at Marol. "I'm glad to see that you've colour coordinated your red hair streak with your glasses and the tie-dye shirt that I can tell you're trying to hide under the lab coat."

"Ha, got to do something to liven up the black and grey streaks. Plus, I've got to say that I'm not trying to hide – but protect my vintage shirt," joked Marol as she glanced in the door mirror, seeing mainly her dark brown eyes gazing back, eyes that were emphasized with the Cleopatra-style eyeliner which was directly adjacent to a wide swatch of red eye shadow blended smoothly into purple. Looking back at them, she asked, "So what is it that you're needing?"

"Hazmat suits," replied Toque, with the slightest hint of a moan.

"Oh, is it that bad? I think there are a couple of regulation size suits here. You can have them."

"What about you?" asked Toque.

"Oh, don't worry about me: there is a size small in a back locker. But now I'm wondering how I'll even get inside the suit." Then, as she brushed back her easy-care hair style with her right hand, leaving several clumps standing at awkward angles, she continued, "A three-quarter length skirt with stiletto heeled boots? Dam. I knew my fashions would catch up with me sometime. There is no way that these boots will go under the suit's enclosed feet. I guess I'll just have to have panty-hose with stocking feet inside the suit."

Brock chuckled. "Well, that way you'll still be sexy and best of all, much closer to the insects."

"Ah, very funny, Getzlaff," replied Marol, calling Brock by his nickname. Then smiling in a self-defacing but agreeable tone added, "I've just about had enough of people asking me if I'm standing in a hole. But seriously, the two suits you want are in the kit under the seat there. But now I've got to check the lockers to find the one with shorter legs. But not a problem, though; I'll be with you in no time."

With that, Marol immediately moved to the depths of the van, while Brock and Toque commenced to dressing in protective suits.

"Right, well ... let's get these on," mumbled Brock, first slipping out of his regulation jacket, leaving on his bullet-proof vest and a light blue T-shirt and his RCMP slacks. He stepped into the suit and pulled it up, slipping his arms into the upper portion.

Toque followed Brock's lead, taking off her jacket and leaving on her bullet proof vest over a white T-shirt and soon had her hazmat suit properly zipped, though the hood was still loose on her back.

"Damn, the zipper is stuck," complained Brock.

Toque continued to watch, hands at her sides, paralyzed, as Brock pulled and tugged at his uncooperative zipper, and complained, "Crap, it's not moving an inch."

Brock continued to struggle and pull, then struggled and pulled some more as he cursed. "Dam it all anyway, I'm wasting so much time!"

Toque braced herself and said, "Here, let me help," as she stepped forward.

They were almost the same height, with Toque at almost six feet while Brock was just under five-ten. They were almost face to face, though not quite.

Her fresh mint breath; his Cedar Forest shower soap: these innocent scents not noticeable except at the distance of intimate personal space, filled their senses: a prickle formed and tickled its way as it moved up each of their spines. Their breathing increased, though only enough for the two of them to know.

As she touched his zipper, she let out an inaudible sigh as she remembered his half-naked form as he worked with the other constables preparing the blankets for the shelter. She could envision his chest under his vest and his T-shirt. She could see a space left between the vest and the shirt. She could see the top of his bulging chest. She could physically sense this man, his overwhelming magnetism, and she could feel his warmth as the scent of Cedar Forest enveloped her. Her knees felt weak.

"Hey," said Brock, in a tone of hushed hoarseness, as if entering an act of fore-play, "I appreciate the ..."

Brock tried to reel in the attraction yet couldn't maintain objectivity. He couldn't help but focus on Toque, her body so perfect: like Botticelli's Venus in many ways. As Toque worked and maneuvered and eased the zipper head, Brock felt the urge to touch back. Yet his mind was overwhelmed by her proximity: though covered with the hazmat suit, it did not disguise what he knew was underneath. Her chest – her breasts, were almost touching his chest, and they moved up and down to the beat of her heart, and her perfect skin – a soft, smooth whitish pink so close he could stroke it; her blue-grey eyes rimmed with long, dark eyelashes, her features were like that of a goddess.

But then flashing through his memory banks was his wife, April, his darling child – Angela – both gone, and all because of him, because of him, because of him. No matter how kind and forgiving April might be from the world beyond, Brock could not let go. And what of his professional manner: he must get a grip! His limbs and muscles tightened with the rejection of the feelings he was having for his magnificent-looking partner, Toque.

And Toque: she felt his warmth, his sexuality, his closeness. His face was like the Grecian ideal with his warm amber skin, his wavy coal-black hair, his strong nose and full mouth, the lips just parted so slightly: his form so perfect: his wide shoulders, flat stomach, just there – where the zipper was stuck, and his entire form was toned everywhere. And his eyes, the colour of a warm blue ocean were upon her: she blanched, but paused. She wasn't sure if she should maintain this contact; and though her hands became colder and colder in the winter temperatures, her interior furnace burnt hot. But then, her hands started to ache from the cold.

Then the horrible ordeals of her childhood flashed through her memory banks: her uncle, and everything connected to that relationship.

Brock's heart was pounding, if not throbbing. He could feel it in his chest, in his throat, and even in his groin. And though fighting with her nightmare memories, Toque's heart matched the pounding rhythm of Brock's and even her groin felt the pulse of the heavy, steady, unwavering beat.

Then the caught zipper released and her fingers touched his clothed torso as, still holding the zipper head, her fingers glided up, across his chest which she touched and could sense was pumped and as was hard as iron. Brock sighed the sigh of the relief of a job well done as Toque suddenly let go, stepped back, and with a slight gasp said, "There you go." The blood drained into her feet and she felt inexplicably light-headed.

Brock tried to catch his breath, as if he'd just run a race, muttering, "Thanks." Then after a pause, added, "Thanks, bud," as he went to pat her on the back but already she was several feet away so his hand dropped down, and alongside.

Then, suited up with their heads sealed into hoods and face protectors, the two of them climbed through the hurling snow and up the concrete stairs to the theatre. As they mounted the stairs, they could see a few lice here and there, rushing off to the darkest crack in any inset area. Once in the grand lobby, the world was alight. The torch-like emergency lighting system augmented what was originally subtle and indirect lighting on the ceiling that had been painted a midnight blue but had also been finished with cedar wooden arcs much like the theatre, only much smaller in scale but nevertheless offered the sensation of being under the great boughs of an old growth forest.

Brock pulled out his RCMP-issue monocular and looked up. He didn't have to search far, and soon saw the fluorescent lice scurrying and jostling for position along the crevices next to the cedar arcs. On the floor, too, on the soft carpet meant to resemble ferns of the great West Coast, the bright back sides of lice could be seen as they tried to bury themselves in the leafy textures of the carpet.

But what was worse was the theatre. Brock paused before entering, glanced at Toque, and recognized that she was not wanting to be the first one in. Without pause, he thrust himself forward, and soon the tail-end of the mass of descending bodies of lice speckled his shoulders.

Toque cringed and shook as if a sudden chill ran through her bones. As she moved, she could hear a crunching noise made as she stepped upon the thousands of lice crawling here and there along the aquarium-like floor, under which the indigenous fish still tried to snap at the insects on the other side of the glass. As Brock and Toque checked the empty seats, they could see that on every surface, lice tried to nudge into any crack or crevice, occasionally joining forces with the next louse so that they formed a conjoined twosome.

A third hazmat suit entered the theatre: by the trademark bounce in her step, and the under five-feet of height, it was obviously Marol Carrier who soon reported, "The custodian is in the lobby if you want to talk to him."

"Let's see if he can take us to the maintenance access route to the cedar arcs above," suggested Brock.

"He'll have the keys, if they're needed," supposed Toque, hoping to escape the barrage of lice.

Soon the four of them entered through a door in behind the refreshment stand where lice floated or sank to the bottoms of the abandoned glasses of various drinks and cocktails. Plates with hors d'oeuvres, also cast off, likewise had blue, green or black lice, finding no available scalp, sought out any crevice they could find.

Still dressed in their cumbersome hazmat suits, on the other side of the doorway, they moved up a narrow, though well-lit stairway, painted in an antiseptic white. Toque, trying to rid her mind of her squeamish reaction, counted the stairs. When they reached the eighty-ninth stair, there was a small landing and an access door, which was under-height, measuring at just over five feet. While Marol walked through this door, the three others crouched down and squeezed onto the cat-walk which was high above the theatre's seating area. Upon the walkway, they could see abandoned piles of string – about fifteen to twenty lengths of it. Along the inner/upper surface of the cedar arcs and stretched across each and every one was a long tube of gauze, all of which seemed to be lubricated with something like blood. The tubes were pulled open along their entire span. In the closest tube they could see the remaining lice, still struggling to find their way to the opening.

Toque tried to keep the top of her hazmat suit from sticking to her, exclaiming, "Wow, it's hot in here!"

"It always is – at the top of the theatre," explained the custodian.

Marol added, "The hazmat suits sure don't help."

Brock crawled over to the nearest arc, grabbed the end of the tube and gave it an enormous tug. With several snaps, it broke free from its duct-tape holds, and showered most of the remaining insects over the seats below but also onto Toque, Marol, the custodian, and to a lesser extent, Brock.

"Oh my gosh, Brock, did you have to?" moaned Toque as she brushed the lice from her hood, face cover, and shoulders.

Brock examined the tube, measured it up against the string, and one could see in his eyes that he'd figured out what had happened. "Look, these tubes were held shut with these strings. Someone pulled them open, then probably ran ... or possibly joined the audience!"

"To sit in there, with the lice falling? If they did, they were insane!" cursed Toque, still brushing the lice from her shoulder and shivering, as if a flu was upon her.

Brock watched another couple of lice crawl from under the fold in Toque's headgear and without thought, reached out his hand, as if to brush them off, but then thought better of it and withdrew his hand, glancing at Marol to see if she had noticed.

Marol looked away: it was unclear as to whether or not she saw his instinctual gesture of helping out his partner. Brock re-aligned his focus to the work at hand. "We'd better bag these gauze tubes, the strings, and get the finger-printing team here."

Marol smiled, inexplicably, then said, "I've also got to get some samples of the insects themselves: and more is better."

"For you, not me," mumbled Toque.

Two hours later, after the finger-print team took over, Toque, Brock and Marol were outside the theatre, peeling off their hazmat suits, then shaking them, to get rid of any hitch-hiking lice.

"Yikes, I'm getting on the rest of my clothes before I turn into a popsicle. I've got uniform-issue undershirts inside if you're as soaked with sweat as I am," called Marol as she hurried into the forensics van, her round derriere bouncing behind her, dressed only in underwear and panty-hose under her wet tie-dyed T-shirt that was then clinging to her torso.

As they were just a couple of feet from the refuge in the warmth of the forensics van, Brock and Toque pulled off their sweat-soaked bullet proof vests. But then they glanced at each other and stopped: a cold stop. And, as if hit by a stun gun, the glances turned to stares – at the T-shirts clinging: his – a pale blue, hers then a transparent white. The ultra-feminine bra was not at all disguised.

He coughed.

She sputtered as she brushed off one more louse, then murmured, "What I need is a hot shower followed by, at the break of dawn, an intense climb in the clean pristine environment of the Peak."

Brock took one more look, which turned into almost a stare, at her white shirt glued to her perfect form, the nipples erect in the cold – under the mauve lacy bra, and then, as he turned away, his voice cracked. "Go for it! Everyone needs time to deal with this sort of thing."

Chapter 19

Mrs. Bean with her ball of white hair, entered CO Grant's office. This day she was at the height of fashion. She wore a shiny purple polyester pant-suit with the reborn retro fashion of padded shoulders. On her feet, she wore mauve suede pumps, cut in such a way that they exposed the upper part of her toes. The pumps were adorned with a V-shaped strip of shiny paten artificial alligator skin.

Grant was even more exhausted this day as he asked, "What's up, Mrs. Bean?'

"Chief Abraham is on the phone. She said she's been contacted again."

Without pause, the CO picked up the phone, saying, "Grant here."

Mrs. Bean turned her back and wobbled her way from the office, moving in the same way as that of a person whose shoes were just a little bit too tight.

Abraham's voice was low, like that which reveals fatigue. "The note-writer is taking credit for the lice at Centennial Theatre!"

"Frogs, mutant lice, and alleged blood! This is insanity!"

"I'm with you on that."

"Evidently every local supplier of lice removal shampoo now has nothing but empty shelves. And there's practically a black market for lice combs!"

"And the lice-removal clinics are working overtime!"

"Crazy! But what are the saboteurs wanting now?"

Abraham moaned. "Now they're talking about leaders being targeted next, unless certain criminals in Scheveningen are freed."

"And what are they going to do next? Attack with mosquitos?" snarled Grant, with sarcasm tinging his tone.

"Or moths? No sock will be safe," added Abraham, equally caustic, "But who knows what these idiots will do."

Grant sighed, asking, "Still no clue as to who the sender might be?"

"Not a thing. Anything at your end?"

"It seems the perpetrators wore gloves. Glove resin on all the balloons tested. No prints on anything."

"I doubt that it was students. They wouldn't be this organized."

Grant grimaced. "I agree. Plus, the lice and frog dumps seem totally removed from the atrocity at the school. We might have a bit of a lead, though."

"Which is?"

"One of our officers, Constable Brock, has been sending in samples of leaked engine oil from each of the three sights. He wondered if it might be a clue so went back to the school after the lice incident to get a sample."

"Good luck on that theory. A lot of beaters leak."

"Fingers crossed. The old saying goes, 'Leave no stone unturned.' Also, we are investigating everyone who was at the performance. Those who bought tickets in advance, and we're questioning if they noticed anyone who seemed out of place. Also, we are checking road cams and witnesses to see if there was an old wreck of a vehicle seen at all three sites."

"Sounds good. We've been asking around the school community if anyone has noticed someone out of the ordinary hanging about."

"Another thing, though. Did you see the VPD bulletin about a train being robbed down at the Vancouver Terminal?"

"Nah. Is it relevant?"

"Probably. They stole a huge shipment of stuff intended for the schools."

"Oh, don't tell me! I can guess!"

"Frogs!"

"I knew it!"

"Yeah, they've also looked into the dozen or so frogs that were released on a city bus –Constables Burdon and Brock actually witnessed it."

"Burdon?"

"Carol Burdon. You know, nick-named Toque?"

"Oh yes, of course."

"But VPD now believes that the box on the bus was picked up by some naïve teen after it had been left behind near the terminal – left by the thieves who took the bulk of the stuff and probably were the ones who did in the basketball challenge."

"Crap! Anything else?"

much. They have a fuzzy image on surveillance of three, four individuals all in hoodies and baklavas. It was dark ng so the image is quite distorted. It could be older teens or young men. Maybe even slender women."

"Cripes! No big leads, then. Hopefully the VPD will come up with something more. Soon."

Grant drummed his fingers. "So, in the meantime, we will continue with the federal policy of not bargaining with blackmailers?"

"No choice, I'd say. And still keep it as a local investigation?"

"Yup. I have several constables on it."

"And several officers on our side of the river."

"In due time, we'll get a strong lead, I'm sure. Although I've got to say that I'm starting to like this less and less."

"Me too, but it does seem that the perps aren't much more than light-weight cat thieves."

"But mean-spirited ones."

"I agree with that."

"No kidding."

"Let's connect as soon as anything else comes up."

"Right."

Chapter 20

It was late afternoon the day after Brock and Toque had been to Centennial Theatre.

As Brock was climbing off the *Angel*, the sun was within half an hour of sliding down beneath the horizon hidden behind the gloom of overcast skies that were threatening even more snow. As he lowered himself onto the pier, an exuberant Rex bounded down beside him, always happy to be accompanying his best friend.

They exited the marina, and Rex patiently waited while Brock attached the lead; then they headed towards Stanley Park, taking the foot path along the waterfront. Near the shore, the water was frozen and only a single female mallard landed, skittering along the surface of the ice, and came to a stop just before she reached the open water. A second duck arrived, a male with neck feathers that would have been a bright fluorescent green-blue, had it been sunny. The male mallard, though, dull in the darkening skies, landed, just a few meters away from the female, and let out a solitary quack as the two of them waddled towards the open water.

Brock and Rex continued along the snowy waterfront overlooking the marina, but once they got to the icy seawall, Brock decided on the route with the softer snow which gave better footing. So, he gave the lead the slightest tug, to show Rex that they were to turn left, rather pursue the usual walk of heading north, past the rowing club's refurbished rustic Tudor heritage building and then on to passing beneath the Lions Gate Bridge. Rex glanced at Brock, a little surprised, but then happily accommodated the change in routine.

Together they moved forward, leaving behind them the seawall where it began its seven-mile pathway around the jewel of Vancouver. Although at this time of day, in this strange early and extreme winter, the park did not seem like a jewel but rather, a seawall-bound forest in which the trees' dark, black-green colour loomed under their premature winter-time coats of snow on this cold, gray evening.

They went through a tunnel which passed under Georgia Street, where one homeless man had already set up his sleeping bag for the night and Brock had to increase his grip on the lead as Rex strained to reach and befriend the sleeping underprivileged.

Once out of the tunnel, they reached a gravel path that formed a fifteen-minute walk around the Lost Lagoon, where weeping willow trees hung their empty limbs over the pathway. On the snow-covered grass beside the lagoon, Canada geese slept in clumps of forty or more and Rex again strained on his lead, wanting to meet the geese close-up. But one sure tug from Brock, and Rex was back at his master's side, happily sniffing his way at any shrub or any potential treasure buried in the snow.

Once they'd cleared the sleeping geese, Brock patted Rex on the head and said, "You're great company, old pal," to which Rex responded with a sloppy lick of Brock's hand.

Continuing along in the end-of-day gloom, Brock continued, "You would have had lots of interesting things to sniff at the place Toque and I visited last night."

Rex paused, and sniffed at a tree stump that had been whittled down by the local beaver.

Then they continued on their way, as Brock continued his one-sided chat. "You know how you like to snack on insects? Well, your stomach would have to be in over-drive from the load there. It was really something. Poor Toque. She's a great animal lover but definitely not keen on insects."

Rex glanced up at the name, Toque. A name familiar, though in his canine brain, was not sure how familiar that name was, at least not when that person was absent.

"But ..." Brock paused and Rex looked up, questioningly. Then Brock continued, "Toque, is ... I don't know how to put it. But I'm just not into establishing a real connection ..."

Rex slowed, then buried his face in a shrub-sized tree and again Brock gently pulled on the lead and they continued on their walk.

Brock let out a huge sigh as the two of them reached the end of the lagoon and crossed over a stone pedestrian bridge to reach the path that would lead back home. Brock almost fell on an ice patch that had crusted over the lumps of snow.

Then, as they left the bridge, Rex again strained the lead, seeing a number of ducks sleeping on the snowy ground just alongside the bridge's under structure. But soon Rex was on track again, although by then it was so dark that Brock had to slow his pace to make sure that his footing was on secure ground.

"You know, Rex, if things were different … but why am I even thinking about her? I am more tied to my memories of …"

Brock's eyes were watering and Rex, as if aware that his master was suffering, nuzzled Brock's leg as they moved forward.

Brock wiped his eyes. "Man, I've got to get a grip. Maybe I should ask for a different partner."

They both paused but Rex continued to listen, as if he understood what was being said. Brock further mused, "But what I do not need is Grant asking why, and wondering if I'm really not up to …"

Brock paused. He could hear the footsteps coming up behind him: a running figure almost upon them … with heavy foot-ware. She stopped. It was Delila.

She laughed as if hearing a joke. "I can't believe you're here in the dark! And on the snow! I had to put on hiking boots to get through this crap!"

"Nice seeing you too," remarked Brock, a little sarcastically.

"Why are you out at this time? This path is so treacherous but it is one of the few that gives me a continuous go of it. I had … uh … er … an engagement of sorts so I'm a bit late – would normally not run at this time, but I'm on the final stretch now … but clearly, you had a choice! You don't need to keep up momentum and could have just as easily walked the more plowed lighted streets in the city!"

Brock looked at her as if she'd just interrupted a sensitive and private discussion, which she had. Rex, on the other hand, lost no time in giving one of her hands a big sloppy lick.

"Ha," she giggled, "I'm onto you! I'll bet you're trying to get away with not picking up after doggy here! This crazy snow will bury any of Rex's droppings in seconds! I'd say you're in luck!"

Brock grimaced, and would have rolled his eyes if he were feeling less emotional. He simply responded, "That's not the way I do things."

"So, what's up?" asked Delila as she slowly lowered the zipper on her training jacket, showing cleavage and the sports bra beneath. The scent of Always Amorous was released as if an invisible mist. Without a second thought of maintaining a running pace, she slowed to that of Brock and Rex's walking speed. Delila moved as close as possible to Brock while still moving forward – they were almost touching.

"There doesn't have to be anything 'up' to just walk in the park. I'm just having some time to myself. That's all."

"I'm thinking that you've had enough time to yourself now," she replied, while slipping
her arm through Brock's, then pushing the adjacent breast onto his side. If it hadn't been the dark of night in an unlit park, he could have seen the goose-bumps forming.

But Brock edged away; pretending that Rex was pulling the two of them offside, but Delila figured out his strategy. "Hey, what's going on with you, anyway? Lots of other guys are thrilled to know me! But you! In fact, most guys make the first move!"

Brock thought to himself, *If it wasn't for April, and then Angela, there could have been a day ... but ...* "I'm sorry to say, Delila, that you're dead right, I'm not like most guys."

"You mean you prefer men? Why do the best-looking guys always prefer dudes?" pouted Delila.

Brock paused for a minute, thinking that letting Delila believe that he was gay might have some merits but he wasn't keen on the idea of dishonesty, so tried to explain, "What I prefer is my own space. I'm happy to be your neighbor but believe me, it will not go any further!"

"I knew it: there is a girlfriend!"

"Much more than that: a wife and child."

"What? I haven't seen them on the pier or anywhere at the marina!"

"And you won't." And to himself, *Because they are no longer with us.* "But let's just say that my commitment to them is ever present."

"Man, some women have all the luck."

Brock winced, thinking, *And some have the worst of luck – like being married to me.* "Hey, let's just leave the topic, can we?"

"Sure, but how about a drink?"

"Like I said, we could be neighbour friends, but it will never be close ones. And in any case, I can't drink now, my graveyard shift starts in a few hours."

"Whatever you say." In spite of her words, Delila thought, *But only for now. After all, when the wife's away* ... "Let's talk when you're more in the mood, but now I should get back. I'm dressed for running, not walking." Delila pulled up the zipper on her jacket and sprinted off.

Unfortunately, being alone with just Rex is the only thing that really works for me, thought Brock, but then, feeling some social pressure, called, "See you round, then."

Just after Delila shot off, Brock patted Rex, and the two of them continued the quiet route around the snowy Lost Lagoon.

From somewhere off in the distance, they could hear the sound of a lonesome train whistle.

Chapter 21

Toque struggled with entering the world of wakefulness just a few hours before her graveyard shift. While half asleep, with her eyelids still closed, she sensed that the oppressive gloom of early evening had settled on the Lower Mainland. And ... it was the day after the fluorescent lice incident.

As she slowly reached greater consciousness, Toque grappled with the memory of her emotion-packed previous twenty-four hours: the infested theatre, the mutant bugs, her squeamish reaction to the disgusting little mites, and the heat in the hazmat suits. But then her angst increased tenfold as she remembered Brock in his pale blue T-shirt stuck to his muscular chest. His slacks riding almost loosely on his naked hips. One could have easily slipped fingers between the belt line and the skin beneath. Toque felt a rush of hormones circuit through her being as she thought of her workmate partner.

She almost wished, and then nearly succeeded in blocking the fantasy that she was lying in bed alongside Brock. But although she fought it, she imagined him lying at her side, and thought that she could feel his warmth, just after they ... her mind blocked the thought.

As her eyes fluttered open, she immediately sensed something different with her surroundings.

As with every day, when on graveyards, there was just a faint glimmer of twilight peering through the venetian blinds. By the end of the month, this time of day would bring complete darkness. Today it was the usual, but she could tell from the light on the ceiling that the cloud cover was dense, though the twilight had an earie glow caused by the white snow that covered the province.

She gripped her mental consciousness and forced herself to think about what happened after her shift: ah yes, the invigorating climb, her climbing friends Joe and Lynn, so kind to avail themselves when Toque explained her need to unwind and re-energize. And the climb was intense: although the snow was deep and they often had to don their snow shoes, the Tusk was more exciting than ever; so much so that she invited her climbing partners back to her place for take-out. To make it even more celebratory, Lynn and Joe powered-up the soiree by chipping in on a bottle of Nova Scotia whisky and a couple of packs of tonic water.

Toque jolted in her bed. The ceiling, as it always did at that time of rapidly waning light, had dulled to an indistinguishable dark grey. But what shocked her was the sense of warmth along her left side and she thought, *What the heck,* as she felt a movement in the bed.

She had company! She asked herself, *A bedmate?*

Looking to her side, she saw the back of a head with dark hair cut in a crew cut and shaved along the sides.

My God, she thought, *Who in blazes have I brought home?*

But then the person in question turned in her sleep, baring a shoulder and one of her bare breasts and Toque didn't feel any better when she saw that it was Lynn. *What have I done?* The memory of the drinking, the laughing, as they had one drink after another, flashed into her consciousness, as did the beginning of a serious head-ache.

Toque regarded Lynn with horror and while she did so, checked her own form for clothing. With hesitant relief she felt her climbing shirt still on her torso but with fear sensed that her bra was missing. With one hand, she felt around her pelvic area and with more guarded and doubtful relief found that she was still wearing her G-string panties, though they were worryingly twisted.

Then, just as she wondered about waking up Lynn, she heard a deep moan from the far side of the bed.

With stealthy quiet and slow gestures of removing the sheets from her form, Toque rose from the bed and looked onto the other side of Lynn. There, under Lynn's left arm and leg, lay the full bearded and red-haired Joe, with the sheet angled down from Lynn to his navel. For all intents and purposes, he seemed naked.

"Shit," whispered Toque, to herself, "What the hell went on?"

Suddenly there were no memories of lice, or Brock, or her nightmare childhood, for that matter. The only thing that motivated Toque was an overwhelming urge to move her ass as far from her condo as possible.

ln't care about how Lynn or Joe would lock up; all she t was removing herself entirely from that more-than scenario. She quietly, slowly removed clean underwear from her dresser, grabbed her uniform from the chair in the corner, then crept from the bedroom and into her tiny bathroom. She heard a brief rustling of sheets moving, but no follow-up foot-steps. In the bathroom she took two pain killers, brushed her hair and her teeth, dressed, pulled on a rancid-mustard coloured toque, (which was how she felt) and then crept past the bedroom door where there was then a pussy-cat like purring interluded with the occasional deep snoring.

She sped through her living-dining area that had been designed for a peaceful effect: the sandy off-white paint, the quiet indirect lighting, and the two love-seats covered with a natural canvas upholstery. Equally tranquil in mood were the tones of identical beige area carpets ornamented with a raised pastel green salal leaf pattern with pink berries; all of which could be seen through the glass tops of both the living room coffee table and matching dining table. Beside the later were four chairs with canvas tops, and wooden frames that were a very light pine, like the floors. One of the living room walls held a matching wooden armoire: inside which was a small television screen, half a dozen picture books on the animal kingdom, and five ivory-coloured Inuit animal stone sculptures, each on a different shelf.

But Toque had no time to enjoy this once-peaceful retreat but rather fled with all the haste she could muster, not noticing that, stuck to a Velcro tab at the back of her bullet-proof vest, was Lynn's dark blue high-waist ladies boxer underwear. The size large tag faced outwards, as if waving for attention.

Chapter 22

Still half asleep, Joe ran his finger from Lynn's shoulder, down her breast, then under the sheet to between her legs.

Lynn, also still half asleep, with her eyes closed, smiled and shifted her position so that the caressing hand could better reach her. She reached down to touch the hand but when she felt its hairy back, she flinched and opened her eyes, saw Joe, and emitted a scream.

Joe's eyes were startled to full wakefulness and to his surprise, there was no gorgeous Toque with her waves of auburn hair but just Lynn, with her dark crew cut. Now he understood why the curvaceous form he was caressing in his half-sleep was so much ampler than that which he anticipated.

"What the hell," cursed Joe.

Trying to cover up her own surprise, Lynn growled, "Who did you expect? You were friendly enough last night!"

"Well," Joe stumbled, "That was different: there was the three of us and I was hoping …"

"You conniving coward!" cursed Lynn as she left the bed and searched around the room for her underwear, "You're as bad as my ex-wife who took everything, and worst of all, our beautiful child."

"Hey you weren't holding back!" accused Joe as he grabbed the sheet and wrapped it around himself as he headed for the bathroom.

"So, I'm not a prude! Big deal!"

"What was going on between you and me? I thought that you prefer women!"

"Hey, just because I know what I like doesn't mean I'm in a rut."

Then as he left the room, wrapped in a bed sheet, said, "Not in a rut but you love rutting! That's a good one. I didn't know you had such a sense of humour."

As he disappeared behind the door, Lynn gave up on looking for her own underwear and with a smirk pulled on Joe's briefs, although they were, for her, weirdly bulky in the front, though otherwise they fit rather well. Once the briefs were on, though still naked from the waist up, without self-consciousness, she stretched the stretch of someone who'd just had a particularly dandy sleep, just as Joe re-entered. His mouth gaped wide, astonished to see the full-breasted display, not noticing at all that she was dressed in his very own clam diggers.

Chapter 23

The Premiers of all ten Canadian provinces, the Yukon, Nunavut, and the North West Territories, were meeting at the conference center attached to the new Capilano University buildings in lower Lonsdale.

Just a few blocks from the water's edge, the conference center was at the top of a three-story building and on one side had an expansive view; on the other, there was a wall-to-wall and floor-to-ceiling sized aquarium alive with local fish and corals. The inlet view on a sunny day included the snow blanketed downtown Vancouver, with all the white, green and blue sky-scrapers perfectly reflected in the gray-blue waters, except where it had iced over near the shore-line. The image of the reflected buildings was drawn into by the passing Sea Buses where each transport trailed its wake of white froth, and further away, smooth ripples. All other boats, pleasure or commercial, including tankers, were moored or anchored, waiting for their next task. From the center's floor-to-ceiling glass walls or its expansive deck, one could also see to the south-east: the white-buried Mt. Baker which would be tinted with oranges and pinks at sunset. In the west, one could see the Lions Gate Bridge and beyond it, the Salish Sea and the white curved hilly shapes of the Gulf Islands and the much larger, Vancouver Island.

The premiers were in their best form, knowing that the media would be recording this attempt at problem solving, cooperation, collaboration, alliance, joint effort and so forth.

Twelve of the thirteen premiers were seated. They very much represented the diversity and heritage of the Canadian culture. Several were of First Nations ancestry, the most senior of which was a woman who represented Alberta while another, from Manitoba, was a male, and was the youngest leader. A third premier who was also indigenous, was born in the north: he was from Nunavut, and was a burly man in his fifties. The female premier of the NWT was of mixed indigenous-Scottish-French heritage.

Quebec's leader was French-Canadian. New Brunswick's premier was a woman of Acadian descent. And yet another, the one that was standing at her marked place at the table, was of mixed European heritage: she was a gay woman who represented Newfoundland/Labrador and was chatting with the KEYNOTE speaker from Capilano University where she worked as an up-and-coming academic.

While everyone in this group of leaders had features worthy of admiration, the Premier of Ontario had ancestors so varied and for so many generations that no one could determine his heritage although everyone agreed that he was so handsome that he could have been a clothing model. Another leader, a woman, was of African-Canadian ancestry and was born and raised in the Maritimes and represented Nova Scotia. Yet another, was a male Sheik-Canadian born and elected in Prince Edward Island. Another was of Chinese-Canadian ancestry, and was elected by almost every voter in her British Columbia riding. And finally, the second most senior Premier of the group, was a man of Persian heritage, born and elected in Saskatchewan.

Unlike previous meetings of premiers, this group decided on wearing similar colours so that the photo records would have a more uniform appearance. But the leaders did show their roots in some ways. In amongst the non-conforming accessories, there was a woman's shawl, pendant necklaces, and men's ties with designs occasionally showing something of the wearer's home ground.

The Ontario premier sat beside the one from British Columbia, who became suddenly reserved in her manner the instant he joined her. The Ontario premier, being terribly handsome and constantly pursued by female fans, was a bit miffed when BC's premier glanced furtively here and there, as if searching for new friends: someone, anyone, other than the man on her side. Her eyes set on the female premier of NFLD, who smiled back, and although it was just a friendly smile, it worried the premier of Ontario. Then, just as BC's leader was to find another person on whom to rest her eyes, she felt a stinging bite on her neck.

"Ouch, what was that?" she cried, as she felt a welt forming on her neck.

The premier of Ontario looked at her with a concerned expression but in seconds, yelled, "Holy cow, what was that?" as he reached for the side of his face where two more welts formed as two flies flew off in another direction.

The Quebec premier, speaking in French to the NB premier, suddenly yelled, "Sacre bleu!" as three flies landed just under his jaw line and each commenced into taking a formidable chunk of face.

Each bite, on every person, was the removal of a hunk of human meat. As the welts formed around the holes made from stolen flesh, the NB premier cursed in French while furiously thrashing at several flies trying to land upon her,.

The NWT premier, in surprisingly quiet tones, spoke to the leaders of Quebec and NB in French. "It is like some of the summers in the far north where my people live. We are more used to it but …"

The Alberta premier wrapped her head in her first nations-designed shawl and tried to convince her neighbor, the premier of NFLD, that there was nothing to worry about.

In response, the other leader cursed, "I can hardly wait to get home to my partner rather that waste my time being eaten here."

The face of the premier of PEI was already puffed from numerous bites, as was the case with Nova Scotia's head of government, though her welts were a little less noticeable, but certainly just as painful.

The premier of Saskatchewan cried out, "This meeting is a disaster! Where in hell did these flies come from?" As he rose from his seat, he looked at the premier of Manitoba as dozens of huge flies descended upon them.

Manitoba's premier likewise rose to his feet as the air became black with flies and he waved his arms to thrash them away, while bellowing, "It is worse than I have ever known, even in the north of the province. I cannot understand why they are here!"

Although the Premiers of Nunavut, the Yukon, and the NWT, had some bites, their eyes were still full open, and unlike the others, not half closed from the swelling caused by excessive bites and chunks of meat removed from exposed skin. But even though they were also hurting, they couldn't help but chuckle at the insane scene before them which was beyond comprehension: millions of man-eating black flies in a high-end city conference center.

In no time, though, it was no laughing matter; the flies were swarming into all human orifices.

Soon, no matter where they were from, all of the premiers, including the press and the body guards, were all badly bitten and the swarming continued, relentless. In no time, all participants were racing for the door, covered with flies and a multitude of angry swollen lumps. For at least half of those present, the colour of their clothing was not even visible, they
were so covered with flies. Everyone was flailing their arms as they exited through and clouds of ravaging insects.

Women and men were weeping, some were yelling, but all ran from the building and into
their waiting limousines and were whisked off to their hotels.

A RCMP cruiser pulled up and skidded sideways in the snow. Toque was driving, and Brock was out of the seat and was running towards the stairs before Toque had removed her safety belt. A young security guard was waiting outside the door, offering advice, "I'm not sure if you should go in there. There are a ton of flies!"

At that moment, as if on que, the forensic van pulled up and also skidded sideways. Marol Carrier jumped out, shouting, "Brock, Toque: wait! I've got some jackets for you!"

Toque looked down the stairs at Marol, and paired her greeting with an observation, saying, "Oh, I'm glad you thought of more than your purple hair streak and tie-dye peasant skirt."

Brock grinned as he quipped, "It's the Cleopatra eyes I'm most impressed with. Makes me think maybe you're familiar with the plagues of Egypt."

Marol managed a cynical grimace. "Very funny. But when I heard about the problem, I knew we'd need these." Then looking at the security guard, added, "Here, I've got one for you too, although it's only on loan from our research lab."

"You sure we need them?"

"I'm sure. From what I've heard of the number of bites, any number of the premiers will soon exhibit the symptoms black-fly fever."

The guard grimaced a half-smile of thanks and struggled with pulling the jacket over his protective vest.

Likewise, Toque fought to pull on the bug jacket.

Brock moved towards her, his consciousness a little too absorbed by the soft white skin at the nape of her neck, and the amber curl of a hair strand that had worked its way loose. As he approached, Toque turned her head towards him as she felt his presence before she glanced his way. Knowing he was almost upon her, she momentarily wondered if she could muster up enough nerve to chance stealing a glance into those eyes that were the colour of a deep but warm blue ocean. She flushed. A mist seemed to rise from her being. He warmed and the cold air on his skin had no impact whatsoever.

In an effort to assist his fellow officer, Brock picked up a wayward sleeve to help Toque slip on the jacket. But he paused, seeing a pair of women's underwear stuck to a Velcro tab on the back of her bullet proof vest ... and the somewhat surprizing, size large tab.

"Wait a minute, you've got your knickers stuck to the back of your vest," chuckled Brock.

Marol and the security guard cast bemused glances.

Toque's flush of attraction and receptiveness turned to that of embarrassed anxiety as she coloured further. "Very funny. You're still trying to live up to your nick name of Getzlaff, I see."

"No, not at all," Brock chuckled further as he gingerly pulled the underwear from the Velcro, using only his fingertips, as if touching something illicit. "Here you are. I didn't expect them to be quite like this!"

As he handed the delinquent clothing to Toque, she blanched. Then as if called upon to defend herself, said, "I don't wear stuff like this! They must be Lynn's!"

"Oh?" asked Brock, still amused but taken aback, with a headache-like chill replacing the warmth he'd just felt.

Still trying to be defensive, Toque asserted herself, saying, "So, what? So – she stayed the night!"

Marol's eyes widened, the guard was even more amused, but Brock's brows furrowed as he asked, "Undressed?"

"What's it to you?" protested Toque, "My private life is simply that: private!"

Brock, Marol and the guard all thought that they had found out more than they ever wanted to know. Brock stepped back several feet from Toque's side and looked anywhere but at her. At that point, the cold weather conditions seemed oppressive.

Toque realized how her life must have seemed to the others, but didn't know what she could say to explain further. After all, she wasn't too sure herself of what went on. But it was no one's business except her own. And possibly Lynn's. And, heaven forbid, Joe's.

She took on an air of pretend indifference, as if this was an everyday occurrence, saying, "Never mind, just let me get the jacket on. I'll stuff the underwear in the nearest trash."

The guard, Marol, and Brock felt as if question marks had formed in their minds but were afraid to make the query, even though their minds were momentarily overwhelmed with wondering about the woman Lynn, who was left with no underwear after she'd spent the night with Toque.

But soon the black fly matter at hand took hold as they all pulled on the jackets, and the guard led the way though the dissembling clouds of flies to the elevator, moving towards the top floor of the conference center.

In the elevator, Marol voiced her greatest concern, "I hope that none of the premiers get Black Fly Fever. Or anyone, for that matter."

"What exactly is Black Fly Fever?" asked Brock.

Marol grimaced under her protective jacket. "It's kind of like the flu only your lymph nodes also swell up. Not fun. For us, there's no reason to get it, as we are wearing the right clothing."

"Thanks to you."

The four of them entered the conference room and gaped around at the huge aquarium, the enormous view, and the abandoned once-sparkling glass-ware, the gold-rimmed bone china plates and matching teacups and mugs. Many of the beverages were almost full or in any number of cases, had been spilt as the owner dashed off to escape. At the food station, pastries and muffins that had been baked fresh for the day had turned stone cold. A variety of beverage dispensers, including various water mixes, juices, and large urns of coffee stood abandoned, while agendas were strewn about, and there were flies: flies, flies, everywhere.

While the guard waited by the door, Toque, Brock and Marol examined all surfaces, took fingerprints and scanned for the source of the flies: under the furniture, in the venting, in every imaginable nook and cranny.

But then Toque looked up, alongside the huge aquarium. "How is the aquarium maintained?"

"From above: roof top access."

"And how do we get there?"

"On the bottom floor, there is an access doorway. You have to walk up two flights of stairs."

"Why not have access from here?"

"Don't know. Probably so that the whole conference center is all show piece."

"Let's go," urged Brock.

In no time, they were climbing the narrow concrete stairs: the guard, then Brock, Marol, and last of all, Toque. Some flies were there, but only a few compared to the swarms in the conference center. Once they were on the roof, they saw that the snow had mercifully been cleared so they were only ankle-deep in the most recent load. They immediately spotted the locked door that had a distinct utilitarian quality and was affixed to a long, narrow structure that was for aquarium maintenance. It was a non-descript one-story unit flanking the back side of the roof and was the length of the entire building, and was about seven or eight feet across. Just outside the door, and in several inches of snow, were seven vac-blower machines.

Once Brock, Toque, Marol, and the guard were inside, they could see flies everywhere in the roof-top aquarium access which was one large room that resembled a bowling alley of about six feet across. There was a standing area of four feet in width which was alongside the top of the aquarium which in breadth was about two feet. On the floor area, six more vac-blowers were abandoned. Along three quarters of the floor's length was a black strip of something that looked like the material of a dirt-bike tire. Alongside, on the top of the conference center's floor-ceiling aquarium, was a gap through which they could see down into the hall that hosted the black-fly assault. The gap was the same size as the black stripping. And from
the floor below there was the scent of the then-stale coffee and pastries no longer wanted and dismally covered with flies.

On the inside of the vac-blowers, their bases were almost entirely covered with a layer of dead flies – the ones that did not survive the transport.

"I guess we know how the flies arrived," remarked Toque.

"And pumped into the conference center," added Marol.

The four of them then proceeded to exit the roof-top access point. Toque was almost out the door, when Brock, who was lined up to exit last, paused as he thought for a moment, then asked, "Can we see the parking lot?"

"Sure. There is a secure area but most of the parking is for the university students and the public," answered the guard.

"Let's see both."

"Let's do the secure lot first," suggested the guard.

After the elevator ride, they entered a long hall at the end of which was a bolted door that also required a push button code. On the other side was the staff and special guests parking lot.

Most of the vehicles were long gone. The lot was almost empty. The guard looked at the few remaining, and pointed out, "These vehicles belong to the university staff – they are the usual ones belonging to the die-hards that live to work here."

As she moved a few inches further away from Brock, Toque glanced at the few remaining cars, then asked, "Where were the vehicles for the premier's conference parked?"

"There were just a few conference cars parked here – the reporters, mainly. Gone now. The premiers and body-guards' vehicles were in the cordoned off area out front but they would have been the first to leave."

"Fine. Let's see the other parking," suggested Brock as he moved entirely away from Toque.

Soon they were standing by a relatively small number of parking spaces, considering that they were intended for all the students and the visiting public.

"Doesn't look like much for such a big university," remarked Brock as he glanced around.

"It's expected that most will take transit. We're very close to the Sea Bus and a major transit hub."

Brock glanced down at a parking spot just a hundred feet from the door, and walked over to it, extracting an evidence bag and sterilized glove from his pocket. He bent over and took a sample of a wet oil leak on the flooring.

"Unusual to see this kind of leak these days," remarked the guard absently, adding, "Most vehicles don't have oil."

"Yes, it is somewhat unusual. Marol, can you get someone in the lab to see if this is a match for the other samples?"

Before Marol could answer, Toque was in the elevator, anxious to leave.

Brock, on the other hand, took his time securing and then passing over the evidence, giving himself much more time than he needed.

Chapter 24

Mrs. Bean, with her ball of white hair, entered CO Grant's office. This day she was dressed in her most preferred fashion: in a V-necked, white collared blue flowered dress with a pattern much like that on Edwardian wall-paper, blue and purple bulbous beads, a button-up polyester purple cable-knit sweater with a rounded neck and aging, flat, purple shoes.

Grant looked up from desk and before he said a word, Mrs. Bean spoke, "Chief Abraham's on the line. She sounds like she's just about had it."

He grabbed the phone, speaking immediately, "Grant here. You got news?"

Mrs. Bean retreated, feeling light-of-foot, happy to again be wearing her comfortable old shoes and yet to still be at the height of what she believed to be appropriate fashion.

Abraham's voice had the quiet and low tone of understatement that can accompany defeat, as she reported, "The note-writer is now taking credit for the flies at the premiers' forum!"

"Why are they always telling *you*, rather than all police forces?"

"Your guess is as good as mine. Any cases of fever from the flies?"

"Yeah. Three premiers, five security people, and one reporter. They all had to have injections. But now, except for the bite marks, they're good to go. Or good enough, anyway."

"That's something, that they got treatment right away. But the red slime on Rockwater, then frogs, then lice and now black flies! Is this some sort of perverted war with non-fatal weapons?" questioned Grant.

"Don't ask me. Did you hear that there were two heart attacks after the frog incident?"

"No. Where was this?"

Grant sounded grim. "It was after the people had left so it didn't actually go on the crime report. One victim was so upset that she had a heart attack in her car while driving home. She lost control of the car and ran over and seriously injured both a man and his dog. Another died at home when he set down his umbrella and a frog leaped out, shocking the gentleman to death."

"All deaths not at the crime scene. The result is that the person or persons who brought in the frogs can't be charged with murder. But certainly mischief. No doubt the people who died were in a weakened state to begin with," lamented Abraham.

"True, but these pranks, if you can call them that, can be extremely unsettling, or in some of the cases, dangerous. When you think about it, all of these not-at-all funny practical jokes can cause fatalities, but in different ways. But tell me, what are the perps wanting now?" asked Grant.

Abraham coughed, then sputtered, "They're talking about more horror involving 'those that count': whatever that means; and are again saying that the next act will occur unless certain criminals in Scheveningen are freed."

"Shit!!!"

"Has your team found anything beyond the engine oil leak?"

"Constable Brock has sent in another sample of leaked oil, now from the site of the economic forum."

"As I said before, there's a lot of old wrecks still sucking up the fossil fuels. A leaking engine block is a weak link, to be sure, but I think we're at the point that I must agree that anything is worth some investigation," grumbled Abraham.

"Yeah, hopefully we'll get a break soon. Also, we still have constables doing ongoing questioning of everyone who was at the performance. We've checked the web cams on the roads but don't know what we're looking for."

"Us, too, although the neighbourhood of the school is a lot more closed in terms of visitors. We've had witnesses, mainly residents in the area, at several locations and at different times, describe what has added up to a total of eighteen vehicles that could be suspicious but without the plate numbers, there isn't a lot we can do.'

"How about sending the descriptions of the vehicles and we can go back to our web cams?"

"Sure; you'll have it within minutes," agreed Abraham, "I suppose you're still in agreement with not bargaining with the blackmailers?"

"Yeah, but it's a tough stance."

"No kidding, but I am starting to wonder about calling in other forces. I'm especially concerned about the threat against 'those that count.'"

"They've already hit the premiers. Who else could they be thinking of?"

"There's a federal leadership review in a week or so."

"Of course! Shit! Our Prime Minister is being replaced! This is incredibly bad timing for her to take early retirement! But at least we have a bit of time before then."

"Thank God for that!"

"In the meantime, while we're trying to track down the friggin' blackmailers, we should make sure that all officers and constables are on hand for the leadership review."

"Agreed: we'll have all 'soldiers' in place at least twenty-four hours in advance."

"Let me know if your team discovers anything."

"You, too."

Chapter 25

Marol Carrier sat in her sterile white cubicle in the lab where she was fixated on the information displayed on her cluster of three computer screens, on which over a hundred documents sat open, overlapping one another. She was scanning chemical analysis data: back and forth, up and down, bringing one to full screen view, then another. The curser moved between the documents as if it had a mind of its own. Every key detail was being taken in by her intelligent dark brown eyes outlined in thick black eyeliner beneath her circular red-framed glasses. Every few minutes, after she compared small sections of the data, she typed in more analysis on a separate document, titled, "RCMP Lab Report."

She typed in the last few digits, then scanned the document she'd compiled: then scrolled backwards through fifteen pages, seemingly reading the whole thing in minutes. Once she was finished reading the first page, she winced a smile of grim acknowledgement as she said to the computer, "Print and staple screen document, 'RCMP Lab Report.'"

With an almost inaudible sound, pages slid from the printer and onto a shelf just beside her knees. The print-out was complete in seconds. And then, as a solid package, the lined-up tops of the printed-out pages were sucked back into the printer, and then the resounding sound of a stapler filled Marol's cubicle, and in another few seconds the stapled fifteen-page document returned to the retrieval shelf.

Marol grabbed the package and, with the usual spring in her step, in spite of the black spike-heeled boots, marched past half a dozen other cubicles, past the lab of technological imaging screens and tables, past the glass-doored cupboards with various potions, weighing machines, and lab paraphernalia, to the exit. As she hurried, her unbuttoned lab coat flowed back, exposing her purple flowered peasant blouse above a three-quarter-length dark purple woolen skirt.

She passed a number of offices, the office pool of eight support staff, including admin assistants, and then stopped right in front of Mrs. Bean's desk.

Mrs. Bean had her bargain glasses perched on the edge of her nose and was using her touch pad to work on information on the screen in front of her.

"Hi, Mrs. Bean, how's your day?"

Mrs. Bean looked up, unused to having anyone make any sort of talk, never mind small talk. "Oh, just fine, my dear. What can I do for you?"

Marol smiled at the older woman, a smile that would make anyone feel as if they were of great intrinsic worth as Marol explained, "I've got the data analysis result for CO Grant."

"My goodness! Data analysis?" Then with a grin said, "Your PHDs are showing!"

Marol reluctantly accepted the remark with an unassuming smile.

"I'll call the boss right away."

Within minutes, Mrs. Bean had taken Marol's arm and while the later stiffened at the much-too-motherly contact, Mrs. Bean was oblivious, and happily moved forward, escorting Marol into their boss's office.

Grant rose to meet the two with a kindly look, wearing a soft brown tweed suit with a beige coloured tie on a chocolate coloured shirt, his belly bulging somewhat, causing the tie to form a downward, then outward slope.

As Mrs. Bean released Marol's arm, Grant took it. Marol stiffened further. Although Grant was not a tall man, at five-eleven, he was well above Marol's height, even with her stiletto heels. It was an uncomfortable contact. And after all, he was her boss and she

could not forget that he had the power to terminate her contract.

As Marol handed Grant her report, he smiled at her, saying, "I hear you came out really well prepared at the theatre as well as at the conference centre. Well done, Marol." As he said this, he patted her on the back, as if she was a pet pony.

If she could have, she would have rolled her eyes, but instead simply replied, "Thanks, I appreciate it, but what I've brought is …"

Grant considered her as if she were much younger and much

less experienced, putting his hand on her shoulder, saying, "It must have been pretty grim …"

Marol stepped away, out of reach, blanched and said, "The report I have is on the blood."

"Blood?" Grant was appalled, as if Marol was referring to woman's matters.

"Yes, blood. It was blood on the school!"

Grant then seemed embarrassed, and returned to the seat behind his desk, exclaiming, "Shit! Exactly what I feared. And exactly what they said. Take a seat, Marol. Tell me what you've found."

"The blood at the school is from three sources."

"Okay … and?"

"Two hospitals were robbed."

"Where?"

"Lions Gate and Surrey Memorial."

"Are you sure?"

"Positive. The hospitals have sent all the data on the donors of the stolen blood. We have analysed the DNA of all the blood samples taken at the school and I have found matches."

"Do you know if any of the samples carried a communicable disease?"

"Fortunately, no. The blood-work people have been amazing with screening donors."

"Well that's something! When I tell our involved constables, and the West Van police, at least they won't have to worry about being infected, though obviously they will be totally grossed out … like everyone else, once the word spreads. But you said there's third source?"

"This is why it took a bit of time. We had to check out a number of sources to determine what we were dealing with. It turns out that some of it is from a meat packing plant in Cloverdale. Human blood was mixed with that from animals."

"That's horrific! You're sure?"

"Entirely. We have done complete DNA analysis on all the samples."

"Why the hell would they mix in animal blood?"

"My guess, and I don't like to guess, because it's based on no facts, but my suspicion is that the vandals wanted lots of blood and there were much greater quantities from the meat-packer."

"Then why bother with the human blood at all? That added a lot of extra effort."

"I have no idea. It's possible that the perpetrators wanted human blood to be a factor."

"Who knows what goes on in the minds of these sick extortionists?"

"Extortionists?"

Grant flushed; he'd said too much. "Never mind, that is classified for now. Don't repeat that, please."

"Sure." Marol looked at her boss and thought that he might have been trying to act like a fatherly figure but really just wanted to get back to the lab and the next task at hand, so made up an unlikely and unnecessary promise. "I'll let you know if anything else comes up."

Grant nodded, then glanced down at the unintelligible report as Marol rose from her seat and quietly exited.

CHAPTER 26

The coffee shop was retro-eighties with brass fixtures, imitation Murano-glass lampshades, golden oak tables, chairs and counters. New age pastries with custards and chocolate squares were heaped inside half of the display cases. The remaining glassed-in shelf area was filled with a variety of fresh donuts that were constantly being made by the donut machine in the corner. There the circular pool of golden oil and the dropping of the cream-coloured tubes of batter was a mesmerizing side-show as they circled around the cooking loop until they slipped out onto a pile in a metal mesh tray where the donuts cooled.

The flavour of the hour was soon to change: cinnamon-sugar donuts were now plentiful and the whole coffee shop was permeated with this engaging scent. Donuts had become a surprisingly poplar treat since the recent discovery that products made with a lot of white sugar in certain proportions with trans-fat had miraculous rejuvenating effects on the human body. As it turned out, the danger to human health was not the sugar and trans-fat in itself, but that it had to be combined in very specific proportions.

Constable Scott was six-foot-five, and still had the remnants of adolescent acne. With a medium, though lanky build, blond curly hair, he sat with a black coffee and a couple of still-warm cinnamon-sugar donuts on a small white china plate. He looked at his counterpart, the other bicycle cop of the district – Constable Brown, who, as he entered the door, lifted off his helmet as he lined up at the counter. Scott took a bite and let the endorphins release in his brain as the simple delicacy melted in his mouth.

Once holding his plate with two Boston cream donuts, Brown stopped at the milk station, dumped an ample dose of cream into his coffee cup, and then joined Scott. Brown was shorter – just less than six feet, and was of small-medium build but every muscle on his body was toned to perfection, showing his interest in Iron Man contests.

He smiled at Scott, asking, "Hey, how's your shift been going?"

Scott, his blue eyes and smallish facial features and pinkish skin gave him a kind of optimistic and expectant presence. He answered, "Not bad. Thank goodness the snow has finally turned to rain. The slush ain't great but way better than the ice or pounding snow. Plus, all I've had is just a B&E to take notes on; otherwise everything is quiet. My biggest grief is getting saddle sores on the saddle sores."

"Saddle sores? You still got that pony racing at the track?"

"It's what keeps me sane. My horse is the best thing that has ever happened to me. But how about your beat?"

Brown took a bite of his donut, showed momentary euphoria, swallowed, then described his shift. "Well, just more of the usual: trying to deal with all the motor homes that try to make their permanent residences on the roads by the water."

"The usual suspects?"

"More or less: mainly the same old but as always, a few go and a few more appear."

"Any bad boys?"

"Yeah, believe it or not, a group of four constructed a home out of cardboard right on the roadway!"

"Bad enough that they take up the parking spots!"

"You can say that again. But there wasn't much new – four motor homes I haven't seen before: two thirty-footers, one fifth wheel and one really old unit called a 'Chaser' that must have been from the sixties!"

"Man, no wonder there's a shortage of parking spots if rigs that old are still rolling."

"A lot of them would be scrap metal if it wasn't for the fact that any number of the owners are jack-of-all-trades and pretty inventive mechanics."

"Yeah, I guess you have to feel sorry for these people who have skills but just can't get a break."

"Sure, though it's a chore monitoring them. I might ask for the odd cruiser to pass by, just to keep these city campers on their toes."

"Wouldn't hurt, especially if their beat is relatively quiet." Scott's face then became more serious as he asked, "Have you heard about what happened to Brock?"

"Brock? Yeah, but just a bit. Do you know the whole story?"

"More or less: he was really beaten!"

"Yeah, I caught that part: as if that guy doesn't have enough problems," sympathized Brown as he pushed back his very short brown hair.

"Brock? Problems? What do you mean?"

Brown had a face that had warm hazel eyes, a straight narrow nose, and a smallish mouth. Seriously, he regarded Scott, then continued, "I heard that he had a wife and child that were killed in relation to some covert operation."

"No shit! Do you think that his recent beating could be related?"

"Who knows? I doubt it, though. From what I gathered, the death of his family was more than a few years ago. Oh, but wait, here comes Matthews and Singh. Maybe they know more."

Constable Singh, like Brock, was not one of the taller cops, but made up for the lack of height by being in good shape and being an all-round good guy. He was a handsome man, with large black eyes, a regular straight nose, and full mouth on a softly rectangular face, under a shock of thick dark hair. He waved at the plump woman behind the bar. "Hey, Muriel, you got any of those cinnamon donut buns?"

Muriel straightened her glasses, putting dough dust onto the corners. "They are next if you want to wait."

"Sounds good. Just give me a tea for now. Three sugars. I'll grab the donut on my way out."

Muriel smiled and looked up at Singh's partner, Matthews. At six-foot-six, and a large frame, he was bigger than most constables. Her eyes paused, for just a few seconds, never passing the chance to appreciate the appearance of a tall, handsome man. "And what's it for you, hon?"

Matthews, with his ivory skin, large brown, almost black eyes, smallish rounded nose, full mouth, and a good set of eyebrows under extremely curly black hair was used to women focussing on him. However, some years ago, he realized that if he catered to the women whose eyes (and sometimes hands) sought him, it would be no short cut to finding a true partner or cohort – someone who would be an essential support in his life of law enforcement. He placed his order, saying, "Hey, how about one of those vegetable gluten-free wraps and a glass of soya milk?"

Muriel rolled her eyes and picked out the largest wrap. "No problem, but sooner or later you'll be paying for your poor choices."

Matthews smiled a smile that would melt most women. "I like what I like: I can't help that."

The other constables laughed, while Brown and Scott were enjoying their donuts and
Singh – his tea, and the anticipation of the donut cinnamon bun.

After swallowing a mouthful, Scott looked seriously at Singh and Matthews, asking, "Have you heard anything about Brock?"

Both Singh and Matthews were blank.

Scott continued, "You don't know? How could you not? It's was even on the news!"

"Hey, in the cruiser we listen to information from dispatch, not the news!"

Singh interjected, "Never mind that. What happened?"

Scott leaned back, enjoying the chance to tell a good story. "It's really hard to believe."

"Yeah, Brock was doing the Dudley Do-Right thing ..." interjected Brown.

"But wait, we have to say first that Brock disclaimed any credit, saying that he really didn't do anything others wouldn't have ..." said Scott, setting the stage.

"Never mind the prequel, tell us what happened!" insisted Singh.

Scott took a gulp of coffee. "So like Brown said, he was doing the Dudley Do-Right ..."

"Which was ...?" asked Matthews.

"Believe it or not ..." continued Scott. He shuffled his lanky frame, trying to get comfortable in the wooden seats. "Brock was walking down the street towards his boat when a toddler got loose from a mom who had a babe and another kid in tow."

Brown added, "And the little tyke ran out onto the road, right in front of a bus."

Scott continued, "The Mom was screaming blue murder but couldn't do anything because she had the infant and the other toddler in hand."

Brown interrupted, "And while you're listening to this, remember what Scott said about Brock saying that all others would have done the same thing if confronted with the same situation."

"He threw himself in front of the bus and shoved the kid out of the way, just in time."

"And the child ran crying to its Mom. But Brock was on the ground and lucky for him, he was dead center under the bus as it passed over him."

"But he was extremely stunned and scraped up by the lower extremities of the bus."

Singh and Matthews together reacted. "Wow! He is so lucky!"

Then Singh asked, "But you said that Brock was beat-up?"

Scott shook his head and anger visited his features. "Yeah, believe it or not, while the traffic had stopped and Brock was semi-conscious on the pavement, three guys wearing baklavas jumped in and hoisted Brock to his feet."

"Except for the baklavas, that might have been good. No?" asked Singh.

"Not at all. One of the thugs held Brock's arms to his back. At first, bystanders thought that because Brock was so delirious that the three men were helping him stand up so that he could get moved off the road. But then the two not supporting Brock pulled out their brass knuckles and pummeled Brock mercilessly while he was not even able to stand on his own two feet. This went on for several minutes before a cop car screamed around the corner."

"So, have the thugs been identified?"

"Not with the fucking baklavas!"

"Baklavas in mid-day? Didn't anyone report them?"

"Here? For one thing, since the pandemic, everyone is used to seeing people masked. Plus, don't forget that we're in Canada and as if that isn't slack enough, we're on the always-asleep West Coast! You should know by now that anything seems to be accepted or at worst, very lightly punished in this dopy town. People all over the developed world still shake heads with disbelief at the number of illegal marihuana shops that existed here before legalization. But let's hope that some of the traffic cams in the vicinity will have caught them pulling off their baklavas."

"I take it, then, that the assholes weren't caught?"

"Unfortunately, they got away. There was just one VPD officer in the cruiser and he ran to assist Brock."

"Shit. I hope we get the bastards."

CHAPTER 27

At five in the evening, it was dark out when Marol left the building. In her high-heeled knee-high black leather boots and her motor-cycle leathers, she walked with the trademark bounce in her step, giving away the fact that, although she was carrying a few too many pounds, she always visited the gym three days a week and worked out hard, as if her life depended on it. It was not that she was a gym fiend: she was only motivated by her love of volunteering for North Shore Rescue and the strength level it required.

Over her right shoulder she carried a motor-cycle carry-bag which held her work clothing; in the other arm resting on her ample hip, she held her helmet that had the word *Mom* painted on it.

She was almost at her bike: after her husband and sons, it was the love of her life: it was what she worked on and polished whenever she had a moment. She had lovingly kept the entire machine in showroom condition: her prized 2030 Breakfree. After almost of month of keeping it locked up, she was almost ecstatic that she could again ride her prized machine, as the roads had once again become reasonably clear of snow and slush.

As Marol fumbled with her carry bag that was sliding off her shoulder, watching her in the dark, behind a huge pile of snow that had been cleared from the parking lot, were three baclava-clad figures who suddenly moved into action.

They charged at her and the sudden movement, although it was a pitch-black parking lot, engaged Marol's instinctual self-preservation and all senses were heightened, like that of a cariboo that is suddenly aware of the presence of a hungry wolf pack.

Except for a horrifying incident on Lions Gate Bridge well over a couple of years past, Marol had not made full use of her karate kickboxing skills at any other time except for competitions. But since the last one, she had great misgivings. It was then that she had competed, and had permanently wounded her male competition. Although she was in no way at fault and had played entirely by the rules, Marol had not forgiven herself. Since then, she continued to keep up her karate skills, but only for fitness and not competition.

In the dark parking lot, the first person to reach her was a lanky individual of five-foot-eight and as he grabbed for her throat, Marol gave him a quick punch to the head and as he raised his hands to protect his face, Marol used an inside foot-sweep, causing her opponent to lose balance, and crash to the pavement.

The second attacker was five-foot-six, and proportioned like a strong man. As he rushed at her from her front, Marol extended her leg, rotated her hips in his direction, then contacted his waistline, knocking him to the ground.

The third mugger was six feet tall with broad shoulders. As he was almost upon her, Marol brought her knee forward, then across her chest, then swung her hip, at the same time extending a leg towards the attacker, striking him in the face with the nasty heel of her stiletto boot. He, too, fell to the ground, with his hand on his bleeding face.

As the third man fell, the first two scrambled to their feet and paused only as they saw CO Grant running towards them.

One of the aggressors, the lanky one, yelled out, "It's not over until it's over, clown-pig!"

Then, in seconds, the two muggers that were upright, were stampeding off – in the opposite direction. And, just before Grant reached Marol, the downed third mugger struggled to his feet, and with a hand still on his injured face, sprinted off – straining every running muscle he had, determined to catch up to his fleeing buddies.

Grant grabbed Marol by the arm and she flinched and threw herself into a continued defensive assault when she, just as her knuckled fist was about to contact his face, realized that this fourth person was not an enemy, but her boss.

Grant's knees momentarily went weak when he saw how close he came to joining the loosing battalia that Marol had just fought off. But soon his grasp on her arm lightened to that of a touch, as he fully regained his self-assuredness, and asked, "Are you alright?"

Marol's grimace-for-survival clenched mouth relaxed. "Yeah, sure: just some local thugs, I imagine."

Grant looked at this under-height woman graced with delicate gold studs on her ears. He wondered how this woman could have fought off what appeared to be three men. As he perused her face, his mind was forced to acknowledge that this was not the person he thought she was: he no longer saw Marol as an eccentric staff member socially removed by so many years in academia. And no more did he see her as a light weight. "What the hell? How did you manage that? Three guys?"

Marol moved from his touch, her eyebrows arched and dark, and on her pale skin, a streak of pink blush that matched her lipstick and, in an almost comical way, restated the same red hue that was in her glasses. Marol glanced away, not wanting to answer.

"So?" again questioned Grant, feeling that he would like to comfort her by touching her shoulder but the memory of her intense defense filled his mind so for a few minutes he remained at a distance and silence filled the air.

Yet men will be men and often bosses will try to comfort their employees so he reached for her again, this time for her forearm. Marol, still full of an attack-generated hyper-alert, was brusque as she stepped to the side.

"What is it I don't know about you?" persisted Grant.

Marol looked back at her boss, disliking the pressure to answer. But after a few seconds, her face took on the appearance of someone being coerced into revealing a secret, and in a very low tone, as if speaking to herself, answered, "Black Belt."

CHAPTER 28

It was at Hastings Park, only a few miles from downtown Vancouver. There the racetrack continued to thrill fans since 1889.

Brock and Scott hurried to an access door on the outside of the boxy venue that was tan-coloured and highlighted with white, taupe and beige. Huge piles of cleared snow rested here and there through-out the parking lot. When they got to the door, Brock noticed a small puddle of engine oil on the pavement just outside the entrance. He pulled sterilized gloves from his pocket, an evidence bag, and took a swab.

Seconds later, Scott and Brock moved through a hall and a couple of doors so that they were soon in the area of the indoor stables, which were illuminated by a single line of naked bulbs along the unfinished wooden beamed ceiling above the walkway. Roughly pieced together plywood walls formed the horse stalls on both sides of the barn-like hallway. Like all stables, the stalls had half-gates facing the walkway where the horses could generally be seen, with their heads facing out. Two out of every three stalls had a seasonal wreath or some sort of garland hanging from their gates. Bales of hay stuck out of a number of the stalls and along the hay-covered concrete floor. Up against the stalls, were metal buckets and the occasional trash bin, and here and there, a few mops and brooms.

Just beyond, were the exterior stables, similar in construction to those inside, although in these stalls, the horses could see out and onto the racetrack area. And two of the horses were lucky enough to have hanging baskets of flowers, though it was a pitiful and straggly display of purple pansies, doing their best to stand up to the dank and cool temperatures of the early December day.

The two constables rushed into the interior stables.

Scott glanced at Brock, as he said, "Thanks for the ride. I bused it today, which is okay for getting to dispatch or going back home. But it would have been bloody slow going getting here from the hall."

"I know it! But, not to worry, responding to steed emergencies is never a chore," responded Brock, with a tone of dryness tinging black humor.

"Especially seeing that you look like shit," added Scott, half staring at Brock's face scabbed over from being under the moving bus and by the follow-up beating with brass knuckles. Brock's right eye was swollen shut and, where it wasn't black, was dark purple.

"Not everyone can be as Aryan as you," joked Brock.

"Not funny. I sure hope we can get those assholes who hammered you. But as for my horse, let's hope this paging is a wild goose chase; maybe later we can go into the casino and have a couple of rounds at the blackjack tables and a brew or two in the lounge."

"Works for me. Might make my throbbing eye feel better. But this place smells gross!"

"It does! But I'm still hoping that my jockey called me here on a false alarm."

"You have a jockey?"

"Yeah," replied Scott, rolling his eyes at the obvious, "At my height I can ride as well as John Wayne but I'm not going to win any races."

"I can see your point. But wait a minute: where the hell are the horses?" asked Brock as they reached the entrance to the indoor stable.

"None of them are looking out – like they always do."

The horses were in their stalls but were not behaving normally. Rather than drinking from their water buckets, some were just playing with the water and not drinking. None of the
horses were eating: the hay was untouched. Some seemed to be straining, trying to defecate. Most were noticeably restless and were pawing the ground. Three or four were rolling in their corrals.

A jockey ran up to them and Scott asked, "What's going on?"

"All the horses seem to have a severe abdominal condition: the vet is testing for the many forms of colic."

"How serious can that be?" asked Brock.

The jockey was noticeably frightened as he answered, "Really serious. All the horses are affected and some of them are now having serious diarrhea."

Mindful of the foulness of intestinal illness, Brock remarked, "Been there. Don't need to return."

"It's worse for horses: if it is colic, there are a number of serious health issues that can result. The horse might go into shock, develop sepsis, and suffer a combination of a number of other conditions. As a final result, the horse might be an unfortunate candidate for euthanasia."

"Shit!" swore Brock.

"Maybe we can do something. Here comes the vet. I hope that he'll have a few ideas."

The vet was a short, dark haired man in his late fifties who looked as if he was related to people from eastern Europe. He wore a grey vest with matching dress pants and his white dress shirt had its sleeves rolled up, past his elbows.

"What do you think?" asked both Scott and the jockey, almost simultaneously.

The vet, still sweating from exertion, shook his head with fear mixed with sorrow. "We have to wait for lab verification, but I believe that it is Equine Colic, most likely caused by salmonella! Deliberately infected – it's the only possibility as the horses do not have the same food source."

"You're fucking kidding me!" cursed Scott.

The jockey looked distraught as he asked, "All of them? But not all of them have the same symptoms: only a few have diarrhea."

The vet saddened further as he explained, "It seems likely that they were all deliberately fed something tainted with salmonella. The diarrhea can come any time in the twenty-four hours following a fever."

"Why would some asshole poison a bunch of horses?"

The vet shook his head. "It's impossible to know. It might be the people who want to get rid of the racetrack. Or it could be someone who had some childhood trauma involving horses. The reasons go on and on."

Scott was visibly upset. All colour had left his face, leaving only a bluish hue where there had been a couple of pimples. With his blond hair, he was totally washed out.

The vet continued, "But for now, we need to get in as many owners, caregivers, and volunteers to help with the treatments. There are way too many really sick horses for me alone."

"Once you tell us what we need to do, I'll call in my partner. She has a long history of being phenomenal with nursing sick animals."

"Do! Call, call anyone who can help."

"Other than getting more people in, what should we be doing first?" asked Scott.

The vet looked at the three men. "To begin with, spend no more than five minutes trying to reach other owners and helpers. While you are doing that, I will be giving every horse
medication that will solve the salmonella but the horse is still in extreme danger because of what has happened to their bodies while they carried the poison. Once they have had the medication, as a group we have to work together: for every horse we have to hook up intravenous fluids. The horses need a crazy volume of liquid and constant monitoring. After the hook-ups, while we are supervising, we can continue trying to reach the owners. Over the next week, they will have to be helping, if we are to have any hope of saving these sick animals. But first, come over to my van and help me pick up the equipment we are going to need."

As they hurried from the building, Brock pulled out his phone, dialled, and before the second ring Toque answered, her voice obstructed by the noise of loud chatter all around her.

CHAPTER 29

In no time, Toque turned up at the race course with her climbing partners, Lynn and Joe. The three of them focussed on Brock, his bruised face, his right eye swollen shut. Mouths dropped.

"What has happened?" gasped Toque, staring.

"Forget it. The horses are the ones that need help."

"And I've brought extra hands."

Brock scanned the three, but glanced away from Lynn as soon as he laid eyes on her, as he tried to cover up his dislike for this woman whose underwear had been stuck to the back of his partner's vest.

"Are you familiar with dealing with intravenous equipment and horses?" asked the vet as he arranged a line full of needles and bottled fluids.

Lynn observed the horse-size intravenous needles, went white, and caught herself on the side of the stable as her knees gave out.

"Ha – look at her! There's a weak link! As for me, my only previous contact with horses was that of my foot being stepped on when I was a kid. Dam, that hurt!" said Joe, almost as if any situation with horses was not to be taken seriously.

"I might not be a horse whisperer myself, but you wouldn't know a horse if you were faced with a line of them," quipped Lynn.

The vet visibly soured. "This is no laughing matter, you two. These horses' lives are at risk if they don't get fast medical attention."

Toque, in an apologetic voice said, "Hey guys, the vet has a point. When you two said you wanted to help, I assumed you knew something about it."

Lynn rolled her eyes. "More likely Joe just wanted to spend more time with the two of us!"

Toque's face was grim. "We're climbing buddies but are not constantly hanging from the same line. Let's not forget that."

Joe winked. "Only climbing buddies? I don't think so! I especially enjoyed the climb with you two the other night!"

Toque visibly squirmed. "Maybe you guys should move on if you're not comfortable helping. I'll find my own way home."

Accepting Toque's not-so-subtle hint, Lynn and Joe turned to leave, but just before they did so, Lynn suggested, "Sure, but let's set up a climb before the week is out."

"You said it. Let's do it!" applauded Joe. He continued the chatter while he and Lynn were still within ear-shot of Scott, Brock, Toque and the vet. Walking as if he had a plastic wrapper on the inside of his undergarments, Joe accounted for his odd stride, saying, "Dam, I've got a rash from the chaffing caused by walking around the other day in climbing slacks without my briefs."

Lynn smiled wickedly, as she offered an explanation, "Perhaps it was the recent activities at Toque's that gave you the rash?"

"Oh, no doubt. But I did search everywhere for them: under her bed, in her bathroom, on her couch." Then, after Joe took in Lynn's broad smile, he continued, "And then, there you were …"

"Ha," laughed Lynn, "I thought you recognized them on me. I borrowed yours because I thought you were using mine! I imagined my sweet nothings would look good on you!"

"Sweet nothings, my ass. But I might as well have worn them! They were just like men's."

"Almost, but not quite, you imbecile!" laughed Lynn, giving Joe a playful cuff.

"So, Lynn, where did your butt-huggers go? Or should I say bloomers?"

"Maybe Toque took them to remember me!"

"Not likely. Not when she has a drawer full of her own – much more tasteful underwear right there beside the bed. In fact, I woke briefly that day and I saw Toque sneak a pair from the drawer when she was leaving."

"Then you should have worn a pair of hers! No chaffing and – nice lace."

"Should have. Those lacy intimates go well on a guy with a hairy chest and a full beard. And the G-strings are the best! Plus, they'd definitely be a souvenir worth having."

"I'm with you on that one!" laughed Lynn.

As Lynn and Joe moved away from hearing distance, Brock's mouth opened in astonishment and his right eyebrow rose, almost to his hairline and he took a step or two away from Toque.

CHAPTER 30

While the vet frantically prepared an over-whelming number of IVs and needles, he explained what had to be done: in teams of twos the intravenous bags had to be attached to the ceilings of the stables, away from the kicking horse; swing hooks would have to be installed in any stables with nothing from which to hang the IV; and then the vet must insert the plastic cable into the neck, just behind the horse's jaw. Then – the unfortunate creature had to be constantly monitored.

The jockey and Scott formed one team; Brock and Toque another, although Brock would have rather been in in the presence of anyone other than his partner who had recently spent the night bedded down with two climbing friends.

In no time, the jockey and the vet brought in step ladders, hammers, pockets full of nails, and ceiling swing hooks, and as many IV bags as there were horses. While the two teams would be setting up the bags, the vet would be running from horse to horse to insert the IVs.

Tragically, in no time at all, the horses had grown much worse.

Scott's horse, Blazer, known for his friendliness, totally ignored them, and while standing there, held his head low, with ears immobile, even at the sound of Scott's caring voice.

Another horse, Gypsy, lay on the straw, her head long and lovely, a chestnut colour with a white marking down the front. But she too, was not herself: a few tell-tale pieces of straw stuck to her head, showing that from the hay-covered floor she had just raised her head to look at the human visitors.

Another horse, Wrangler, had cramped himself into the back of the stable, rubbing his rump upon the back wall.

Yet another was the horse, Magnolia, that was fighting to get back on her legs.

Several others were attempting to kick at their own bellies.

A few would repeatedly lie down, then struggle at rising.

In addition, one sad creature, Colt, was lying down, with his long beige snout on the straw covered floor, eyes at half-mast.

One handsome dark brown horse, Diesel, had his head outstretched, so even his jaw was on the floor; his eyes were totally closed.

Yet one more, Pecos, was flat on the floor, including his head that lay sideways, with eyes unfocussed.

But worst of all, one depleted horse was lying sideways, with ribs starting to show.

Scott and the jockey took one row of stables while Toque and Brock took the other.

Toque grabbed the ladder and hurried into the first stable, where Gypsy was lying on the floor. "You watch Gypsy here and I'll hang the IV bag. There is already a hook there."

"Yeah. Sure, but I don't think she's going anywhere: she's totally wiped."

The bag was installed in just a few minutes and Toque practically ran down the ladder, grabbed it and hurried into the next stable. Brock followed, focusing entirely on the horse and the task. "Looks like Wrangler's IV bag will need a hook installed. I'll do this one."

Brock winced in pain from the brass-knuckle pummeling as he brushed past Toque, moving as if she were a complete stranger and started up the ladder.

Toque cringed at Brock's slight, but asked, "Do you want me to hold the hammer while you get the nails in place for the swing hook?"

"Nope. I'm good," answered Brock as he awkwardly balanced his aching body on one of the ladder's top steps, with the hammer held under his arm, up against his body.

Toque's face showed the sting of the hurt caused by Brock's subtle cold-shoulder, but she put that feeling to the side as she forced focus on the job at hand. She moved close to Wrangler, and stroked his nose as he pressed himself against the back wall in a futile attempt at putting some sort of healing pressure on his internal pain. Toque tried to sooth the suffering animal, saying, "We'll help you fella. Don't you worry."

Although he struggled with doing the job on his own, Brock got the bag hung without accepting any assistance from Toque. In minutes he downed the ladder, charged from the stable, pushing his way first.

"You hold Magnolia. I'll do this one also," determined Brock as Toque rushed after him.

"Why not take turns up and down the ladder," suggested Toque, the hurt colouring her tone.

"I'm already on it," replied Brock.

Toque held Magnolia's lead, and gently stroked her nose, as she asserted, "I'll do the next one. It's Colt. If you could just …"

"I know what I have to do."

"Don't you think that we would be more efficient if we take turns?"

"Whatever you want. You're the boss."

"Sure …" Toque seemed inexplicably saddened. She was pretty sure that she knew why Brock was upset, but could not bring herself to explain the Lynn and Joe sleep-over, in part because of her sense of personal space – but also, because she, herself, didn't know what had really happened.

After Brock had hung the IV bag in Colt's stable, he handed the hammer to Toque, who almost dropped it, as Brock backed away much quicker than expected. She took the ladder from Brock and scrambled into the next stable, determined to do the same as Brock, even if it meant her balancing dangerously on the top of the ladder.

While Toque installed the swing hook, Brock focused on Diesel lying on the stable's floor. As he inspected the suffering once-majestic creature, Brock's jawline firmed, as he grumbled, "I wish that this was on our turf, and not that of Vancouver. I'd love to get the bastards that did this."

Toque looked down from the ladder and on her face was the picture of troubled agreement.

Although Toque and Brock worked as if she was carrying leprosy, they maintained the momentum of getting their share of the IV bags hung, so that they finished at the same time as Scott and the jockey. Then, both pairs lost no time in proceeding to tackle what was next: the exterior line of stables.

136

Soon the four of them were completely done, and the vet was just a few feet behind, inserting the IV needles.

Once the vet was finished, Brock asked, "Is there any more that I can do?"

"Until more owners turn up, I need a couple of people to monitor the IV's to make sure that the horses don't shake them out."

"I'll do it," volunteered Toque.

"Me too," said the jockey and Scott almost simultaneously.

"That will work: that means each one of us can pace up and down an aisle of stables until more owners and jockeys arrive," The vet looked at Brock's swollen eye, grimaced, then continued, "Brock, thanks for helping, but you don't need to hang around unless you want to help out Toque."

The vet might as well have suggested that Brock help move a hive of killer bees. Brock held himself back from groaning, and an awkward moment ensued.

"I'm fine on my own," stated Toque, knowing that Brock was still reeling over the Lynn and Joe sleep-over.

With that, Brock turned on his heel and left, without even thinking that Toque might need a ride home.

If it hadn't been for their intense concern over the severity and horror of what had been done to the innocent animals, both the jockey and vet would have been surprised at Brock's quick departure from the woman for whom most men would trade in their car keys.

***

As the next days progressed, a covert observer would see Toque driving through the pouring rain, the huge puddles formed by the massive snow melt, and past the seasonal lights indifferently blinking while on her way to visiting the suffering animals. When not on shift, she was there, initially holding out some form of feed to any horse's mouth while the ailing creature lay pitifully on the straw floor, unable to rise.

After two days passed, there was a sign of health returning: as Toque entered the long hall, on either side of which were the stables, one recovering horse, Colt, greeted her by clasping its feed bucket in its teeth – and holding it out towards this return visitor who had become a much-appreciated care-giver.

And by the third day, when most of the horses were considerably better, any observer would see any number of them lovingly muzzle Toque as she replenished their food and water.

CHAPTER 31

The garage at the Vasiliev household faced one of the city's main arteries: Capilano Road. Like all new homes, the interior of the garage was finished with dry-walling, inset pot-lights, and a motion sensitive spot-light in each corner, for which the main control switch was in an *off* position.

Yana tentatively knocked on the garage door, even though it was her house, or at least it was the home she shared with her husband, Alik, and their two children.

"Fuck off," sneered Borya.

"Please, can we talks?" pleaded Yana.

"Why would I want to talk to you?"

"Please, I cannot hear you through the door. And a neighbours could be ..."

"Ah, you're too fucking paranoid. Okay, but wait a minute."

Yana could hear rustling: plastic or perhaps fabric being hung, or folded, or something ... it was hard to tell for sure.

After a few minutes she heard Borya snarl, "Come in, then."

Yana opened the door and paused before she entered, surprised at the change in her garage which had been empty, save a few stored lawn chairs, when Borya took his unwelcome possession. As she entered, she could see that one wall was lined with several dark grey crates – the type made out of recycled plastic; and alongside were what had to be at least a dozen garbage bags and a couple of sheets that all covered what might have been aquariums ...

But no, that isn't possible, she thought.

The rest of the garage was made into a make-shift office/living room. Taking up the bulk of the space was a stained, old, grey upholstered sectional that looked like it had been slept upon, with a dark maroon quilt marked darker here and there with what may have been food spills, and a pillow, with a matching cover scrunched and indented from use. Facing the cumbersome shape of the sectional, on the wall across from the crates, sat a wooden packing case on which sat a lap top and a small printer.

On either side of this work station, alongside a couple of unfilled plastic boxes, were fold-up white plastic tables covered with diagrams, maps of what might have been the Netherlands, and articles from a variety of web-based news sources.

"What the hell are you wearing?" cursed Borya.

"It is the top and bottom legging set. Everyone here wears it."

"That's not how women are supposed to dress! And your pregnant belly should never be even hinted at!"

"That is old fashions! But in any case, I do wear the dress or skirt and heels when I go out, including to work, even though sometimes the clothing slow me down when I'm doing certain experiment. But as for being at home, you should know that here there is no needs to care about what others might think."

"But you were outside to reach the garage door! What if someone saw you?"

"Don't worry about that. It's not me, but the sight of you that will make people talks," defended Yana. And then, with the slightest touch of sarcasm added, "Plus, you don't need to worries about the fashion I wear. I am very cautious of being non-offensive."

"So, well I know. As for me, the uninformed doltish public here wouldn't know me from their local MP. Or probably their Prime Minister! I can't believe you've asked me to leave," grumbled Borya as he gathered up pieces of paper, forming them into piles to be packed.

"Borya, you are putting us all in dangers by being here. You are the wanted man!"

He scanned his sister's face: her clear whitish-pink skin, her delicate and arched eyebrows, her long black eyelashes that in tone alone stood out because of the contrast to her highlighted auburn hair: all of her facial features seemed to contrive to emphasize her fearful dark eyes. That she was clearly scared, angered him. He inwardly seethed. "So how could *that* possibly effect you? You weren't at all involved! If they come and get me, what's it to you?"

She looked back at him, seeing eyes like her father's, though slanted with an all-encompassing dogma, as she replied, "I just have the really bad feeling about what will happen, especially considering the type of peoples with whom you associate."

"That's a laugh," snarled Borya, "You and your spineless husband! Running from our homeland! And when asked, Alik did not want to even know about my business, never mind pitch in!"

"Alik has his own works! And you forget that we just wants to live in peace in a country that honours individual freedoms!"

"Huh! You're ignoring the needs of our homeland! Alik is a builder and could be doing so much back home. But selfishly, he got his degrees, then sold out. And, as for my work, I could have used …"

"Borya," pleaded Yana, "You have far too much hate! I fear for you!"

"Ha," jeered Borya, "The only one in this garage that is 'too' anything is you: you're far too weak. But you are a woman, so I expect as much."

"Why not contact the polices and turn yourself in? Maybe they will go easy on you."

"You can't be serious! In the next breath you'll be telling me to call up that cop-turd."

"Why not? He has been very kind to us."

"I can't believe you! He is beneath contempt. He is the complete figure of all that I hate in westerners."

"What? Not Constable Brock?"

"Yes, that piece of horse-shit. He alone was almost entirely responsible for ruining my career! Because of him, I am a wanted man!"

"It was his job. He really is the good person."

"You should know that the only gesture I'll ever make to that swine is that of cutting his throat … or better still, his nuts … if I can find them! Ha! I can only hope I can get that rumoured paranormal knife – I think it is called the Firuz. It will be really useful if I ever again run into that piece of horse-shit!"

Yana bowed her head in great sadness and shed a tear as she held her belly, a gesture common to so many women expectant with child.

Borya cursed, threw papers into the waiting container, then further badgered his sister. "I cannot believe that you are forcing me to leave when you are nothing. Your work is of no importance. I have real work to do. You are a traitor to our homeland.

And worse, with your attitude, your children will be nothing but more capitalistic dogs using democracy to weaken the line of our ancestry! And what's worse, you cheated me! It was agreed upon! I was to get a child … a boy. You and Alik promised me when I, alone, helped you get out of the country. But you have failed to keep up with that bargain."

"Stop it! It is not my fault that I lost the babe that was to be yours! But it was just wrong … from the start," sobbed Yana as she sank onto the couch.

"You know I had plans for that boy … my son! Now that opportunity is gone. I bet you did it deliberately! And now you can do no better than to bare another for your asshole husband! A girl! After this one, you'll be too old and worn to give me what our family – what I am due! You are a disgrace!"

Tears ran down Yana's cheeks as she hung her head. "Please, Borya, we just want to lives in peace with our children."

"Your brood! You have brought shame and ruin to our genetic lineage!" spewed Borya as he dropped a final pile of papers into a waiting unfilled box.

"It is you, not me, that is a … a shame to a family," objected Yana.

Borya slammed the lid onto the box he'd filled and lifted it over to the bins on the other side of the garage. "You will regret even thinking that. But what I will not regret is taking into my own hands the problem of defectors in the family!"

Like muscle spasms cracking through one's limbs or lightning through the sky, alarm flashed over Yana's features, as she begged her greatest fear. "What are you plannings? You surely will not hurt us?"

Borya laughed: a cruel, cold, biting laugh. "While you can, enjoy living in peace with your children."

"No, you cannot mean …"

"Why not call your friend, Constable Brock? I'm sure he'll come running!"

"There is nothing wrong with having the friend with the polices. But what are you thinking? Tell me!"

Borya went over to his lap-top, folded it shut with a snap, then disconnected the printer cables, and placed these items in the second empty box. "Let's just say that your children, including the one that's growing inside you – are deprived of the values of their real homeland. An example needs to be made for all of our countrymen who have deserted their homeland ... an example of a first born or ... ha ... this is good ... a gaggle of firstborns ... might attract some attention ... kind of Biblical, don't you think?"

Yana fell to the sofa, weeping, "No-o-o-o-o-o-o-o-o-o-o-o!"

As the sound of voices emerged from the other side of the garage door, without even glancing at his sister, Borya ordered, "Get out! Get out of here, now! My friends are here to help me move. They cannot see you looking like a whore! Get out, and quick!"

CHAPTER 32

After briefly knocking and getting the okay-to-enter grunt, Grant's assistant entered his office. This day, Mrs. Bean had a particularly electrified fuzzy ball of white hair. She was wearing a strand of white beads, a blouse patterned with miniature forget-me-nots, of which the darker tones were identical in colour to her suit jacket and matching three-quarter-length navy skirt, and comfortable black wedge-heeled shoes.

Grant peered up from his computer terminal as he asked, "Hey, Mrs. Bean, what's up?"

She straightened her dark-framed glasses, answering, "Marol Carrier wants to speak to you."

Grant grimaced, as the remembrance of Marol fighting off three muggers came to mind. Then he cringed, as he remembered his own hand clutching her arm and her instant reaction to defend herself, cut short at the last minute. Then the thought of his request, his demand – of an explanation – which she held back, but was finally coerced into telling him that she had a black belt. A sudden sense of inadequacy permeated his entire self-awareness.

Mrs. Bean regarded Grant questioningly, waiting for a response.

Grant's face then showed the smile of a man caught in a daze, then mildly offered what was a true explanation, though not for the current lapse. "I wish that I could leave my door open for staff, but you never know when I might have sensitive information on the screen or a call that is restricted or confidential."

"Of course," she said in acknowledgement, but then reminded Grant of her purpose in the room. "Marol Carrier is here with some lab results."

"Oh – right. Do send her in. Immediately."

Marol walked into the office still wearing an open lab coat over a tie-died pink and purple shirt under a red vest and over a red and maroon peasant skirt. A choker necklace with flowers made of tiny red beads wrapped around her throat. With her black spike heels, she almost reached Grant's shoulder. Her hair was in grey spikes, except where she had sprayed on red colour.

She adjusted her round red-framed glasses, through which the observer could see her generous coating of black eyeliner under red and purple eye-shadow.

Just as she opened her mouth and was about to speak, Grant asked, "Are you alright? I mean, after that attack?"

"Just fine, thanks," replied Marol, "Though I suppose I am a bit out-of-sorts. Up until I was attacked, and that famous but horrible night on the bridge, I used karate for only occasional teaching or more seriously, for competitive fighting, which used to seem okay when any opponent had the same training."

At the very thought of Marol's defensive skills, Grant felt a chill and his limbs felt weak.

Marol continued, "But I'm not doing the competitions any more: just teaching it to kids – and only if I'm needed."

Grant then rallied himself together and again became the supportive boss. "Well, it's darn lucky that you have those skills. Unfortunately, we've not had any luck finding those three thugs."

"I just hope that they don't jump someone else."

"Me too. Fingers crossed that you scared them. But Marol, what have you brought?"

"The results are in on the oil spills that Brock collected."

"What did you find?"

"The oil is identical from all five sites: Rockwater, Cap U, Centennial Theatre, the Economic Forum, and at Hastings Park."

"The same vehicle?"

"There is no way to know for sure but as there are so few oil-lubricated engines now, the chances are high that it is the same vehicle."

"This is a huge clue! Captain Abraham and I didn't think that Brock was onto anything but it isn't the first time that his instinct has proven him right."

CHAPTER 33

Toque and Brock were moving along the side street from the dispatch building, just having started a shift that was once again in the pouring rain. Toque sat reasonably upright, but as the car turned onto Lonsdale, her inclination leaned towards Brock, and her pulse increased as she breathed in a faint trace of Cedar Forest scent. She snapped down her armrest and stared out, knowing that her pulse would increase even more if she happened to glance directly at her partner.

Brock's right eye could open now, and the bruises had lost some of their anger. As he drove, he leaned towards the door adjacent. His chest still ached from the pummeling, although it was better than it had been. But rather than focusing on those who attacked him, he thought about Lynn and Joe's conversation and their remarks about spending the night with Toque: the same night, the same bed. He could not get the situation from his mind but knew that he had to re-build a solid trust with his partner.

"Umm-m-m-m, been climbing lately?"

"No, but I've been kind of busy on my time off," replied Toque.

"Anything worth talking about?"

Toque twisted in her seat, wondering if she should speak about spending time with the recovering horses, but then thought that it might seem as if she was trying to get Brock to volunteer as well, or worse, that she was trying to make him feel bad for not helping more. So, she answered elusively with, "Oh, you know, things to do, things to see."

Brock paused, at a loss as to how he could re-establish a buddy-type relationship with Toque, who in the past, had disclosed so much ... about her childhood, but at this time, was clearly trying to avoid chatting about personal time. *Perhaps she senses my disapproval of*
her relationship with her climbing partners? Or, unless, he reasoned,

She is again involved in something that she is uncomfortable talking about – this time, perhaps it's something she's chosen to be part of – something kinky – like a continued sexual relationship – a threesome or maybe even more. His mind bolted. *Toque, poor Toque, to have suffered such terrible abuse as a child and now she has run to the refuge of not one lover, but probably at least two.* He imagined Toque in bed with Lynn and Joe. Then started to wonder about who was the dominant one and exactly what formations they preferred. Then Toque's phone's buzzer sounded.

She glanced at the call display and answered, "Hi there. Any news?"

Brock could hear only a muffled male voice on her phone.

"Sure, I'd love to be there later. I just can't have enough of personal contact."

Brock could hear the male voice chuckle, say a few words, and the sound of another person, a woman, giggle in the background.

"Oh yeah, I can bring that. It's only been used a few times. It will still be good. Especially if she's in the upright position."

Brock's lip curled as he thought, *What is she talking about? My good old partner's professionalism has gone straight down the tube.* His face reddened, though he tried to suppress his angst.

Then she gleefully continued, "But you mounted her this morning? Excellent! I'll try it as well when I'm there after my shift. You'll be there, too? Great! I can hardly wait!" The voice at the other end made another remark unintelligible to Brock though Toque's reaction had a distinctly positive tone, as she recalled, "She moved so gracefully yesterday!"

Brock focused on the traffic, wishing that Toque would keep conversations to herself when her phone rang again.

"Yeah?"

Brock could hear a blurry voice – a woman's voice this time.

"Thanks for letting me know," then glimpsing at Brock's clenched jaw added, "I'm on shift right now. Got to go."

The two constables continued up Lonsdale. A car from a side-street pulled in front of them, without warning, and Brock braked suddenly. Toque glanced at the errant vehicle and observed, "The plate sticker is out of date."

Brock, relieved that some law enforcement business fell into their hands, put on his flashers and siren, and pulled over the errant vehicle. In no time, Toque was out and talking to the uninsured vehicle's driver.

When she returned to the cruiser, she reported back. "Claims he is on his way to get the sticker. He just got his license renewed via email, after having a medical halt on his driving privileges."

"He's okay now?"

"Yeah, the insurance corporation was holding his license till his condition was stabilized by meds. He's paid the insurance from home and just needs the sticker. A slight transgression, only, his first in fifty years of driving. I think he's okay."

"I agree. Let's go over to the Highlands area."

"Sure. And by the way," Toque tried to sound casual, as if the information she was about to impart was old news. "You know the sick horses?"

"Yup. Poor sods."

"It turns out that their colic was caused by being fed salmonella tainted food."

"All the horses?"

"Yeah, someone deliberately poisoned them!"

"That makes no sense! What kind of sick person would do that?"

"Like you said before, someone who is truly demented."

"Where did you get this information? Was it on the radio? I haven't seen any news yet – today."

"Me either. The source is VPD forensics."

"More and more, it's seeming that the scope of these pranks is far greater than that kid Peanut could have organized."

"Probably, but maybe we should have another look at his home and friends, just to make sure."

"Why not?"

The two constables continued driving down the road, swallowing the bile-filled information on the cause of the suffering of the racetrack heroes. Both Brock and Toque were immediately lost in their own thoughts, wondering why anyone could be so cruel as to poison innocent, harmless animals.

CHAPTER 34

Mrs. Bean, with a ball of fluorescent red tinted hair, entered Grant's office. This day, her fashions were clearly influenced by those of Marol, though her face looked particularly pasty when adjacent to the brilliant red hair colour streaks and under the dark-framed glasses. Atop her traditional grandma-style green and red floral-patterned dress speckled with gold flecks, on her shoulders she wore a red scarf patterned with appliqued Christmas trees with little golden bells on the top of each tree. The scarf was worn like a shawl and it kept slipping from its wrap-around position, jingling as it moved and as she wobbled into Grant's office on shiny red spike-heeled boots.

Grant was grey with fatigue but his eyes rounded as he saw his changed assistant, and asked, "What's new, Mrs. Bean?"

Mrs. Bean flicked an escaped end of scarf back across her shoulder, only to have it fall forward again, as she faltered forward. "Chief Abraham is on the phone. She said she's been contacted again."

As Grant reached for his phone, Mrs. Bean wavered her way from the office, the scarf bells jingling a cheery song quite irrelevant to the pressing work of law enforcement. As soon as she'd closed the door behind her, Grant groaned in anticipation as he picked up the phone. "Grant speaking."

Abraham's voice, as before, was low, like the tone of a person who's fighting an over-whelming challenge. "The note-writer is taking credit for the equestrian colic!"

"What? The writer is contacting you about something he or she did in Vancouver? Don't they know about police jurisdictions?"

"They also sent the note to VPD."

"And left me out? If this wasn't so important, I would feel hurt!" moaned Grant, with black humour tinging his tone.

"Yes, it would be funny, if it wasn't so serious."

Grant moaned quietly, then loosened his tie. "So, what is the latest?"

"They again are threatening 'those that count,' whoever that means."

"Could they have been referring to the horses? After all, there was that human-interest story on the news a week or so ago about horses being able to count."

"Maybe. But because ... in part, they're already taking credit for the colic infection, I believe that this threat is a new one."

"Because ..." prodded Grant.

"Because they have now threatened with the names of potential victims!"

"No! Anyone I know?"

"Your constables, Brock and Burdon."

"Crap!!! What about *your* officers?"

"Just your two were mentioned."

"Brock and Burdon, aka Toque."

"Exactly. The email said that the two of them will be targeted if the investigations are not halted and again, unless certain Scheveningen criminals are freed."

"Are they serious? Scheveningen again? Did they give names?"

"No: no names."

"And did they say which investigations?"

"Yup. Teams investigating the mischief at the school, the university, the theatre, the premier's conference, and the racetrack: all. Oh, and another thing – the writer said something about female slime in the police force. Perhaps they're again referring to your constable, Burdon, as she was already named. But on the other hand, have you had any suspicious activities with regard to your women employees?"

Grant thought about Marol being jumped by three men. "Don't tell me that that is connected."

"Who? What?"

"One of our lab team members was jumped but she's a black belt so they didn't get anywhere, thank God."

"Bonus marks for her! But it's becoming more and more apparent that these pranks are a lot worse than simple mischief."

"But with regard to the lab team member, she has now reported that the oil found by Constable Brock was identical in all five sites."

"Rockwater, Cap U, Centennial Theatre, the Premiers' Economic Forum and at Hastings Park?"

"You got it."

"Anything on the eighteen vehicles spotted near the school? Have you had any matches with those seen around the sites in North Van?"

"That one is time-consuming. I've got a constable on it as we speak. I'm just hoping I won't need to add more men to that job.."

"Should we call in external law enforcement?"

"It just doesn't seem quite serious enough to bring in the army. Yet the request for the prisoners' release is a mounting concern."

"It is. And it does not seem that it is a passing and idle threat. We are definitely getting near the stage of calling in federal assistance. Bad enough that they have now attacked a staff member and are threating constables. But it seems that they are light-weights with the type of crime with which they've been involved."

"Agreed, but let's step things up. Maybe we'll get them before any more harm is done."

"Hopefully."

CHAPTER 35

Alik climbed down the stairs in the basement of the dispatch building lugging two large bulky trash bags. Of all the tables that lined the room, each and every one was covered with pre-checked and now folded blankets. And there were plastic bins awaiting filling and delivery. Alik's warm brown eyes scanned the area, searching for a face he recognized amidst the volunteering constables, all of whom seemed overly heated because of the furnace blasting away in the adjacent room. Most were wearing just T-shirts over yellow-striped uniform slacks. All five constables present had black shoes shinning as a constant reminder of the expected dress code. In seconds, Alik focussed on a person he well recognized.

"Hey, Brock, nice seeing you!"

Brock looked up, just after taking a gulp from an alongside cup which was labelled with the logo of Muriel's take-out coffee. He smiled as he greeted Alik. "Good to see you, too, and thanks in advance from all of us for offering to drop off the blankets."

"Agreed," chorused the other members of the blanket-folding team.

"A pleasure," grinned Alik. Then further addressing Brock, "But what happened to your face?"

"Ah, a little bit of a run-in. Not an issue." Brock then reached into an orange cellophane bag sitting on the table in front of him, just beside a pile of blankets, and threw a Cheesesnack into his mouth. Then, in seconds, right after the piece of snack food was consumed, Brock continued the exchange, "But Alik, what's the deal with the bags? I hope that you're not delivering garbage to the dispatch hall."

Alik laughed. "Hardly. I didn't know if you guys tag the blankets or anything before they go to the shelter."

"We just fold and check them," explained Scott, "But did you collect all of those?"

Alik beamed over the large contribution stuffed into the bags. "I'd love to say that I am that generous but have to give credit where it is due. A number of people from where I go to church want to help out with your 'Adopt a Shelter Program,' even though our place of worship is over town.

The blankets here are in quite good condition. Some members of the congregation have even gone out and bought brand new ones."

"Hey, that's great that they are keen to help," praised Scott.

Alik accepted the approval, saying, "Of course. We all feel for the homeless. Some of our contributors are struggling, themselves, but in spite of personal difficulties, they want to help those less fortunate."

"There's a community that's a great part of any neighbourhood," remarked Brown.

"Thanks. Like all churches, charity is a big part of our mandate."

"Sometimes we spend so much time on the differences that we don't notice the similarities," observed Scott.

"Say, Alik," said Brock, "I'm glad you got these to us today. Just leave the bags where you are and we'll fold what we can. We'll get most of them ready while your truck is being loaded. Even though it's raining rather than snowing, these blankets are really needed."

"I thought that might be the case. I was just holding out for one last contributor who, as it turned out, had broken a bone in her foot and couldn't get to the church. One of us would have gladly gone to pick up her donation but she didn't want to put us out. She just said that she'd bring in a couple of top-quality blankets as soon as she could."

"That's impressive," commended Singh.

"You don't know the half of it," explained Alik, "When she did come in, she came with a walker and travelled on a bus and then, to make her efforts even more commendable, struggled along the five-block hike that was from the bus stop to the church."

Matthews' eyes widened. "Sometimes I feel like my efforts are nothing more than a joke compared to what others go through."

"Ah, you're too modest," remarked Singh, "Every time there is a charity, you're there helping."

"Nothing better to do," responded Matthews, forever humble.

"Is there anything else I can help with before I go? You want me to fold a few before I load up the bins?" offered Alik.

"No, but thanks. We've got to get what we can to them asap. We plan to make another trip later in the week, anyway, because there are a few more being dropped off in the next day or two," responded Brock, "But by the way, how is Yana doing?"

As Alik was about to reply, on the other side of the room, Scott called to Brown and Singh, "You guys going to see the game tomorrow?"

"What? *The* game? You got tickets?" asked the feeling-excluded Matthews.

"On our wages? Surely, you're joking!" laughed Brown.

"Come on Matthews. You have to know that the guys meet at the sports bar down by the tracks."

"Oh, you mean ..."

As the four constables made plans to watch the next hockey game, Alik, sensing that he was able to speak surreptitiously with Brock, explained, "Well, seeing that you ask, she seems rather preoccupied – but isn't talking."

"Could it be her workplace? The robbery?" asked Brock.

"No, I don't think so. The mess at her workplace is all sorted out and new samples are arriving daily."

"I hate to ask," said Brock, "But might she be feeling badly about the loss of the unborn child?"

Alik blanched as he replied, "It sure wasn't easy," He then paused, awkwardly, then continued, "And she really hoped that the babe would be a kind of ... uh ... er ... new life for her brother, Borya. There is no question that she suffers the loss. But there seems to be something else that she isn't saying. Well anyway ..." he trailed off, as he turned to leave.

Brock felt badly for this alienated husband as he suggested, "Let's just hope that it's the excessive hormones of pregnancy that are bothering her."

Then, as Alik stepped away, he answered, "I sure hope so. But shall we get these blanket bins into the truck?"

"Right! Hey guys! Let's load her up. I think that the shelter staff are hoping to get what we can put together in time to make up tonight's beds!"

In no time the table tops in the detachment hall were almost empty, and Alik's truck was piled with the bulk of the blankets loaded into plastic bins.

Then, as Alik pulled away, Brock called out, "Thanks again, Alik. Scott and I will follow you in a cruiser."

CHAPTER 36

Located down by the railway tracks just a few hundred meters from Burrard Inlet, the red brick pub was architecturally designed to be like a British train station. While The Randy was situated far too close to a quiet middle-class neighbourhood, its location was made even worse by the fact that it was practically on top of a huge sewage treatment plant. There, the neighbours once complained about their proximity to the pub, and succeeded in putting a stop to the proposed construction of a big-box store across the street, although that, along with the noise from the Randy, had become a distant memory of what would have been a better community.

Brock passed under the twenty-foot red awning of the entranceway, trimmed with white blinking seasonal lights, and stepped into the dark inside. The Randy smelt entirely of beer, though, at least it was fresh beer. Brock's injuries resulting from the pummeling were on their way to recovery and although his face still had some bruising, he had returned to moving with a casual all-muscles-are-tuned saunter of an athlete. He walked past chewing gum machines that had been converted to ones that dispensed regular and barbeque peanuts, along with curried fingerling pretzels. He scanned the room. In behind the mahogany bar were two bartenders, dressed in shorts, T-shirts, and aprons, even though December blew cold rain just outside the doors.

Brock didn't recognize anyone amongst the seven men perched on bar stools watching the four screens above the completely stocked bar – numerous meters in length, holding double-decker rows of bottles that contained anything anyone could want or imagine. Strung just above the bar were blinking multi-coloured twinkling Christmas lights. He smiled at the figure seated at the end of the bar: it was a wooden sculpture of a popular bar-fly character from an eighties TV series. Someone had stretched a lighted Santa hat onto the sculpture's head. Brock then scanned the rest of the first room. Lots of laughing and animated faces but not one that he recognized.

The pub was packed and the customers who mixed socializing with keeping a keen eye on the games being shown on the monitors hanging from the ceilings and placed in every nook and corner, save the red glow from one lit casino machine and the occasional fabric crest of a widely known team. Over half of the big screen monitors were tuned into the home hockey game and the entire pub cheered as the home team scored. Ninety percent of the room was male. As more beers were being ordered, Brock maneuvered himself past the many dark wood tables crowded with empty glasses, froth still visible on many of the drained tumblers.

The only passageway to get through the pub to its second serving area was that directly adjacent to the bar, where the servers picked up orders. There Brock moved around a lit Christmas tree, then crossed from the shaded wooden floor and onto an area of murky tiles, on which lay a large midnight blue carpet entirely covered with the logo of the home hockey team: the Canucks.

Finally, in the second section of the pub, an area that held another thirty or more people, Brock could see faces he recognized, in a corner where several framed sports heroes' uniform shirts hung up against the almost obscured red brick wall. Seated there was a good representation from both West and North Vancouver detachments.

He saw Toque before anyone else. In fact, for a moment it seemed as if she was the only other person in the room, in spite of the loud chatter and cheering of the lubricated crowd. On her right side was Trembley; on the other, an empty chair, then Karimi. Toque waved her acknowledgment of Brock's entrance, as if to show their location.

As soon as he was within a few meters, she called, "Hey, Brock, I saved you …"

Brock forced a smile and said, "Ah thanks, but there's something I have to discuss with Scott."

He seized a chair just vacated by another customer who grabbed his coat as he exited the room, saying, "See you," to his friends still seated.

Across the table from Toque, Brock pushed his chair into the too-small gap between Matthews and Scott, asking, "Hey, Matthews move over, will you?"

As Brock sank into the dark tan faux-leather seat, all male faces at the table looked upon him with surprise while Toque was distinctly embarrassed.

Karimi laughed at what he perceived was an opportunity, and without hesitation, moved onto the seat that had been reserved for Brock.

In seconds, someone at the adjacent table, understanding the meaning of Karimi's vacated seat, grabbed it and waved at some new arrival just entering the room. No sooner had the chair been taken when those at Brock's table spread out to fill the gap.

Then the conversation commenced as if nothing out of the ordinary had taken place.

Trembley's arm crept across the back of Toque's chair, just before Karimi feigned a yawn, stretched out his arms, planning to rest one on the very spot that Trembley's upper limb then occupied. In fact, Karimi's arm almost touched Trembley's, but when Karimi realized he was about to make physical contact with a fellow male officer, he withdrew with the same speed that one would if a burning beam had landed upon his outstretched limb. Karimi then took on the same expression as that worn by a dieter who had just missed out on the free chocolates.

Toque shifted uncomfortably. Brock watched from across the table and his jaw clenched.

Scott, unaware of Brock's focus, greeted him with a friendly punch. "Hey Bud, thanks again for helping with the horses."

"Always happy to help."

Scott smiled, then said, "Yeah," and looking at Toque, appreciatively added, "And Toque went beyond the call of duty!"

However, because Toque was leaning at an angle and forward towards the table so that she could speak to Singh and Brown on the other side of Karimi, she didn't hear Scott's remark, nor did she realize that Trembley's arm rested behind her on the back of her chair.

Brock relaxed his jaw momentarily and looked bewildered, wondering why Toque would rate an extra accolade. As if to explain, Scott continued, "The jockeys are totally smitten with her!"

Brock tried to maintain his composure but couldn't help but think, *I can't believe it! First, it's her climbing team and now it's the jockeys! Am I going nuts or just plain jealous?*

Brown broke away from the conversation with Toque while Singh asked, "Anything new on the blood, lice and other sicko stuff?"

Brock acknowledged the question, answering, "Grant recently found out that the same vehicle was likely at all scenes."

Karimi raised one of his dark eyebrows. "Oh?"

Brock explained, "The same oil was left at each site."

Trembley, who was following Toque's every breath, momentarily turned from her and added, "Then ... that's got to exclude Peanut, that Rockwater kid, as a suspect."

Brock barely paused to consider the remark, then suggested, "He can drive, can't he?"

Trembley considered the question, then answered, "I doubt it's him because he's got an electric car. Parents gave it to him for his last birthday."

Acknowledging that, Karimi added, "Seemed like kind of a reward for bad behavior."

Trembley's eyes hazed as his mind clearly moved onto another topic: his arm resting on the chair slowly made its way towards Toque's shoulders. Simultaneously, Brock rounded his fists and glowered.

Toque, flinching at the touch, nevertheless maintained her composure insofar that she realized that it would be best to not embarrass a fellow officer. As a ploy, Toque feigned a smile to disguise her message from onlookers, then whispered in Trembley's ear, "Don't take this personally, but I really want to keep things more professional."

Brock saw her smile and unclenched his fists and tried to focus on his conversation with the guys, though he found it hard to swallow the beer that now seemed bitter.

Trembley felt Toque's warm breath on his ear and felt his whole system engaged.

Brock's eyes were glued to the interaction.

Trembley smiled. "Certainly, my Cherie. We will meet alone soon, just you and I."

Brock tried to ignore hearing the remark and responded to Karimi, "What about his friends' vehicles?"

Toque, knowing that meeting Trembley privately was as likely as an icy fire, allowed Trembley's remark, but then smiled again, though this time it was in relief as Trembley removed his arm. Brock winced at her gestures that seemed to be positive acceptance.

Trembley, almost beating his chest at what he thought would be a future relationship with Toque, couldn't stop smiling or – inwardly panting. But then, rejoining the world of policing said, "We'll look into what his friends have access to."

"Good. Let us know if you find anything," returned Brock.

Scott's pinkish skin paled with thought and the old acne scars became more visible, making him seem too young to be in uniform, never mind sitting in a bar. As he reached for his beer, before drinking, he pointed out, "But clearly, Peanut is a suspect for all of the assaults: blood – because he's already hit on the school once, and the frogs, lice, and flies simply because of the nature of his prior, a targeted mini-infestation."

Matthews agreed, "Exactly. Peanut has experience."

"Ha," responded Brock, "Chaos by creepy creatures."

Everyone at the table grimaced a smile at this black humour.

But then Singh challenged, "But there is more than one perp needed in the delivering of the blood, the insects and the frogs."

"Okay. So, let's again consider his friends – those ones in STAGS," suggested Brock, "You said previously that all of them had alibis for the mealworm incident about a year ago?"

Karimi explained, "Yeah, we were really suspicious of them but the parents and friends covered for each and every one – except Peanut's parents. We couldn't prove a thing on the others. But yeah, it's very likely they were in on it and got off – blame free."

His blue eyes searching for relevant clues, Brock looked straight at Trembley, asking, "What about the receipt that was found in his friend's locker?"

Trembley answered, "Nada. It could have been a link to the balloon bag that you found. But believe it or not, the father of the kid with the receipt is a high-stakes lawyer and said we have no right to question a minor, besides which – lots of school supplies are in that price range, including chocolate bars – which apparently the kid loves."

Brock moaned, then uttered a sarcastic, "And we're supposed to believe that he bought fifty-three of them?"

There was a group moan, marking agreement with Brock's sentiment.

Meanwhile, Toque inwardly fought with the anxiety of unwanted affections but still joined the conversation. "Doesn't Peanut have a connection to the university that had the frogs? Doesn't his brother go there?"

Karimi confirmed Toque's observation, saying, "You're right on that one."

Brown brightened. "Didn't principal Bothe indicate that Peanut's parents are high profile contributors to high-stake politics and various causes? I wonder if they might be connected to the Premier's event and the benefit concert at Centennial Theatre."

Trembley considered Brown's thoughts, then said, "Worth the question, for sure."

"Is there anything that could connect him to the horse poisoning?" questioned Toque.

Trembley thought for a moment, then answered, "Not sure. But Peanut definitely has the brains to pioneer it."

On the TV monitors showing the hockey game, a penalty was called for tripping and the pub crowd moaned.

Karimi, though, had not noticed the exchange between Toque and Trembley regarding his arm on her shoulders. Instead, and after the fact, he happily observed that both of Trembley's arms were resting on the table. Not wasting any time, Karimi let his knee fall against Toque's and placed his hand on her thigh. Toque flinched. Although Brock could not see the under-the-table contact, he was pretty sure that Karimi's hand was on Toque's leg. Brock again clenched his fists, though not quite as vehemently as with the initial interaction of Trembley's arm extended right behind the seated Toque.

Toque paused, thinking. Although her first thought was to flip Karimi onto to the ground, she hesitated, wondering about how to deal with this latest jerk move on her.

On the monitors, the visiting team was getting the penalty shot, and with ease an opposing player shot the puck into the net.

The pub crowd moaned.

Toque, oblivious to the game, considered her own reaction to the inappropriate advances. Soon she decided and showed considerable restraint when she gently warned, "There's a time and a place for everything but here is not the place for what you have in mind."

Grinning widely, Karimi took this dismissal as simply a postponement, though in Toque's mind, the interpretation of postponement would be true only if contact was possible in another lifetime.

Brock unclenched his fists and instead clenched his teeth. Still watching Toque, he thought, *What the hell? First her climbing partners, then the jockeys, now these two! She's definitely great looking but ... shit! But why am I wasting time – even thinking about it?*

Then interrupting Brock's thoughts, Trembley suggested, "Brock, why don't you and Toque visit Peanut tomorrow? We've tried, but haven't got anywhere. It seems there are a number of unanswered questions. Maybe a new team – from another detachment – will catch him off guard."

"Of course, we will!" said Toque, without pause. She glanced at Brock who immediately turned the other way and she was pretty sure that he had misread her actions but didn't know how to right the error in his judgement. Trying anything, she leaned across the table and asked her partner directly, "But Brock, do you ..."

At that point, Lily Sun and Nat Boucher made their way over to the table. Lily smiled as she said to Trembley and Karimi, "Hey, are you guys consorting with the enemies?"

Everyone grinned.

Brock managed a half-hearted smile, as he rose and pushed away from the table, saying,
"Glad to see you two. You arrived just in time. I'm on my way. Flip a coin as to who gets my seat. And Toque, I got to go. I'll see you next shift." Then, as if she was a distant associate, added, "I'm sure you're going to have lots of fun with the group here."

Sun and Boucher paused by the then empty chair, not sure who had first dibs on the seat.

But Toque thought only of Brock's sudden departure. She felt a chill as she briefly glanced into his eyes as they changed from the colour of a warm blue ocean to that of the Arctic waters when encompassing a glacier.

With his short verbal dismissal of Toque, Brock left his beer two-thirds unfinished, grabbed his coat, and hurried to the door. Everyone at the table looked on with disbelief at his hurried exit – except for Toque who wished she could run after him but knew it would seem odd, so instead, stayed unhappily seated. Karimi and Trembley simultaneously leaned closer towards her, and she felt trapped by their unwelcome and claustrophobic presence.

But Lily, with the instinct of female team spirit, said, "Hey, Nat and I want some girl chat. Trembley and Karimi, let's switch around. Karimi, I see a vacant chair just two tables over, why don't you grab it and the two of you can squish in by Brock's chair?"

Begrudgingly, Trembley and Karimi rose from their seats, though they moved as if they had lead weights in their shoes.

On the monitors, the home team scored and the whole pub, except Trembley and Karimi, cheered as if their team had won the Stanley Cup.

CHAPTER 37

North of the Trans-Canada Highway, and just past a huge lighted Christmas tree which filled the entire space of what was usually a generous manicured flowered area, Toque and Brock were driving along Taylor Way – heading to what was known as the British Properties. On one side of the two-lane road was a boulevard with trees devoid of leaves, having shed their foliage for the winter. Remnants of snow ground-cover was here and there as the rain continued to dissolve its icy mass. On the other side of the road were modest ranchers, backed by enormous cedars, hemlocks, and firs. Every driveway had a residue pile of snow from shovelling the result of the freakish November weather. Ornamental shrubs and trees also occurred in profusion, in many cases, hiding much of the appearance of any house or structure.

Turning left just after a mile or so and onto Southborough Drive, it was as if one were driving along a paved two-lane piece of treed wilderness, except for the areas of lawn with neatly manicured shrubs. Occasionally Toque and Brock would pass entrance gates to an estate, often totally hidden from eyesight. Yet a number of the homes were the originals: ranchers or modest two-story houses, though here and there were the huge houses, owned by the rich. But whether a modest home or an enviable mansion, hedges and shrubs continued to obscure most of the homes from the eyes of any passerby. Occasionally a house might show itself or a roof, or some part of the whole that could be a brand-new Tudor-style home or one that was ultra-modern in design.

Turning left onto Highland, the domestic trees had shed their leaves as they stood on the park-like street corner, where road-cleared piles of snow sat alongside the bright green grass and the large dark cedars behind. On Highland, sighting homes and their address labels continued to be a challenge as many were buried in the greenery. Intermittently, Toque and Brock would see the gates to a property but often it was difficult to find any address. For much of the drive, except for the trimmed grass strip here and there along the roadside, it was as if one continued to be driving through the forest.

And then they saw it on the corner of Cedar Drive and Highland, on the upper side of the street. Behind a five-foot-high white stone fence with turrets and behind a newly planted cedar hedge, the house loomed with a rounded marble staircase leading up to the closed wrought iron gate. Every inch of the roof-line eavestrough was ornamented with icicle-style Christmas lights, and on the roof, a giant star – so huge that it had to be the one that could be seen from Vancouver, across the harbour, miles down the hill. The house itself was white: every square inch; three stories high and with a flat roof. Every corner of the house had a camera mounted. Over the entrance way was a three-story high rounded pagoda-style ceiling supported by four Romanesque columns. And another rounded pagoda structure, also supported by columns, was two stories high, and was on the west side of the house. The front of the mansion was covered with windows, to appreciate the view that it no doubt had of the whole city that lay beneath.

Along the side of the house was the snow-pile lined driveway, leading to a four-car garage and adjacent to a paved area with additional parking.

Toque and Brock pulled over to the side of the road, let themselves in through the iron gate, past the lawns spotted with snow, and gardens on either side of a walkway, up five more steps to the main entrance, and knocked at the huge ornate doorway painted in glossy white. Brock glanced to the east of the house and into a treed-in area through which he could see the corner of what appeared to be tennis courts. As they waited by the door, they could see the corner of a swimming pool adjacent to the shorter pagoda structure, while at the same time could hear approaching footsteps from inside.

The gigantic door opened. Standing on the other side was the daily Happymaid employee, a tiny woman of four-foot-eight, dressed in a traditional black dress with white apron and trim. Her brown face was covered with the sheen of exert-caused perspiration.

Toque began, "We would like the speak to Mr. and Mrs. Cudmore, the parents of a Rockwater student named Pearce."

"And why would that be?"

"We need to ask them about their son."

"And what is the reason?"

"It's school related. We believe he's nick-named Peanut."

"Ah yes, we all call him 'Peanut,' but his parents do not have time to discuss school issues."

"We are doing an investigation of a number of serious cases of willful mischief: damage that may have an untold cost."

"That has nothing to do with the Cudmores, I can assure you."

"Good to know. But we still wish to speak to them. And then, we want to talk to Pearce and, as is required by law – in the presence of at least one parent."

"They are not free to talk to you now."

"By law we can and will question them," insisted Brock

"Then you will have to come back. They are not here."

"We can wait."

"In your car, then; not here."

"Can you give us a time frame?"

"I never know. They may not be back till well after most people are in bed."

"So, who acts as a legal adult in this house?"

"All I can say is to phone before you come." With that little bit of non-help, the Happymaid employee closed the door in the faces of Toque and Brock.

"We'll see," said Brock, with a frown.

The two of them turned, and from their perch on the landing leading from the top stair, they could see the complete panorama of the lower mainland. Down five stairs, they saw in the home's exterior kidney-shaped pool, a remote-controlled mechanical swimming gargoyle with long paddles of feet. It had sharp pointed teeth and snapped intermittently as it moved forward.

"What the hell?" questioned Brock, "Maybe we should see what's going on here."

"What, without a warrant?" worried Toque, though somewhat remiss to even question her estranged partner.

"Why not? This mechanical monster may be a public hazard."

As they reached the pool, they could see a youth who was operating the floating beast with a remote control. Behind him was the parking area, and the enclosed garage, beside which was a back-up generator, presumably for the whole house.

The youth pulled a lever on the control and the beast snapped up a floating beetle.

There was an inordinate number of such beetles in the pool as the machine moved about, biting them into two pieces. Alongside the teen was a pet carrier that held three baby chicks.

"Are you Pearce Cudmore?"

"Whose asking?"

"You can see that we're cops."

"I don't have to answer anything."

"Who says we're here to question?"

"Better still, who says *you* have any rights here? You're not even in your jurisdiction. And you're on private property," smirked the teen.

Brock surveyed the sky, as if asking for help from above, then glanced away from the youth where, if it wasn't for his surly nature, anyone, including potential pool users, could enjoy the view of the harbour and the city.

"We only asked your name."

"Why should I tell you anything? You guys should f ..." the youth paused, looked at Toque, then changed his wording, "You guys should move on."

Toque, sensing that she might have some leverage, tried to be pleasant. "Hey, buddy, we know you need to have a parent with you when questioned but we just wanted to see your cool mechanical creature."

The young man pulled a lever on the control and the mechanical fiend snapped another beetle in half. The teen glanced tentatively at the caged chicks, as if willing their cage door to open.

Toque put on her best pretend smile. "So, what have you got here?"

"It's an invention."

"You made this? I'm impressed," smiled Toque.

"It's nothing," scoffed the young man, though he glowered with pride.

Brock attempted to join in the conversation. "So, what's the deal with the beetles?"

"Nothing," sighed the young man, as if it should be obvious.

Before anyone could say another word, a V12 Range Hero passed alongside the house and entered the garage. In seconds, the driver was marching towards them.

In her forties with a generous mane of blond hair tied in a pony-tale, she was wearing the latest top-end jeans, tight against her butt and legs, and showing a body that was no stranger to rigorous gym work-outs. She wore red stiletto heels, while above the jeans, she showed off what had to be extra-large breast implants bursting out from under a red wrap-around T-shirt. Her over-full lips formed a pout briefly, but then her mouth opened with a snarl as she demanded, "Peanut, what are these constables doing here?" Then she glowered at Toque and Brock as she crossed her arms and glared.

"Ah, Mom, don't worry about it. I've got the situation under control."

Mrs. Cudmore sighed, as if this was not possible.

Brock, trying to overlook the rude challenge to their presence, introduced themselves, "This is Constable Burdon and I'm Constable Brock. We're trying to track down a few things and thought that your son might be able to ..."

"My son doesn't need to answer any of your questions. He is a minor, as if you don't already know."

"Sure, but with a parent present we might be able to get some assistance from – is it Pearce?"

"Peanut," corrected the young man.

Mrs. Cudmore curled her lip in scorn. "So, you *have* to question minors?"

Toque attempted to explain, "We are trying to investigate the blood on the school and possible ties ..."

"Tell me about an investigation worth caring about," muttered Peanut.

"And you think that *my* son knows something about infantile defacements? Don't make me laugh!"

"We only wanted to ask a few questions."

"Like what?" snarled Peanut's mother.

"Where were you on the night before the school was blood-bombed?" questioned Brock, looking at Peanut.

"You're being way too melodramatic," moaned Mrs. Cudmore, sighing and rolling her eyes.

"I was at home."

"Alone?"

Peanut nodded but his mother interrupted again, "So what's the problem with that? He's seventeen now. That's legal!"

Brock continued, "Another thing, Peanut, we found a receipt in one of your friend's lockers showing a purchase of fifty-three identical items priced at $2.98 from an unnamed store and …"

Mrs. Cudmore broke in, "My son isn't responsible for everyone else in the school, friend or not. I'll have you know that my Pearce is brilliant and when he's finished with high school, will have his choice of the best universities in the world!"

Peanut's chest pumped as his mother reviewed his strengths but then returned to the matter at hand, and in a tone of contempt, joined with his mother's mood and he laughed the laugh of scorn. "What a lame question! Haven't you yet covered proper questioning techniques? The receipt is probably for rubbers. But then, again, it could be nylons. They're really handy for making stocking faces for animations!"

Mrs. Cudmore smiled the smirk of those in an alliance of derision. "Yeah, Peanut and his friends might be planning a stocking face puppet show!" Then sarcastically added, "Arrest them all! I'm sure that in your book it's a major felony using nylons, not for leg covers but to make puffy potato-patch faces!"

Brock's face was cold and impassive. "We're only following any possible lead."

"And Peanut was involved in a mealworm incident last year," added Toque.

"So, he's a criminal for life? Give me a break! It was a one-off adolescent prank!"

Brock eyed Toque in a gesture to suggest their departure as Mrs. Cudmore added, "Here I am just coming back with dry-cleaning because of that frog incident at Capilano University and you're still fucking around with a high-school prank."

"You were at *the* game?"

"Of course! Our other son is on the team! You must have heard of him! Pearce's brother is the best power forward they've ever had!"

"Good for him," remarked Toque, dryly, but lost no time in asking, "But was Peanut at that game?"

"Pearce has no interest in his brother's life as a college basketball star. While we were at the game, Pearce was at home, doing his homework, if you have to know."

"What about the Premier's Economic Forum? Were you there?" asked Brock.

"Listen, I've had enough questions. Peanut, we're going inside," ordered Mrs. Cudmore.

"Just another question or two, please," probed Toque.

Mrs. Cudmore turned her head and curled her over-plump lips. "I think that you two should leave and if you have any more questions, I want my attorney present. And I want to know why you are here asking questions. You two are not West Van cops!"

CHAPTER 38

Reflected in the sparkling harbour amidst the mirror images of bobbing white boats was the crisp clear sky behind the backdrop of dark blue mountains. A brief reprieve from the rain.

Like a child at the end of a long day at school, from the pastel green cockpit Rex bounded, past the blue-detailed white hull under the shining teak tow-rails.

Though he almost laughed with understanding Rex's joy of life, Brock yelled, "Hey, wait up," as he fumbled with the lock on the teak hatch-cover.

Rex, with his lead held in his mouth, went only as far as the end of the first slip and then bounded back to Brock as he clambered from the *Angel*. In seconds, Brock had joined his furry friend and within minutes had flicked the latch of the chain-link gateway so that the two of them were onto the seawall.

As Brock attached the lead, Rex patiently waited, although his keen eyes, without pause, darted here and there, sizing up all moving people and animals – preferring the later (except for his master). Once the lead was attached, it was as if Rex had been given an additional surge of energy as they moved forward, past the parking lot on one side, and the marina on the other. When they reached the spot where the roadway met the pedestrian seawall, rather than leading in the direction of the later, Rex lurched around an over-full trash container, surprising Brock and catching him off guard so that he stumbled ever so slightly, just missing the glass of a smashed bottle that had fallen from trash.

Then the lead tightened as Rex let out a single bark, then leaned towards an approaching person. Brock took his eyes from the broken glass and looked in the direction of Rex's interest and saw his boat-neighbour, Rita, approaching, struggling with her rotund weight, and too many bags for one person. There were mesh bags hanging from her arms and two canvas bags clutched to her chest while her shoulder bag stuck out at an awkward angle above a cloth carrier. She seemed flustered, with her greying hair falling out of the knot she'd fixed. Her unfastened green canvas jacket was riding up above her belly, along with what had been a low hanging yellow flowered blouse, worn over a once-mauve T-shirt blotted with oily stains. Her colourless muffin-top mid-rift and what must have been the top of her undergarments were showing, above the elastic waist of a rusty-brown corduroy skirt, below which were her budget black and white running shoes.

Brock hurried across the bike path and onto the sidewalk leading from the Denman Street shops and offered, "Let me help you!"

She gave Brock the once-over and although a look of recognition visited her features, she grunted, "Don't need help," just as one of the bags balancing on her ample bosom dropped a small clump of carrots and a box of crackers.

Brock caught the crackers in mid-air while Rex helped himself to the carrots, believing that the orange delectables must have been dropped for him.

"Well maybe I could do with a little bit of help," Rita conceded, as she loaded her canvas bags onto Brock, then slipped one of the mesh bags over his wrist, keeping one for herself.

Rex swallowed the last carrot, saw Rita with one hand hanging free, and hurried over and in seconds his long pink tongue ran the full length of her hand.

Rita held back a smile until Brock glanced the other way as they headed toward the marina. As Brock eyed up the shortest route to their vessels, Rita gave Rex a scratch on his head to which Rex responded with another lick of her hand.

It was then that personal safety was blinded by innocent affection as Rex trampled
through the broken glass, totally absorbed with walking with his master and the neighbour.

Poor Rex let out a yelp as a piece of glass sliced into his paw. Brock turned, saw his limping companion, laid Rita's bags down as he gave his injured friend instructions. "Sit! Rex sit."

"What could be the matter with him?"

Brock frowned, expecting a burr or stick but coloured with anger when he saw the glass sticking out of Rex's paw. "Dam it all, anyway. I don't get why people keep piling trash on top of trash."

"Too lazy to carry a bottle to the next bin."

"Or take it home, for crying out loud. Will you stay with Rex while I go and get some tweezers?"

"Of course."

"Rex, stay. Rita, I'll drop off your bags on the way."

With that, Brock hurried to the marina. Rita knelt down by Rex, stroking his fur. "You'll be alright, boy, not to worry."

Rita glanced down to the marina and saw Brock board the *Angel,* then momentarily glanced at the seawall leading from Stanley Park. Every hundred feet there was a person or group, enjoying the crisp, beautiful day.

The walker closest to her paused, to stare at Rex, then asked, "What is wrong with your dog?"

Before she looked up, Rita replied, "Just a cut paw. From someone's trash – a broken bottle." But then, as she struggled to rise, she reached out her hand for assistance, and started to ask, "But could you …"

But as she spoke, her face turned to the stranger and her heart stopped.

While Rita floundered with rising from her kneeling position, the man backed off, making his hands inaccessible by moving them behind his back, and looked entirely humourless while he said, "People here need to better police their garbage."

In spite of receiving no cavalier assistance, what she first saw was a handsome man: his hair blond, though sandy where it was short above his ears, his eyebrows full, though not overbearing, his well-spaced hazel-brown eyes, his moist heart-shaped lips, with the top lip ever so slightly elongated, his aquiline nose; his face a longish oval, and the cheeks slightly flushed upon a flawless ivory complexion. His build was what one might call meso-ectomorph, a build that was not heavy-set but had every muscle toned and ready for action. Of any sort. Momentarily, in her mind's eye, Rita became a young beautiful woman and she felt an erotic pull to this stranger.

She smiled her best smile while the stranger's face became even harsher as he said, "Back home they shoot injured dogs. Injured? Not worth the time of day."

Then staring at Rex, the stranger's perfectly shaped eyebrows furrowed, his eyes tensed and his mouth formed a cold thin line. In seconds, Rita's feeling of attraction evaporated and she again became an aging overweight and defensiveness eccentric. And then, the sudden shock of an unpleasant recognition visited her features and rather than eroticism, cold fear charged through her veins.

She wanted to call out but knew that Brock was unlikely to hear from inside his vessel.

Recognizing Rita's frightened bearing for what it was, the walker, a man we know as Borya, turned and increased his pace, to that of being almost speed-walking, and going in the direction of the shopping area just up the street.

Although it was less than five minutes when Brock returned carrying a first-aid kit, when he cleared the marina gate, Borya was already crossing the main road, Georgia. In seconds he dissolved into the crowd of shoppers starting to get ready for the coming Christmas.

"He was here!"

"Who?"

"The man I told you about who was asking for you!"

"Where?"

"He must be on Denman by now. I doubt you'll find him."

Brock leaned forward, in a body stance as if to start a race, but as Rita picked up Rex's injured paw, the suffering animal let out a loud whimper.

Brock strained at seeing far into the distance, willing himself to locate the person whose features resembled those of Borya, but it was more than clear that he had vanished.

Rex let out another heart-breaking whimper. And just as Borya had vanished, so did the thought of his presence. Brock, summoned to the role of caring for his best friend and sole companion, said, in as soothing a tone as possible, "Don't worry Rex, I'll have you fixed up in no time."

CHAPTER 39

Brock sat in the cockpit as the December sun lowered itself towards the horizon, filling the crystal blue sky with bleached-out traces of orange and yellow upon newly forming cirrus clouds. At his feet, Rex lay sleeping fitfully, his paw bandaged. Brock thought about how people with nine-to-five jobs would be soon heading home, cooking meals, and having conversations with caring family members. His blue eyes darkened at his revisiting sense of loss and he gazed northward, seeing the dark ultramarine mountains like massive beings, monumental in scale and slouching down towards the tiny human structures built on the treed mountain base, where the waters of Burrard Inlet lapped at the boats, docks and shores. His focus wavered as he saw a hooded figure approach from the adjoining pier.

The person moved hesitantly, and was bent over slightly, as if in pain. He or she was wearing a black hoodie, grey baggy sweat pants and cheap black flip flops. To begin with, Brock wasn't certain whether or not the person was male or female, but when he perused the face he could see that it was a woman. What should have been brown skin was a washed-out colouration much like stale porridge, her lips were parched, and her eyes had a black and deadened presence, and what could have been a well-endowed chest was almost indistinguishable under the extra-large black hoody. A strand of blond hair fell from beneath the hood and it was with surprised shock that Brock realized that the person now standing by the *Angel* was no other than Delila.

Natural human concern coloured his reaction and he asked, "Are you okay?"

Delila, too ill to consider potential ramifications of Brock's question, replied, "No, not good at all."

"Sick?"

"Really feeling unwell. I switched my anti-depressants because the medical insurance plan switched my prescription drug for a generic one."

Brock rose from his spot in the cockpit and reached out his hand to help Delila on board. He wracked his mind for something he could offer. Then remembering seeing in the back of the kitchen drawer a bent, probably out-of-date pack of chicken soup, offered, "How about some soup? But if it doesn't make you feel at all better …" Brock searched in his mind for the next step, knowing that he didn't want to get too involved with Delila, so added, "You'll need to go back to the doctor."

Delila slumped to the side of the cockpit seat while Rex stirred, opened one eye, closed it, and attempted to resume his nap.

"Come inside," suggested Brock, as he effortlessly moved down the ladder and into his cabin, then turned to help Delila with her descent.

"I'm good enough to climb in on my own," said Delila, her state of health making her uncharacteristically distant.

Forty-five minutes later, in front of the two of them on the galley table sat two empty soup bowls, an almost full package of rye bread, and three empty bags of Cheesesnacks. "You're looking better now," observed Brock, seeing that the colour had, in part, returned to Delila's face, though he could not get over the change in her appearance.

"Yeah, sure," mumbled Delila, as she reddened at seeing her sloppy choice in clothing, and added, "I'm a mess. I'd better get going."

"No rush," replied Brock, glimpsing at the clock, knowing that he should be leaving soon. "I don't have any tea. Or anything like that here – but I could offer you a beer, though I can't join you in having one because I'm on shift soon. But oh, yeah, I have some non-alcohol beer that I bought by mistake."

"The non-alcoholic would work better with the new meds. Jeez, I just don't feel good mentally. It's all coming back to me." Her hand shook as she reached for the can of stale, warm beer.

Rex lumbered over to Brock and placed his head on his master's knee. As he scratched Rex's chin, Brock inwardly sighed. On one hand, he wanted to help, but then again, this was Delila sitting there. "You say it's coming back to you?"

Delila took a sip, then grimaced. "Yeah, I had a couple of break-ups that I didn't do well with."

Brock thought about his wife April, their babe, both taken from him and looked at Delila with sympathy, as if he understood.

"The first was one of my high school teachers."

"High school teacher?" repeated Brock, with disbelief.

"Yeah, we were seeing each other a lot. We kept it from everyone because it wasn't acceptable for students to date teachers. But we got really serious. There was a little room under a stairwell in the school that we called our 'love nest' because no one ever knew we were there."

"In a school? How could that go un-noticed?"

"Oh, we'd meet at night when there was a game on in the gym. Because of that, it was almost always week-nights. But I thought that it really was true love."

"What school was this? Was it local?"

"Rockwater: a place that I now wish I'd never heard of!"

"Rockwater! And you had the relationship in the school building?"

"Mostly, but when we couldn't get into the school, he'd crawl into my bedroom late at night."

"Didn't anyone notice?"

"No, he came after midnight when everyone was asleep and stayed just an hour, at most."

"So, what happened to the relationship?"

"His wife came to the school one day because he forgot his phone. School was in session and I was in his class when she came to the door. I was so upset that I had to run to the washroom to throw up."

"You could press charges."

"He told me later that he and his wife had a plutonic marriage and that he loved only me. I believed him and we continued our relationship for another few months."

"How did it end?"

"One day in our 'love nest' he left for a few minutes to go to the washroom. His phone was in his jacket pocket and when it rang I picked up. On the other end of the line was a little kid's voice saying, 'Can I speak to Daddy? He was supposed to pick me up fifteen minutes ago from Cubs. Has he gone to get my sisters from Brownies first?' I was shocked. I had no idea that he had children."

"You *should* charge him."

"I don't want to spend another second on that dirt bag – unless it's revenge and I don't have to tell you that a rape court case is more about defaming the woman accuser than the perpetrator."

Brock swallowed. Couldn't think of anymore to say. Glanced at the clock, knowing that he would have to soon leave. "I hope that this hasn't permanently wounded you."

"It has. And he wasn't the only one!"

"I hope not!"

"Well, it happened again. My next 'love' was my Cap U equestrian coach."

"Another person in a position of power."

"I guess that type is my weakness. I'm telling you now, though, if I ever again screw a guy in a position of power, it better go my way or he'll regret ever laying eyes on me!"

Brock gulped. "What happened with the coach?"

"His name was Bud: he and I were really hot for each other. We were together constantly: in the bathrooms, in his car, behind the coat racks, anywhere."

Brock sat, fixated.

"We planned to be engaged. Every waking moment I thought of Bud. When I dressed, when I ate, when I tried to study: every moment. In lecture halls I would doodle his likeness in my margins. When I could, I'd page through photos of him on my cell phone."

"And?"

"And then I thought that the engagement ring had to be on the way. That we would marry, settle down, have children, have a life together, and live happily ever after."

"But?"

"When we were at a training session, I told Bud that I had to leave early for a medical check-up. We said our good-byes and I left. But I was just about on the bus when I checked my calendar and realized that my appointment was for the following week."

"So, you returned?"

"I still wonder if it might have turned out different if I had got on that bus."

"What happened?"

"When I got back to the stables, all of the equestrian team were on the horses, practicing but I couldn't see Bud out front, coaching, like he generally did."

"And ..."

"So, I searched the stables. And then I saw them in a stall, rutting like hogs in the straw: Bud was with one of the female jockeys."

"Not that it's much of an excuse, but could it have been an unplanned moment of weakness?"

"Not at all. When I stood there, I asked, 'Bud, what the hell is going on?' and she, the bitch, answered, 'The same thing that's been going on for months now! Go back to your school books, girly.' And sneered, then laughed!"

"That must have been really hard to take!"

"You have no idea how much I hate that bitch, that asshole, and their looser kid."

"Kid?"

"Yeah, it was born about three quarters of a year later."

"When was this?"

"Three or four years ago. I think that the kid is in daycare now – you know the one in Edgemont Village – called All Faiths Family Daycare?"

"I do. But it's called 'All Faiths'? I didn't realize that there was a religious element. Or is there? How could they include every possible belief?"

"They can't. Basically, what it really means is 'All faiths loosely based on some version of the Old Testament.' I can tell you, that their kid certainly needs some religious input with the parents she's stuck with."

"I can see why you're bitter and am really sorry to hear about what you've been through. I'm not surprised you dislike them so intensely."

"Horses too. Bud would have never met the bitch if it wasn't for the fucking horses, would he? But I've talked too much." Delila maneuvered herself to her feet. "I feel like I need to go and forget all this. Again." Delila looked in the mirror by the galley and frowned, pulled a lipstick out of her sweat pant pockets and quickly applied a coat.

Then, although her face was still a greyish hue, it was as if she had a second wind, put her hand on Brock's wrist, saying, "Thanks for listening," then climbed out the hatch.

Chapter 40

Captain Abraham leaned back in her plush aqua chair, looking around her computer terminal and down West Vancouver's 16th street. She was not a big woman and her chair was boosted a little higher than that which most would need. But though not tall, she was in perfect shape and wore her navy suit like a soldier: perfectly pressed and as crisp as it was the day she first wore it. Under her right-hand sleeve cuff, was just the edge of a tattoo with a thick, bold application of dye. Though only partially uncovered, it was clearly the edge of a First Nation's design. Addressing the few loose strands that needed attention, she smoothed, then into a knot retied her straight long black hair which had only an occasional strand of white. Serious and thoughtful, she then focused on the view from her window, her concerned dark eyes demarked by a generous application of black eye-liner, and the red lipstick on her mouth formed a troubled line.

Dusk had set, lights were turning on ... everywhere.

From her seat, she could see eight blocks down to John Lawson Park bordering on the dark grey waters of English Bay and the homes and sombre blackness of the trees and gardens in the Point Grey area across the bay. She could count five freighters at anchor. Two of the five had a rather meagre display of Christmas lights. But granted, it was a least an effort at this dark time of year. A sixth freighter was being ushered by two towboats generously trimmed with red Christmas lights, including a matching lit tree strapped to each of the decks at the bow. She knew that the tugboat-escorted freighter was on its way to the Vancouver docks, on the other side of Lions Gate Bridge.

She sighed, and clicked onto a blinking email icon. She'd checked that folder just seconds ago.

The new email opened. "Those that count will pay! Negotiate now or remuneration begins before the next sun sets."

She scowled, looked out at the tugboat-assisted ship that was then passing under the bridge, and absently reached for the phone. But then, mentally revisiting her last talk with CO Grant, shook her head.

On her computer keyboard, Captain Abraham clicked *delete*.

CHAPTER 41

Toque and Brock went to their respective homes after their shift, one full day after his conversation with Delila about her past. For Brock, the first order of business was taking Rex out for a walk around Stanley Park's tree-shrouded Lost Lagoon.

It was when they'd just finished their walk, and Brock was about to unlock the marina gate, when he heard a voice calling, "Hey, neighbour," not far behind him. Rex, at Brock's side, turned briefly, but soon refocused on the water, watching a small flock of air-borne Canada Geese move downwards, soon skittering across the waters as they landed, leaving V-shaped ripples behind them.

Brock turned to see Delila coolly walking towards him, a woman changed from their last meeting. Through previous interactions with Brock, she suspected that a restrained and indirect approach would be her best chance at entering the light of his favour.

Adding to her allure ability was that the previous emotional turmoil seemed to have vanished. Not only was the old spring back in her step, but her appearance was again enticing, although in a way that showed discernment. It was the kind of attractiveness that can creep up on a member of the interested sex, but then explode: rather like the flavour of a dessert that, when tasted is found to be heavenly – with endorphins being released by the multitude.

Brock's first reaction was a desire to run but then he sensed something different. Her make-up was less conspicuous; but somehow, to his inner instincts, made her natural beauty much more seductive. Likewise, her sexual appeal was enhanced through subtlety and the power of suggestion and imagination: the sensuality of her shapely body was only hinted at by unisex fashions – a sheep-skin lined brown suede jacket over bleached-out jeans which she wore like the promise of a hidden dream to be won, then secured. Shaking his head to rid his mind of these thoughts, he then remembered Delila's unwell state the last time they spoke, and her disastrous relationships while in school.

"Feeling better today?" he asked, trying to be congenial, as he held the gate for her.

She smiled as she slowly approached him, bringing with her the faint but noticeable aura of her cologne, Always Amorous. With an unwavering stare, she met his eyes, the colour a deep but warm blue ocean then answered, "Much better, though a little light-headed. But thanks. And how was your day?"

He looked back into her dark eyes and was momentarily speechless. His voice was verging on being hoarse. "Not too bad." Although her skin was the colour of health, and her blond hair was tied back in a pony tail with playful wisps escaping here and there, he couldn't help but remember how ill, how victimized, how vulnerable she was just the previous day.

Once the marina gate was open, Brock fought with himself to withdraw his mesmerized focus from Delila. Forcing himself to tend to his pet, Brock bent over and unhooked Rex's lead. Rex promptly ran off, down the ramp, and onto the pier where the family of geese sailed by.

With dismay, Brock watched Rex, then the geese. "Shit! How could I have not noticed the geese!"

Delila, sensing that dog discipline was in order, stepped to the side of the ramp while Brock rushed down to the floating pier, yelling, "Rex! Stop!" Rex stopped. "Rex! Sit." Rex sat, but looked longingly at the geese nonchalantly sailing by, as if there would never be a threat at any time in their lives.

With Rex then behaving himself, Brock turned to Delila who was just about to step onto the pier. It was there, on the last inch of the ramp that the non-skid wire mesh had broken free from its stapled attachment and had curled so that it caught on the pump heel of the left foot of her brown leather ankle boot. Delila tumbled forward.

Brock, with a reaction as fast as a rabbit in heat, jumped forward and caught her, and in seconds set her upright. Delila, embarrassed, chuckled. "The things I do to catch your attention!"

Brock smiled but before he could react further, Delila's knees seemed to buckle and as she crumbled towards the pier, Brock again caught her, mid-collapse. The colour drained from her face and as he righted her again, she leaned on his arm for support.

"Honest to God, I've never reacted like this to new meds!" said Delila, holding onto Brock for support.

In her touch, he could feel her tremble. He looked down the pier at the *Angel*: just four boat lengths away. Then he scanned over several piers to Delila's vessel. It was much, much further.

She let go of his arm and her expression of fear and confusion melded into that of a person feeling their way back to health. She gazed at Brock's face. Intensely. Those eyes! And his warm amber skin, his wavy almost blue coal black hair, his wide shoulders, broad chest, and the solid hips, just noticeable under his blue bomber jacket. She thought for a moment, and then, as if a new idea occurred to her, asserted her health by saying, "I think that I'm pretty good now. Just a little dizzy."

Brock had his doubts. "Don't get the wrong idea, but I am here if you need a friend to lean on. I've got a fresh bag of coffee, if you want me to make you a cup. You know, Muriel's coffee – but it's all I have – other than beer – the real thing and the non-alcohol. Oh, and Cheesesnacks, of course."

But then she clutched him with a grip so firm it made Brock wonder about her physical stability.

"How about a coffee, then?" he asked.

Delila paused, as if counting to ten before she answered, "Sure, for just a few minutes."

They continued along the pier to the *Angel* where Rex still sat, but now watched his master with a woman, a woman with her arm through that of his master's, and his arm around her waist. Rex let out a wide yawn.

At the *Angel*, Brock climbed into the cockpit, then reached down to help Delila manoeuvre over the toe-rail. He unlocked the teak hatch and again Brock went first, turning around to again help Delila. As she moved down the ladder and into the galley, he held his hands on either side of her, to prevent a fall, his hands lightly riding along her legs, her hips, as she lowered herself into the main cabin. As he thought about moving his hands away, he briefly touched the skin of her torso, then feeling his pulse quicken, moved his hands back to her jean-covered hips.

She turned, quicker than he anticipated and his hands were still on her hips. She could smell his Cedar Forest scent.

She held his hands in place and gently moved him, face to face, into the forward bunk cabin and as they passed through the galley, Brock had almost the time to think about his regrets when he felt her hand slip under his belt, undo the snap at the top of his pants, and then, with her hand on bare skin, reach down, much further.

"Like I said, I don't want to be involved … ah … my wife, April …"

"Don't worry about her … I promise you that this is just for now. Her fingers touched his penis that was already rock-hard. His whole body tensed, and his head filled with a passion long lost and for that moment, the memory of his wife and child was like an ancient radio
wave then light years away and getting fainter and fainter.

***

Whereas Brock encountered Delila upon his return from his shift, Toque also came across a person with whom she had recent contact.

In her silver six-year-old electric economy car, Toque was heading for her parking spot at the back of the boxy four-story fifty-year-old rental apartment building in which the once-rust coloured wooden siding had turned to a splintery grey and the adjacent tan stucco was stained with lichen and black trails formed from run-off water. She parked without hesitation and as she exited the car, she pulled the toque from her head, unknotted her hair, then shook her head, allowing her hair to fall free.

Within seconds, she rounded the apartment building, approached the entranceway and with surprise saw him, slouched by the front door.

Although his full height was understated just a little by the fact that he was leaning on the wall, the size of Joe's hulking form could not be mis-interpreted. While he had the genetic gift of a six-foot-seven height, broad shoulders, an expansive chest, he also had massively developed muscles in his legs and arms, as if he spent hours on daily work-outs.

If he were to be a basketball player, the ball would seem to be a child's toy in his mammoth hands. On his feet were hiking boots, a size that was beyond that which was sold in most stores.

With his mane of curly red hair and untrimmed full beard, he had the bearing a man who'd just arrived from a logging camp. He saw Toque as soon as she rounded the corner and with the expectations of a would-be lover, saw her untied auburn hair flowing down onto her shoulders and over her perfect form. He was waiting to see the most attractive woman he'd ever known – Toque – and her unleashed presence was over-whelming. His entire interior filled with the sensation of sparking electricity while the pounding of his heart became so loud he wondered if it could be heard by Toque, herself.

Toque considered Joe with apprehension, if not fear: she remembered when he and Lynn were at the stables and left that terrible impression on the others, including Brock, but worse, she remembered waking up in bed with Lynn beside her and then, Joe beside Lynn. Not smiling, she asked, "Joe, what are you doing here?"

Joe braced himself, as if he were about to enter the most important exchange of his life. "Toque, I just want to talk. I feel like our friendship is spiraling downwards." He looked at her, and couldn't help but notice that the top button of her shirt was undone and the second button was straining to pull open.

Toque reached for her door key while blocking Joe from entering the building, even though his size was daunting. "I've had a tiring shift, Joe. I'm sorry, but I really just want to hit the sack right now."

Joe flushed at the thought of Toque lying in her bed but fought to control his rampant emotions. He almost fell to his knees as he pleaded, "Toque, please, that night Lynn and I stayed over – that wasn't what I was planning. It just happened."

Toque scowled. "Listen Joe, let's discuss it at another time."

"Toque, I really want to talk about us."

Us? What us? thought Toque. *Other than the one really bad night, we are climbing partners: nothing more – distant friends, at best.*

Joe placed an enormous hand on Toque's arm. "I just want to be on good terms." In his other hand, he held a peace-offering, a decorative bowl of toffees.

Toque pulled her arm from his hand, as irritation triggered by being cornered resulted in her temper moving up a notch. "You have a funny way of trying to be friends. What about when you and Lynn were at the race track and were blabbing about staying overnight? Do you have any idea how that would have sounded to my partner, Brock, and the others who were there? Do you know how embarrassing that was?"

"Honest to God, I'm sorry." Then, as a couple of Toque's neighbours smiled and passed by her to get into the building, Joe continued, "But waking up with you and Lynn …"

Toque's neighbours slowed, trying to listen, and would have turned up their hearing aids had they been wearing any.

Toque interrupted. "Joe, for heaven's sake. There you go again!" She let out an exasperated sigh. "Okay, if you're wanting to talk, let's do it inside. In private." But to herself, Toque thought, *Fuck, now I've invited him in. Shit! What am I going to do now?*

Joe managed a small smile, assuming that the gate was now open to the path of a successful shot. "Sure, I was really hoping that you would hear me out." He gazed down at her, unwilling to let his eyes tear away and couldn't help but notice that the second button on her shirt had come undone.

Toque's neighbours disappeared into the elevator while Toque stalled, getting her mail from one of the slots in the building's lobby, with Joe alongside, waiting with nervousness mixed with anticipation.

Soon they were seated in her apartment: Toque on one love seat, Joe on the other. On the coffee table in front of them was the bowl of toffees.

Joe tried to put on an air of being at ease as he sat, completely filling the love seat. His arms casually draped over the armrests, and his knees stretched so wide apart that physically he totally took over the entire area. "Honest, Toque, I think that we all drank a bit too much."

Toque surveyed her hulking guest. "No kidding! But you two staying was a huge mistake."

"It seemed like you were okay with it when we headed into the bedroom."

Toque coloured, thinking, *What the hell DID happen?* "All I remember is feeling really tired and that I'd had way too much to drink. All I wanted was to go to sleep. I thought that you two would simply continue drinking." Then, with accusation in her voice, added, "But then you both must have followed me!"

Joe raised his eyebrows, surprised at the accusation. "It seemed like you were leading us into the bedroom."

"What!" she spat, "My head was spinning from the whisky and I needed to lie down, you idiot!"

Joe seemed like a scolded red-haired Bernese Mountain dog. "Geeze, I'm sorry, I was pretty loaded as well. At the time, it seemed that both you and Lynn were leading me into the bedroom."

Toque momentarily gazed out the window. *What now? I love climbing rock faces with Lynn and Joe. But what happened that night? I dread even wondering about it. But maybe I am too paranoid.*

"Toque, I promise you: it will never happen again!" He paused. "I mean, the three of us."

Toque studied Joe's brown eyes. She wondered about the meaning of his last sentence. But he seemed sincere, with his bearded woolly face almost like that of a teddy bear.

"Well, maybe we can keep up the climbing but I don't want it to go beyond that."

His sexual imagination worked overtime: maybe that wasn't a complete *no*. Hope formed on Joe's face. He smiled as he squarely faced her. "Agreed. But there is one thing I was hoping to ask you …"

Oh no. What now? Toque's feelings on her worried face were more than apparent.

"It's not a big deal. Well, I guess it is, sort of."

"What?" asked Toque, with deep trepidation.

"I'm hoping that you will come with me to the party selection meeting. It's in a few nights."

"What, the election of the party leader to replace our retiring Prime Minister?"

"Yeah." Then straightening, he explained, "I've been active in the party for years. Believe it or not, I'm going to be one of the contenders."

Toque's eyes widened as she gasped, "What? With that hair and beard?"

Joe laughed. "I am an on-again, off-again mountain man. Occasionally I clean up and look just like I've stepped out of a catalogue sales magazine – though for the oversize crowd. But my beard grows faster than cooking a steak on the barbeque so I can be mountain-man whenever the mood suits. But over the last month, things have changed for me. People in the party have approached. The result is that I will be cleaning up in a big way in the next day or so."

"You never mentioned anything about politics before!"

"They say never mix politics. Plus, climbing frees me from all the shackles."

Toque relaxed – a little. "I know what you mean."

"So, you'll come?"

"Sure, but only if we are just friends."

"Great!" Joe almost clapped but held onto self-restraint and leaned back in the loveseat. He at first looked, but then couldn't blink as he was totally transfixed by Toque's appearance: her smooth whitish-pink skin and her thoughtful, soft blue-grey eyes. He remembered the night that he and Lynn had stayed and then fantasized that the shirt Toque was currently wearing would strain further and open by yet one more button. He wished for it, and stared at the third button, willing it to spring open as a result of the mystical electricity emanating from his focussed desire. But the button held, so he turned his gaze onto the sleek, feminine arms, the tapered fingers, the supple mouth and full lips, the mesmerizing eyes. "And Toque …" His voice went hoarse. He paused.

Toque's expression of forgiveness and starting anew changed to one of concern as she glanced over his massive form. In his loose-fitting cargo pants, there was something that bulged – it couldn't be – but riding from his groin and just above the crease that runs towards the hip, and above the thigh, it seemed as if he was carrying a good-sized salami that extended on his left side – reaching almost as far as the bottom of his hip pocket.

Toque eyes widened. *What IS that? It couldn't be! S*he wanted a better look but couldn't possibly bring herself to openly stare at his
family jewels. She felt faint. Her head spun. She thought back to the night spent together. *My God! Joe and Lynn did seem entirely naked ... and my bra was off and my underwear crooked. Was it a threesome?* Nausea rose in her throat. *I have to get a grip on myself,* she thought, as she reached to the bowl of mouth-size toffees, thinking that the melting of one of the smooth, round forms of buttery sugar on her anticipating tongue might distract but ...

Joe leaned forward, towards her. He smiled. His pupils dilated.

Toque tried to peruse any direction other than that occupied by Joe, but his very scale was so overwhelming it was like trying to ignore a cement mixer in her living room.

Her hand froze just before she managed to pluck out a toffee.

He leaned forward a little more, gently touching her hand with his.

It was as if a bolt of lightning tore through her limbs. Toque took another fleeting look at Joe's bulging pants. Her throat closed. Her whole body started to tingle and perspire. Nipples hardened and became erect. Her hands started shaking.

She leapt from the canvas love seat, knocking over the bowl of toffees, then fled through the door, her auburn hair streaming behind her.

Joe sat astounded for just a few moments. Then, as he moved to stand, he straightened his pants and inner apparatus, and the shape that seemed a lot like a salami ... almost entirely disappeared.

CHAPTER 42

Laden with tormented emotions, tears ran down her cheeks as Toque drove through the snarled Vancouver traffic, first crawling along bumper-to-bumper on Fourth where the traffic frequently slowed to a stand-still while cars attempted to parallel park. She then moved onto Burrard where wide bicycle lanes had reduced those for cars to a fraction of the original city road plan. In most of the commercial buildings, the Christmas decorations were in full display seeing that December had arrived. But no tinsel or seasonal lights helped Toque's mood.

Then, in the black void of her emotional state, as she drove she thought about the extent
of her agitation. *I've got to talk to someone. But who can I go to? Am I ever going to be able to establish a real friendship?*

As tears blurred her vision, she had to force herself to focus on the task of driving and at the last-minute, cut into adjacent traffic to avoid a bicycle that swerved out to pass several slower cyclers. *Dam, I should have anticipated that!* She cursed to herself.

She thought back to Joe, left in her apartment. *I can't even join a climbing group without them coming after me! Shit! And what the hell was in his pants? I've seen smaller on horses!*

She slammed on the brakes, narrowly missing a vehicle that had turned into the traffic from a side street.

From Burrard, she turned onto Robson and while passing through the first blocks of high-end designer stores, she again braked suddenly, this time when a taxi stopped mid-traffic to take on a signaling fare.

Her entire body trembled as frustration and anxiety acted like a horrible flu that had attached itself to the essence of her being as her car crawled along. She wished for any reprieve. With wet eyes, her vision was clouded and her mind was in a fog of emotion that prevented rational thought. Tremors from angst riveted her being as she neared the end of Robson Street and chose turning right, purely out of the habit of travelling this route to work.

But then, as she reached the lights on Georgia, she momentarily touched her forehead, wondering where she could possibly go at this hour. As the North Shore was heavily associated with her work, and what she needed was some reprieve, she elected to go straight and, as soon as she crossed the intersection, swung into the parking lot alongside the waterfront. *Oh my God, what am I going to do?* Tears flowed down her cheeks as she rested her head on the steering wheel.

How can I go on? First, what happened many years ago. I'll never get over that. But things have never gotten much better. Everywhere I go, some guy is trying to hit on me. I can only get through a day if I hide my hair under a toque. And even then, I still get men, and sometimes women – wanting me. I feel like – I'm always filthy.

Toque raised her head and saw the darkened marina in front of her. *Wait a minute! This is where Brock lives! He is one of the few guys who has never hit on me! Maybe he'll make me feel better!* With that, Toque left her car, waited until a marina resident was exiting, showed her badge, and gained access through the locked gate.

As she approached the *Angel*, she thought to herself, *Damn, the boat seems to be in darkness. I can't wake him with my troubles. Perhaps if I have only a quick look. Just to see if he is awake – maybe reading by a pen-light or maybe watching a small screen movie.*

Then climbing into the cockpit, she saw the half-asleep Rex, who groggily perked up and licked her hand as she boarded the vessel. Then with the stealth of a considerate visitor, Toque slowly slid back the hatch.

Suddenly the cabin lights were ablaze.

There was Delila, with her hand on the light switch, and the scent of Always Amorous in the air. It was a vision that would shock any church-going citizen.

Facing the hatch and Toque's amazed face, Delila stood with legs spread and with both hands placed on her hips, as if in command and owner of the vessel. Gone was the look of sophisticated elegance. Instead, she was dressed in a black lace open-nipple bra and her breasts spilt over the confines of the tiny lace garment. Beneath the ample breasts, she wore hot pink split-crotch panties cut open right up to a black lace flower stitched onto the hip-hugging bikini waist band. Although Toque passed only a fleeting glance, it was clear that Delila had a *Brazilian*, probably through laser therapy, and the brown skin of her privates was private no more. Delila turned from Toque, revealing that the split of her panties extended all the way up her totally exposed butt, only to be closed by a discrete second black lace flower at the top by the supporting hip band.

"Hey big boy, we've got company! You got it in you for another go? We got a threesome now!"

Brock opened the door that separated the toilet area – the head, and stepped out, holding a bar of Cedar Forest shower soap. He was totally naked. Stripped, he was even more amazing than when Toque saw him with his shirt off at the detachment hall. There was no debating it; even the chest scar acted as a come-on.

Toque's eyes rounded. However, faster than the speed of light, her first instinctive reaction of fascination changed to that of resistance.

Just as instantly, Brock felt the chilled breeze of torn emotions, and what was, at first, a retained and partial erection, changed quickly to a shape resembling a fallen acorn. His tan-coloured face turned red, and he stammered a few unintelligible sounds. Then grabbing a towel to cover up, ingrained manners emerged. "Oh Toque, let me introduce Delila."

Delila beamed with the look of a cat that had caught the mouse.

Toque gasped, and for the second time that evening, ran.

She leapt into her car and tore off, and through a pile of almost dissolved snow, spewing the icy mush in twin sprays behind her.

Brock fumbled for his trousers but as he did, Delila ran her hand across around his thigh, gently massaging.

"I have to go," he croaked, "As I said, I don't really want this to go anywhere."

"Trust me, she'll be fine," crooned Delila.

"I don't think so," he added, trying in vain to raise his pants as she lowered herself and planted her lips around his member.

"Just trust me. You'll be fine."

His legs weakened and together they sunk to the floor of the cabin.

An hour later Delila and Brock were back in the forward cabin. She ran her tongue down the length of his body, pausing here and there, and he smiled the smile of guilty fulfillment. "I guess I didn't see you in that underwear the first time."

But for Toque, her inner turmoil stormed through her veins as she drove along Georgia, the traffic somewhat lighter in the eastbound direction, the high-rises mainly dark and the streets almost empty. In no time, she was parking on Homer and was knocking on the door of a Yaletown townhouse.

Her climbing partner, Lynn, opened the door, saw Toque's tear-stained face, and reached out to Toque's shoulder, pulling her into the townhouse.

"You poor baby! What happened?" she asked, as she closed the door, then slipped her hand under Toque's shirt so that she held Toque around the waist, around her naked torso.

Toque looked at this sometimes friend from her climbing trio. Standing too close. Her clear pink cheeks, her watchful light brown eyes, and her recently washed, then dried hair: its velvety close-cropped sides beneath the silky longer dark brown hair above.

They were standing so close.

"It's just that men are always ..."

"Men. We don't need them," murmured Lynn as she undid the third button of Toque's shirt. Just one inch taller than Toque, Lynn's lips were seconds away so that they seemed to breath as one.

Lynn's breath was warm and smelt of chocolate liquor; Toque's of fresh mint.

Lynn's second hand joined the first that was still under Toque's shirt and in seconds Lynn undid the back of Toque's bra.

Toque's head spun: out-of-control passion stormed through her entire form as if she had lost all control of personal desires, emotions, and sexual preferences. Images of Joe, Brock, her uncle Kane, Trembley and Karimi, all spun into a crazy kaleidoscope mosaic.

Then hesitating briefly, but in seconds with a kind of sad resolution, Toque reached up under Lynn's T-shirt and touched her velvety and generous torso, the bounteous and rounded flesh, the soft and ample breasts, and then the hardened nipples.

Their lips met.

Their shirts unbuttoned, and their bodies came together.

CHAPTER 43

That evening, Toque and Brock were back on shift and moved down the road, leaning as far away from one another as was possible in the confines of the cruiser. Some of the commercial buildings on Lonsdale had seasonal decorations but the rain had already set the depressed mood initially caused by their individual sexual misadventures. Not a word was being spoken.

What could he say? That one female hand down his pants and he was a taken man? Besides that, he bemoaned the conversation between Lynn and Joe at the racetrack wherein Toque's participation in a threesome was obvious. Even though he blanched at Delila's suggestion of a threesome; he considered that it was likely an enjoyed past-time for Toque. *Oh, for the innocence of the love he had for his wife, April! And hers for him! So innocent, so pure, so perfect.*

Yet Brock was enveloped in Toque's aura: her essence alone made the cruiser seem full. But add to that, her sexual appeal – and he felt an inescapable arousal. He inhaled the increasingly familiar scent of her complete being – and also, that of her fresh mint breath. *She seemed so clean, with such worth ... but,* he kept telling himself, forcing his legs together, *This is a woman who has no bounds in terms of relationships. Sure,* he told himself, *She had a terrible childhood. Perhaps that has made her incapable of a solid one-on-one relationship. Well, for me – Delila,* he told himself, *But that was a one-off ... or so to speak. Whereas for Toque, ... I don't know. But there is Delila. I have to get across to her – that there is not going to be anything long-term. But I have a feeling that that conversation will not go well.*

Toque sighed, engrossed in her own thoughts.

Brock continued his reflections. *But why did Toque turn up last night? She appeared bedraggled. God knows what kinky stuff she's been into – climber friends she couldn't have known for long – and not caring about commitments. Climbers! Sex for the same thrill as climbing. Or worse! No doubt. It's no wonder that she might have*

196

run into some problems. I wonder if she has a dose. Or pregnant. Or, I wonder if there has been more than three at a time. This is what I do not need to think about! Even though I should have never slept with Delila, I did try to make it clear that the first night was a mistake. But in her mind, that was before ...

Toque glanced sideways at Brock. *So that's his type. A woman who dresses like a sex queen. Not my preference in clothing, for sure. Perhaps Lynn has a good idea of wearing boxers. She is so kind, so comforting.* With a smile, Toque remembered waking up alongside Lynn, the sun shining on Lynn face, as if showing the way to a new and better life. *But Brock! I thought so much more of him!* Toque could smell the faint scent of his Cedar Forest shower soap and felt her pace quickening. *Forget this guy. He's not on the same wave-length at all. And that his lover, or should I say, his screw, wanted a threesome! I've never heard of such a thing!*

Well, sure, Joe and Lynn joked about it but ... well, I must admit that I don't really know what happened that night when they stayed over. But then again, with the size of Joe's salami, I can't imagine that he could get into anything other than a horse! But then, did he screw Lynn? But she is my partner now. But did he have me as well? What does that make our relationship? Oh, man, this whole thing is making me think crazy stuff!

But what happened on the Angel *is without question! Brock is definitely involved with that woman who likes the idea of a threesome and who knows what else! What diseases might she have shared with him? Or was she just a hooker? And maybe one of many? And how often does he get them down to his boat? Every night? Several times a night? Who knows where his personal tragedy has led him.*

Brock glanced at Toque the same time she at him: both looked at each other as if they carried the plague and they leaned even further away from one another.

The cruiser's call system crackled and would have brought relief except for the message, "Constable Burdon should be behind the steering wheel right now. Report back when this is the case."

Both Brock and Toque raised their eyebrows. Brock responded, "Toque is driving. What's up?"

"You're both directed to report to the detachment hall right away."

The two of them were taken aback by this out-of-the-ordinary demand. Toque answered, "What's going on?"

"Don't know. The CO's order."

Less than fifteen minutes later, Toque and Brock were at Mrs. Bean's desk. They had never before seen it manned at night.

Yet there sat a male night-shift constable, temporarily assigned to the spot. Something was definitely wrong. Then, as soon as he paged the boss, Grant was at his door, as if waiting for Brock and Toque.

Grant's face was tired, showing the wear of having had to get out of bed in the middle of the night to answer the call of duty. But he was otherwise expressionless, rather like a person with really bad news but was holding it back, momentarily.

Grant looked at Toque and said, "Why don't you go for coffee? Come back in fifteen minutes."

Toque, at first confused, paused for a moment, then replied, "Sounds good. Brock, I'll be in the staff room."

Grant, still without expression, gestured for Brock to enter his office, and then, again, to take the visitor seat on the opposite side of his desk.

Without a word spoken, Brock knew that something not good was going on. His mind raced. *Did something crop up from a previous case? Something in connection with his intelligence work? Had someone, who was imprisoned, managed to escape and was out looking for him? Or much worse, was he going to be asked to keep out a special guard for Toque, because she was being threatened?*

Grant looked at Brock in the face. "You are being relieved of active duty effective immediately."

Brock's mouth fell open. "What are you talking about?"

"There was an anonymous tip-off. VPD found what seems to be cocaine on your boat. Lots of it."

"What? On the *Angel*?"

"Yes. Exactly." Grant's face showed almost no emotion as he tried to hide his disappointment with the current turn of events.

"Is Rex okay? Did they do anything to him?" worried Brock.

Grant's eyes were sympathetic. "I'm sure he's fine. It's yourself who's in trouble now."

"You know it's a set-up."

"That's what has to be proved. But for now, I have no choice but to put you on desk duty until the situation is resolved."

CHAPTER 44

While Toque and Brock served the shift that ended much before Brock anticipated, down at Coal Harbour Marina, four members of the VPD were let in the gate by the marina's dock-master. The police lost no time in moving along the ramp and then across the pier leading to the *Angel*.

"I haven't had a search warrant for a vessel here in years," commented the dock-master.

"It's not common in this marina, but there are other places that we visit frequently."

"Couldn't you pick a better time? I was dead asleep when you woke me."

"A crime scene doesn't sleep."

"I don't suppose you can tell me what this is about?"

"Nope – only that we had an anonymous tip-off. This is it?"

"Yup. This is the *Angel*."

A sleepy Rex in the cockpit rose and greeted them with a bark.

"Don't worry about the dog. I've never had a problem with him."

"I'll take you at your word," responded an officer has he gripped a stanchion, preparing to mount onto the vessel.

Rex let out a resounding growl and the officer backed off. "I thought you said that he was safe with people!"

"Beats me. Hey Rex, come! Come to me!"

Rex momentarily measured his options. He studied the policemen, growled again, then regarded the dock-master, recognizing him as one of his marina friends.

"Come Rex, come on!"

Rex paused, then leaped from the boat and onto the pier.

"Come over to my boat, Rex. I have something there for you." Then, to the attending policemen, the dock-master asked, "Let me know when you're done and I'll bring Rex back to the cockpit."

"Will do. But someone might have to watch out for him."

"But ..."

Before the dock-master could complete his thoughts, the four cops climbed on board, donned sterile gloves, and forced open the lock.

The still-suspicious Rex viewed them with distrust, growled, but continued moving away with the dock-master.

Inside the *Angel*, the first policeman to touch the floor of the galley went straight into the head, slid back the medicine cabinet door, and there under the top shelf holding a razor, hair brush and comb was a middle shelf where – squished beside a bottle of pain killers, and a deodorant stick, was one extra-large zippered clear plastic bag packed full of hundreds of clear chunky crystals, each sealed in their own small sac. On the bottom shelf was an unopened packet of Cedar Forest shower soap, alongside a box of medical-grade plastic gloves, and a second box of small re-closable sacs.

He whistled with surprise, then called out, "Got it! Come and look, then I'll take the pictures before we confiscate what sure seems like dope. And let's bag the boxes of gloves and two-mil sacs!"

In the crowded galley, each cop, one at a time, poked their heads into the tiny locker-sized room holding the head, the shower, the sink, and the cabinet with the suspicious contents.

"Gotta be crack," weighed in the second policeman.

"Rocks."

"Same stuff," added the third, "Crack, rocks, candy, hail, ice cubes, sleet, whatever – all the same stuff: just different names."

"Sure looks like it. Is he stupid or what, to leave it like this?" asked the fourth.

All faces were grim but the third cop added, "You'd think."

Shortly thereafter, the officer who first found the questionable substance took pictures with his cell phone, commenting, "This is too much stuff for evidence folders, to say nothing of the box of re-closable bags."

"I'll get a container from our cruiser."

"Right. In the meantime, let's search the rest of the boat," said the cop closest to the galley sink, as he picked up a half-eaten bag of Cheesesnacks, inspected the inside, then did the same with an adjacent coffee cup from Muriel's.

Then the complete search began. One officer opened the top drawer of a cabinet just next to the entrance to the forward bunk cabin, only to see the drawer filled to the brim with bags of

Cheesesnacks, some individual sized, and some jumbo. The second drawer held coffee filters, one almost full pre-packaged bag of Muriel's coffee, and from the same establishment, two take-out bags – one holding two and a half stale donuts, while in the second bag were three almost-as-stale donut holes. The third drawer – the bottom drawer, held two six packs of local beer and four non-alcohol ones lying alongside.

Another cop opened up the chart drawer under the table and pulled out the contents: three charts and a zipper-lock bag containing bank statements. He eyed the statements, took in the contents with surprise, then said, "Would you believe that this guy was worth $1,000,000,000 at one point?"

"You're joking! And living on this boat?"

"Yeah, he had a huge chunk of change: $999,998,650.00 for just over a year."

"These dealers do well!"

"But imagine being so stupid as to keep it in a bank."

"Just dumb. It's amazing he hasn't been caught sooner."

"Yeah, you'd think he'd at least hide his bank info."

"The greed of these pricks!"

The cop holding the bag continued, "Then, about a year after the initial huge amount, he added to it and then, just a few months after that, withdrew it all."

"When was this?"

"It was withdrawn late March, 2035."

"A few years ago."

"Bet you that he was buying foreign property or hiding it in an account in Switzerland or the Channel Islands."

"Who knows? The closest we'll ever get to that amount is right now, looking at this asshole's bank statement."

"Whatever. Let's bag them as evidence. You don't get that kind of money for nothing."

Shaking their heads with agreed-upon disdain, all four continued the search, examining every surface and storage area: the hanging locker, the book case above the galley dining nook, the adjacent railed shelf, and the galley cupboards.

And then the drawers, the stove insides, the lockers under seats, and the back cabin where stored boxes were opened, emptied, then filled again, though without care or order. In the forward bunk cabin, the search continued to the lockers beneath the berths and even the small raised shelf.

Even the galley garbage was emptied and sorted. The cop on garbage detail wadded through the trash, finding the occasional piece of donut, empty beer can, more Cheesesnacks wrappers, rolled up bags from pre-made salads, a soup mix wrapper, and a filter's worth of cold, wet coffee grounds sticking to every piece of garbage, including the stained take-out bags from Muriel's.

"This guy sure knows how to eat. If we're not sure of his appearance, all we need to look for is a guy with Cheesesnack crumbs on his chest and donut grease on his fingers."

The others chuckled.

Then the officer who'd left returned with an evidence box, put it on the galley table, then climbed into the engine room separating the main cabin from the aft. There he clambered around the smelly diesel engine, examining the area for any hiding spots and even shone his flashlight into the bilge, making sure that there was no second stash of a dubious substance.

After a couple of hours of searching, the four of them gathered in the galley. Two were perspiring, though the night was cold, and sat on the ends of the dining nook while the other two stood, facing their seated counterparts.

"Looks like we found the stash in the first few seconds."

"All the rest of the time searching was a big waste."

"Had to check, though."

"Has anyone looked under the carpet?"

"Not me."

"Me neither."

"Likewise."

"Okay. Let's pull out the table so that we can peel up it up."

In seconds, the table was disassembled, its round steel support soon resting on the wall, while the table top leaned on one of the seats.

One pulled up the carpet and shook it while the others peered down at the floor where various particles of dirt, Cheesesnack, and donut crumbs collected. And as they peered, they saw crystals, not a lot of them, but between the four of them, they found seventeen separate, though small, chunks.

"How could he be so sloppy as to have this stuff on his carpet?"
"Probably half high himself, is my guess."
"Likely."
"These lowlifes know only their fucking habits!"
"Who is the sleaze bag who lives on this dump, anyway?"
"I heard that he's RCMP!"
"You gotta' be joking."
"That's what I heard, too!"
"If that's true, he should serve twice the time."
"You said it. I hope they throw the book at him."
"It's this type of asshole who makes the rest of us look bad."
"As if the job isn't tough enough."

With that, the four officers climbed from the *Angel*, then with a box containing the evidence, and headed for their two waiting cruisers.

As they walked, one asked, "What about the dog?"

"Let the dock-master figure that one out," replied another and then with disdain added, "A dealer's dog isn't worth the time."

CHAPTER 45

Some hours later, when morning had arrived, a group of Rockwater eighth-grade boys thundered into the change room after their homeroom period. Gym class was next on their agendas.

One lad threw a half-eaten apple at the head of another, who in turn, punched his neighbour in the shoulder. Two others wrestled one of the smaller kids to the tiled floor, twisting his arm behind his back until he cried "cat dump." Yet another bully – a large and over-weight fellow, grabbed the shortest student's pack and threw it to the tallest kid who looked as if he'd grown a foot in the last fortnight. The taller, gangly one, tossed the pack onto the ledge above the eye-height cubby holes built for storing students' belongings.

The student deprived of his packsack, cried, "Oh you guys, why can't you take it easy?" as he grabbed a chair at the end of the change room and moved it to a spot beneath the cubby holes where he could reach the abducted pack.

The heavy student went to grab the smaller one's chair when a teacher's voice boomed into the room. "You guys are due on the floor in two minutes! Move it, or you'll be doing extra laps!"

Then moving away from his smaller peer and his step-chair, the large and over-weight student swore. "Shit!" He then hurried to unbuckle his belt, then positioned himself on the changing bench, where he struggled with pulling off the too-tight pants from his legs.

Relieved at having the chance to retrieve his pack, the smaller student climbed the chair and reached out. But then paused, saying, "What the?" as he pulled a small plastic zipper bag from the back of a cubby.

The large boy looked up, succeeded in removing one of his pant legs, then hopped forward in his stocking feet, and snatched the packet from the smaller boy.

"Hey, I had candies at Christmas that looked like this – it's just that they were round and wrapped separately in a blue wrapper." With that, he opened the pouch and popped the crystal into his mouth. He tasted, thought for a moment, then said, "It doesn't taste like the other candy. The round one tasted like licorice!"

By then, several boys were searching the cubby holes and some brought in more chairs to inspect the backs of the higher storage niches.

Before any time passed, the whole class was finding the tiny bags, each with a little crystal inside.

The large boy eyed up the multiple bags and with speed that was surprising for his cumbersome form, grabbed half a dozen bags from the neighbouring adolescents, dumped the contents into his hand, then threw the small pile of crystals into his mouth. "Maybe if I have a fist-full, the flavour will be more noticeable," he said, justifying the quantity he was attempting to consume.

As he did this, half of the class had bags of crystals and those that didn't pass them on to friends, quickly swallowed theirs, following the example of their large classmate. All takers were soon trying to discern the taste of licorice.

"I don't taste anything like candy," complained one.

"Me neither. I sure don't want a second," said another.

Briefly, the large boy sucked on the fistful of crystals, then swallowing, added, "If that is candy, it isn't worth anything. Even a fistful doesn't taste like licorice. It's not sweet at all. In fact, it's bitter!"

He grabbed another boy's find, opened the bag and complained, "And it smells funny. What the hell is this?"

The teacher's voice bellowed again, "You guys have one minute!"

Plastic zipper bags were dropped, soon to be forgotten, as the class fumbled to don their gym strip and appear on the floor in time.

***

An hour or so later, all of these students were sitting in their Math class, with the middle-aged teacher using a laser pointer to mark a specific rule for calculations. But symptoms of multiple illicit drug ingestions started to appear: some students put their heads down
on their desks, others were restless, some complained of heartburn, yet others were confused, while several ran to the bathroom without

permission; but worst of all, was the large boy who felt extreme nausea, light headedness, had cold sweats, and then complained of a severe chest pain, just before he collapsed from his desk and onto the floor.

***

"How could this have happened?" asked Principal Bothe as the last ambulance left the waiting area in front of Rockwater. His face was bleached, as if he had been ill himself.

The administrative assistant and the math teacher stood beside him while further behind, the girls of the class, watched, whispered, and pointed. Two or three boys stood even further away, talking to one another in hushed tones.

"I have no idea," moaned the math teacher, "They seemed a little off when the class started but after about fifteen minutes, various symptoms started to appear."

"You didn't see them eating anything?"

"Nothing other than the odd sandwich."

Bothe raised an eyebrow.

"You know kids, especially boys – will often try to get a head-start on lunch."

"None of the girls ill?"

"Don't think so."

The small boy who had his pack taken moved forward. "Sir …"

"Not now, son," responded Bothe.

"I think I know what happened."

"Speak up, then."

"In the change room there were little plastic bags with a clear candy in them."

"Candies?"

"Well, we thought they were but the guys who ate them said they tasted funny."

"Good God! Your classmates ate an unknown substance?"

"Most did. Mine was taken from me. It was …"

Bothe interrupted and signalled to his administrative assistant, saying, "Get the custodian to clean that change room! And tell him to keep an eye out for any small plastic bags and substance that might
have been mistaken for candy!" Bothe spoke thirty decibels too loudly, as fear and exasperation mixed on his features.

The math teacher asked, "Are you going to call the police?"

Bothe moaned. "I've had it with the police for now. That blood balloon episode cost us a number of students who were pulled out. As you know, the parents here expect the best. The blood bath just didn't fit the picture."

"Are you sure we shouldn't involve the law?"

Bothe sighed. "I'm going to give it a day or two. If the police hear about the drugs, and turn up, parking their cruisers anywhere near the building, it will be in the news in no time because every kid who looks out a window will be posting cop car pictures on the web. Then more parents will want to pull their children. I have to see if we can solve this at the school level. First stop will be Pearce Cudmore, aka Peanut."

The math teacher was clearly upset. "Good luck with that. I just hope that none of the students suffer any long-term damage."

"Of course. That goes without saying."

Chapter 46

Grant, still grey with fatigue, sat mulling in his office. *Brock dealing crystal meth? I can't believe it! Yet the evidence is indisputable, and with four officers witnessing – it is inarguable. Shit! Right in his medicine cabinet? With pieces scattered on his carpet? Brock has been a CSIS agent, for crying out loud! Even if he possessed the contraband, there is no way he would leave it in his medicine cabinet!*

Grant reached a hand to his balding head, as if to push back hair no longer present. *There is no way that Brock would be so sloppy. But even still, evidence is evidence and protocols have to be followed and charges have to be made. He'll have office duty for the next forty-eight hours. During that time, I hope that something surfaces to prove that he was set up. Unless, of course, if the press finds out about this – in that case, he will be assigned unpaid leave until his innocence is proven. Shit! But who the hell could have set him up? I wonder if this is connected with his CSIS work.*

A knock on his door broke his line of thought. Grant responded, "Enter."

Mrs. Bean, with a mixing-bowl cut of straightened white hair, entered. As if told to tame down her fashions, this day she was a changed woman, wearing institutional black pumps, a navy-blue skirt, matching jacket and white collared blouse. Not a whit of jewelry.

Grant glanced at her, raised his eyebrows as she spoke, "Captain Abraham is on the phone, really excited." With that, she quickly exited, almost military in her gait.

Grant picked up. "What's going on?"

"Another email that says more damage has been done. You know of any other infestation?"

"No, not here. Not that I know of, anyway."

"They might be just blowing gas. But the night before last, they said damage would be done before the next sun sets."

"Odd. All the other assaults were right in our faces."

"But what really concerns me is that the current threat says that there will be an attack on – wait – the wording is, 'Those that count and count big will soon face a desert fate unless prisoners in Scheveningen are freed.'"

"No way! Have you organized your part in the extra security for the election of the new Prime Minister?"

"Of course. And you?"

"Likewise. But the emailer expects all prisoners released? Is he nuts?"

"Not all: just three. This time names are given: Kliment Voronin, Lev Kuznetsov, and Gleb Oblonsky."

Grant's head sunk and he raised a hand to his forehead. "No-o-o-o-o-o-o-o-o!"

"What?"

"I've heard those names before."

"When?"

Grant explained, "Before he joined my detachment, one of my constables was in CSIS intelligence and was directly involved in busting a sex-trafficking operation. It was a big international sting."

"You're kidding me! That guy? The Canadian that was in on the apprehensions? Now in North Van? That's a huge surprise!"

Grant confirmed the unknown reassignment of an intelligence agent to the North
Vancouver detachment, replying, "Yes. He is full of surprises, and was also key to the
success of the Lions Gate incident."

"Crap! I'm glad we've got him on our side."

"I wish! Unfortunately, he's on desk duty."

"Shit." Abraham paused, wondering about the famous intelligence agent. But then she continued with the business on hand, saying, "But whatever. What now?"

"Even if the constable in question is put on active duty, this is way beyond our scope, given what has happened so far with regard to the blood, the lice, and so on. Now our next Prime Minister may be at risk."

"If it wasn't so serious, I'd say that might be a bonus."

"Good one. But what about the comment that said, 'More damage has been done'?" asked Grant as he glanced at Brock's re-assignment form on his desk.

210

Abraham shook her head. "Other than the forwarded racetrack report from the VPD and your reports on Cap U, Centennial Theatre and the Premier's Forum, all I have is my officer's report on Rockwater."

"Nothing more on that front?"

"Haven't heard anything, so I'm assuming they're dealing with the blood incident the best they can, probably hoping that we'll come up with the suspect."

"Back to the threat of the possibility of them hitting the leadership convention."

"We have to call in reinforcements."

"Agreed. I still have the contact in CSIS. I'll call him."

"Do it. Let me know if you need back-up. And, call immediately if anything else comes up," requested Abraham.

"You, too."

As he disconnected the phone, Grant looked at the re-assignment form in front of him. On it was the name of his constable being assigned to desk duty. "Brock," Grant said to himself, "We need you now. But shit, what can I do?"

Captain Abraham, as she hung up the phone, for the umpteenth time, read over the incident report regarding Rockwater and muttered, "Let's hope that the blood will be the only atrocity your children suffer."

Chapter 47

As soon as he hung up, Grant quickly scrolled though staff phone numbers and dialed.

"Burdon here."

"Are you able to speak privately?"

"Not a problem. I'm in the car on my way home: I had a couple of things to pick up after my last beat."

With Grant on the line as a reminder of her work life, Toque squirmed, in emotional turmoil over Brock: everything about him – his being blamed for storing dope, his intense attractiveness, but worst of all, was his relationship with Delila. *I've got to get over this guy,* she told herself.

"Ah, Carol, I need to speak to you as soon as you start your next shift. I'll stay late so I can meet with you before you start."

"Of course. What's this all about?" Then hesitantly, with her voice cracking ever so slightly, asked, "Brock?"

"To some extent, but the real reason is to let you know about persons of interest in the incidents we've been facing: the same individuals that were part of a case that Brock was involved with – before he joined us."

"What kind of case?"

"I'm not going to go into detail on the phone but I can tell you that it involved sex-trafficking."

"I remember a high-profile case in the news when I was still training."

"It *was* huge news. Has Brock spoken of it at all?"

"Brock? Involved in that? Jeez, no. Not a word."

"Whatever he said or didn't say, I want to talk to you about it."

"No problem. But you know that Brock should be at our meeting if we're discussing a previous case in which he was involved."

"Unfortunately, not as long as he is on desk duty. And if he ends up getting suspended, there is no way he can be involved."

"Damn! What abysmal timing!"

"You're right on that one. So, I will see you in my office at the start of your next shift?"

"Right. See you then."

CHAPTER 48

The grey-white office area of the detachment building held sixteen work stations, complete with computer terminals with triplicate screens. Half a dozen office employees worked the swing shift in separate nooks. At one of the stations Brock sat, not dressed in his uniform, but rather, dark jeans and a white-collared shirt taken from the dressiest section at the Jeans-Are-Us store.

Scott, in civilians, entered the building's foyer and was about to go down the stairs to the change area, and had just about passed the glassed-in office area when he saw Brock at one of the computer terminals. He stared in with surprize. As he paused, Brown entered the building, also planning to head downstairs, as his shift, too, was about to begin.

"Hey! What's up with Brock?" puzzled Scott.

"What? Is that him in there? Maybe he's researching something in connection with his last beat."

"Doubt it. Never seen him in there, except to ask a question."

Then, with the arrival of Singh and Matthews, the wet chill of the cold December evening moved into the foyer.

"Hey, either of you guys know what's happening with Brock?" asked Scott, nodding at Brock in the office work area.

Singh paused, as if thinking about whether or not he should provide the details of the circulating rumour.

Matthews, his partner for several years, saw Singh's expression of not wanting to give away information. "Come on Singh, what's up?"

Singh grimaced, still reluctant to speak.

"Come on, let's hear it," cajoled Matthews.

Singh continued to pause, his large black eyes thoughtful. "It's only a rumour, but Brock's on desk duty."

"No rumour, I can see that!" observed Brown.

"Spill it, will you? What have you heard?" demanded Matthews.

"Supposedly they found a stash on his boat."

"Of what?"

"Dope. Don't know what type. It's all hush-hush until it can be thoroughly investigated."

Brown sighed an objection. "I don't believe it for a minute."

"Likewise. The only question is who would have tried to set him up."

"I'm going to ask him myself, to set the rumours at rest," said Singh. He then entered the office area and was soon looking at the computer screen in front of Brock. He asked, "What are you up to?"

Brock glanced up, answering, "Searching for those guilty of animal endangerment, aggravated graffiti, and major event interlopers."

"Very funny, but really?"

"You know the incidents with horse poisoning, blood, frogs, lice, and flies?"

"Yeah, like everyone."

"Well, on the left here, we have tapes from Rockwater. On the right, we have traffic cams at Cap U, Centennial Theatre, the Cap U at lower Lonsdale, and from Vancouver I've got one from Hastings Park."

"So, you're looking for?"

"Any repeat vehicles."

"Good luck on that!"

"I got to say that there is a shitload of vehicles going past those buildings!"

"You taking notes?"

"You betcha. See the notes on the third screen?"

Singh considered what was in front of him.

"So far I found a postal vehicle and a private parcel delivery service as repeaters."

"No surprize there. Tell me if you find anything out of the ordinary."

Brock sighed. "I know what you mean. But if I'm diligent, I will find every vehicle that has been in all locations and on the times in question."

"Hopefully you'll figure it out soon. Say, er ... why aren't you on the beat tonight?"

Brock paused, as if remembering lines from a script, answering, "Internal stuff."

"Oh. You can't talk about it."

"Like I said, internal stuff."

Singh gave Brock a playful punch. "Hey, you know you can call on any of us if there is anything we can do to help."

"Thanks, I'll keep that in mind," Then, trying to change the topic, asked, "Anything new in the rumour mill?"

"You heard about Marol?"

"Marol Carrier?"

"Yeah. She was jumped in the parking lot!"

"Is she okay?"

"Couldn't be better. It was actually a laugh. I wish I'd seen it!"

"What! Are you sick?"

"No! She creamed them!"

"You're kidding me!"

"Did you know that she has a black belt?"

"Oh, yeah. Right. But sounds like she made good use of it!"

"Yeah, so funny except for the fact that the bastards jumped one lone person innocently leaving the detachment."

Brock thought about Toque and a feeling of apprehension settled in his bones. He voiced his concern, "It could have been anybody. Were they caught?"

"Unfortunately, no. And Grant got there just a little too late to help. I gather he grabbed Marol after the fact and bruised her arm."

"That's too bad, but lucky she was good on her own. Is there a description of them?"

"Not great information: the bastards wore baklavas. Three guys. Two around five-ten; one a little taller. Both had narrow builds, though one of them had a noticeable paunch. The third was over six feet tall, with slender hips, wide shoulders, and was like … better toned."

Brock thought for a moment, and looked increasingly worried and, as if remembering a bad dream. "Shit. I hope that everyone will be diligent about watching out for them."

"Yeah, everybody is going to be in line with this. Those assholes won't be setting foot on our lot again."

Brock's eyebrows furrowed with uneasiness as he said, "Hope so. Another thing though, are we still 'on' for taking the remaining blankets to the shelter tomorrow?"

"Oh? They're letting you out and into the real world?"
"Not funny. But yeah. I can do charity work. For now."
"Shit. Hope this thing gets cleared up soon."
"Me too."
"We'll see you later."
"Right, have a good one!"

CHAPTER 49

Just a few hours before Brock spoke with Singh at the detachment hall, Toque lay in her bed in her apartment in the popular Kitsilano. There was the faintest, almost undiscernible glimmer of twilight peering through the venetian blinds. Aside from the pounding rain that she could hear from the other side of the window, she could tell from the light on the ceiling that the cloud cover was practically black and the light of the ending day was barely different from that of the night. Breaking the illumination of gloom on the ceiling, was the flickering of three large candles on white pedestals set on her dresser beside the bed as their scent of floral bouquet permeated the bedroom's presence.

Toque snuggled under the sheet, in spite of sensing that the bed was warmed more than usual, then by the fact of the two bodies lying in it. A white down comforter covered their hips and the far side of the crisp pink sheet was carelessly draped over the other recumbent form.

Lynn's dark eyes opened, she smiled, as she moved her hand and ran her forefinger along Toque's shoulder, down her right breast and over a pale, pinkish-tan nipple, then down her unblemished soft, smooth, whitish pink skin, then rested her hand on Toque's hip. Toque managed an uncertain smile, although her expression gave one the feeling that something else was on her mind and she turned sideways, facing away from Lynn. Toque's auburn hair spread out on the pink pillow as if a beautiful halo and replica of that which could have been seen had Botticelli's Venus been resting there. Lynn gently brushed the hair to the side as she crossed over to the side of the bed where Toque lay. Lynn moved up against Toque, so that there was no space between them and their bodies formed as one – the whitish-pink of Toque's skin was an analogous compliment to Lynn's less opaque, but distinctly rosy skin. Toque could feel her heart-beat quicken. Lynn's hand reached down towards …

There was a loud knock on the door that landed like a crack of thunder.

"Don't answer that, Hon," murmured Lynn.

"It could be an emergency."

"Surely they would phone."

Toque thought about Brock: could he have come to the door? Did he need to talk about what was found on the *Angel*? She thought of Brock's eyes the colour of a deep but warm blue ocean. She remembered his wavy coal black hair; always looking as if he'd just had the perfect haircut. She thought of Brock with his shirt off: that welcoming bronze chest, the broad shoulders, the flat stomach, the belt buckle just a little loose on those solid, rugby-player like hips. She could visualize the space between his belt buckle, the fastener at the top of his pants, and his naked abdomen. She remembered him naked on the *Angel*.

Her nipples hardened and Lynn moved her hand towards the erogenous zone, whispering, "Just stay here with me, my love."

"It might be Brock. There was an issue ..."

There was another loud knock on the door. Toque worried that the noise would bother the neighbours or worse, the building manager – who was always hoping to evict any resident in the hope of jacking the rent.

"An issue with Brock? The only issue with guys is below their waist. Why do you think men are sometimes called 'pricks'? It's because that is what they are governed by. I tell you, your cohort is nothing but a low-life guy who will screw anyone, anytime, just for the pleasure. And in their minds, if there is no commitment on either side, all the better."

And then Toque remembered Delila on the *Angel*, in her seductive undergarments. Then Toque's whole being felt chilled. Even so, she defended her working partner, saying, "He's a good guy."

"Thanks for trying to make me laugh."

Toque and Lynn's bodies separated.

"He is! In his spare time, he's out helping the homeless."

"Don't underestimate his male self-absorption! Without question, it is just one more male power trip! And pretending to be helpful to those who need real charity! Sickening!"

Toque frowned as she reached for a T-shirt and sweat-pants. She looked at Lynn and wondered about whether or not she had made a bad choice and that if, perhaps, she should cool the relationship.

"I tell you, your partner Brock is just another male asshole! You were right to call me!"

Another loud bang on the door and a male's voice resounded. "Toque, are you in there?"

Toque pulled on her sweats, half hoping, and half dreading that it would be Brock.

When she opened her door, she was both bewildered and disappointed. There stood Joe, towering above her. At first, she didn't recognize him because his beard was gone – he was clean shaven, and his hair had been cut back to that of a respectable businessman. Instead of climbing gear, he wore tan coloured dress slacks and a navy-blue collared shirt, with the long sleeves rolled up to just beneath the elbow. He was a changed man.

"Is it your boyfriend, Brock?" called Lynn, with sarcasm icing her tone.

"Joe! What are you doing here?" asked Toque, blushing at Lynn's remark, and the exposure of the sexually oriented scene into which Joe had stumbled.

Lynn stepped out from the bedroom, the sheet wrapped around her like a pink toga. She chuckled. "Oh, are you here for more, now that I'm here as well?"

Toque blushed. "That's not going to happen."

Lynn was taken aback and speechless.

While unphased by Toque's den of iniquity, Joe apparently had something else on his mind. He stammered, "I just came to apologize for the other day." Though at the same time, he was unsure exactly what he was apologizing for, then added, "I feel that we got off on the wrong foot."

Toque remembered the salami-sized shape that seemed to be in his pants and again felt ill at ease and, like Lynn, though for a different reason, was speechless.

Joe continued, "For one, I think that the three of us were having a great time as a climbing team."

Lynn's face confirmed her agreement, while Toque just stared at him, at this man who seemed so changed.

"I'd hate to give up the climbing group. Can we agree on that?"

"Sure, why not," answered Lynn, "How about this Sunday if it's not raining ... or snowing?"

Joe seemed relieved, answering, "I'm in!"

You wish! Thought Lynn, cynically.

"Shu-u-u-u-u-u-u-re," agreed Toque, hesitantly.

"But another thing, Toque, you said you'd come with me to the leadership race."

Toque glanced sideways, away from Joe.

"Well, can you still join me?"

"Um, I'm not sure that ..."

"Hey, how about me? I can go with you!" interrupted Lynn.

"Good to know, but I did ask Toque first."

"She doesn't want to go; can't you see it?"

"Come on Lynn, how about letting Toque speak for herself? What's is it, Toque?"

Toque still looked uncertain.

Joe added, "It would mean a lot and I promise you that it will be strictly friends, if that is what you want."

"Okay, I'll go, as I said before."

"Well," harrumphed Lynn, "In that case, Toque, I expect you'll go out of your way to join me at the upcoming all-nighter at the Christian Climbers Elemental Assemblage."

"Both of us?" asked Joe, clueless.

Lynn moved close to Toque and slipped her arm around Toque's waist. "No, Joe, just us ladies at this one."

"Maybe. I have to check my schedule," said Toque, with hesitation colouring her tone.

CHAPTER 50

On her way to start her shift, on her first night without Brock, Toque approached the traffic lights at Denman and Georgia. After that intersection, there was only two choices of direction: the long circular route arcing through Stanley Park at the speed of thirty kilometers, or straight through the Stanley Park Causeway at racing speed and, whether you wanted to or not, onto Lions Gate Bridge. There was absolutely no turning around until one had crossed the bridge, then fought their way through a set of annoying multi-turn traffic lights after traversing a good-sized block or two on the North Shore.

Instead of proceeding on one of those routes and directly to work, Toque moved into the right-hand lane, turned onto the north end of Denman, and soon pulled into the parking lot adjacent to the marina where Brock moored the *Angel*. Toque grabbed a flashlight as she swung out of her seat. Nervously, she stared down at Brock's vessel. It was cloaked in blackness. She let out a sigh of relief and proceeded to walk through the parking lot, covering one parking spot at a time, examining each inch of ground with her flashlight. It didn't take long: in about ten minutes she found a wet oil stain. She reached into her bag, pulled out an evidence sac, plastic gloves, and took a sample. Once done, she again looked uneasily at Brock's boat, remembering the day she went for emotional support, but instead found Delila and Brock carousing in their nakedness. Toque shook her head, as if trying to get rid of the memory.

Once in her car, Toque was soon on the Stanley Park Causeway. As she drove, she used the auto-phone system to call dispatch.

"Carol Burdon calling."

"Toque?"

Toque sighed. "Yeah, sure. Is Marol Carrier still in the building?"

"Just a minute. As you probably know, she often works late. I'll check the lab."

A few minutes passed as Toque boarded the ramp of Lions Gate Bridge, with the rain pounding on her windshield.

The phone rustled with the sound of the person in dispatch reconnecting. "Sorry, she's gone. I can try to connect you to her private phone. She might pick up."

"Yes, please. Try to connect."

To Toque's relief, Marol's voice answered on the first ring. "Marol here. Is this dispatch calling?"

"Yes and no. It's Carol Burdon."

"Carol Burdon?"

"You know, Toque!"

"Oh! Of course!" Then there was the pause of a question mark.

Before Marol could speak further, Toque stated the reason for calling, "Marol, I have a huge favor to ask."

Marol eyes rounded with surprise. "What kind of favor?"

"I suppose that you heard that Brock has been put on desk duty."

"I was shocked! Yes, I did hear. Drugs, wasn't it?"

"Yeah, VPD found crystal meth on is boat. A lot of it. But I'm working on the assumption that he is innocent and has been set up so have looked around his marina parking lot for clues."

"And?"

"I know it's a long shot, but I found some leaked engine oil. I'm wondering if it is a match for the oil Brock collected at Rockwater, Cap U, Centennial Theatre, the Premiers' Economic Forum and at Hastings Park."

"Not that I don't want to help, but there is a specific team that does the sample testing. For this sort of thing, I'm the one who later does the met-analysis."

"I know. But the team doesn't start work until tomorrow. Right now, there is a huge likelihood that if the story of the stash on Brock's boat hits the news, he will be relieved of all duties. Then, once his reputation is in question, it will take forever to regain it."

"Temporarily looking not so great has happened before with other cops and it didn't mean the end of the world."

"I know. But things will not be good for him for a long time. Plus, I have a bad feeling about these assaults, infestations – whatever you want to call them. And Brock and I are the only ones who were involved in all of them."

"I can understand how you feel, losing your partner, but I wonder if you're jumping the gun. In due time, those assaults will be solved, regardless of the specific cops working on it. And eventually, Brock will be cleared, provided he is innocent – as we all suspect."

"But something else has cropped up – some names in connection with a case he worked on before I joined the force."

Marol thought for a moment, but drew a blank. Only Grant knew of Brock's intelligence work. After a pause, Marol responded. "I haven't heard anything about Brock's earlier work."

"Well, I can tell you that some names have come up: bad players, from what I understand. And I have a hunch that there is a connection to those who have it in for Brock. If this is the case, believe me, there's no telling what they will do next."

"Shit. So, you want me to do the lab work for your oil sample and then check to see if it is the same as the others?"

"Please."

Marol, although knowing that this would mean a lot of extra time, felt the flush of determination, similar to that when she, and other members of the North Shore Rescue team had an urgent call. Marol agreed, saying, "I'll meet you at the detachment office."

"Thanks so much. And Marol, would you promise in advance to call me on my cell as soon as you get results?"

"You know the results all go to Grant. But sure, I'll let you know as soon as I do."

CHAPTER 51

Borya gingerly touched his face where the wound from the heel of Marol's boot had left a large sore that had not totally healed, then being only partially scabbed over with half of its surface still wet with yellow pus. A small portion of his baklava was embedded in the abrasion. He grimaced at the touch on his painful wound, then looked at Egor and Ras with severity. Their rain coats dripped from their walk through the continuous downpour. Their faces were in shadow from their hoods still over their heads.

"What the hell happened to our party in the RCMP parking lot with that bloody motorcycle mom? I loved the idea of taking her down a peg or two!" griped Borya.

"Me too! But it turned out that it was our pegs that were kept down!" bemoaned Egor.

"Kept out, you mean. I don't know how we got fucking beaten when we tried to grab her!" added Ras.

Egor sneered, "I want another go at her. I'll be prepared next time."

"Well prepared," added Ras.

"I am sickened by these capitalistic sluts and hags, marching around as if they are worth listening to. And then that cunt using some sort of weird kick-boxing moves! What kind of creature is she? Not a woman in my book! That she even lives, galls me!"

"So, you want to go back and show motorcycle mom what we can really do?" asked Ras, smiling and rubbing his groin.

"Sure, we can fit that in, and fit you in. In fact, we can all fit in, though not together. I'll go first."

"No, you guys are after me. I'll get her ready for the two of you. Then you won't have to stress yourself, though with the size of your tiny pegs, it won't be a problem, no matter who goes first," laughed Ras.

But Borya shook his head. "Maybe later we'll deal with her. Show her what a real assault is. I'd like that: light entertainment. But, given her fighting skills, we *will* have to be prepared. And with equipment, including that fantasy knife you told me about. Luckily,

I'll have it in my hands soon." Then, looking even more serious, continued, "But what I want to talk about is that we need to consider an increased scale for our *real* work. I guarantee that as before, you will benefit beyond the captures. Benefit in every way."

Ras and Egor smiled the smiles of the perverted anticipating illegal pornographic horrors. "Sounds good; but holding and distributing is a problem when there are just three of us."

"As I've said, I do plan to have others."

"The inmates we spoke of?"

"Who knows: maybe. But a much surer thing is Kliment, Lev, and Gleb."

"You're kidding! Are they going to be released?" questioned Ras.

"Can't say, at this point."

"That would be huge, if they join us again!"

"I'm planning on it. The law here is pure fluff! No real consequences. And their resolve is shallow. Anything goes! All is forgiven in no time. We can use that weakness to regain ground and get our members back."

"We're with you, one hundred percent!"

To himself, Borya thought, *Once a loser, always a loser. But useful losers ... for the next while. I can keep them reined in now that I know the kind of liabilities they can be. And it won't be like before. And once they've served their purposes, I'll enjoy being the cause of*

their wishing they'd never been born. Borya continued, "And, just for the fun of it, as a special gift in thanks for your continued service, I've been planning a private live show that you'll never forget!"

"A show? We get movies in prison!"

Borya threw his head back and with a jeering laugh, explained, "This one will be interactive! You'll never participate in anything like this in a *male* prison!"

"What?"

"Just wait and see. But for a while, I'll continue to think about how we can again be a group of six. As you've said, with just three we can't do a lot in terms of acquisition and distribution."

"So, it's a wait-and-see?"

"Yeah, but in the meantime, I have plans for that constable asshole, Brock!"

"Let me in on whatever you do to him!"

"We'll see."

"What are you going to …"

"Not just Brock, but that slut of a partner. They call her Toque. She's relatively new on the scene but will be a worthwhile catch!" smiled Borya.

"Yes. YES! Me first!" panted Egor.

"We'll see," smiled Borya evilly.

"I get your meaning! We'll take turns … and take turns watching!" laughed Ras, salivating.

Chapter 52

With her hand, Lynn preened the longer portions of her hair as she entered the three-story mixed-use commercial building with a pharmacy on one side of the main door and a learning center flanking the other. Through the glass front and across the beige tiled floor, she could see the elevator that would take her to her destination. Nervously, she entered, tucking into her navy slacks the freshly ironed matching pin striped white shirt, and then checked out her navy loafers for dust. Soon she was on the third floor, and walked down the hall, then entered a door on the right at the end of the beige carpeted hallway.

Just inside, in a waiting area that held four sage-coloured upholstered seats, was the receptionist sitting at a shiny mahogany desk. She was a beautiful young woman of Chinese heritage but seemed too young to hold any position of responsibility. However, in seconds any misgivings that a client might harbour were dispelled. When she spoke, she immediately stood out as forthright yet kind, and business-like, yet humane: a perfect combination for the person on the front line of a family law office.

"Ms. Lynn Ashton?" asked the receptionist.

Lynn signalled her presence, though without a smile.

"Dr. Lakewood is waiting for you."

"Doctor?"

"Yes, that is the title that all new attorneys are going by now."

Lynn entered a large office to the left of the receptionist. There, behind a huge gleaming mahogany desk partially covered with a green blotter and tandem computer screens sat Lynn's new attorney: a middle-aged woman with greying hair cut in a short bob. On one wall beside her was an enormous mahogany bookcase, sparsely filled with white stone sculptures of the human figure, made by a local artist. One shelf, however, was filled with black binders labelled with some unintelligible system. On another wall was her framed degrees and membership to the British Columbia Bar Society.

Dr. Lakewood stood and extended her hand as she said, "Ms. Ashton, I'm glad to meet you. What can I do for you?"

Lynn found it hard to make eye contact but started in, in spite of her interminable feelings of deprivation. "I have been denied custody of my daughter, Nikki, and I would like to revisit it."

"Why did you not get custody initially?"

"Dr. Lakewood…"

"Call me Bella."

"Right, let's use first names. I didn't get custody because of a few issues. I've come to you because from your photo on your website I can see that you're a senior lawyer and …"

"Not exactly. I don't want to mislead you. I was just called to the bar earlier this year."

"What? This place looks well established!"

"I took over the office from another lawyer – an outstanding game changer who moved on to other aspects of law. I only hope that I can follow in his shadow."

Lynn looked at the door and paused. "Well, seeing that I've taken the Canada Line all the way out here, let's see what you think."

"You said that you were denied custody? Often, when the child is a girl, the mother is given serious consideration, especially if the mother is the primary care-giver."

"To explain, there are two moms. My ex and I were a gay couple."

"I see. Your ex's name?"

"Carla Rivers."

"So, the reason why Ms. Rivers got the custody is?"

"Well, I had a bit of a problem with violence."

"That would probably go against you."

"But I have made amends! I haven't threatened Carla in the last year."

"That's an improvement! Just what did you threaten?"

"Death, but it was kind of tongue-and-cheek."

"I doubt a judge would feel like laughing. Any other threats?"

"I might have bashed her around a bit."

"Recently?"

"No – when we were together. But she was hospitalized just a few times."

Bella shook her head. "This is not likely going to go your way. Did you also hit the child?"

"Absolutely not! She was only one when we split! There was no way she could have provoked me the way Carla did!"

"How did Ms. Rivers provoke you?"

"Lots of little things, but the worst was that she acted like she knew everything and that my opinion wasn't worth the time of day. Or when she always had her head in her books or marking and acting like I was an intrusion when I walked into her study."

"Any other behavior on your part that I should know about?"

"Well, I stalked her but I haven't done that for over a year now!"

"Better, I guess. Anything else?"

"Well before, I was pretty intense with my save-the-planet efforts."

"And you did something I should know about?"

"Well, before Carla and I broke up, I was implicated in the torching of one of the oil freighters that had come in to pick up cargo."

"The inferno up against the pier that was burning for over a week? Those creosote-covered pilings that wouldn't go out? You were involved in *that*?"

"Well," acknowledged Lynn, "More than involved: it was my plan."

"Pardon my bluntness, but to save the planet you caused a fire that had smoke so toxic that the fire department had to issue a health warning for the entire city?"

"Well, not exactly entirely me: I was only involved in the initial stages of just talking about it. In fact, as punishment I got off lightly: I was given house arrest."

"Even so, the custody is not likely to go well for you."

"But as I've said, I've been on good behavior for a year now! I even joined a Christian group and have started a really solid relationship with an RCMP constable."

"That might help. But is there anything else that might go against you?"

"I'm currently unemployed."

"Job skills?"

"I've worked as a cashier in a few different places, done some of their paper work, and a little bit of job training for the newbies – mainly at home improvement stores. I was at the last place for a couple of years and was on my way to management but since the fire episode, I think that I've been blacklisted."

"That's not legal."

"It happens. It's all covert and can't be proved."

"I can help you with asserting your right to a position. But for now, if you're not working, how can you afford to live in Vancouver?"

"I have an inheritance from a great Aunt. That, by the way, is why I can afford to pursue this issue of the custody of my daughter. But also, another asset, though probably temporary, is that my parents have an investment property where they're letting me live. It's a definite bonus except for the fact that I have a couple of brothers who are pissed that I'm getting accommodation for free. They want their share."

"Back to you not getting custody, does Ms. Rivers have any issues that might go against her guardianship?"

"No, she's sickeningly perfect. First of all, she excelled as a physics teacher at Rockwater, then advanced to Capilano University."

"Anything else to her credit?"

"She's always going beyond: doing this, doing that. Can't sit for a minute and pass the time of day. Lately, she's been organizing her students to provide sandwiches for the homeless. Carla is tireless when it comes to trying to be important and climb the ladder."

"Is it possible that Nikki might be getting the short end of the stick with regard to childcare?"

"If she is, it's the gold tipped end. But maybe, depending on your point of view. Nikki goes to a really nice daycare in Edgemont Village – All Faiths. But I was doing great as a home mom. Though when we were together – the three of us – being with Carla, it was often just plain intolerable, living with a self-important teaching machine …"

"I see. But is there anything else you can provide that would make your child's life better than it is currently, under the custody of Ms. Rivers?"

"Absolutely. Like I've said, I've been and will be really good as a home mom and I expect that very soon I can introduce Nikki to the best ever step-mom. And this may happen really soon! The absolutely wonderful woman I'm seeing now, as I've mentioned, is a cop – a person with a respected career and with no marking."

Just bullets, thugs, and criminals, thought Bella.

Lynn continued, "It is my hope that we can start a family, beginning with Nikki. Maybe with your help, I can even get back to work – possibly even management – and then do different shifts from my new partner and we won't need daycare! In our times off, we can both be home-moms."

"Do you have a commitment from this new partner?"

"Not spelt out. But we are definitely an item."

Bella took the remark in consideration, though she looked skeptical as she advised, "Maybe if you were to re-marry, along with the home-mom argument, there is something we can work with. But I'm telling you now that I think that you don't have much of a chance, particularly considering your record of violent behavior."

Lynn mentally sought out and thought she sensed a faint, though almost impossible, glimmer of hope. "But you think it's worth a try?"

"Anything is possible. I just want to give you a sense of the likelihood of success."

"So, we'll go for it?"

"Sure, as long as you understand what you're getting into, within the limits of the law, I'll do everything I can to help you."

Chapter 53

Toque pulled over as soon as she saw the five-foot-high white stone fence with turrets, the newly planted cedar hedge, and in behind which – affixed to the lawn with guy-wires – loomed a two-story-high inflated snowman, complete with a red and green striped scarf. The giant balloon structure seemed to hover in front of the three-storied-high house and the rounded marble staircase leading up to the closed gate.

Choosing to not make use of her knowledge that along the side of the house was the driveway, leading to a four-car garage and adjacent to a paved area for additional vehicles, Toque parked behind an almost disintegrated pile of plowed snow, on the side of the narrow curb-less side street where the indefinite edge of the asphalt road was formed by an irregular and patchy line of loose gravel bordering the shoulder grass.

At the entrance-way to the house, Toque passed under the circular pagoda-type ceiling that was supported by four Romanesque columns. Windows that covered the front of the house were all alight, as if a party was in progress.

In no time, she let herself in through the wrought iron gate, passed the shadowy lawns and gardens on either side of the walkway, climbed up five more steps to the main entrance, and knocked at the huge ornate doorway painted in glossy white.

Although the house was brilliantly lit, no one came to the door, so after waiting five minutes, Toque turned around, and glanced for a moment at the spectacular view of the night-time twinkling lights of the city of Vancouver. Then, just as she anticipated that within seconds she'd be climbing back into the cruiser, the speaker in the surveillance system came to life, with a greeting that sounded like a demand. "What do you want?"

Toque recognized Peanut's voice. "Hello ... um ... er. . . Pearce, I have just a few questions, if you've got a moment."

Peanut sat on a kitchen stool at the white marble island. In front of him was a steaming plate of macaroni Alfredo. Peanut was watching the screen mounted beside the white windowed cabinets. On the monitor was a live video stream of Toque at the door.

He, like most heterosexual males on the planet, was taken by her appearance, even though he could see only the uppermost part of her torso. But what he saw was pure beauty, though he felt that it was ridiculous that it should be existing under the cap of an RCMP constable. But in the light of the front porch, her blue-grey eyes with long dark eyelashes and perfect arched eyebrows were calling. Her dream-like face, her full pink lips, her seductive neck moving down to ... *Heck,* he thought, *A cop's uniform hiding what even an idiot would instinctively know were firm, rounded breasts and a great bod.* Peanut flushed. He was about to say that he did not have to speak to her without legal representation but instead he said, "You're here alone?"

Toque paused, thinking about her answer. *I don't need to worry about being alone with this kid. There is no way that he is a threat to me. He is just a scrawny teen. Plus, he might be smart but he is also extremely naïve. At worst, he's a somewhat perverted insect killer and bug pusher. But in every way, he's just a kid and an underdeveloped one at that.* "Yes. I'm alone. It will take just a few minutes."

Peanut thought to himself, *Mom will kill me if I let anyone in. She'll take away my internet. For at least the week-end. She hates it when there are strangers in the house. But she's at another benefit. She's always out till late when she goes to those things. She doesn't have to know.*

Peanut took the remote and flipped through the camera feeds from various locations around the exterior of the house, paused on the cruiser parked in front and then moved back to camera focussed on Toque. Botticelli's Venus on his doorstep. Alone. He dumped the pasta into a zippered plastic bag, spilling just a little onto the cuff of his sweat-pants. He then threw the steaming once-a-meal-mass into a random kitchen cupboard, and placed the plate in the dishwasher.

"Hold on, I'll be at the door in a minute," responded Peanut, lowering his chin slightly so that his voice was an octave deeper than that with which he'd originally answered the intercom system.

When the door opened, Toque was struck by Peanut's youth: he seemed barely beyond puberty. Although adolescent growth spurts had given him almost as much height as herself, under his wrinkled T-shirt, his shoulders were still those of a child, and his track pants that barely hung on him, were baggy from excessive sitting. He stood tall, though, and held his narrow chest out to maximize its size and then, once in the kitchen, crossed his arms and placed his hands under his bicep muscles so that they seemed larger.

But to Toque, he was an adolescent with many more years to grow before manhood.

Toque took a bar stool at the kitchen's island, wondering about the scent of Alfredo sauce.

Peanut deepened his voice as low as it would go. "What kind of questions do you have?" he asked, moving onto the stool beside her.

She focussed on his washed-out blue eyes, his pale, blanched indoor skin, his sparse thin brown hair, his peanut-shaped skull. "There's no rush, just a few questions. But before we get to that …"

Peanut looked at her expectantly, sensing her fresh mint breath, then sneaking a peek at her chest, cruelly [to him] covered by her bullet-proof vest and jacket. He gaped at her neck, her blue-grey eyes, her long eyelashes. He glanced at her well-formed, toned thighs, his pupils dilating.

"I was wondering how you are doing with your insect-eating invention."

"It works fine, just like I designed it."

"Just for the fun of it?"

"What else?"

"Oh, I don't know," stalled Toque, "It just seems so incredibly clever. It's kind of a waste to not sell it to someone."

Peanut thought for a moment. "I hope that you're not thinking it's just a toy."

"Not at all. It's really an ingenious invention!" exclaimed Toque, trying to sound enthusiastic.

Peanut's narrow chest swelled from the compliment. He smiled, showing his undersize teeth that seemed to be all the same shape, unlike most people who have larger incisors on the top.

"I want to go over the night before the defacement at

Rockwater."

"I already told you and … the other cop my answer. Nothing has changed. I was at home. Alone."

"What would you say if I told you that it was blood?"

Peanut shrugged and gave away nothing.

"Okay, Pearce. It's clear you're a really bright guy."

Pearce glowed from the complement. "Remember, just call me Peanut."

Toque smiled, then continued, "And I've been wondering about a group you belong to – the Society To Advance Global Species. Sounds interesting."

Peanut leaned back, spreading his legs, as if to predict his coming manhood, as he added clarity to her remark. "More like *important*!"

Toque smiled, trying to become friends with this teen. "Sounds cool. Can you tell me about it?"

"Do you realize that the oceans contain more weight in plastic than in fish?"

"Yes. It's horrifying. Is your group trying to improve the situation?"

Peanut paused, though pumped from her compliments. But then he smiled. "You can bet on it! But not plastics this time, we're working on getting the government to delineate a substantial increase in funds for bitumen clean-up in our waters."

"Getting anywhere with it?"

"Don't worry, we will!"

"Oh?"

Peanut glanced at the ceiling and laughed the laugh of one who knows but isn't sharing. His eyes refocussed on Toque. Then thoughtfully, with measured words, as if he'd made a choice, moved the topic over to that of Rockwater. He leaned back while still seated on the bar stool, with the assuredness of one in the know, then added, as he put his hand on her arm, and Toque grimaced as she thought that she could smell ear wax, but her eyes widened when Peanut uttered the words, "I know that you want to ask me about the crack."

Toque almost fell off the bar stool, thinking, *How could he know about Brock's boat?* She leaned away from Peanut, purposefully moving just out of his reach. "Crack?"

"Yeah. In the PE cubby holes! The stuff that made the guys in the grade eight Math class sick!"

"You're kidding me!"

"Yeah, there was a ton of it in the cubby holes and the stupid grade eights ate it! Those little nit-wits got what they deserved! They really are nothing more than ankle-biters. Imagine eating it!"

"My God! Was anyone seriously ill?"

Peanut smiled more broadly, realizing that he had new information and again leaned towards Toque, sharing again the ear wax scent. "Yeah, most of the kids are over it, but one is still in a coma and the grade eights are super bummed-out about it. It was quite the show – the front of the school was bumper-to-bumper ambulances!"

"When was this?"

"Yesterday morning."

As he finished his sentence, thinking that he was now a key informant, he leaned even closer to her, this time placing his hand on her knee. The groin of his sweat-pants suggested a swelling underneath. But before Toque could react to his touch and arousal, Peanut's mother threw open the kitchen door and with one quick glance saw her son with his hand on the knee of the female RCMP officer. Her mouth opened in astonishment, forming a red *O*, as she noticed the bulge in his pants and lower down, on the cuff, the suspicious sign of the Alfredo spill.

"What the hell! What kind of cop slut are you to be here after my son?" screeched Mrs. Cudmore, her firm breast implants barely moving in her semi-transparent evening gown cut open to her navel and slit up the legs to her hips.

Peanut's hand removed faster than it would have, had he had it in a flash-fire, and his penis retreated like a snail that was prodded, and his lychees shrunk down to the size of two shelled pistachios, leaving the sweat-pants just bulgy and with not an iota of apparent content.

Mrs. Cudmore shook her blond mane in anger, her eyes visibly blazing, even though they were partially covered by one hundred coats of mascara.

"This is the crust on a shitty night, after I go to the bloody benefit at the daycare that has to end almost before it started because the useless staff felt they should be up before dawn to tend to the children," she whined, toning the last word with biting sarcasm.

Peanut's mother continued, "Like being a little tired hurt anyone! Lots of people do just fine on a few hours of sleep. They should be glad they have jobs. But what's worse than the complainers, are the ones who are sucking up for reasons unknown. I'm sure they just want to get something for free or step on another worker to get ahead."

"Anyone come to mind?" asked Toque, though reluctant to interrupt the rant of this crazed socialite.

Mrs. Cudmore, seeing a chance to up her vindictive skills, relaxed a little, to spill out a gripe. "Yes: her name is Petra. She should have stayed in her homeland. She seems to be just too friendly. Always sucking up for unknown reasons. And almost horny ... I'm sure you've come across this sort of thing. But I don't even want to think about that. But totally suspicious! No one acts that caring ... all the time."

Toque tried to act professional, asking, "But you said you were at a benefit at a daycare?"

"Seeing that you ask," groaned Mrs. Cudmore, "All Faiths bloody daycare. They didn't even offer us a drink!" She snorted with disdain. "And after the donations we've given them!"

"I have just a few questions for uh ... er ... Pearce," said Toque as she gestured at Peanut and briefly looked him in the eyes.

That brief glance sent Peanut cascading into a sexual fantasy. He gazed back at Toque: at her face, her chest, her thighs: he was spell bound. His pupils dilated. His member swelled. A lot. With shock, Mrs. Cudmore stared at her son's metamorphosis, then again eyed the creamy substance on the cuff of his sweat-pants. A sudden, though incorrect conclusion formed in her mind, and her toned-down rancor turned into full-bore venom.

"No, you don't, you RCMP cunt. But what is that fucking smell? Don't tell me you two did it in the kitchen! The maid is going to have to sterilize the whole fucking place! But why is the smell over there?"

With that, Mrs. Cudmore threw open kitchen cupboards until she came across the still-warm pasta in the clouded-over plastic bag. Her eyes narrowed as if a thought was about to form, but alas, only rage controlled her frontal cortex. Then malicious, she pulled out Peanut's dubious cuisine, and threw the warm mass onto the white marble counter, splitting the bag open so that the contents vomited all over, still steaming, and onto the white tile floor.

She glared at Peanut. "Why can't you be something other than a little nerd? You're a continual embarrassment to me and your father. Why can't you be like your brother? How are you ever going to manage at university? The only part of your brain that works is the school brain. For now, consider yourself canned. After you clean up this mess you can sit in your room. With no internet! And think about what you have done in your little soirée here!"

"Mrs. Cudmore, I assure you, nothing inappropriate has been done!"

"Was I hallucinating? I saw what I saw! Pearce, go to your room now! I'll call you when I'm finished with this embarrassment to the police force! Then you can clean up! And it better be good!"

Pearce stood, and moved towards the door of the kitchen, head down. But just before he
exited, he chanced a glimmer of a smile at Toque, but at his mother then cast the look of unabridged hatred.

Mrs. Cudmore did not see the look as she was then totally focussed on Toque. "And what I'd like to see NOW is your tart ass getting out of here! Don't be surprised when my complaint goes through to your superiors. I won't rest until you are fired! And disgraced! And serving time for molesting a minor! I don't need to imagine what went on before I walked in. How stupid do you think I am? I will be contacting my lawyer immediately. Now get out!"

Mrs. Cudmore then turned her back on Toque and went to the wine refrigerator and extracted a bottle of chardonnay.

Toque, not needing further instructions from Mrs. Cudmore, headed for the door, feeling a mixture of relief with that of being affronted and insulted.

***

Within five minutes Toque pulled onto the yellow striped *No Parking* zone just behind the loading area at the front of Rockwater. The adjacent parking lot was as empty as a graveyard on a stormy night.

As she stepped from the cruiser, in front of her, in the darkness, was the long two-story building. Above the gloom of the building, the clock tower was alit, as if time was important, even when school was not in session. In the deserted night, the front steps gave a feeling of vacuous spaciousness; the grandiose entrance acted as a shell of tribute to the school days' busy activities.

Toque pulled out her flashlight and perused the parking spots of the loading area. Within minutes, she found what she had been looking for: leaked engine oil, not more than a few days old. First time lucky. Holding her evidence kit, she took a sample, then bagged it.

Just a few meters away was another spot where oil had leaked – probably a couple of weeks earlier – it had been smeared around – most likely by the school's snow plow, before the current trend of rain. She thought to herself, *This is where Brock took a sample*. She then continued to search the parking areas for the entire school, found nothing more, but was unconcerned, as she had already bagged the reason for the visit.

CHAPTER 54

Delila leaned back on her bunk, running a twelve-inch lime green glow-in-the-dark vibrating dildo down her naked torso, leaving behind an oily trail of lubricant. She thought about Brock; his eyes the colour of a deep but warm blue ocean, his wide shoulders, his flat stomach, the warm amber six-pack, and the amazing muscle tone everywhere. She smiled, then thought about Toque; her statuesque form, her warm blue-grey eyes and her soft smooth whitish-pink skin. Then Delila smiled even more. She relaxed into a totally recumbent position.

As she reached the dildo further down her torso, the touch of the device on her pelvis was like a trigger of a memory and any iota of pleasure was displaced by the tormented recalls of her first sexual encounters; the disastrous experience in high school followed by that in college. Her face distorted with the pain of the remembrance of the fake shows of love that had so overtaken her and just when she gave all, the pretend love walked away as if she were nothing.

"Could be a better show, you imbecile."

She looked at Borya and remembered when they had met: he was hanging around the marina, pretending that he didn't notice her. But then when she asked him if he was waiting for someone, he seemed at a loss for words. But then their eyes met: her dark eyes, his well-spaced hazel-brown eyes under eyebrows full, though not overbearing. And his moist heart-shaped lips, with the top lip ever so slightly but aesthetically elongated, his aquiline nose, his face a longish oval, with cheeks slightly flushed upon a flawless fair complexion. His hair was blond, though sandy where it was short above his ears. At over six feet tall, with slender hips, he was really well toned, and seemed an unbelievably perfect match to her entire appearance, including her body shaped like that of a gymnast. At first, they spoke in awkward snippets but even with their minimal dialogue, the two managed to meet for tea almost every day for almost a week but before the week passed, the tea was an afterthought to the passion they'd soon experience in her bunk.

He shared with her what he said were all the positives of a successful and happy life: he claimed that for all intents and purposes he was upper-end management, with many people working under him. He spoke of only one of the negatives – that there was a person who was the worst of enemies.

In turn, she shared with him the story of her life – her romances that turned to cruel fakery. He swore complete revenge on her previous lovers that had so callously betrayed her. She asked to meet at his home, but he delayed, saying that it was not fit to visit but that soon his circumstances would improve and then she would have a ring on her finger. She swore to be his life-long helpmate and act at his every beck and call.

Despite the fact that after several weeks, the romance seemed to be waning, Delila still had hopes of it rekindling. Even though, at this time, she found it hard to look at Borya because the wound on his cheek was like a cold sore gone wrong.

"I said, come here. No, you don't need to get dressed. You're not done," ordered Borya.

Delila attempted to assert herself, saying, "I've done enough."

"Guess again. You've already fucked him once while you and I are committed to a relationship. So, it's not like you're preserving yourself exclusively for me. That you've already spread them for that asshole has set the stage. At this point, the number of times you screw him makes no difference. It's like rain on wet paint, with even one drop, the paint is
never the same."

"Not the same? You think our relationship is spoiled? You promised it wouldn't matter! You said that I was doing you a huge favour and that our future would depend on my doing it – with him."

Borya turned his head so that she couldn't see his smirk and his rolling of the eyes, as he thought, *Like I'm going to marry this sleaze.* But instead, he said, "Couldn't care less. It's only sex. It's the necessary means to an end."

"Don't you care that I'm with another man?"

Borya approached her and passionately kissed her, his tongue seeking out hers, as he put his hand on one of her nipples and stroked. "Of course, I care, but like I said, you have to do this. But most important, we've got to cinch him in." Borya stepped back.

"Ha, I wish I could have seen his face when he was accused. But we're far from finished with him. We need to have him naked, again and again, and so used to it that he will be a perfect target. If he's aroused, so much the better," snarled Borya, as he sat again at her galley table, surveying her form as if it was merchandise. "Come over here and have some of this stuff: it should improve your performance."

Delila rose from the bunk and moved over to the galley. Totally naked. Her ample breasts, the toned form, her even brown skin, the red lips, the dark eyes surrounded with eyeliner, the platinum blond hair. Most men would have traded their new car for simply a glimpse.

But not Borya. He was in work mode. Delila hesitantly sized up the two lines of powder set out for her. Borya rose, grabbed her torso from behind with one arm, overwhelming her with his hips that pressed hard against her buttocks, his hazel-brown eyes turning dark. For a moment, though clothed, he banged up against her, hard and fast with his hips. Then he laughed, saying, "Later, if you're lucky." As he stopped the humping motion, with his free arm, forced Delila's head to the table, demanding, "Snort, it! Don't be such a prude!"

Borya thought to himself, *I should get an acting award for calling this slut a prude!*

"How can you treat me like this? We are engaged to be married!"

"That is exactly why you must make my enemy yours and prepare. It entertains me anyway. I like to see you naked with your rubber toy. It makes me want to be with you forever. Truly. But you must do as I say, and ... as you promised. Plus, that's the way it should be for a man and a woman. The man decides. So, you have to! Come on. It's easy. Not a problem. Just snort it!"

Delila breathed in but the dust barely moved.

"You stupid cunt! Pinch one of your nostrils first, you moron!"

Was this the man she loved? Was she making another mistake?

Delila pinched her right nostril and drew the powdery line into her left: her memories faded and her mood visibly changed.

"Save the rest. You'll need more in half an hour." Then he shoved her towards the bunk, fingering her crotch, then patting her ass, as she floundered forward. "Now go to it! Show me that you can do what was in the film!" ordered Borya.

Then, as if in a trance, Delila ignored Borya's presence, thought about Brock, and then of Toque. Delila's nipples hardened, her eyes rolled back, and she engaged the dildo.

"Better. Keep going," he ordered, "But faster! What a fucking simpleton you are! Let me show you," he growled, caustic hatred tinging his speech as he rose from the table, fists clenched. He marched over to her side, roughly placed one hand on her stomach and with the

other, grabbed the dildo. But before he could move it, there was a tap on the hull.

His hand, raised in the air, just above her groin, paused in mid-air as he listened. Delila closed her eyes and enjoyed the cocaine's effect of euphoria, as if entering a dream. Silence surrounded them until they could hear the lapping of the waves on the pier and then the rain started again.

Borya gripped the dildo so hard that it was dented by his fingers. He was just about to apply the devise when again there was another tap on the hull, although this time it was more of a knock. He handed the dildo to Delila as he turned to the entrance hatch, clenching his fists.

And then there was a voice, calling, "Delila, are you in there?"

With apprehension, she stared at the closed hatch as she whispered, "It's Brock!"

For a moment, both Delila and Borya were motionless.

But then she moved: she first reached for, then pulled on her semi-transparent red negligee while at the same time she placed the dildo in the pocket. She then attempted to slide past Borya. But he grabbed her wrist so hard that there were white pressure points on her skin from his fingers. Then, with fierce urgency he ordered, in a hoarse whisper, "If you allow him to see me, I won't be seeking revenge on those assholes you dated. You have to prove to me that you are worth it!" He briefly considered the second line of cocaine still on the table. "And likewise, don't let him see inside! Go fuck him on HIS boat! That will toast his tiny mind. Just get him out of here!"

"Why do you keep suggesting THAT? I am YOUR future wife!"

"Do as I say. If you want that ring on your finger, don't waste your breath even asking!"

Delila listened, expressionless, and reached for her coat. Borya blocked the reach, saying, "You don't need that. I'll tell you if you ever need to cover up. Not now." He planted his mouth on hers, with a kiss that was to her, overwhelming.

Then, looking resolute and with energy beyond her pre-cocaine state, Delila left the cabin while Borya stayed behind the closed door of her bunk area.

Brock, in the rain, was despondent. Rex stood beside him, but in contrast, was exceptionally happy, because he sensed he was visiting a person who seemed to be a friend of his master.

But then, when Brock saw Delila, in her negligee, he almost forgot about being given desk duty and the threat of being suspended ... or worse.

"Hey Brock, so glad you've come by. But the place is a mess. Let's have a visit at your place." As she spoke, Delila slipped her arm through Brock's and aimed him in the direction of the *Angel*. The scent of Always Amorous enveloped the two of them as she leaned upon him, letting her breast press against his arm. But as they moved, she felt the dildo moving against her far leg, and glanced down, then saw it though the transparent negligee. While she leaned on Brock on one side, on the other side she removed the dildo, then dropped it behind her, hoping that it would bounce into the water and then, simply float away or better still, sink.

"I think that we need to talk ... but are you sure you don't want to wear ..." he said, looking at her through her sheer garment and for a moment became spell-bound, but then noticed that her feet were turning pink under the icy light of the fixtures built into the cold concrete pier.

"You're right. We do need to talk. The *Angel* will warm me up. Let's get going," she urged, as she unobtrusively guided their two forms towards Brock's vessel, the rain soaking
them as they went.

At first, Rex moved towards Delila, sensing that he might get an extra pat or two. But then he saw the dildo on the pier, just a few meters behind his human owner and the female friend, and with relish hurried and retrieved the device, and because it was soft yet firm, found that it felt much better in his mouth than any of the sticks he'd ever found.

When they reached the *Angel,* Brock turned to check on Rex and the obedient pooch dropped the dildo at his master's feet. Brock's mouth opened in amazement and Delila started laughing and couldn't stop.

Rex pawed at the dildo and with a toenail, unknowingly turned on the vibration feature. Rex jumped back, peeled back his lips into a snarl, showing his teeth, and growled at the vibrating devise. Rex crouched, like a bird dog, growling at the gyrating green shape that might as well have been from outer space as far as Rex was concerned. Delila continued to giggle, unable to stop. Brock looked just plain bewildered. The dildo continued to vibrate, working its way to the edge of the pier. Brock stared at it, as if in suspended animation. Then, with one last jiggle of a vibration, the dildo toppled from the pier and into the water with a splash. Surprised, a brown mallard duck snoozing on the underside of the pier let out a quack and with both feet flipping, managed an immediate take-off, quacking all the way as she flew off into the gray blackness of the rainy evening.

Delila's giggling subsided, and embarrassment replaced her levity, though she tried her best to act innocent, saying, "Where the hell did that come from? Let's get inside before I freeze to death."

Brock still perused the sky, as if the mallard might reappear, but then turned his mind to that close by and wondered if he should fish the dildo from the waters, but then Delila was already in his cockpit and leaning forward, exposing her naked breasts, including both nipples, hard from the cold, as she reached for Brock and pulled him into the warmth of the *Angel*.

"But …" stammered Brock.

Hours later, when he woke, Delila was beside him and as he looked upon the face of this sleeping bedmate, he noticed the smallest trace of white powder on the side of one of her nostrils.

CHAPTER 55

It was late afternoon when Toque turned up early for what would be her graveyard shift. She hurried into the detachment building and went straight into the forensic lab. Most of the technicians were already gone, done for the day, but as Toque passed the various emptied work stations, she could see Marol's spiked grey and red streaked hair just above one of the work station dividers.

"Hey Marol, did you get to that sample I dropped off last night?"

"Yes, I did! Lucky you got it to me right away. It didn't take as long as I thought it would. The testing team had everything set out, ready to go, and I had the lab to myself. Also, it was a bonus that there was no one around to slow the process with questions and what not."

"Are you saying that you've managed to check them both?"

"Yes, I have. They all a match."

"That's got to be a lead of some sort," responded Toque, hopeful.

"Seven samples the same can't be just a coincidence."

"Agreed. Are you okay on the two of us going to talk to Grant before you leave for the day?"

"Absolutely. He's already got the analysis."

"Let's do it now, then."

Mrs. Bean had already left for the day and Grant was just turning off his work station computer when Marol and Toque knocked on his door.

From the other side of Grant's door, they heard the resounding, "Come!"

Marol opened the door and the two of them entered the office. Grant sat behind his over-size aluminum and wood desk. It was considered to be modern when it was purchased in 2020, but at this time showed the scuffs and chips of age. Although it was the end of the day, his grey suit looked relatively unwrinkled, like his white shirt and dark grey tie. He placed his hands on his bit of a paunch and seriously regarded Marol and Toque. "You're here to discuss?"

Marol carried a folder full of data analysis. "You got the lab results I emailed earlier today?"

"It's a while since I worked with that stuff – it's all numbers, charts, and graphs. I've done it a hundred times, but it's a lot faster to have a written summary."

"Sorry about that, but not a problem now; I can easily give you a verbal summary," stated Marol.

Toque then added to the agenda, saying, "Plus, we need to talk about the implications of the results."

One of Grant's eyebrows went up. "So, there is something new about oil spill leaks?"

"Yes," responded Marol.

Toque continued, "Marol has examined two more samples ..."

"Other than those Brock brought in?" interrupted Grant.

"Yes. One from his parking lot, that is, the marina parking lot," added Toque.

"Adjacent to his boat?" asked Grant.

"Right. And another sample from Rockwater," added Toque.

"But there was already a sample from the school," observed Grant.

"This is a different one. A different spot. And fresh," explained Toque.

Grant eyes widened at the new information. "So why did you bother to check again?"

Toque continued to explain, "I was interviewing Pearce Cudmore for a second time and ..."

Grant's eyes widened, thinking about an abuse-rape claim made that very day by Mrs. Cudmore.

But Toque continued, "And I found out about an incident in which crack was planted in most of the cubby holes in the boys' locker area. It seems that a number of kids got sick and one is still in a coma."

"In a coma! This happened recently?"

Toque nodded, answering, "Yesterday."

Grant deliberated. Then the notion of a connection flashed upon his face. "So why wasn't I told about this? Hold on for a second." Grant grabbed his phone and touched the icon of a contact at the top of a list.

248

After a few rings, a voice picked up. "Abraham. Something new?"

Grant wasted no time with formalities. "Crack in the boy's locker room at Rockwater."

After a brief pause, Abraham replied, "Haven't heard anything recently but let's face it, drugs in the schools are a problem everywhere."

Grant clarified: "The dope was planted. Kids were hurt. Yesterday."

"News to me. I'll check it out. Let me call you back," replied the now even-more concerned Abraham.

Grant, hanging up the phone, regarded Toque and Marol. "Right. I can guess why you two are interested in the locker-room crack. But tell me what you've been thinking."

Toque was dead serious as she explained, "It was planted in the same time frame as when crack was found on Brock's boat. Likely both happened at night when no one was around!"

Grant's interest was piqued. "You mean the night Brock was on patrol with you, then was slammed onto desk duty?"

"Exactly," responded Toque.

"Carol, I get the feeling that you see some sort of connection to the oil leaks," prodded Grant, with the semblance of someone who has a strong suspicion of where the discussion would lead.

Toque looked at Marol. "Go ahead and explain what you found out about the samples."

Marol took on her best scientific voice and proceeded. "Both samples from Brock's parking area and the school are likely to be the same vehicle."

Toque joined in. "And, as both samples are from the sites of the planting of the crack, it is very likely that the perpetrator was the same person, driving the same vehicle."

Grant placed his hands on the desk while reaching a mental exclamation point. "And because he was on the job, Brock couldn't be directly involved with the dope at the school, and if the crack was planted by someone parking the same leaky vehicle on the same night, as at the school and the marina parking lot ... Brock was set up."

With the smallest hint of a smile, Toque responded, "Exactly."

A more positive demeaner set on Grant's features as he continued, "Definite facts that give reasonable doubt if not a huge doubt with regard to Brock being involved with crack. But Marol, you have a lot more data recorded here than for two samples."

"That's to show that the samples also match the oil samples Brock collected from every infestation, or whatever you want to call the assaults."

"All of them?" asked Grant.

"All of them: the marina, the first and second samples from Rockwater, Cap U, Centennial Theatre, the Lower Lonsdale Cap U buildings, and the racetrack in Vancouver.

The phone rang, and Grant took note of its call display, then picked up. "Hey, Captain, find anything?"

Abraham lost no time with her response. "Sure did. Phoned Principal Bothe. They're trying to deal with it by themselves. That's why we didn't hear."

Grant scowled. "Hear exactly what?"

Abraham continued, "A grade eight class found plastic bags holding crack in the PE cubby hole lockers. Believe it or not, a number of the kids tried eating it, thinking that it was candy. Their symptoms starting showing up an hour or so later when they were in a math class."

Grant leaned back in his chair, glancing at the ceiling. "You're kidding me! And kids in the eighth grade are old enough to be babysitters!"

Abraham sighed. "Yeah, pity the babies. But a number of the eights got quite sick. One is in a coma. We're still waiting on that. Very worried."

Grant cursed. "Shit!"

"It looks like the threat against 'those that count' might be the grade eight math class."

Initially surprised, Grant paused for a moment, but then verbalized what he thought might have happened. "I suppose the perpetrators could have calculated how long the crack would take to get into their systems after finding it in the cubby-holes."

"Could have. A bit of a long shot, though. Who could guess that the kids would eat it? How did you hear about it?"

Grant explained. "One of my constables was interviewing a Rockwater student, Pearce Cudmore."

"No surprise there. We've also talked to him but didn't get much. You guys get anything?"

"We're exploring a link between oil spills."

"You mean the blood on the school and the leaving of crack might be connected?"

"Might. We're just in the initial stages of checking it out. I'll call you back as soon as we've got the whole picture documented."

"Right," said Abraham, just as she hung up the phone.

Grant rubbed his forehead; the day had been so much longer than usual. Exhausted, he focussed on Marol and Toque.

Toque sized up her boss. "So, what do you think about Brock?"

"From the very beginning, no one could believe that he was involved with crack. But we needed time to prove it. And, as you know, it takes a while. But what has gone a long way to proving his innocence is your discovery of the matching oil samples, combined with the fact that the blackmailer has now said that more damage has been done, with probable reference to the school. So, for now, Brock is vindicated: the oil spill samples show that it is very likely that it was the same people who set up the crack on Brock's boat and at the school.

"Is that enough to bring him back into active duty?" asked Toque.

"I think so ..." mused Grant, then after a pause, said, "The evidence is mounting that proves that Brock was a target. Another indication of his innocence is that the bits of crack found on his carpet have no evidence of his DNA. Another questionable part is the mental state of the officers who searched Brock's boat: they were really rabid about his bank statement. Only thing is, I know about the cash in question, and I know that it was legit. But
that is a different story and is Brock's personal business. All things considered, though, I think that we'd better bring him in and see if he's ready to go back on active duty. Until, and if, something else comes up."

Toque smiled, but within seconds the smile changed to the look of someone who stepped off an un-perceived curb, as she remembered Brock with Delila on the *Angel*.

"Either of you know if he's still here?"

While Marol shook her head to indicate that she had no idea, Toque glanced at her cell phone, checking the time. "Don't know. But probably, if he's still on swing shift."

"He is. Let's go talk."

Seconds later they were within sight-range of the cubicle assigned to Brock. And there he sat, his keys, wallet, and cell on the desk beside the keyboard. Brock was hurriedly typing in commands as if it were second nature to him. He was oblivious to their presence.

"Hey, Brock, we want to tell you …"

Brock typed a few more strokes, pressed *Enter*, then glanced up. "Check this out," he began, "I've just finished the list of any repeat vehicles to the sites."

"Good work. What have you got?" asked Grant.

"A pizza delivery, a postal vehicle, two private parcel delivery services, an exterminator van, a grocery delivery, a plumbing outfit, a home internet provider's truck, a catering service, and a green motor home."

"The same motor home in all of those locations?"

"Suspicious, I agree. For one thing, none of the sites are included as points of interest on local tourist maps, and are certainly not listed as campgrounds."

Toque, Marol, and Grant grimaced at the joke as Brock continued, "But seriously, we need to track down that vehicle, but, then again, let's face it – any of the vehicles could be questionable."

"Definitely something for our team to further consider."

"Help will be appreciated."

"On the topic of your assignment …" started Grant.

But he was cut off by the visual blinking of a new message on Brock's cell.

All four looked at the phone. On it was the image of the sender: Delila. Seductively posed and dressed in red lace string undergarments. The message started with, "Hey lover."

Marol seemed surprised, and Toque turned away.

Grant cleared his throat, but continued, "Thanks to Carol and Marol, there's now enough information to indicate that you were set up with the crack. Effective immediately, the desk job will be done by someone else. As soon as you finish this shift, you'll be on the beat again, partnered with Carol."

CHAPTER 56

As Marol took a few steps towards her work-station to pick up her coat, Grant blocked Toque's exit before she could move or before Brock could rise from his chair. Grant looked at the two of them seriously as he said, "Carol and Brock, I need to speak to you before you go."

The two constables faced their boss, listening.

"There is a threat from someone who claims to have been doing the blood, frog, bug and other assaults. The threat is against the two of you."

"Surely not the sex-trafficking group," moaned Toque.

Hearing this, Marol turned around and asked, "A threat? Is it possible that I, too, am somehow included? Is that why I was attacked?"

Grant grimaced, answering, "Possibly, but Brock and Carol are acting constables for those incidents. Plus, as I indicated to you on the phone, and to Carol in the office here, we already suspect that there is a connection between the infestations and a previous case in which Brock was involved."

"What? How?" asked Marol.

Grant's face was grim as he spoke, "Someone or a group of people are making threats – trying to blackmail law enforcers into releasing three convicts from Scheveningen."

"Names are?" asked Brock.

"Kuznetsov, Oblonsky and Voronin," replied Grant, grimacing.

"And their cohorts are on the North Shore? It can't be!" exclaimed Marol.

"Unfortunately, could be," summed up Grant.

Brock's face cringed with concern, wishing that he didn't know those three names all too well. After a moment of internal searching he asked, "Those three with active contacts here? There's definitely something wrong with this picture!"

Toque groaned, more than worried.

"But whoever the perps, with the threat to you and the seriousness of their probable current activities, I want you to be especially careful when you are out there," continued Grant.

254

Toque understood his point, and without a smile responded, "Thanks for the warning. We'll be careful."

Brock's facial expression also showed acknowledgement of the gravity of the situation, as the three staff members then turned to leave.

***

But before any of the three moved another inch in the direction of the exit, Grant had one more piece of unfinished business.

"But Carol, I need to speak to just you for a second – in my office ... and now is as good a time as any."

Toque hesitated but knew she had no choice, as she answered, "Sure. Yesterday you said that you wanted to speak to me first thing on my next shift."

Grant replied, "Yes, but that was about the threat to you and Brock. Something else has come up ... concerning only you."

Seconds later they were alone in his office and Toque stood back a few feet to avoid personal contact. Grant understood, took his seat, waved his hand at the seat on the other side of his desk and began, "You should know that a woman named Mrs. Cudmore complained that you abused and likely raped her son and that she had physical evidence on the boy's track pants."

Toque blushed. "I assure you ..."

"Never-mind defending yourself. It is a non-issue because the son spoke up and said that he'd washed the garment that was evidence, and that he was simply cleaning up after a pasta spill."

"Pasta?"

"Alfredo, evidently. But then the son added that nothing happened. That his mother was wrong. The mother went berserk in my office, cursing her son for contradicting her. She was super annoyed, and stomped off, leaving the son to scramble after her."

"So that's all you wanted to tell me?" asked Toque, both horrified and relieved.

"Yup. That's it. Just wanted you to know in case you come across either of them again."

CHAPTER 57

Their lips sealed in the most intense kind of kiss known: one tongue searched the other while their long legs wrapped around each other. Then, with a movement as subtle as an hour change, the hands of one moved onto the other's breasts, who, in sync, softly moved her hand past her partner's breast, then held her buttocks, so firmly there were ticklish dimples in the soft but well-toned cheeks.

Toque, with her auburn hair streaming around her like waves in the sunset, gently removed her tongue and her blue-grey eyes smiled, though with some uncertainty, at her lover's light brown eyes.

It was Lynn who then moved her head back in an almost swoon as she whispered, "It's easy. Keep going. Just like I showed you before."

Toque's rose-coloured tongue, moved down, caressed the nape of Lynn's neck, then onto the left breast, slowly circling it.

Lynn smiled. "Yes! Yes! Exactly like that! You're so perfect."

Then Toque moved on to a nipple flushed pink: sucking, licking and a gentle nibble, then trailed her soft wet tongue to the other breast; around it, onto the equally flushed nipple, sucking on it gently so that it, like the other, reached a state of erection.

"You are so marvelous," whispered Lynn. Her hands were on Toque's back, gently stroking, rubbing, massaging: hands that were tempted to again reach around the front.

Toque continued, down the ample more-than-Rubens-like torso, lingering when she reached the navel.

"Keep going. Please keep going," murmured Lynn when Toque hesitated.

Toque moved her right hand to Lynn's groin.

"Down there. Down there. Use your imagination."

Toque glanced up.

"Please, please, just do it!" begged Lynn.

Two of Toque's left-hand fingers inserted and her tongue moved down, over the soft tummy.

"You are the absolute best," sighed Lynn as her head moved back in ecstasy, her pink cheeks glowing, her brown eyes bright, as if heaven had been reached. "Now use your tongue, darling, please. Just inside. Please. Please"

Then, just as Toque reached the soft texture of hair she again paused, then stopped, the mood suddenly disrupted by the thunderous crashing of someone rushing in the door. The erotic aura vaporized like the smoke from a candle, which had been too briefly aflame.

Toque looked over her shoulder at the door to her bedroom while Lynn tilted her head forward, to see, and possibly defend themselves against whoever had just entered the suite.

"Doesn't anybody lock their door anymore?" asked Brock as he approached the bedroom. Then, as soon he cleared the doorway, saw Lynn and Toque in what was an entirely compromising position.

At the entranceway to the bedroom, Brock stood staring at the two naked women as if his eyes were experiencing a total lockdown from all motion: the skin on both women was flushed with arousal, and Toque was on top of Lynn. But in seconds, Brock exclaimed, "What the hell?"– more or less rhetorically, as his voice cracked and then went up an octave, all in the very last vocalized word.

"What are you doing here?" cried Toque, rolling to the side and pulling the sheet and comforter over both herself and Lynn, aghast at having this observer.

Though shocked, Brock couldn't help but pause at the sight of his gorgeous partner stark naked and radiating a sexuality that should have been reserved for the gods. For an insane moment, he considered tearing off his own clothes and joining in. But social etiquette took hold, though he couldn't totally hold back the sex-drive portion of his brain that had jumped into over-drive, attempting to sabotage expected workmate behavior. He thought, *If only ...*

But alas, this notion was immediately interrupted.

"You have no fucking right to walk in like this," growled Lynn, though when she turned her angry face from Brock and returned her gaze to Toque, Lynn couldn't help the immediate change in emotion and facial expression. She smiled and couldn't help but move her hand to Toque's shoulder, almost on her breast, and massaged ever so gently as the sheet and comforter slipped downwards.

Rather than gawk at the descending sheet and comforter, Brock fought the urge, and to be polite, tried to focus on an invisible spot on the ceiling as he announced his pressing purpose.

"I've been trying to call you for hours. You and I are starting now – as partners, as usual. Everyone is to put in overtime!"

"Partners?" growled Lynn, "I don't think so! Toque and I are the only partners in this room! I'm the only overtime partner in her life!"

"RCMP partners," clarified Brock, his voice cracking again.

"My God! I've never been called in like this before," explained Toque, as she grabbed the top sheet, and pushed the quilt onto Lynn, whose right breast was left totally exposed. Brock couldn't hold himself back from stealing a peek now and then. In fact, if proper decorum had ruled, he would have left the area and waited in the adjacent room. But he was numbed by the erotic scene in full display, and stood as motionless as a potted plant. As for Lynn, she took on the facade of one who didn't care – didn't mind being caught indisposed, as she sat upright, crossing her arms under her totally naked breasts.

Toque, on the other hand, attempted a complete shroud, but unsuccessfully covered just one and a half breasts with the bunched-up sheet, leaving totally exposed the soft pale skin and auburn hair just above her thighs that left a space just wide enough to slip in whatever he might have in mind. He couldn't help but look and …

Brock flushed, his pants tightening. Lynn, too, watched Toque's attempt at rushing for her clothing, her watching eyes dilating with stimulation.

"Give me a few minutes, will you?" asked Toque.

Brock, fighting every sexual instinct within his being, turned, then said, "I'll wait in your living room."

Brock and Toque were in a cruiser just ten minutes later. Toque blanched, then asked, "So what's going on?"

"All cops are supposed to be on deck – as long as possible because there is a new threat."

"Which is?"

"The exact words are, 'Before the fire of our wrath, the gregarious will arrive.'"

"Has a weird kind of Biblical tone. The second part doesn't sound so bad but what about the fire of wrath?"

"Doesn't sound good, that's for sure."

"But given the lice and flies, I'm not crazy about another batch," reflected Toque, scratching the back of her neck.

"Another bug attack is particularly disturbing when one considers that they also had the
sick desire and know-how to spread equine colic."

"The insects were super annoying but animal cruelty: I can't handle that," added Toque, still scratching.

"We'd better visit Yana first. Perhaps there is some connection to the insects stolen from the university."

"Worth a visit."

As they drove, silence pervaded. To begin with, both played out in their minds the horrors of what they were trying to solve. But as the miles passed under the tires the attraction between them again surfaced. At first his arm brushed hers. Their skin prickled. Then her hand touched his, when both reached to reset an icon on the cruiser's computer. The breathing shortened. Their pulses increased. That fluttery feeling in the chest that precedes a sexual encounter pervaded.

Brock thought about Toque undressed in bed with Lynn. Her nakedness; more perfect than he had ever imagined – but only when his resolve was weakened by fatigue. Then, when over-tired, he'd find himself thinking of such off-limit things – putting himself in the danger of losing his grip on his decision to not drag another woman into his life. But at this time, when he'd just seen her naked … so close he could have almost touched her. But then, he thought of her bedmate.

Clearly, Toque had made a choice. He knew he had to stop thinking of her sexually, so said, "Glad to see that you're establishing a strong relationship." *God,* he thought, *Why do I want to encourage her?*

Toque, still aroused by her proximity to Brock, felt deflation taking over her entire body. She answered, "It does seem we are getting along." But then she paused, thinking, *What am I talking about? Lynn has been so kind, so supportive, so loving. Yet, do I want to act like this is the commitment of my life? But even so, in spite of that concern, I do feel absolutely wonderful when I am with her. But on the other hand, I react to Brock as if he's a magnet: it's as if Lynn is only a bus stop and temporary, at best.*

Brock paused, trying to find the right words. "What about Joe?" Brock waited for the answer, afraid of the potential reply.

"Oh, Joe, he's just a friend."

Brock raised an eyebrow.

Toque, wishing that Brock had not found her in bed, said, "Platonic," wondering if she might have said the same thing about her relationship with Lynn, had Brock not found them having sex.

Brock paused, commenting, "So, just the two of you."

Toque frowned, *What IS he thinking? That I have threesomes all the time? I need to set him straight.* "Yes, just like you and Delila."

Brock cringed, remembering when Toque had dropped by, catching him and Delila in the cabin of the *Angel* sans clothing, sans everything that involved personal privacy. "Well, I don't know how serious we are going …"

"You know what," Toque exclaimed, suddenly smiling, "Why don't we go on a double date?" And as she asked, she put her hand on his knee, instantly engaging unchronicled erogenous zones on both sides the cruiser's mounted electronic computer control unit.

Brock raised his eyebrows and his eyes looked upwards. The warmth of her hand felt like a body of stimulant, and the resulting erotic warm feeling flashed straight to his groin. "Shu-r-r-r- r-r-e-re. You and Lynn," His voice cracked as he continued, "And me and Delila. I'm sure the two of you will love Delila." But to himself thought, *This will be crazy. And what do I say to Delila about the non-relationship I've been pushing for?*

Toque smiled the smile of misgivings.

Then in seconds, all personal talk halted as they pulled up in front of the home of Yana and Alik Vasiliev.

Chapter 58

Grant scratched his balding head, worried. His kind face was hardened by lines of concern deepened by the effects of middle-age. He rested his hands on the bit of a paunch which was just barely visible under his dark gray suit, slightly wrinkling the darker gray tie beneath. What was usually a relaxed aura – much like that of a kindly father, was displaced by the attributes of one who had to move onto a mounting and sobering problem.

He spoke into the intercom. "Mrs. Bean, would you come in here?"

In seconds, his assistant hustled through his doorway. As an older married woman who had worked her way up in the detachment offices, starting with years of volunteer service, she had earned the privilege of her unique civilian position. Within a couple of minutes, she stood across from him, looking at her boss with a question mark in her eyes. Somehow, she was a spark of positivity in the office, with her mixing-bowl cut of straightened white hair, dark framed glasses, sturdy mid-height black heels, and a brightly coloured dress covered with a pattern of tiny yellow flowers.

"What's up, Boss?"

"Will you get me everything you can on the international sex trafficking operation that was broken about five years ago?"

"Oh? The one where the Bogdanov brothers were sentenced?"

"That's the one."

"Weren't they part of a group that had some guy who got away and is still out there? What was his name? Oh yes, I remember putting up the poster in the constables' area: I'm pretty sure that the name was something like Boris Mozorov."

"Close. It is Borya Morozov."

"Oh, right."

"Three other members of that group are now in Scheveningen," added Grant.

"Don't tell me that those are the cons that the local infestation perps want freed."

"I don't want to remind you that – that is extremely confidential information."

"Of course," assured Mrs. Bean who then looked at Grant expectantly but getting no more information, asked, "Anything other than what I can find on that group?"

"Yes. As soon as you're at your desk, will you connect me with the director of CSIS?"

Within minutes Mrs. Bean paged Grant. "Director Sandford Graham on the line."

Grant introduced himself as soon as he picked up the line. "Director Graham, it's CO Grant from the North Vancouver detachment."

"Right. Your assistant said as much. Haven't spoken to you since the Brock Edwards directive, and the following crisis."

"A while ago, yes."

Graham typed in a few commands on his computer. On the screen appeared the headings: Top Secret. Secure Access Only. Then after a few more prompts, a few more codes, then another prompt which required an iris scan, the screen momentarily wavered with lines. Then it cleared, showing the title, Identity Security. He asked, "Is this about Brock?"

"Not directly. What we're really concerned about is the upcoming leadership review."

"What? For the next prime minister?"

"Exactly."

"And?"

"There is an ongoing investigation into six probably related incidents, with a number of possible perpetrators. One group we're not ruling out is one that Brock was working against when he was one of your agents."

"What was the case?"

"Sex trafficking."

"Tell me you've got a lead on Borya Morozov."

"I wish. Right now, there's no sign of him but what has reared its ugly head are connections to others that were part of his nasty group."

"What? Those two locked up near your jurisdiction?"

"Yes: Egor and Rasputin Bogdanov were recently given ten-hour passes to work outside the prison."

"You're kidding me."

262

"Not funny from my perspective. Their sentences were relaxed because at the time of their offence they were considered to be 'culturally deprived' and could not be expected to understand or follow our beliefs and laws."

Graham paused before he responded. "I agree that it's no joke when those two lowlifes are now literally having lunch with the public."

Grant proceeded, trying to explain the change in the fates of the Bogdanovs. "Well, the thing that was considered to be in their favour was that they have become models of totally assimilated Canadian behavior."

"And the people who agreed to their work passes just forgot about the videos of them with the kids?"

"You're not the only one who can't believe it! I'm still pissed that we weren't able to extradite them and have them tried in an international court, which is what should have happened. But as you know, because they were in disguise, there was no solid proof of that dirtier stuff so we got stuck with them."

"Too bad you didn't get a confession."

"I wish. Given that the two can hardly walk and chew gum at the same time, it's embarrassing that we got nothing on them for their marketing and probable multiple assaults on the sex slaves. All we could get was the transporting of foreign citizens for the purposes of illegal immigration."

"I remember."

"Sometimes I wonder if the enforcement of the law here needs some sort of amending."

"Yeah, it often works, but too often doesn't. But what exactly is your current concern with the Bogdanov brothers?" asked Graham.

"It's only conjecture, but since they have been on work permits away from the prison, someone has been demanding that we release three prisoners who are in Scheveningen."

"Cripes! Don't tell me. I can guess!"

"You probably got it! Kliment Voronin, Lev Kuznetsov, Gleb Oblonsky."

"Those fuckers! What are the extortionists using as leverage?"

"The incidents I initially mentioned."

"Which are?"

"Infestations of insects and frogs; and the poisoning of horses at a local racetrack."

"Are you joking?"

"I wish. However, I have to say that what might clear the Bogdanovs, is that just before they got their work permits, there was an incident with a school being covered with blood: it was followed by an email that matched those sent right after the other occurrences."

"Maybe there are others involved. Or the emailer jumped the gun and just claimed to have done the blood thing when it was possibly just a school prank. But tell me, aside from making a few people squeamish, what exactly happened in each of the incidents?"

"Live mutant lice were dumped onto the guests at an elite fundraiser at Centennial Theatre, live black flies released into the Premier's Forum at Cap U's new conference center. All the horses at Hastings Park had their lives on the line when they were deliberately made ill with equine colic. And ..." Grant paused as he wiped perspiration from his brow, even though his office was quite cool.

"Continue."

"And there was the blood, though a questionable connection, to the brothers, as I said. Blood balloons were tossed all over a local school: Rockwater Christian Secondary."

"Crap. I hope that the blood wasn't infectious."

"It wasn't. And then there were the frogs: a couple of hundred were released into the North American basketball championship at Cap U."

"I saw the frogs at the basketball championship on the sports channel," Then, with a caustic tone, "Short game. But hell! What kind of weirdos do you have? Although, at least it's not a mass shooting."

"That's true. But one more thing: crack cocaine was planted in students' storage lockers at Rockwater and in Brock's vessel, as if to frame him."

"Shit! Brock's boat? And crack planted in a school? Are the kids okay?"

"We're still waiting to hear about one. It doesn't look good. Sounds like he had more than his share."

"And you think the crack is associated with the biological incidents?"

"There is a likely connection: as I said, all the assaults are followed by a threatening email claiming credit, although in the case of the crack, the email simply said that more damage has been done. But also, in all cases, including the crack, we found oil from an engine leak, probably from the same vehicle at all of the sites."

"Was Brock involved in any of the investigations?"

"He was working on all of them, up until the crack was planted at the school and on his boat."

"It isn't the first time that scum have had a go at him."

"Luckily, he's strong. I've just been given enough information to make it obvious that he was set-up. As a result, I've taken him off desk duty and …"

"You had *Brock* on desk duty?"

"Briefly. No choice." Grant paused as a momentary and awkward silence ensued.

Graham shook his head in disbelief, and he scanned through the paragraphs under the heading of "Identity Security." On the document's second page and buried in text, were Brock's full names: his birth name and that assigned to him for identity protection: "Isaac Bruce Strong: Brock Thomas Edwards."

Grant continued, "But just re-assigned him to active duty. He's again with the partner he's had since he rejoined the force."

"Good call. After this amount of time together, I'm sure that the two of them instinctively understand each other … probably better than we can imagine. Add their close connection to
the fact that Brock has experience as a trained agent having dealt with these assholes … and
you've got an outstanding cop team for this job: just like they were at the Lions Gate crisis."

"I know it."

"And you've contacted me because of the threat to the Prime Minister?"

"Yes."

"And the whole thing might be connected to the Bogdanovs who may be the ones who are demanding the release of Voronin, Kuznetsov, and Oblonsky?"

"Right. But again, we need to keep in mind that there are a number of others who could be the perps, to say nothing of individuals that aren't even on our radar."

"I get it. But have the saboteurs threatened with another specific attack?"

"Believe it or not, the threat is, "Before the fire of our wrath, the gregarious will arrive."

"What the fuck! What kind of horse apples have you got?"

"Rotten ones."

"You've increased your people on patrol?"

"Yes; West Van, too. All personal leaves are cancelled for the time being, and everyone is expected to put in overtime."

"I'll get a team involved. Send me everything you have. One of us has to find a clue as to where these idiots are and the location of their next prank," said Graham, with resolve.

"Right. You'll have everything within an hour."

"Good. For now, you couldn't have a better person than Brock on this. Make sure he has all the help he needs. Make him full detective if that will help. His partner too, if you think it will get faster results."

"I think they're good for now in their current roles."

"Your call. Let's hope we have a day or two before the gregarious arrive and that the fire thing is symbolic."

"I'm with you on that."

"I'll be back to you within twenty-four."

***

Just over twelve hours later, a sleepless Grant was lying in bed in the darkness of the night, his eyes awake. Beside him, he could hear the soft breathing of his wife, unaware of the latest worries plaguing her husband. He turned onto his side, closed his eyes, but seconds later his eyes again opened. He knew that there was little likelihood of getting to sleep.

Beside his bed was a phone and within seconds of its ring, Grant acknowledged the caller's name as he picked up the phone and said in a hoarse whisper, "Just a sec," as he moved the bed sheets to the side and walked into the study across the hall.

"Hey Graham. You've reviewed everything I sent?"

"Not only that, I've got the team ready."

"Good. More people involved increases the likelihood of us finding them."

"And protecting the next Prime Minister. What I'm most concerned about is that the offender seems to like spectacle-type assaults."

"I know. The only one-off was Brock being set up. But even then, the crack on his boat was possibly set to intentionally connect to the distribution in the school cubby-holes, possibly to put further blame on Brock. The perps didn't think that the very connection would suggest a set up."

"Glad to hear about that quick resolution. From my end, I've decided that in addition to a couple of agents working on it from here in Ottawa, to assist the RCMP Protective Policing Service, I am sending half a dozen agents to the Federal Leadership Review in your neck of the woods. They'll be flying in later today."

"Good. Hopefully we'll catch them before the next ..."

"That's the plan. Fingers crossed, but for now, let's put off any negotiations for the release of Voronin, Kuznetsov, and Oblonsky."

"Agreed."

Chapter 59

Overlooking the Burrard Inlet and the sparkling lights of the Port of Vancouver stood the North Shore Convention Center with its glassed-in conference hall taking advantage of the glorious view. Above that great hall was a high-rise hotel, fully booked as it was the venue for the much-publicised federal leadership race. The current Prime Minister, having served one and a half terms, totalling six years, had decided to retire early. Although she released no reason for her resignation, speculation was that health was an issue.

On the evening preceding the day of the big vote was a glitzy dinner and dance wherein all the candidate hopefuls would be schmoozing in an attempt to win undecided votes from the party's political elite. Party members were dressed in their best formal attire: women in formal gowns with corsages, the men in tuxedos with a rose or a carnation on their lapels, and all were in earnest about their role in the voting in of a new leader that would move directly from the party's election and into the role of being the next Prime Minister.

This skip-to-the-top was a rarely used circumvention of the usual electoral process: a general election. This shortcut to the highest-ranking government position was afforded only when the existing Prime Minister chose to or could not continue as leader for his or her full term. It was going be a relatively unique coup for someone present, even though a Prime Minister chosen in this manner rarely lasted much more than a year. But whatever the case, it was an easier win than when the whole country made the choice. As it stood, only those that had paid – the party faithful – would be making the leadership decision for the rest of all Canadians.

And security: it was everywhere and included CSIS agents that, like the guests, were dressed in formal attire.

Toque entered the lobby adjacent to the conference hall, her arm through Joe's. All heads turned. Her hair was up and the best she could substitute for a toque was a cap-shaped fascinator with a simple bow that covered about half of the cap's circumference.

From there, a wide-weaved mesh fell down, over her left eye then gracefully curved up, just beneath her right eyebrow. The mesh did nothing to hide her eyes, but somehow made them even more visible. In spite of the veil, by toying with the uncovered state, the simple head ornamentation made her blue-grey eyes more seductively entrancing – eyes that were further emphasized by her perfectly arched light-brown eyebrows. Though her auburn locks were tied-up and back, a large wave of amber hair curled loosely over the right side of her forehead.

As usual, on any of the rare occasions that she might attend a formal event, her lips were covered with a simple pinkish lip gloss. With her make-up understated, it made her into a dream-like image, but one towards whom everyone in the room felt the surge of magnetism. The silk covered fascinator, like her small evening bag, and her fitted silk gown were all the colour of soft sage. The fabric of the skirt was draped down from her backless dress on the left and formed long graceful folds. Just where the skirt fabric was gathered was a bow, simple in shape, like that on the cap, and had the effect of softening the back of her narrow waist, beneath her alluring uncovered pink skin. On her feet, when she moved, her shoes became visible: clear, stiletto sandals, leaving Toque's height just a fraction shorter than Joe's.

Toque had bought an ensemble that she thought would be subtle and unrevealing. But when she moved, the opposite of her plans occurred: the sensuality of her form was magnified, much like the human nude can be made more erotic by the addition of a clothing prop. On her left wrist, rested a very lucky corsage of white roses.

With Joe on her arm, they seemed as if they had been co-ordinated. The reds in his hair were a match for some of the hues in hers; on his lapel, a single white rose was like those in her wrist corsage. With the beard gone, he was a handsome guy with a rectangular Nordic face with a straight nose, clear blue eyes and ample eyebrows. His hair was in a standard cut, though it was a little longer on the top so that its natural wave was apparent, then emphasized, with hair gel. His single-breasted black tuxedo jacket lay flat on his broad shoulders, the lapels a smooth silk, his sleeves fitted to reveal just the right amount of the cuffs of the white dress shirt underneath. A white handkerchief in his breast pocket was folded as if sculpted. His black silk bow-tie was perfectly centered. The silk braid that lined the outside seams of his trousers matched the lapel facings, and the black shoes were like a counterpoint to her minimal look. Through a strange coincidence, his waistcoat was the exact colour of her dress. Or was it a coincidence? After all, he had asked her what colour she'd be wearing.

As people stopped to stare, Toque glanced around at the others attending. Most of the women, like her, were in long gowns, setting the tone of luxurious formality. A few women, though, wore gender-neural tuxedos and extended the event's tone to one of inclusivity. The best family jewelry had been brought out of the safes and safety boxes for this occasion. Several men and women stepped forward to shake Joe's hand, and to thank him for throwing his hat into the ring of candidates.

Cocktail servers glided by, pausing to offer a glass of champagne or an hors-d'oeuvre. The voices of those there were that of subdued anticipation. The music from the adjacent hall was the almost-new genre of music called Chamber Rock.

There was a casual movement of the guests filtering into the conference hall.

The convention center was gorgeous. Huge sprouting indigenous potted plants and ferns were everywhere. But what was most impressive was that in one corner of the great hall, around which the room had been built, was a massive and flourishing arbutus tree. Miraculously, the wonderful result of the array of foliage was that the hall held the scent of new architecture mixed with mature green growth. From all the plants hung silver, white and red Christmas bobbles. The centre's hall was the equivalent of sixty feet high. Half way up its walls and encircling the grand room was a silver wrought-iron balcony-like pathway with Christmas-light-covered stanchions that were shaped to resemble the graceful branches of arbutus trees. Above this great hall was a huge chandelier supported by a delicate but strong silver-plated metalwork structure from which suspended hundreds of glass sheets which were etched by a team of artists who created an interlocking design inspired by the fluidity of the ocean's undulations comingled with rippled sand, all hung amongst thousands of miniature LED lights. The chandelier was over thirty feet in height, and hung from a midnight blue ceiling speckled with an untold number of pale-yellow discs, varying in size, to emulate the appearance of a clear night sky.

Along the walls opposite the curved floor-to-ceiling view windows, were huge tapestries; those on the lower walls went from floor to the balcony; those on the top went from balcony to ceiling. All of these wall hangings were designed by First Nations artists depicting images from their traditional worlds, bold in design, though subtle in the choices of colour: three different tones of gray. Under the chandelier was a hardwood dance floor, stained a dark grey. It was flanked on the inside wall with a long table facing the water and city view, with a dozen chairs for the existing Prime Minister, her husband, and other top government officials.

On the other side of the dance floor was the band, facing inwards. At either end of the stage were round tables centered with healthy bouquets of white flowers with holy and red-
berried arrangements that matched those on the head table. As an accent to the elegant white tablecloths, the upholstered skirted dining chairs were slip-covered with pristine pale grey textured seat covers, which were fastened with cloth-covered buttons at the backs. There were ten places set at each table, white napkins on the silver-trimmed white bone china plates, and glistening utensils on either side. In a circular pattern on the round tables and a linear pattern on the head table were lines of candles which augmented the light of the chandelier and the perimeter dimmer controlled spot-lights set under the balcony walkway. On the two far ends of the table areas were the press galleries, mainly full of Canadian news reporters and cameras. And security. Everywhere.

When the meal was about to commence, all seemed to be in order. The mass of waiters and waitress had delivered wine to all the guests. And in front of everyone, sat their first course: an appetizing salad with a nut and seed topping or crab, depending on individual preference. Conversation was muted, but a positive tone permeated.

Toque, seated beside Joe, smiled awkwardly as she placed her cloth napkin on her lap. Joe smiled back, thinking that he had successfully lured this amazing woman to be his companion for the night, in every sense. He thought to himself: *The leadership and Toque – both will be mine – if not within hours, certainly before the next sun rises.* The wave of amber hair that curled loosely over the right side of her forehead seemed to be a teaser and an unspoken agreement that he would soon have her entirely, and in that moment of unabridged passion, her auburn locks would cascade down in all their glory. She had to be ready; one only had to look at her, with her breasts flush forward and so alluring, her behind shaped like a sweet promise. Her eyes, her mouth so seductive.

His eyes moved from hers, then to her glistening lips, then down her pink throat, her neck, her firm, round breasts, with a hint of the nipples almost showing. His eyes paused, hoping for more, and his slacks tightened. It was through an effort of magnanimous self-control that he didn't slide his hand across her naked back, then further towards her front to touch where civilized men never stroked … or licked … in public. So, he moved his hand under the table cloth, under her napkin, then onto her thigh, then under one of the fabric folds of the skirt of her dress, hoping beyond reason to find his way onto that area where the soft stomach meets what he hoped would soon be yielding thighs. It was as if her silk dress was part of her entire sensual being and was made of no separate fabric at all.

Toque shifted uncomfortably, trying to determine her next move in this setting of the dignified, highly polished political elite.

Then suddenly, as if a judgement from above, over one million locusts surged through flanged flexible tubing that was duct-taped to the back of the trunk of the arbutus tree, soon swarming the conference hall, spilling out of the tubing like high-pressure water from a source dedicated to an entire city, immediately swarming every living or cut plant, then chewing voraciously until anything that once had soil-bound roots, including the salads, was being entirely devoured. As the locusts exited the tubing, the shocked musicians stopped, so that what momentarily filled the air was a loud rustling crackle from the wings of the onslaught of the insects. Some of the chaotic swarm landed on the women's corsages, the roses or carnations on the men's lapels, the table bouquets, and even the edges of the filled wine glasses. Half a dozen inexplicably landed on the Prime Minister's hair and started ravenously devouring her fascinator. The hall was overrun. Momentarily, the astounded guests were silent in their shell-shock.

Band members realized that their services were no longer required and began to pack up
their instruments to take flight. In that moment of traumatised silence, once the insect masses had landed on their prey, the entire hall was filled with the sound of the locusts eating: a noise that was like the sound of electronic static or perhaps that of cellophane being crinkled.

But then, the screaming started.

Corsages and boutonnieres were torn from wrists and garments. Some guests had the wherewithal to actually unpin the once-lovely floral decorations. Chairs were spilt over as a mass exodus of humans began; the majority of women hiking their long dresses to knee height, as they attempted to make a dash for it and were held back only by their stilettos, which, at best, afforded them a wobbled path to a bug-free zone. Several threw their shoes in any direction so that they could escape barefoot. Waylaid locusts buzzed onto arms, down cleavages and some onto hair and various women's legs, clambering upwards, then holding on for dear life as the panicked legs carried them out. The men thrashed about wildly, though their gestures were futile, as no one had an insect zapper.

Toque watched the ascending swarm with amazement while Joe rose and ran to the door, abandoning her. She'd never heard him scream before. It was higher pitched than she would have guessed. Every plant and everything that once grew was covered with devouring locusts. Some of the insects, the confused or possibly satiated, disappeared into slip-cover folds after crawling about on the seat coverings of chairs – some of them standing and some turned over.

Toque stood, and with a calm gesture brushed the half-dozen

locusts from her arms, pulled her cell from her bag, and speed-dialled Brock.

Brock, sitting with his usual dinner of beer, Cheesesnacks, and salad, sat at the *Angel's* table area alongside Rex who was happily eating his own meal. Brock glanced as his phone, saw Toque's formal surname, raised his eyebrows at getting her call, and answered, "What's up?"

"Another attack! Locusts! I'm at the new Convention Center."

"What the hell? Isn't that a closed event? Were the insects invited?"

"Not funny, Getzlaff. Joe invited me. He's one of the candidates."

"The lumberjack? You're kidding!"

"He's different now. But it's chaos here. Security is trying to help the Prime Minster but it looks like she's barely conscious."

"Where the fuck is Joe?"

"Don't know. Ran off. But can you come here now? All the cops and special security agents are going crazy trying to keep the conference guests from stampeding out of here! You won't believe what is going on. People are bashing each other around, trying to get to the door."

"Crazy. But I'll be there as fast as I can."

In seconds, Brock was in his uniform, closing the hatch of the *Angel* but as he did so, his phone again beeped a message. It was from dispatch. "All available officers, on duty or otherwise, report to the North Shore Convention Center."

Brock ran to his beat-up, bleached-out, red four-by-four with one black fender and a blue hood over the engine. He threw open the tail-gate and pulled out the portable emergency vehicle light bar and slapped it on the roof. He was at the conference center in thirteen minutes, parked illegally in the front where a shivering and traumatized crowd stood. Many of the women were weeping.

Brock moved quickly through the crowd and into the lobby where he immediately spotted the tallest couple present: Joe and Toque. Joe had returned to her side just minutes before Brock appeared. They still looked like a couple paired up by a fashion magazine, especially if one could ignore Joe's panicked

274

facial expression. But Brock paid little attention to Joe, except for bristling at the sight of that huge man at Toque's side. But then Brock took a serious look at his work partner – in her dress: she was impossible to ignore. He felt the flush of desire but then, as Joe placed his arm on Toque's, Brock looked down, scowling.

Joe had momentarily returned to Toque's side, but in no time was off again – some party official had latched on to him. This second departure was a non-issue for Toque, although Brock thought that the running off was a sign of Joe's blatant insensitivity.

With Joe gone, Toque showed Brock around the conference center. Locusts crawled everywhere, though hundreds were squished on the floor. Every plant that had once lived was gone. The venue was ruined: chairs were all askew, glasses and dishes were on the floor, white table cloths were pulled and stained all over the place – and looked especially grim where red wine had been splashed as guests thrashed their way to a hasty exodus.

As Toque and Brock looked for the entrance point of the swarm, locusts rose from the devoured plant life, then hovered. The air was infected as if a million wood chips hovered here and there, but every single one of these chips was searching for another growing thing to ravage.

It didn't take long. Soon Toque and Brock discovered the tube that had ushered in the starving insects. As Brock fingered the flanged end, a gentleman in a black suit who introduced himself as the conference center's manager, joined them – just as Brock clambered over the arbutus to further examine the tubing.

Toque extended her hand. "I'm Constable Burdon. Until minutes ago, I was a guest. Brock here is my partner."

Brock climbed back over the arbutus and shook hands with manager while asking, "What's under the floor?"

"Why, the car park, of course. Directly underneath is the parking for the caterers.'

Then as if on cue, a man in a black tuxedo with a white bow-tie and waistcoat, rushed towards them, almost shouting, "I am Monsieur Jacquet, the caterer. Let me assure you that I had nothing to do with these insects."

"Let's have a look downstairs," suggested Toque.

Monsieur Jacquet sized up Toque with appreciation, a misdirected gesture caused by his not knowing that she was a cop.

Brock interrupted his thoughts. "Constable Burdon is in plain clothes and is helping sort out this mess."

Monsieur got a grip on himself and refocussed on the disaster. In seconds, the four of them tore down the emergency exit stairs, then into the parking lot beneath the conference center. At the distant end of the lot, in the locked-off parking area beneath the conference hall, were nine twenty-foot-long catering trucks parked in a cordoned-off area. All were covered with matching custom vehicle wraps. The parking lot itself was unexceptional except for the shadowed and barely noticeable portion of the trunk of the cherished conference-room arbutus tree, up against which one of the catering trucks seemed pressed. No one seemed to see or care that the delivery truck was so close to the tree. Except for the truck up against the trunk, uniformed security personal stood guarding, with their backs to the vehicles.

Instantly, Brock assessed the mass of high-end limousines and cars waiting in the
protected lot, eyed up the delivery trucks, then asked the caterer, "How long have those nine catering trucks been sitting there?"

"But Monsieur, there should be only eight catering trucks!"

Brock ran though the lot that was filled with the expensive metal that we call luxury cars and manoeuvred himself alongside the catering truck that was pressed up against the trunk of the arbutus. On the rear of the vehicle, the cargo roll-up door was open about four to five inches. Several wooden boards had been set there vertically to block most of the opening, leaving only enough space for the circumference of a round flexible duct: tubing originally intended for venting. The tubing left the truck's cargo area and ran to the back side of the tree's trunk then reached up, towards the
ceiling, duct-taped to the smooth trunk. At the parking lot's ceiling, the tubing had been partially collapsed into a much flatter shape so that it could pass through the narrow slot adjacent to the trunk, the slot that led past the parking lot's ceiling and to the floor area above. Tossed to the far side of the truck and against the wall were

the three traffic cones that had been originally placed by conference center staff in front of the tree to prevent anyone from parking anywhere near it.

Brock pulled the tubing from the truck, causing the roll-up door to further open. A blast of heat came out from the truck's box. As he opened the tailgate more fully, a sprinkling of locusts flew out, and Brock could see the warm glow of a propane-powered heater. He grabbed the tubing. Four locusts fell out and as the tubing passed near his nose, Brock could smell something: it was the faint scent of vegetation. He then knew.

"The locusts were attracted to the scent of the flowers and plants in the conference hall. They must have been bred, kept in an over-crowded box truck, then starved. That would have caused the swarm."

Toque, who had been looking at the vehicle's custom wraps, made a perceptive observation. "Look, compared to the adjacent delivery trucks, the colours of the locusts' truck are in the warmer range; the greens are less blue, the reds and oranges just a touch warmer. The colours are not quite the same as the adjacent trucks."

Brock stood back, eyeing the row of catering vehicles, then also saw that the locust truck was the only one of the fleet with a colour anomaly.

The four of them then realized that somehow this truck of locusts had entered the conference center under the almost perfect guise of being one of the catering fleet.

CHAPTER 60

"Sandford Graham on the line."

"It's CO Grant from the North …"

"Right. North Vancouver RCMP. It's all over our information feeds: our Prime Minister's life is in question. What went wrong at the leadership race?"

"As you no doubt know, the Prime Minster had a heart attack and is unconscious in the hospital. Numerous other high-ranking ministers are in a state of shock. The voting for the new leader has been postponed until at least two thirds of the party are able to participate. We're thinking in about a week. But it may be longer. Until then, the country is vulnerable."

"How the hell did this happen?"

"A box-truck with fake wraps managed to get in with the train of catering trucks. The wraps were reasonably convincing."

"And the security didn't have a count of expected trucks?"

Grant continued, "Screwed up. Lost count or didn't count or figured the extra truck was simply that."

"And they didn't see anything?"

"Security had their backs to the vehicles, keeping their eyes open for incoming problems."

"Shit. Was there a shortage of normal size brains in the year those guards were born? How exactly did the bugs get in?"

"There is a tree around which the centre was planned. Its trunk passes through the corner of the parking lot. The tree is slated to have special padding around the ceiling and protective concrete blocks around the base, but for now it was only sectioned off by traffic cones. The guys with the locust-filled truck just threw the cones to the side and constructed venting into the conference area. It would have taken almost no time at all."

"Did you catch them?"

Grant moaned. "No idea how they got out. Guesses are that they were in catering uniforms and just blended in with the staff coming and going, then probably managed enough of a change of clothing to give a new impression – then they just took off,
probably from the lobby. The truck rental name is bogus. We're

now questioning all the legitimate catering and delivery staff to see if they noticed anything different about the guys from the extra truck. But as the delivery staff were mainly occasional workers, concerned about their work, it seems that we're not going to get anything that will help us."

"Crap."

"But, like I said, we're on it."

Graham proceeded with an unexpected disclosure. "Now that locusts have also been used, I think that I can illuminate your understanding of the perpetrators. It's not much, but it might help."

"What do you mean?"

"Ever heard of the ten plagues of Egypt?"

Grant was puzzled. "What? Ten?"

"They're in Old Testament based faiths."

"A religious act of hatred? You've got to be kidding me!"

Graham went on, "You wish. As you probably know, a number of religions are based on the Old Testament. The Jewish and Christian faiths both have the same ten plagues that
occurred in the time of the prophet called Moses."

"And they're using the Old Testament?"

"Most likely. The first eight plagues include blood, frogs, lice, flies, livestock disease, boils, hail (which is also known as crack), and locusts."

"I can't believe it!"

"So far, in terms of the Biblical order, they've missed only the plague of boils."

"Is it possible we missed seeing them?"

"Unlikely. As I said before, the perps seem to like spectacle-like assaults. Don't know why they missed the boils. Maybe later, unfortunately."

"Crap! I guess I'd better unearth a copy of the Old Testament."

"But what's worse, is what might come at the end: the death of the firstborn."

"Shit!"

"Let's hope it doesn't go that far! But in the meantime, we know we're probably after someone with some knowledge of the Bible."

"Likely. But as you said, it's not much."

279

Chapter 61

Sun, Boucher, Trembley and Karimi rushed into the parking lot while Toque, Brock, the conference center manager, and Monsieur Jacquet stood scrutinizing the colour difference between the locust vehicle's customized wraps and those of Jacquet's fleet.

Trembley and Karimi saw Toque in her sage-coloured fitted silk evening gown and edged each other in an attempt to be the one to stand beside her. Toque's nipples had hardened in the cold parking lot and their shape was visible under the soft fabric of her gown. She turned sideways to make an aside to Brock as Trembley and Karimi approached and saw the backless feature of her dress and practically pushed one another to the side so that they could stand the closest. A real clown act.

Brock, however, focused entirely on the locust truck, had almost forgotten Toque standing there, but then he saw the guys gaping at her chest. Brock paused. Looked. And then felt a poorly-timed stirring inside his core. But in seconds, he reined himself in, pulled off his jacket, and then wondered if he should drape it over her shoulders. Touching her? Possibly his fingers on her naked skin? Near her breasts? He shook some reason into his head and simply handed her the jacket, as if passing her a sack of potatoes.

Toque hesitated, pausing to wonder what innuendos might be taken from her accepting the jacket, and almost as bad, if Delila was the last female to handle it. But as Toque felt December's cold air slide right though her light-weight formal wear, goosebumps formed and her bones chilled. She didn't pause long. In seconds from her wrist she removed the half-eaten white rose corsage, then grabbed Brock's jacket and pulled it on. Then, just as she was about to stuff the wrist corsage into the jacket pocket, from behind a rose, a locust's head popped out and sized up the surroundings.

Trembley, seeing this, took one step back, and whispered to himself, "Sacre blue!"

With the back of her hand, Toque brushed the insect from the corsage, then wiped her mouth with the same hand, removing her pinkish lip gloss. Toque then pulled the fascinator from her head, unfortunately releasing her gorgeous mane, and, as the hair started to fall, she faltered. Brock, knowing that head coverings were her way of life, offered his hat and without pause, she accepted it with the relief of a person who'd just found their keys. She didn't think of Delila this time, but instead from the pocketed corsage, hurried to pull an elastic, and with it managed to fix her hair into a knot, over which she positioned the RCMP cap.

"Thanks," she blushed, while trying to project the tone of someone who'd been offered a shovel to help with the digging.

Tremblay and Karimi seemed at first displaced by Brock being the chivalrous one, but soon rallied.

Boucher asked, "So what have you got?"

Toque looked at the four of them, wondering if they had been at the conference site for long. "Been upstairs?"

"Just arrived."

"Hundreds and hundreds of locusts released into the site of the leadership race through the duct taped to the tree there," reported Brock.

"Locusts? You've got to be kidding!"

"Not a word. And the brass just phoned with a theory as to what is going on. They're wondering if someone is trying to re-enact the ten plagues of Egypt."

The essence of a distant remembrance passed through Tremblay's face. "What, from the Old Testament?"

"That's it. So, there could be a link to someone who practices Judaism or Christianity."

"What are the plagues that they're thinking about?" asked Karimi, looking worried.

"Water turning to blood, frogs, gnats or small insects, flies, livestock pestilence, hail, and now – locusts," explained Brock.

"Some of those are in the Qur'an," observed Karimi.

"Yeah, the brass wondered about that, but felt it's more likely Christian or Judaism based. They didn't elaborate, though. Does the Qur'an have all of the plagues that have happened here?"

"Yes and no, but common interpretations definitely include flood, locusts, qummal, toads or possibly frogs, and water turning to blood," explained Karimi.

"Totaling a possible five?"

"Right, though some waffle on including other possible plagues and some also include drought and famine."

"Well, aside the non-existence of drought and famine, what do you think are the biggest similarities?"

"So far? Locusts. Blood. And a close third would be the frogs, which, as I said, is more often believed to be toads. The other plagues are debateable. Plus, the Qur'an plagues are in a different order than has been happening."

Sun joined in. "Surprising similarities, though. But the blood on the school was a really gross interpretation."

"I'm with you on that. But how can the blood be interpreted as water turning to blood?" questioned Toque.

Boucher smiled a grimace. "Given any thought to the school's name?"

Toque's eyebrows went up. "What? Rockwater?"

"Didn't you see the huge painting in the lobby?" asked Boucher.

Toque thought back, while Brock immediately recalled, "Of a stream, a rock and a stick; right?"

"I can see your religious upbringing was different from mine. In the Old Testament Moses hit his staff on a rock and water rushed out," informed Boucher, "So, the painting illustrates a biblical passage but also the school's name."

"Of course!" said Brock, with the look of surprise, but then a deeper understanding.

Karimi looked taken aback, then added, "Water from a rock happens in the Qur'an also, only the prophet is Mūsā."

Boucher took in Karimi's observation, then said, "The staff in the painting is a reference to a miracle that gave the believers what they really needed: water."

"And so, the school's name," observed Brock.

Sun confirmed, saying, "Exactly. Rockwater Christian Secondary."

"The thing that doesn't make sense at all is the threats West Van dispatch has been getting about setting some prisoners free," puzzled Toque.

"But that too, could be considered related because the plagues were brought on when Moses was wanting the pharaoh to set his people free," explained Trembley.

Karimi further considered the faith of his ancestors, then disclosed, "In the Qur'an Mūsā also wants a pharaoh to set his people free."

Brock, at first thoughtful, then scowled. "I get it, but I'm inclined to side with the brass
thinking that the perpetrator is Christian or possibly Jewish. The perp is unlikely Muslim, because of the use of what seems to be adding up to being an enactment of the ten plagues of Egypt and not the lesser number."

Brock mulled further. "Now, that two incidents have happened at Rockwater, Cudmore, our little Peanut, seems to be our guy." He paused for a moment, thinking. "But why would a high school kid want prisoners sprung? It makes no sense. And another thing: the rig that was at a number of the sites leaked oil. Peanut's car is electric."

"Leaks?" Sun visually surveyed the lot, then asked, "What's that over there on the first parking spot across from the bug truck?"

Reaching for one of the extra evidence bags that Brock always stored in his inside pocket, Toque moved over to the spot, saying, "I'll get a sample."

"But why would the perps be here in another vehicle?" wondered Sun.

"Darned if I know. Scouting it out, maybe. But that's further proof that it wasn't Peanut."

Sun looked serious. "That might be true, but it turns out that Peanut has more connections than just the school."

"Such as?" questioned Toque and Brock, in unison.

"VPD called to say that in interviewing the regular clients of the racetrack, one high-end businessman said that he often gives his seats to an associate. Turns out it's Peanut's father."

"I think we need to revisit him," said Brock, "We already know that Peanut has no alibi for the night of the blood: he was home alone. Even still, all the dots just don't connect … for the kid."

Karimi scowled and forewarned, "Good luck with getting his mother to allow him to talk."

Chapter 62

Captain Abraham sat upright in her plush aqua chair, and briefly glanced out the window, past her computer terminal, and then beyond the street below. She sought a moment of refuge. She focussed her dark eyes through the light rain and onto the handful of freighters sitting quietly at anchor in English Bay.

From the back of her neck, she wiped a few beads of perspiration that had formed there, under the tie on her long black hair. She then ran her finger under the collar of her perfectly pressed white shirt and then flattened the blue tie that already lay smooth under her dark blue suit.

She picked up her phone and pressed a pre-programmed number.

"What's up?" answered Grant, his face set with anticipated aggravation. Already his dark gray suit was wrinkled, his matching tie loosed around his neck.

"Another email."

"And..." Grant ran his hand over his balding head.

"They're taking credit for the locusts."

"U-huh," acknowledged Grant as he picked up a pencil and pressed the tip to a notepad so hard that the point broke off.

"And again, they're saying we must spring the same three ..."

"Voronin, Kuznetsov, and Oblonsky in Scheveningen."

"You got it. And if we don't..."

"Go on."

Abraham looked at her hands on her desk rather than out the window. The view meant nothing. "The actual wording is, 'without mercy, the oldest in care will be struck.'"

"What the hell does that mean? Is this supposed to be the tenth plague of Egypt? And are they talking about the students at Rockwater or a senior's home? And what about the threat of the fire of their wrath?"

"Don't know about the fire bit, but with regard to the oldest in care, I doubt that the target is Rockwater. As you know, the students are all from reasonably well-off families, if not just plain wealthy: the parents, like their kids, feel entitled and know their rights. Not easy targets; they'd fight back."

"Yeah, I guess. But do you know if there are special needs kids there?"

"Are you kidding? Rockwater screens their students so that they have only the academically elite."

"How do they get away with that?"

"Wish I knew. But for now, we have an explosive concern."

"What the hell! 'Without mercy, the oldest in care will be struck.'"

"Exactly. You've got it. Word for word. We need to focus on care facilities, including for the elderly and …"

"Retirement communities …"

"Or any place with an age rage that provides care …"

"Any school …"

"Including independent facilities with special Ed programs …"

"And hospitals …"

"Shit! This list goes on and on."

Chapter 63

It could have been part of a courtship in which a shivering fair damsel in her flimsy dress donned her suitor's jacket, and with an arm of assistance, gracefully slid into the passenger seat of a shiny high-end car. But no, it was Toque clambering in her stiletto sandals and struggling with the long gown as she fought her way over the missing running board, then into Brock's dinosaur of a wreck with its unmatched fender and hood.

When they were approaching his vehicle, Brock had paused, thinking that he should be chivalrous and assist his partner. But then, in his mind, were the images of Toque with Lynn, the imaginary image of Toque with Joe and Lynn as a threesome, but worst of all, Toque's facial expression when she saw him undressed on the *Angel* when he was with Delila. Was it his body that so appalled her? His scars? The two shortened fingers? How could he know for sure? So, he let the thought go, deciding that it was best if she was treated like one of the guys.

Even before she closed the door and fastened up the passenger seat-belt, the truck filled with exhaust as Brock revved the engine, then slipped into gear.

Waiting for the manager, one of the valets stood in front of the convention center, eyeing up Brock's illegally parked wreck. With suspicion, the inexperienced valet focussed on the displayed transferrable police decal and portable emergency light bar. But it was as if this valet was invisible when Brock and Toque arrived and unlocked the wreck of a four-by-four. As they did, the valet's hand reached for his cell but before he could reach a contact, Brock and Toque roared away, leaving the entrance to the center in a cloud a putrid exhaust.

As they left the lower Lonsdale area and started to move up the street, Toque's cell phone rang.

Just milliseconds after Toque picked up, Grant spoke, "Marol's on her way. Bring the oil sample right in."

Toque replied, "You don't lose any time."

"The convention center manager called and asked how long it would be before we knew something. He described you in detail. Less information about Brock but a lot about you. He was impressed. Anyway, he told me you got another oil leak sample."

"We're on our way."

"Put me on speaker."

"You're on."

"The two of you should know that already one person is taking credit for the locusts and is now threatening the oldest in care."

"What the hell does that mean? The tenth plague?" grumbled Brock.

"I'm very worried about the hospitals, care facilities, and schools, including those for the handicapped. But how can we know who is next? The army is going to assist with guarding all possible targets."

"Is it possible the Prime Minister who is already out of commission, and her staff, might be hit again?"

"They will be very heavily guarded. And ... hopefully ... with help from the Feds, maybe we'll get a break locating the perps."

"Hopefully," muttered Brock.

"But another thing worth thinking about ..."

"Yeah?"

"Is the next plague, if you want to call it that."

"What's coming?" asked Toque.

"My guess is that they'll catch up on the one they missed: the plague of boils!"

"How is a plague of boils possible?"

"Unfortunately, these guys are resourceful."

"Let's hope that if they do it, that it's confined to one location," said Brock.

Grant moaned but agreed. "Exactly. But you need to know that Captain Abraham, Sandford Graham and ..."

"Graham is now in on this?" interrupted Brock.

"Just hear me out. We're increasingly suspicious that Egor and Rasputin Bogdanov really are involved."

"I can't believe those lowlifes can still cause problems!" griped Brock.

"There are links. As you know, the three Scheveningen prisoners were part of the trafficking ring with the Bogdanovs."

Brock moaned.

"Too much is adding up. Because of you being the key agent in their arrest, there's a solid reason why they would have it in for you. This could explain the threat to the two of you, and more recently, the crack set-up on your boat."

"But the Bogdanovs? Surely they can't be involved! And why would they have any issues with Toque? She was still in cop training when they were tried!"

"Don't know about her inclusion in the threat, but the Bogdanovs …" began Grant.

"But aren't those two losers rotting in prison?"

"Sort of … but they are a risk because …" continued Grant.

Brock fuming, interrupted. "What? How in hell could those two morons be doing anything serious from their prison cells? Aren't they being watched?"

"The Bogdanovs were given ten-hour day-passes to work outside the prison," explained Grant.

Brock scowled as their cruiser turned a corner, just before the detachment hall. "Those assholes out on day-passes? What the hell!"

"Good behavior. Don't you remember they were considered culturally deprived?"

Brock smouldered. "How about those kids? And the women? And the special agent they killed? And his family?"

"You know how it goes," responded Grant, sounding both depressed and defeated, "But one thing that goes against their involvement is that the whole thing started with the blood-balloons, and that was before the Bogdanovs were given their day-passes."

"Shit! Now I have a really bad feeling about those two," mumbled Brock.

Then, as Brock pulled into the RCMP parking lot, he briefly thought about his neighbor Rita, talking about a person asking for him – a blond person with a pale complexion carrying a Bible. Brock thought to himself, *Could it have been Borya Morozov – the sixth member of the trafficking ring? If he is around … but how could one guy have done all that damage at Rockwater?*

But then, in seconds, Brock put that question to the side and moved his attention back to arriving at the detachment hall, saying, "We're here now. I can see Marol's bike already parked."

Toque reached for the door seconds before Brock pulled up the brake handle.

"Okay," replied Grant, "Drop off the sample. And tomorrow, come by my office before
you start your shift. Let's hope Marol can get the lab work done by then."

Chapter 64

They were again on graveyard. In a cruiser, Toque and Brock were just pulling out of the detachment parking lot. Yet another downpour was drowning the city.

Brock grimaced. "Egor and Ras: free for ten hours a day! I could puke."

"And we both know of a person who is a blood relation to their friend, Morozov."

"And that blood relation works in a lab that studies insects," added Brock.

"Our friend Yana, the unfortunate sister of Borya Morozov."

"Let's see if she's home."

Soon Brock and Toque pulled up to the home of Yana and Alik Vasiliev.

Yana was looking out the window as the police cruiser pulled up and by the time Brock and Toque were approaching the house, she was standing at the door between the garage and her home. There, in the lighting of the covered vestibule between the garage and the house, Brock and Toque could see that Yana's eyes were red, as if she had been crying.

"Yana, I'm sorry to say that we've come by in an official capacity."

Fear and worry clouded her brain and her face went pale, though she tried to be nonchalant and calm, asking, "About?"

"We just dropped by to ask you a few questions about the break-in at the university."

Yana seemed relieved, then replied, "Oh? As I mentions to you, before – we files already the report."

"Right, but you mentioned to us that samples were taken. Is there a record of exactly what insects?"

Yana thought for a moment, then answered, "Yes, there are records. But I can tell you ... there were the egg of cockroaches, black fly, locust, lice, blow fly, and June beetle."

"And the larva was of ...?"

"All a same."

"Any frogs?"

"No, just insect."

290

"Any bacteria like salmonella?"

"No, like I said, just insect. What is this all abouts?"

"We're wondering if the insects from your university could be the source of the infestations."

Yana flushed. "I must admit, I wondered about that as well. But if they are connected, we had only insects eggs and larvaes."

"Yeah, we thought of that, but we still need to get all possible information," added Toque.

"But also," questioned Brock, "Do you remember two of your brother's buddies, Egor and Ras Bogdanov?"

"I remember their name from that sex trades incidents some year ago. But no, they have not been touching with me. But I do not understand: I thought that they were at jail."

"There's a matter that we are interested in …"

"You don't think that they are connected to an infestations?" asked Yana.

"We're just getting together all the facts we can."

Yana glanced down at the flooring along the perimeter of the deck and almost gasped when she saw a locust emerge from a crack under the garage door. Then, when she edged her way towards the insect in such a manner as to not attract attention to the gesture, the locust scurried away, encouraged into disappearing from the lighted deck.

Yana then, in an effort to hide her trembling hand, pushed it into her pocket. Toque watched.

Brock also observed the gesture, and with concern asked, "I'm sorry to ask you this, but if Borya, your brother, ever surfaced, do you think that he would reconnect with the Bogdanovs?"

Yana's mouth dropped open slightly, as if her recent contact with Borya had just been uncovered, but then took on a demeanor of nonchalance. "I only wish he are still alive. But even if he are alive, I have no way of knowing if he would ever want to connect with those two." She looked to the side and sighed, and her shoulders slumped with the weight of the memory of Borya's threat and his hatred of her children, including her unborn.

"But Yana, are you alright? You seem bothered by something," asked Toque.

Yana paused, as if considering volunteering information but then her face hardened with the resolve of a person defending their own kin. "Oh, nothing to say. Moms always worry about their children."

Brock remembered his own child. *She has no idea.*

It was then that a second locust scurried from under the door, and darted into the shadows of the dark evening.

Both Brock and Toque stared, as if it were a plague-carrying rat, whereas Yana harrumphed, illogically thinking that a verbal intrusion would ward off any suspicions.

"So, what's in the garage?" asked Brock, "Locusts don't live around here."

"It might be the grasshopper," lied Yana.

"I don't think so. It's way too cold for them at this time of year. And last time I checked, it's moths and not grasshoppers trying to stay warm in my woolens," remarked Brock.

Toque glanced to the side, momentarily, taking in Brock's version of humour, but then her face became dead serious as she repeated his question, asking, "But again, what's in the garage?"

"Nothing to interest, I am sure."

"Let's have a look and see for ourselves."

"No. No. It is a mess in there. Maybe another times."

Upon that remark, Alik emerged from the house. Hearing Yana's refusal, he said, "My love, Brock and Toque are our friends. They won't care about a bit of mess. Also, I'd like to see it myself. I've been wondering ever since you said that it was off-bounds for your private pre-spring gardening plans."

"No. Not now," urged Yana.

"Oh, come on, we're adults. We promise to not disturb anything. Right, constables?"

"Let's have a look," repeated Brock.

With that, Alik opened the door and as the four of them took in what was inside, they could immediately see four stacked plastic bins and nine aquariums.

"What's all this? I thought that you were keeping the garage to yourself to prepare for the gardening season. I've been parking outside for this junk? It doesn't even take up that much space."

Brock's brow furrowed in thought, as he observed, "The aquariums are from the university: several have their labels. Is it usual to have university equipment at home?"

Toque glanced at Yana, then at Brock.

Yana stammered, "Oh, I was going to try some experiment here but then the university got robbed."

Toque glanced at the wall behind the aquariums and saw two dead black flies, practically on top of one another, and a third, then a fourth – further along the wall. Then looking at Yana for her reaction, said, "I think that we are going to have to fill out a report and have the aquariums confiscated."

Yana's initial expression of surprise when seeing the aquariums soon changed into that of anxious concern as she tried to explain, "I assure you that ..." Yana paused, taking in a breath, "That it is okay for me to have all these."

Brock's face was serious as he responded, "I hope so."

"What is going on around here?" questioned Alik, looking bewildered.

Yana reddened and looked down at the garage floor.

Later, when Brock and Toque were in the cruiser, pulling away, Toque said, with surprise in her tone, "I think she's lying and hiding something."

"I agree; and worse, from the expression on her face when we asked, I can't help but wonder if Borya really is nearby."

"He's wanted internationally and he turns up here?" asked Toque.

Brock was mindful of this skeptical question, but frowned as he remembered his neighbour's concern about a stranger. "A while ago, there was some guy looking for me at the marina. I've been wondering if it could have been Borya, but the neighbour's description was extremely vague."

Toque summed up Brock's remarks, "Could have been one in a million."

"Practically."

Chapter 65

Delila held onto the railing that led to her cockpit while Borya pumped her from behind. Her ample breasts, her shapely gymnast-like form, and her tied-back platinum blond hair might have spelt out a partner from an erotic fantasy except for the dark eyes that were deadened by coke – an effect that was unfortunately emphasized by the generous application of black eyeliner.

Their bodies met: back and forth, back and forth. Their contrasting skin tones glistened from perspiration.

"Oh-h-h; it hurts. Can't we lie down on the bunk and meet face to face and have real sex?"

"This is as real as it gets. Get used to it. This is what I want," he insisted as he plunged as hard as he could, his slim hips back and forth, his shoulders broad, but his handsome features set with hatred.

"But it hurts, so much."

"You want to please me, don't you?"

He shoved and thrust and finally his face expression changed to that of climatic euphoria and he threw himself back onto her settee around her galley table, first wiping his penis dry on the upholstery. He poured another line of white powder on the table. "Now snort this. Like I told you. Then clean yourself up! You smell like a hooker. And get ready for that prick, Brock. Use the douche and for the sake of every whore on the planet, show what whoring is really about. And wipe your fucking nose. Can't you even snort a line and get it all inside? You know how much that stuff costs?"

Delila cowered, and went to the washroom.

"Put on more of that fucking stench you call perfume and that see-through gown you wore before."

"I just don't know if I'm ready for another man tonight."

"Tell me something I care about. When I say go, you go. You haven't fucked that asshole for over a week. He has to fall for you. And big time. Wear that red dress thing."

"I need a coat, not a negligee."

"Don't be so fucking weak. You'll warm up soon enough. He should be back soon. Go wait for him by his boat."

294

"I'll freeze – waiting. How can you be so mean? You promised we'll be married!"

Borya rose from the galley seat, and caressed her breasts. "Listen, my love, you know that I said we have to rope in that Brock bastard. I'm sorry if I am harsh but I am really stressed and I need you to help with this." He glanced away from her momentarily, as the expression on his face became that of grim resolve. Then he lowered his head to suck on her nipple while he reached down to her crotch.

"But Borya," she stammered, as if unsure, "I want to be with just you."

He raised his hand to her cheek. And caressed it, while he pressed his naked groin to her hip. "I need you to do him. Repeatedly. You have to trust me." He planted his mouth on hers: a long drawn out kiss, his tongue inserted, then withdrawn. "If you want to be my wife, (like that's going to happen, he snarled to himself), you'll do it to please me – but also, because I need you to do it."

"There has to be another way!"

Borya again looked away from her and sneered. Then his face changed to that of angry
passion as he turned towards her. "For me, you must!"

"Come on, there has to be another way."

"There isn't. You have to realize that I know what is best. And you must accept it. I have a stronger drug if you can't do it. But I don't want you to seem doped when you're with him."

"Never mind; I'll go as I am."

Borya reached through the opening in her negligee and again stroked her genitals. "And make sure you appear to be in the mood. Just remember that I love you but I really need your help. Focus on this. Only this."

As he stroked, she closed her eyes and as pleasure encompassed her being, inexplicably, the image of Toque formed in Delila's mind and she imagined touching Toque on the cheek then the neck, then unbuttoning the collar, then their lips meeting – but when Delila opened her eyes, the lips on hers were those of Borya.

Shortly thereafter, and as luck would have it, as Delila approached the *Angel*, Brock was just boarding his boat after walking with Rex. By the time she was near, the second line of cocaine had kicked in and she walked as if she were on a cloud, floating towards Brock. She gazed past him and smiled. Then focussed on Brock himself: his warm ocean blue eyes, his wide chest and she imagined his tender love-making. *He isn't that bad. I can do this*, she thought.

Brock didn't notice that she was high: all he could see was this voluptuous woman approaching his boat. The eroticism was tangible.

Rex, on the other hand, immediately realized that a patting or chin-scratching opportunity was likely imminent and without pause, leaped onto the pier and raised his chin in anticipation. Delila, disinterested in anything other than connecting with Brock, gave Rex a cursory pat, which was enough to satisfy the friendly canine. In fact, Rex would have smiled if he could have but instead simply let out a satisfied wide yawn and moseyed back and onto the *Angel*, considering that his job was done.

But then dawning on Brock, was some sense of reality as to what Delila must have been feeling.

"What are you doing in such a flimsy garment? It's fucking freezing," swore Brock, as he helped Delila up from the pier, removed his uniform jacket and pulled it over her shoulders. Her breasts, being covered with a negligee of such a sheer silkiness, soon tingled at the touch of the very fabric that still felt cozy from having been on Brock.

She snuggled up towards him and the scent of her perfume, combined with her shivery form, caused a heart-felt concern but also ... desire. But motivated to help her return to a normal body temperature, he held her as close as he could. *But nothing more*, he told himself. Her almost naked body was pressed against his clothed form. Her breasts and her flat stomach were soon returning to that of warmth; his chest – at first cooled at the contact, became temperate from their continued embrace. Then, in only a few minutes, they left the cockpit of the *Angel*, and climbed down and into the galley.

Rex watched them descend, but with little interest, and instead became preoccupied with the latest spider that was moving towards a drain hole in the cockpit. But soon his long pink tongue extended, the gangly spider was gone, and a contented Rex again yawned as he reclined, stretched out his limbs, and entered the world of doggy dreams.

Once inside and the stove lit, Brock grabbed the sleeping bag from his forward cabin, unzipped it so that it formed a huge comforter, and wrapped it around his almost naked guest.

He thought about the double date that Toque had suggested but internally thought, *No, this cannot be.* "Delila, we need to talk ..."

But she was not to be dismissed. She reached to him, undid the top fastener on his slacks after undoing the belt buckle, pulled his pants to his knees reached down to his member ...

One hour later they were in each other's arms on the bunk in the forward cabin.

As they lay there, the thought of Toque again flashed through Delila's mind and her whole core was filled with sexual arousal. Internally, she shook her head, and could not readily accept or understand the same-sex fantasy. So as the image of Toque filled her mind, she again reached for Brock.

Brock was exhausted, and felt fulfilled ... though momentarily. In seconds the image of his wife April, filled his mind and guilt took over his being.

He began to spill his feelings. "Delila, I just don't know how long we can keep going. As I told you, I have a wife."

"It doesn't matter. She's not here, is she? Let's do what we can – and as much as we can."

"Delila, I gotta say that I really enjoy being with you, but I must be up front. This relationship will not go anywhere."

Delila removed her hand from his torso, bemoaning, "Great! Another rejection by another power figure."

"But I've told you that I'm not at the stage of being able to establish a relationship."

Delila sighed. "First the high school teacher, who pretended that he wasn't married, then the university equestrian coach – the man who promised to be my husband but was cheating on me practically as he put the ring on my finger."

"Delila, I am truly sorry that you've had such a rough time but we have to call it quits before we get any further involved."

Delila thought about Borya and how disappointed he would be. "No. Now I am going to take control. To hell with power figures. This relationship will end when I say it will."

Brock winced.

"Maybe later. Much later. Maybe in a month or two. When I decide," replied Delila as her head moved down towards his groin.

Brock went to rise from the bed but already his member had made the decision on his behalf. It then seemed possible that he might be going on that double date, after all.

Chapter 66

Brock and Toque were stopped in the detachment hall just as they were about to start their day.

"Got a minute?" asked Gant, "I have a couple of things to go over with you."

Toque glanced at Brock, and he at her: both a little surprised at this request for a private interview with the boss.

"Not a problem," answered Brock, as Grant managed a trace of a smile, though his face immediately turned back to an expression of seriousness, as if there was impending doom.

Grant gestured at the two chairs waiting by his desk and once Brock and Toque were seated, he slipped in past them and was soon at his workstation, facing them. Grant glanced down at a notice on his screen, then up, at the two constables looking expectantly at him. He began, "I just want to update you on a couple of recent findings from our lab."

Toque moved forward, just an inch or so – to hear, while Brock's face showed his full attention.

"The engine oil sample from the convention center matches the others – from the school, university, and so on."

"Shit."

"Yeah, so it's something we have to keep our eye on. We've got personnel investigating the vehicles you tagged when you were on desk duty but so far we haven't found any that are leaking."

"Have you checked with local garages?"

"We're on that, too, but it's a bit like a needle in a haystack because anyone can buy oil. Plus, a vender doesn't necessarily know the person buying or the vehicle being used, or if the oil is even being used for a truck, car or whatever."

"But you have someone on it?"

"Definitely. Another thing. Do you remember the partial label on a balloon bag found at the school?"

"The one Brock had to scale a tree for?"

"He did? I'd like to have seen that," smiled Grant.

"It was no big deal," remarked Brock.

For a second, Grant raised his eyebrows. "But back to what I was talking about, that label turns out to be from one of the franchised stores called Cashdiscount."

Again serious, Brock asked, "Like the one in Cap Mall?"

"Could be. That's what I was wondering," acknowledged Grant.

"Well, there's a place worth visiting. We can see if the receipt without a vendor's name found in the kid's locker is the same as those used at the Cap Mall outlet, and if that same store currently carries bags of balloons and for the prices listed."

"Good idea. They're probably open until nine."

"Worth a look," agreed Toque.

"And also, could you drop by the shelter that is receiving our blankets? Marol Carrier is there and says there's a problem."

"On our way."

CHAPTER 67

Toque and Brock drove in a south-westerly direction, down West Keith Road, alongside the green boulevard. The local government had decorated larger trees with multi-coloured seasonal lights. Near the bottom of the road, half a dozen shrubs interspaced a few trees, a few evergreens and others naked for the winter. On the other side of the road were parked vehicles and homes with yards landscaped generously with manicured shrubs.

A number of homes were brightly decorated for Christmas, utilizing a variety of lighting displays and inflatables that included reindeer, penguins, snowmen, cartoon trees, jumbo candy-canes, and, of course, images of Santa. As they moved forward, they passed park-like greenery on the right, and then again were passing houses with yards outlined with hedges or any of a range of fence types, including cedar with lattice tops, or white picket fences. And more Christmas lights and inflatables.

Once at the bottom of Keith, they came to a multiple lane and multi-directional intersection and turned south-east, onto the third of five possible routes. As they swung the cruiser onto a road called Bewick, they couldn't help but notice two men crossing the road. Judging by their worn sneakers and unkept clothing, it seemed likely that they had come from the shelter. But what was disconcerting about the two was that both men's faces were red with swelling. Unbelievably, it looked as if their faces were marred with boils.

Once onto the side road, across the street was a car wash, while beside them – on their right – was a fifteen-year old apartment building next to a bulk no-frills food outlet. In front of the outlet were three more men, obviously dressed in shelter-supplied clothing, cowering from the rain by practically clinging to the portion of the building that had an extended roof over-head. The faces of these men, too, were red and swollen with what again, looked like boils. Just a little further beyond these three and across the next road, was a small building-supply shop and on the other side, the shelter for which the detachment had been gathering blankets. Toque and Brock knew that beyond the shelter were train tracks, the North Shore Rescue Society, small commercial buildings, work yards, and various industrial supply yards, alongside windowless concrete buildings behind chain-link fences.

The shelter was a three-story apartment-like building, shaped like a cedar-plank box, only with windows and a few feet of decorative brick beneath the first-floor windows on the front of the building. On the windows, holy leaves and bells were painted, along with cut-out paper snow-flakes. On the door was a simple wreath made out of the branches of local trees and decorated with pine cones and a few sprigs of red berries. On the roof, they could see an oversize fenced-in ventilation duct. Alongside the shelter was the Spirit Trail that extended along the entire North Shore. Blocking part of the trail, they could see the parked crime scene forensics van. Leaving the door were two people in raincoats, their faces red from fever and Marol in a hazmat suit following them, calling out, "Wait, you are probably contagious!"

"I'm not staying in that hell-hole," yelled back one of the men, as they crossed the street against the light.

As the men made their escape, Marol waved at Toque and Brock, then signalled for them to go to the forensics van, directing them, "Get on a hazmat suit, then come in."

In minutes they were inside another nightmare. Every unfortunate soul in the shelter was covered with boils, swelling, and some with weeping or draining wounds. Many were softly moaning. Some had a rusty-yellow crusting on their skin; others clearly had chills and sweats.

"This first room has the victims who are least affected."

"What the hell! How did you come across this?"

"I was on my way to the rescue society and thought I'd drop off a few late donations of blankets. When I saw the residents, I went back for the forensics van."

"And this infection has been unmonitored?"

"None of these people are registered for medical insurance. They were going to just ride it out!"

"Crap!"

"You don't know the worst of it. The residents are in much more danger as one moves up in the building. Come and see on the second floor." As they reached the top of the stairs, they could see that the non-paying tenants were bed-ridden. Too soon the three of them saw that all the cots on the second floor were occupied by the seriously infected, all ridden with pus-filled boils. "These guys also have either cellulitis or are having trouble because they have antibiotic-resistant infections."

"How did this happen?" asked Toque, with her voice trembling, revealing her over-whelming sympathy for the infected residents.

"It was all initiated by a contagious staph infection that has effected the whole center," Marol sadly explained.

"What's on the third floor?" asked Toque, though afraid to ask.

"It's where the infections are the most out of control. Those people already have septic shock or have sepsis because the bacteria have moved into the rest of their bodies. Two have flesh-eating infections."

"And boils?"

"On everyone."

"How could a staph infection get this extensive?"

"As I mentioned, staph infections are contagious. The staphylococcal bacteria can live on objects long enough to be caught by another person."

"But how could everyone be infected? I've never seen or heard of so many boils anywhere, anytime."

"It is likely that it was done deliberately."

"But how?"

"Good question. That's why we have to swab everything that these people touch and see if we can find the source. Let's go into the van and I'll set you up with more swabs than you have in the cruiser's kit."

Once in the van, Brock and Toque watched while Marol grabbed packets of sterile swabs.

***

Several hours later, in the cruiser, Toque shook her head and moaned. "One gross thing after another."

"Yeah, but there's no oil leak here. Perhaps the boils are not related."

"Maybe you missed the leak."

"Could have. I'll look again in the day-light but so far, nothing."

As they moved away from the site, several news-cast vehicles screamed past them, then came to an abrupt halt by the shelter.

Brock cursed under his breath. "Bad news travels fast."

CHAPTER 68

Mrs. Bean, with a mixing-bowl cut of straightened white hair and purple framed glasses, entered Grant's office. She wore institutional black pumps and a navy-blue skirt, matching jacket and a purple long-sleeved T-shirt. From her ears hung multi-stranded purple beaded ear-rings that stopped just short of her shoulder. From her neck hung about five pounds of matching purple beads.

Grant was grey with fatigue and dark shadows seemed to be permanently under his eyes. However, he cheered somewhat when he saw his changed assistant. "The conference call set up, Mrs. Bean?"

"Captain Abraham and Director Graham are both the line."

Lifting the telephone's receiver, and without a greeting, Grant jumped right in. "I take it you know about the latest plague: boils."

Both other leaders groaned an affirmative sound at the same time.

Graham then summed up: "That's sixth in the Biblical order of the plagues, but is the eighth attack!"

Captain Abraham leaned on her desk while sitting in her plush aqua chair. She looked out the window, briefly focussing her concerned dark eyes through the light rain and upon the freighters in English Bay but then used an electronic command on her keyboard to close the blinds so that her room was closed off from the harbour view. She loosened her subtly patterned grey scarf worn over a lighter grey shirt, removed her dark grey jacket, then spoke. "I've got another email."

Grant moaned. "And?"

"The sender takes credit for inflicting the boils and now threatens that we must release …"

Grant completed Abraham's report. "Kliment Voronin, Lev Kuznetsov, and Gleb Oblonsky – from Scheveningen."

Then, before Abraham could say another word, Graham also interrupted, saying, "Right. And if we don't …"

"Did they again threaten the oldest in care?" asked Grant.

Abraham gazed at her hands on her desk as she said, "No. Don't know what they're thinking about that. But the latest threat ... I'm guessing it's flooding of some sort. The actual wording is, 'Noah's ark you will need, if our people are not freed.'"

Grant was astounded. "Flooding? I can't believe it! I'm not a Bible person but from my Sunday-school days, I can't remember flooding in the ten plagues of Egypt."

"You're right. There were no floods in the ten plagues. But there is the Noah's Arc incident. It happened earlier," remarked Graham.

"So, either some jerk is compiling random Old Testament disasters or, possibly, the perps are including plagues from more than one faith," hypothesized Grant.

Abraham sighed. "Maybe ... some other faith somehow connected to the Old Testament ... or just mixing it up, to suit themselves or perhaps what resources they can get their hands on. But whatever their reasoning, now we have a flooding threat!"

"As I mentioned to Captain Abraham after the locust infestation, another loose thread is the threat of fire – the warning that originally came with the locust threat," mulled Grant.

"As you can probably guess, with the one-way email communication, I didn't get to ask them about inconsistencies, although as the three of us previously considered, the fire one might be just symbolic," replied Abraham.

"Maybe. But with the unfulfilled threats of death, fire, and now the flooding, there are three good reasons to figure out where they're coming from. Yet ... with regard to the Old Testament and the ten plagues, like Captain Abraham suggested, we could be looking for a pattern when there isn't one. It may be just random mischief in the mind of the deranged. There may be no logic at all," surmised Graham.

Abraham sighed, then asked, "The question now is, should we consider contacting Scheveningen regarding the release of those prisoners?"

"It's tempting but ... against everything that ..." began Graham.

"I do wonder if we may have to bend."

"But what will happen if we don't set them free? It could be worse than horrifying!"

"Either way, it will be horrifying."

"Can we attempt to negotiate a middle ground?"

"Like what?"

"Perhaps we should bring in some negotiators."

Graham determined the next direction. "I'll check into it, and in the meantime, we need to consider which areas are vulnerable to flooding. We have to have every dam or dike-like structure secured. I'll contact the armed forces and get extra people brought in."

Grant thought for a moment, cringed, then added, "But for the next few days, we'll stick to our policy of not giving in to blackmailers."

"And pray that we get a break with finding out who is at the bottom of this," added Abraham.

Sandford, dead serious, gave final direction, "Too bad it's nearly Christmas and that people want time off. But everyone, on every police force in the entire area of Greater Vancouver, has to be on active duty sixteen hours a day. No leaves. No time off."

Grant and Abraham reacted, almost together: "We're on it."

CHAPTER 69

The stairs to the detachment hall were lit by the paltry-glow of the grey skies that marked the beginning of nightfall just after sunset. Toque and Brock were just about to mount the dimly lit staircase when the door from the inside opened and Marol Carrier stepped out. Her lab coat was gone and she was dressed in her motorcycle leathers. In spite of the gloom, one could easily make out the entire name, *Mom* printed on the flames painted on her brilliant red helmet which was tucked under her arm like a football.

Toque smiled at Marol. "Hey. Anything new?"

Marol forced a glimmer of a smile but was clearly uncomfortable. "You don't know the half of it."

"What's going on?" asked Brock.

Marol jumped into an important disclosure. "I just got the lab results back for the homeless shelter."

"And?" asked Toque.

Marol continued, "The outbreak in the shelter was caused by infected towels."

Brock interjected, "What the hell?"

Marol reasoned out the probable scenario. "It is likely that about a week ago, all of the towels were sprayed down with the virus."

"Where the hell would someone get access to a virus in a spray container? Do you think it could have been developed in the aquariums confiscated from the Vasiliev home?"

Marol sighed. "No, we've already checked them. Definitely not the source of staph. There was only evidence of insects: the same as those being experimented on at the university."

"Any guesses as to how the virus could have been developed?"

"Actually, not that hard. The virus can be found even in a healthy person's nose. Or, in a boil – then cultured in petri dishes. It would take just a couple of days."

"It seems that someone must have had a little bit of scientific knowledge, do you think?" asked Toque.

"Anyone with a high school biology course could do it. But as for the towels, to begin with, we weren't a hundred percent certain, because they were washed and sterilized as they are every day – but then, as luck would have it, one of the shelter residents had tossed a used one under his bed, then pushed his storage bin in front, then left for a couple of days, probably forgetting about the towel. Because the bed was in the corner, and the towel was behind the bin, it wasn't noticed till late yesterday."

Toque was a little surprized, and questioned, "They're allowed to leave a bed vacant for days?"

Marol explained further: "He's a long-time resident and legitimately had to leave: he was shipped into the hospital."

"For what?" asked Brock.

"He had a compromised immune system to begin with, and then he tried to clean an open sore with the infected towel. The result was that within hours he experienced a ton of pain, swelling, and he had a severe fever. There was some fear that he'd developed a flesh-eating infection. The hospital had him isolated."

Brock continued searching for all the facts. "He's recovering now?"

"Fortunately, he is responding to antibiotics but he's being closely monitored."

"There was just the one sample? Just one towel?"

Marol answered, "No. Another resident left a towel in a locker. He figured it was good for several days."

Toque looked puzzled. "So how in heaven's name did someone get access to the shelter's towels?"

Marol agreed with their bewilderment. "That's what I wondered and I called the shelter to ask them about the process of getting clean ones."

"And?" asked Toque.

Marol went on, "Every day the shelter gets a new delivery. The company that brings them in comes before wake-up, so the towels are left in a covered area in the lane behind the building."

Brock thought for a moment, then asked, "So, you're certain that someone deliberately sprayed them down with a virus that caused the infections?"

"Unfortunately, yes. All of the shelter occupants are infected with some degree of staphylococcal bacteria. The towels infected many of the residents right away because any number of the homeless have compromised immune systems to begin with. And making matters worse, was the shared contaminated surfaces existing in the shelter."

"Holy crap," retorted Brock

Marol grimaced. "I can't imagine anyone so perverse as to start an outbreak in a homeless shelter."

Toque looked at Brock and wondered if they were both thinking the same thing, just before she suggested, "Would you say it's time to again try the home of the Cudmores, and see what Peanut was up to over the past week?"

Brock scowled, answering, "Definitely worth a visit. I'm more than curious about his reaction to all this. Yet the oil leak thing has me miffed. I rechecked all the parking areas by the shelter and there is no evidence of a leak as there was at all the other sites."

"Perhaps the oil leaks aren't a real clue."

"Certainly possible," said Brock, "All we can do is keep looking and asking questions."

"I'm with you on that. Why don't we first drop by the Cashdiscount at Cap Mall, then visit Peanut?"

"Good idea," said Brock, then after a brief pause added, "And even though I can't see how a person who is doing a great job of becoming a new Canadian would be involved in Old Testament plagues, why don't we go see Yana Vasiliev after the store and the Cudmores?"

"Why not? Might strike it lucky in one out of three."

A few hours later, in the family's stately West Vancouver home, Peanut sat on an overstuffed beige leather recliner: eyes momentarily glazed over as he fixated on Toque who sat across from him, on a matching leather love seat. Beside her sat Brock, though in Peanut's mind, Toque might as well have been sitting there alone. In his blind-sighted imagination, he was alone with her. He imagined himself pulling her towards him: in his mind's eye his underdeveloped scrawny form changed into that of a lean, mean, and desirable man.

Brock cleared his throat. "We're wondering what you were doing in the early mornings
over the past week."

Toque's lips parted and Peanut's fantasy re-emerged. He imagined his lips on hers and her body pressed against him. Her bullet-proof vest that was mattress-like and squarish under
her regulation cop shirt, replaced by a lacey pink camisole, her nipples hardened under the imaginary soft silk in the room that, in his mind, had turned just a little bit cool. His bare chest against hers. His groin against ... but then, in the real world, she spoke, "For our records we need to know your whereabouts when ..."

Reality crashed in on poor Peanut but he tried to present himself as a dignified man of the world who knew his rights. "I do not have to answer your questions because ..." For a minute he considered the excuse of being a minor but then glanced at Toque – how he longed to touch her, to measure up. He grasped at words, thought for only seconds, of saying that his mother should be present but then found in the recesses of his mind a more adult response. "Because I have a right to legal representation."

Brock held back the urge to moan, but inaudibly grumbled, "Of course."

Peanut smiled at the success of his excuse, then gave Brock the once-over, seeing a man who clearly was a babe magnet.

Toque smiled. "Yes, but we just wanted to speak to you because I am hoping ..." She looked Peanut directly in the eyes.

Peanut almost quaked when she directly addressed him, glanced at Brock, then mentally dismissed Brock as a mere service person, probably wrongly celebrated as a hero in the Lions Gate incident of terror. *In fact,* thought Peanut, *Both these cops are lower in cast than I am – after all, I will be a great scientist someday.* Toque continued to look at him, eyes fixed on his. *She wants me, I think she instinctively knows my true worth. Or perhaps she has access to my school grades and knows what a catch I am.*

Peanut straightened, pumped his scrawny chest and boldly stared back into Toque's eyes. Brock was again of no consequence in Peanut's mind. As he spoke, Peanut tried to deepen his voice, saying, "For you, I could answer a few questions, but understand that it is a personal favour ... to you."

"Great!" resounded Brock, ignoring the 'to you.'

Peanut ignored Brock's remark but continued his gaze upon Toque.

Toque, realizing that she was the object of teenage raging hormones, smiled. "So, what about the early mornings last week? Between six-thirty and seven-thirty?"

"Give or take an hour," added Brock.

Peanut smiled as he leaned towards Toque. "Unfortunately, I was alone in my queen size bed between six-thirty and seven-thirty."

"Anyone to back-up your statement?" asked Toque.

"And before and after that time frame?" repeated Brock.

Peanut frowned, as if having to ward of an annoying insect, but then another thought rifled through his mind and a glimmer of a smile formed on his face. "You mean was I sleeping with someone?"

"Exactly," added Toque, playing along with Peanut's fantasy.

"No, on my own, this time round," replied Peanut, in a tone that implied he'd had various trysts in his queen size bed.

Brock raised an eyebrow, but nodded as if he believed in Peanut's sexual exploits.

"Peanut pumped his chest further, thinking that he was being taken seriously, "On my own ... last week."

"The property surveillance cameras can prove that?"

Peanut's eyes narrowed. "Of course. But I've already said more than I should. If you want the recordings from the surveillance system you need to get a warrant and I will have to involve legal counsel."

"As you wish," responded Toque, gaining another lustful smile from the high school teenager as he leaned even closer. Ear wax smell again.

"But while we are here, could you tell us if you drive anything other than your BMW?" asked Brock.

Peanut looked exasperated as he replied, "I wanted a Ferrari but all my parents would get me is the beamer."

***

Two days later, in the cruiser, Brock remarked, "So, the Cashdiscount store implicated young adults buying a ton of balloons the week of the blood on the school."

"Yeah, the store clerk remembered a handful of teens who acted like they thought they were going to get away with something. Unfortunately, she wasn't sure if there was three or more."

"But she did think that Peanut might have been one of them, but said she couldn't say for sure."

Toque frowned, adding, "Unfortunately."

"Plus, the tapes at Peanut's property showed that he was at home when the towels were done at the shelter."

"Peanut does seem like a dead end and there was nothing new at the Vasilievs." Toque felt the back of her neck, as she added, "Though I was glad that there weren't any more creepy insects."

"Not even her brother."

"So, you're still thinking that Borya might be around?"

"I'm worried about it. I think I'd better again talk to one of my neighbours, Rita, who complained about a strange guy at the marina."

"Similar to Borya?"

"Could be. But shit, I just remembered that Rita said she saw him again a second time – when Rex hurt his paw. But I was mainly focused on Rex. Rita just might be able to add to her story."

"You want me to join you?"

"Nah. Rita's kind of shy. I'll let you know if she comes up with anything."

***

Sitting in his four-by-four beater in the marina parking lot, Brock could see the multitude of boats decorated with Christmas lights. One sailing vessel was all in red: lights all across the cabin,

all the way up its two masts, the halyards, and all around the entire toe rail. Another boat owner had built a huge multi-coloured Christmas tree from his mast, on top of which was a lighted angel. Owners of yet another vessel had formed a huge star that went all the way from the deck to the top of the mast. The star pulsated and rotated through the colours of white, red, purple, blue, and green. In all, at least two-thirds of the vessels had some sort
of display.

As soon as Brock opened the marina gate, Rex pounced, euphoric at the return of his best friend, and was soon happily licking Brock's right hand.

"Hey boy, how's your day been?"

"Woof."

"Great." Then, just as Brock reached the base of the marina's ramp, Rex turned towards the pier leading to the *Angel*.

"Rex, wait – first we're going to have a little visit," said Brock as he headed towards Rita's boat. Dutifully, Rex soon turned and joined alongside.

Within a minute, Brock tapped on the hull of the vintage wooden vessel named Fusilier. Then, no sooner had the tap resounded when a voice crackled from within, sounding as if those vocal chords hadn't been used in the last week. "What do you want?"

"It's your neighbour, Brock."

Then the sound of hasty rustling ensued. In seconds, the generously proportioned Rita threw open her cabin door and emerged – dressed in a multi-coloured Kaftan garment appearing as if it had been just shipped in from India. On her feet were fur-lined ankle-height slippers while her V-neck front gave more than a hint of the ample breasts beneath. But because the neckline was low and because the slit up the side of the garment's lower half showed nothing but bare skin, there was the distinct impression that the only thing under the Kaftan was Rita.

Brock glanced at the spans of skin between the top of her slippers and her hip-line and coughed.

"It's you!" she said. Then changing her tone, asked, "What can I do for you?"

Brock grimaced a smile. "Sorry to interrupt, Rita. But you mentioned that when Rex was hurt, you again saw the man who had been asking for me – and that he ran off?"

Rex heard his name and his ears perked up.

"Sure – the guy with the accent."

"Do you remember anything more about him?"

"Yeah. I thought about it quite a bit after I saw him that second time. I was meaning to tell you but I didn't see you again …"

"Not a problem. But you feel that you might be able to add something?"

"I think so. Although he was repugnant, if you could get past that, he was actually quite handsome, although at my age …"

"You said he had fair skin and hair."

"He did. And hazel-brown eyes."

Realizing that not much was happening, Rex sat down, with a bit of a harrumph, and then eyed a couple of mallards passing by.

Brock, though, was more interested in what Rita had to say. His eyes opened wider. "Oh? Anything else? You thought that he was just over six-feet."

"I think so. That was probably the case. But wait, now I remember … his build … he looked strong but not heavy-set. And as I said, initially kind of handsome. But never mind, I'm an old woman, and in the end, he was revolting."

"Revolting?"

"Yeah, I again started to get a bad feeling about him. And he bad-mouthed Rex." Rita glanced away, then buried her hands in her pockets as she chilled in the December air.

Brock thought about Rex, and reached down to scratch him in one of his favorite spots, just under the collar. "So … an accent, fair skin, hazel-brown eyes, just over six feet,
reasonably good looking and a lighter-weight build?"

"That's it."

Brock scowled as he thought, *Like Borya*.

"Why? You know him?"

Brock shook his head. "I hope not. But you said he had a Bible?"

"You've got a good memory! But yeah, at the time I thought

that it was odd, him carrying it. I think that it was the type with the Old Testament ... and like I probably told you, it was bookmarked."

"Could it have been less than a quarter of the way through?"

"Oh, let me think ... probably less than that."

Brock smiled. "Thanks, Rita. Let me know if you think of anything else."

Rex eyed Rita, hoping for more of a visit, but to his disappointment, with a slight smile Rita accepted the thanks, then moved back down her hatch. "Sure ..."

CHAPTER 70

Brock leaned back on a wooden chair at a window table in Muriel's. The warm Murano lights of the coffee shop were a welcome warm contrast to the wet, dark outside.

He fumed. "Boils! What kind of sicko would infect a homeless shelter?"

"As if those people don't have enough to deal with," added Toque.

"Exactly. Things seem to be taking a nasty turn."

Toque sighed. "And I really hated seeing those horses suffer. Bad enough to torment a human target. But hurting a defenseless animal is just plain sick."

"Absolutely. The locusts caused less suffering, but it was still pretty shitty."

"Well, yeah, but the lice were really gross. I had to put everything I had on in the freezer which in itself wasn't that big a deal, but I had to empty it to get everything in."

"But you know the word is on what's next in line?" asked Brock.

"Something new?"

"Yes: a flood."

"No!" Toque paused, thinking, then asking, "A different threat? What happened to the oldest in care? And how does flooding fit into our Bible series – the Plagues of Egypt? I wonder if the flood is like Noah's Arc? But the mix is confusing."

"That's what the brass are trying to figure out."

Toque grimaced. "I wish someone would figure out what the hell is going on."

"You and me both."

"Could it be that someone is working loosely from the Old Testament?" suggested Toque.

"But why? If some extremist is wanting some sort of vengeance, he's not going to be consulting a Bible as a play book."

"Exactly. And who's walking around with a book-marked Old Testament?"

Brock's eyes widened as a remembrance suddenly occurred: "Shit! I DO know of someone!"

"You've got to be kidding!"

"Borya!"

"You're back onto the topic of Borya again?"

"You can bet on it! I just I revisited my neighbor, Rita, about the stranger, that, with every additional detail, sounded more and more like Borya. And what's even more crazy is that he was carrying an Old Testament!"

"No way!"

"And it was book-marked near the beginning: possibly in Exodus, which is where the Plagues of Egypt are located."

"Crap! Have you told the brass?"

"I sure as hell will, now."

CHAPTER 71

Toque sat in her condo thinking while studying her computer screen.

A flood! But how could a flood be engineered? A water main breaking? Let's look at a geographic map of Vancouver – no – West and North Vancouver are where most of the so-called plagues have been happening – now where could a flood be caused? The waterfront? Bombing the seawall – nah – no significant collateral damage. Start an avalanche on one of the mountains? Probably not. After all, it's only snow and again, on the North Shore: not much potential damage in terms of real estate or large events but maybe – if the snow could be released, it could wipe out a line-up of skiers. But no, the ski runs are too hard-packed. What else?

Toque stared at the map on the computer and her eyes fell onto the reservoirs. First she eyed the Seymour reservoir but thought, *No, too far from development.* Then her eyes fell onto the Capilano reservoir.

H-m-m-m-m-m. Could that be it? But there isn't much built beneath the reservoir's dam. There are a few houses near the base of the river, plus a few high-rises, but they're so far away: at worst, their basements would be flooded from a breach in the dam. Whatever: I should check it out, just to see if there is anything not apparent from the satellite map. I'm probably totally off track. But just to have a better picture in my mind, I'll stop by the dam on my way in tonight – to see if I'm over-looking anything.

Just a couple of hours later, Toque arrived at the Capilano River Regional Park. She stopped in the almost-empty parking lot, where sat only a couple of lonely blackened cars, seemingly abandoned. And off in the darkest corner was a parked motor home. *Perhaps someone is illegally staying here over night,* she thought. *I'll check it later.* Toque then focussed her eyes on the pagoda-style building which was an access point to the pipeline that channeled this reservoir's water into that of Mount Seymour.

It doesn't seem that many homes below could be flooded, if any. I looked around at the few streets on the way and there's very little there. And the high-rises at the foot of Cap are too far off, and West Vancouver has only a few homes and they're well above the likely water level, thought Toque as she climbed the wide stair case, then onto the pea-gravel path leading across the rolling grassed park grounds. She reached the crest of the path, took a few steps forward on the grass, and looked out over the lake-like waters of the reservoir where by moonlight the mountain peaks quietly stood above their shining reflections.

For the briefest of moments, Toque thought that she heard the sound of a something other than the noises of the park ... but then entirely filling the blackened air, and almost drowned out by the rush of water cascading downwards from the face of the dam, were the resonant swishes of the towering giant firs, cedars, and hemlocks.

As Toque climbed the hill, Borya, Egor and Ras had just reached the top of the stairs that ran alongside the dam itself.

"Is that the bitch cop?" questioned Borya.

Ras smiled. "I think my moment has come."

"Stop thinking about your prick – what if she is onto us?"

"All the more reason to shut her up ... after some fun."

"Think again, asshole," cursed Borya, "We can't risk a cop seeing the three of us together. It was a really bad choice to jump that motorcycle mom. But at least she wouldn't have recognized us."

Egor scowled. "Our day passes are up in an hour. This is a great spot for a meeting but now we've got to get back."

"I'm sure we have time," argued Ras, "Plus, how will anyone know it's us scouting around?"

"You assholes! The cops here have ways."

"But where's the cameras?" asked Ras, "I tell you, these jerks can't even tie up their own shoe laces ... or zip their flies!"

"But you have to admit that it would be cool to do that cop. Maybe help out with the breeding here," drooled Egor.

"Ha, ha. Good point. We can film it and send it to that shithead cop," smiled Ras, as he fingered the growing member in his pants.

"We can stick it on the net! Man, that would be great!" added Egor.

"Idiots! Then they'll know that we were the ones that did her!" snarled Borya.

Ras snorted. "The camera's not going to be on our faces. All they'll see is the parts that count – and – they'll see her face ... we can wait till she's conscious for that. You know, there's money to be made in snuff films. A cop being done, then snuffed will be worth a fortune. Especially that cop!"

Borya narrowed his eyes. "If I let you do this ..."

"But we all get a turn," interrupted Egor.

Borya scowled. "I'm out. But you two can have your jollies but I'm not plugging into any cop trash. If we go with this, the final stage of the plan must go as I say."

"You mean no touching the children?"

"Exactly, especially my nephew. Throats only. The knife will be able to take care of it in no time."

Ras shook his head. "I really don't know. You've said yourself they're no better than a liter of hogs, worse in many ways, than their parents."

Egor frowned, saying, "Get a grip, will you? The worst of all, are defectors like Borya's sister and husband who were raised to know better."

While Borya continued look annoyed, Ras sighed. "Okay. But I get first dibs on the cop cunt."

With the search for detail as part of her training, Toque proceeded along the grassy knoll over-looking the reservoir. She was almost upon a staircase that led down and onto the top of the dam which was both road and pedestrian walkway. There, just out of her sight range, were the waiting three men.

Flanking the lane leading from Capilano Road to the dam was a grove of trees in which hid Egor, Ras, and Borya. Having climbed the staircase alongside the dam, they hovered while waiting for their prey.

When she reached the bottom of the stairs leading from the grassy area over-looking the reservoir, Toque paused on one of the darkest patches of the empty lane. Briefly, she glanced in the direction of the hidden threesome. Then, without seeing any movement, focused her attention on the dam ahead, and was about to proceed in that direction.

But Ras smiled with anticipation, then sneered a starter's command, "Now's the time!"

The three of them rushed Toque and before she had time to react, the men had her pinned to the ground.

"Get your cell phone flash-light in her eyes. Then she can't identify us, if we let her live. If! And put your cell on video record and I'll go first," ordered Ras as he reached for the zipper on her jacket.

Toque screamed for all she was worth but before seconds passed, Borya had his hand clamped on her mouth as he spit out, "Shut up, you fucking whore!"

Egor tugged on Ras's collar. "Fuck you, I go first. You record it."

"Why? It was my idea!"

"Because you're a cockroach, plus you know everything that goes right for us is because of me!"

Borya forced a belligerent snarl. "Oh! And what a success you are!"

"Me, first," Ras insisted, still getting nowhere with Toque's zipper.

Toque writhed and kicked but was no match for three men.

Just seconds before the three of them rushed Toque, Sun and Boucher moved into the vicinity in their cruiser, down the gravel road from West Vancouver, then stopped in the turn-around on their side of the dam. Just as Boucher opened the car door in readiness for a look-around, they heard Toque's scream.

"What was that? It sounded like a woman's scream!" shouted Lily.

"I thought that this stop was going to be another big zero but that *was* a scream!" asserted Boucher.

"Call for back-up. And let North Van know we're crossing into their zone."

The cruiser tore off, covering the few hundred yards across the dam. Siren blazing. In the light shed from their head-lamps, they could see three individuals and a fourth person downed. Borya, Egor and Ras stared at the approaching vehicle, momentarily stunned at seeing a car in so isolated an area. But their motionless gaze soon turned to fear for their own survival and the three turned and fled, running through the circles of light shed by the occasional street lamp along the road of the darkened park.

Another West Vancouver cruiser arrived and tore down the gravel road, bringing in Karimi and Trembley.

Brock, in North Vancouver, was on his way to his shift when heard the call. As was often his habit, he had his cell connected to the vehicle's blue tooth and the software channel for those on active policing duty.

"I'm on my way in and am on Cap Road, almost at the turn-off to Highway One. Any one active near me?" asked Brock.

Dispatch replied, "All cruisers are some distance away or are engaged. Can you take it?"

"I'm on it!"

As Brock sped up the road, there were few cars around. However, there were half a dozen vehicles, two of which Brock had to tear past in the oncoming traffic lane, with fist on the horn, forcing the vehicles into the bicycle lane. Then, just as he passed the fountain that benchmarked the crossroad to Edgemont Village, coming from the opposite direction, a speeding motor home streaked around, then past him.

He flashed through his memory banks as he recalled the list that included a motor-home at each site. For a second he considered a chase, but realized it might be nothing more than a wild goose one, at that. So, he only cursed them, though he did try to see the driver. All he could discern was that each of the front seats was occupied. He caught a brief glimpse of the driver, but it was only a glance.

In minutes, Brock careened into the space between the road and the gate to the park and skidded sideways as he slammed on the brakes.

Two men who had been running towards the gate, came to an abrupt stop, realizing that they'd just lost the three who'd tore off in their vehicle. It was Karimi and Trembley who were then standing still and annoyed at missing an arrest. They had arrived in their cruiser just a little too late, although they'd put in a good show trying.

Brock bolted from his seat, yanked open the gate and in no time broke into a sprint, and in seconds caught up to Karimi and Trembly who were then running towards the victim. They came to a halt beside Sun who was holding the downed Toque while Boucher rested a comforting hand on Toque's shoulder.

Brock, Karimi and Trembley where shocked, seeing the face of the victim. It was Toque!

She was shell-shocked: at first no words would come, though in earnest she tried to stand. But as she did, she tried to take control of the state of her inner chaos, croaking a few words of self-assertiveness, saying, "I'm okay. I can get up."

Sun and Boucher stepped back. But then Toque wavered and looked as if she was going to fall, and as Brock swung forward to help, was pushed aside by Trembley who was also trying to assist, as was Karimi, who was on Toque's other side. In no time, Karimi and Trembley were on either arm, trying to help support her.

"What happened?" demanded Brock.

"Three guys jumped her," explained Sun.

"But we got here in time, just after she was downed!" added Boucher.

"Shit!" swore Brock.

"It's okay. I'm alright," said Toque, half whimpering, making it obvious that she was shaken. She tried to pry herself from Karimi and Trembley's grips but they held tight.

Brock was deeply disturbed by the assault, feelings that were exasperated by the two male officers, on either side, who also needed to back off a little. He frowned but then with appreciation looked at Sun and Boucher while he said, "Sure glad you two got here on time."

Toque managed to verbalize, "Me, too," though was too overwhelmed to express any more.

"I expect one of you will phone in a report?" questioned Brock.

"Will do, but it isn't much. They were running before we reached her. Didn't see them well enough to get an ID," explained Sun.

"Yeah. And by the time we got here, the three guys were almost at the parking lot," explained Trembley.

Brock frowned. "Okay. Report what you can. And Toque, I'll drive you to the detachment hall. We'll get your car later when you're feeling better."

Toque tried to move, yet Karimi and Trembley held fast.

Both Sun and Boucher watched and inwardly flinched.

Brock, too, reacted. He stepped forward and crowded their space as he said, "Okay. Thanks, guys." And then, after a pause, added, "I'll be taking her in."

Brock clenched his jaw as he reached for Toque's arm. Almost simultaneously, Karimi and Trembley let go, and stepped back. Brock, too, dropped his hand because at the very moment she was released, Toque suddenly gained her where-with-all and strode – almost sauntered, towards the parking lot and the general area where Brock had left his vehicle.

By the time Toque and Brock reached the top of the staircase leading to the parking lot, Sun and Boucher had already started their cruiser. A little slower, Karimi and Trembley paused in the darkness of the gravel turn-around, sensing some undefinable loss.

CHAPTER 72

Toque and Brock, both in uniform, sat in Muriel's Coffee Shop. Brock had his usual coffee: black, no milk, no sugar and Cheesesnacks, an item Muriel had started stocking for Brock's benefit. Toque had her usual: rose hip tea and a carrot muffin.

Brock faced Toque, thinking about the attack she'd suffered in the park. "You're looking a lot better – your colour is back to normal."

"Yeah, but it was bordering on devastating! I felt so helpless!"

"Got to give the West Vaners credit for combing the back roads."

"Thank goodness for that, especially Sun and Boucher."

"But my hat's off to you – very few could bounce back and then put in a full shift."

"You know better than anyone what I've been through in the past. That those three didn't get anywhere, made it less excruciating ... that is ... compared to ..."

"Still ... it had to be traumatic."

"Yes ... it could have been the end to any peace of mind that I still ..."

"Or worse." He focussed on Toque's eyes, relieved that she was still more or less together mentally ... and alive. But then he spoke more in her direction than to her face, "You described the attackers to the brass?"

"I don't even want to think about it again but ..."

"But what?" Brock asked.

Toque heaved a sigh and closed her eyes, as if by closing them she could erase the image of the assault. "It was dark ... and I could be mistaken ... but ..."

"Come on. Spit it out."

"I think that there was a resemblance to the Bogdanov brothers, and ..."

"And who? Not ..."

"The third could have been Borya," said Toque, confirming Brock's unspoken suspicion.

"Another indication that he could be here: just like the two sightings at the marina. But there he was, as if he had just appeared out of nowhere – bothering poor Rita. Sort of like a demon – except in Borya's case, he's more like a bottom feeding form of low-life."

"That attack in the park was a real-life nightmare!"

"It had to be terrible! But it makes me think: that you, Marol and I were all jumped by three …"

"I know! But unlike with you and Marol, the guys who got me weren't wearing baklavas."

"Maybe you were just at the wrong place, wrong time."

"Maybe …"

"But, at least that Borya might be around is now being taken seriously. But unfortunately, the status of Egor and Ras is unchanged: they still get ten-hour passes every day. And there is no lid on whoever attacked Marol, like the guys that brass-knuckled me on Denman. So, unless you can …"

"Like I said, Brock, I thought that it may have been them. But making a positive ID is virtually impossible, if I had to swear beyond any doubt – not only was it dark, but they shone a cell phone flashlight in my eyes. I was blinded."

"I get it. But shit, let's just hope that when Borya is caught, we get a confession about the assaults … and the infestations – the ones that they could have been involved with," mused Brock.

"That's a lot to hope for. There is a strong likelihood that whoever did the infestations and sabotage is someone different altogether. Plus, Borya is like a snake in the underbrush."

CHAPTER 73

Approaching the glass wall separating Vancouver airport's customs and immigration was a wiry man with a pale pitted complexion, who was wearing a taupe suit and a collared tired-looking black shirt that had faded to almost grey. As the shirt was wrinkled and unbuttoned, one could see a little of his hairless bleached-white chest peering out beneath. On his feet were well-used dress shoes, that were brown and bent with slightly curled-up toes and the edge of the heels were worn almost to the sole of the shoe. Over his shoulder hung a cloth bag woven with a geometric pattern in a variety of tan-coloured threads. The bag held specific herbs to aid the man's purpose, and two dog-eared hard-cover books, no bigger than small pocket books, with pages yellowed and worn by age and use. Just inside the front cover of one of the books was a yellowish hand-made piece of paper, seemingly shaped to match the scale of the undersized book that acted as a carrier.

Being an international airport, no one even glanced at this mousey arrival.

As he exited the airport, Ras rushed out, then ushered the visiting enchanter to the waiting parked green motor home, with Egor at the steering wheel.

Egor sized-up the new arrival, then without a greeting, ordered, "Sit in the back."

The visitor looked insulted as he responded, "I have come all this way from my distant home, first travelling by bike, then freighter, then plane, to grant your request. And I can tell you now that there are lots better things I could spend my resources on than travel business attire. Making myself inconspicuous! Why? Even second-hand, it set me back. I cannot understand how you even got the knife, never mind my home number," complained the self-taught enchanter.

"We find out lots of interesting stuff in prison, though we're pissed that in the daytime we're stuck on the outside with a mandated supervisor: a barely-awake parole officer."

"Stuck here? Surely you could make it to the border somehow or another? There has to be any number of ways you could get out of the country if you really want."

The motor home exited the parking area and was soon moving down the road. Egor dismissed the stranger's suggestion, grumbling, "Easier said than done. Getting smuggled out of the country is almost impossible with no contacts, to say nothing of the fact that we have almost no cash and that the authorities will be after us in no time if the parole officer misses us or we don't make the regular check-in."

"So now I'm dragged into your miserable lives. Without question, I would not be here at your request if it wasn't for your second cousin who sought me out and threatened to expose my practice."

"Of course. We asked him to give you a visit you'd remember." Ras smiled at his thinly veiled admission.

"Threatening my family – that was just too much!"

"So, you saved them and your practice! You're almost done with us. You'll be home as soon as you do us the favour!"

The enchanter scowled, saying, "Favour! Hardly! As I said, I am here only because of your cousin's threats. If it was just me, I would have stayed home and suffered whatever he planned. But your cousin threatened my sister, and her children. I have absolutely no desire to be involved in your evil plans."

"Sucks to be you," smirked Egor.

The motor home moved down the road further, pulling into a bar-restaurant overlooking
the Strait of Georgia and the runways of the Vancouver International Airport.

"It is because the knife has already been enchanted, that additional incantation conditions will be much shorter than the originals, though they will be an appendix to what has already been written," explained the reluctant visitor.

The three exited the vehicle and walked over to a picnic table. The noise of the afternoon crowd in the bar flaunted the seriousness of their meeting.

"A list of incantation conditions! I'm not happy about that at all," muttered Egor.

The enchanter thought to himself, *What a self-absorbed ignoramus,* but said, "You'll have to live with it. That is the way it works. I have brought the incantation conditions with me, and as before, they are written on a piece of aged papyrus from the Nile Valley and are written in Edwardian script."

"Oh, crap! No way!" asserted Ras.

"You two would rather I not proceed?" asked the enchanter, thinking to himself, *If only ... This knife is too important to be in the hands of these slack-jawed stooges.*

Egor snarled. "Shit! Go ahead, then. After you're done, we can get out of this miserable damp cold and get back before we're missed."

The enchanter accepted the go-ahead and paused briefly while he mentally readied himself for the process. Then, the incantation began: he chanted, he sprinkled dusty powder on the knife. He chanted more, and, at the same time, sprinkled another batch of powder, then waved the knife back and forth while chanting. Then he reached into his cloth bag and extracted three packets holding mysterious materials, extracted some, and threw them onto the knife and spit on the powder, then rubbed it with his middle finger, as if trying to force the material into the knife. Then more chanting, followed by a flailing of the knife. Then silence.

Then there was an enormous cracking sound from the gloomy skies above and the whole world went silent. Not a sound. Even from the adjacent bar crowd. A minute passed. Five minutes passed. An inexplicable heat formed suddenly so that an uncomfortable stickiness formed between their bodies and clothing. Ten more minutes passed and a distant rumbling seemed to shake the soil beneath them.

It was when five more minutes had passed when the three could hear the road and air traffic noises and the sound of the people in the bar. With the return of the familiar noises, the enchanter stood, picked up the knife, and handed it to Egor, saying, "I have now completed the knife's re-enchantment. As before, the text on the knife must be read and recited by the user of this weapon. Once read, the enchanted knife is powerful and ready to use. To cancel that power, the conditions are given in this verse:

The vice of the knife will not waken
If held by a lover who is much deceived
And says these words to be relieved,
'The evil here by good is taken.'"

***

Later that day, the enchanter sat in the brightly lit room of the boarding area at one of the gates in the airport.

Meanwhile, Egor and Ras drove along a twilight-grey highway.

"We can toss this stupid poetry shit out the window," laughed Ras.

"Light it on fire – first," smirked Egor.

With a grin, Ras lit the aged papyrus on fire, and tossed it from the window, and had it not been for the sudden onslaught of rain, might have been a problem. But all was safe in the wet landscape as the written conditions settled into a murky ditch, where the ink bled into not even a hint of what had been recorded there.

In just under an hour, Ras and Egor were back in North Vancouver, returning to Borya the well-used green motor home.

As they exited the vehicle, they glanced at the box on the floor behind the seats and smiled, though Borya just eyed the shape for a minute longer than he might have ... otherwise. In another life, he might have gone as far as cheering, though at this time, his mood was entirely dominated by his now-permanent sour frame of mind.

CHAPTER 74

Toque stood by her clothes dryer with the end of a wet towel in her hand, the bulk of it still in the dryer with the other wet linens. She frowned, thinking, *Dam! I forgot to turn on the dryer!*

Then, while stark naked, and dripping wet, her phone buzzed. She shook her head as she moved over to her dinette set and paused without sitting on any of the four canvas-topped, wooden framed chairs. Her hair shed drops of moisture, still present from the shower and a multitude of other water drops dripped down her form, but especially on her back, rolling down, then dropping to the floor and leaving their glass bead-like rounded formations on the pale pine flooring. On Toque, goose bumps formed, especially on her arms while her nipples hardened from the chill of having just stepped out the shower.

Her cell beeped again. She picked up the phone. Her mood suddenly crashed when she glanced at the phone's message.

Crap! Lynn and Joe are at the door! I don't even want to think about what they are here for!

She hurried back into her bathroom and grabbed a dark-flowered robe, and tied it closed with a wide over-size matching belt, then slipped on a pair of worn purple with brown polka-dot terry-cloth slippers, dashed into the bedroom, tied her hair into a quick knot, then stuffed it under a mustard-green toque. If she could have gotten away with putting on clown-like sunglasses, she would have done it.

Just as she tucked a delinquent strand of hair under the toque, there was a knock on the door, followed by the too-anxious ringing of the doorbell. As she hesitantly moved towards her entrance, Toque wondered if she should just pretend that she wasn't home. But before giving the idea serious thought, leaned towards the door and peered through the security peep-hole. There they were.

Lynn seemed less butch than usual, although her hair was extremely short. She wore an ensemble which looked brand new: a crisp white collared shirt covered with tiny fleur-de-lis and a soft green angora cardigan over slacks, and a loose scarf.

Joe was still like a poster boy for his current role as a federal party leader candidate: he had a handsome look. His broad chest seemed to bulge under his light blue casual shirt unbuttoned at the collar, with a hint of curly auburn chest hair visible.

The two of them could have been a couple, had it not been obvious that Lynn preferred mainly women.

Toque cringed at the sight of them. The last time she saw Joe was when he disappeared, disserting her at the convention center.

As for the last time she saw Lynn – it was worse: it was when they were in bed together and Brock walked in.

Toque's hand paused at the door handle, as if she might not open it. She hadn't said a word to let her visitors know that she was home. As she tried to get herself stabilized, on the other side of the door, Lynn spoke, "Hey, Toque, it's your climbing buddies! Are you still sleeping off your work day?"

"Not at all," answered Toque as she opened the door, though with considerable reluctance.

"Well, come on then. Let us in!"

"Yeah, Toque," added Joe, "We want to talk to you about something serious."

In seconds the three of them were sitting in Toque's living room: Lynn sat on one of the canvas love-seats; Joe on the other; while Toque had brought in a dinette chair and was sitting facing them and the coffee table that held the bowl of toffees brought by Joe on a previous visit.

Lynn jumped into the conversation first, saying, "Joe and I have been having a disagreement with what is going on between the two of us."

"You and me?" asked Toque.

"Of course," replied Lynn, eyeing Toque's ankle that was bare under the robe as it shifted and opened, exposing one whole calf and knee. And water droplets on her ankle, and a few moving down her calf.

Momentarily, the visitors eyed the lucky droplets.

"But what about the two of us?" interrupted Joe, further perusing the casual opening of Toque's robe, and wishing for more. He continued, "Except for the bloody locusts, that convention seemed like it was the beginning of something serious."

Lynn's eyes narrowed.

"You should have seen the people looking at us. We were perfect," exclaimed Joe.

"Well, uh," stammered Toque.

"But, another thing, don't you remember when the three of us …" started Joe.

"I remember much better when it was just Toque and I," interrupted Lynn, "It was the best!"

"I don't know … but …." mumbled Toque as she leaned back, unintentionally causing her robe to open at the top, showing cleavage.

"Come on, darling, I know you were into it," prodded Lynn, leaning towards Toque, grabbing a toffee, depositing it in her mouth, then leaning forward further, resting her hand on Toque's uncovered knee.

"Listen, if you want to be a dyke, that's one thing: I understand. I prefer a twosome myself. But, what the heck, I'm open: the three of us were once about to become really good together," said Joe as he, too, reached forward, brushed aside the robe that still covered one of Toque's legs, then planted his hand firmly on Toque's freshly-uncovered knee.

Toque stood up, and hands fell away while she re-wrapped her robe, tightened the belt, moved her chair back a couple of feet, sat down, pulled her knees together, and raised her voice, "Listen guys, I think I need a time-out."

"What? You're throwing me over?" questioned Joe as he, too, grabbed a toffee, and tossed it into his mouth.

"Is there another woman?" asked Lynn.

"Or guy?" asked Joe as he glanced at the drip marks left when Toque stood naked by her dinette.

Toque thought briefly of Brock, and wished that he was there, and not the two in front of her, but then Toque shook her head, as if she could shake away her thoughts.

"Or both a guy and a girl?" questioned Lynn, looking more worried, also noticing the drip marks.

"No. I just want time-out!"

"Don't you realize that you could be a prime-minister's wife?" asked Joe, as if offering a prize.

"Oh, so you think you're going to be moving to Sussex Drive? You haven't won anything yet!" snarled Lynn.

"As a matter of fact, I will win. And I will move to Sussex Drive."

"In your dreams!" sneered Lynn.

"It doesn't matter. I just need time out," insisted Toque.

"How about the climbing?" asked Lynn.

"Not likely, for the immediate future, anyway. All I know is that I need time to myself. Alone."

"By yourself? Great! You're just as bad as my ex. Poof! It's suddenly over! And I'm left with nothing!" moaned Lynn.

"Isn't that what you started out with?" asked Joe, sarcastically.

"Let's forget the wise cracks, and just stop. Maybe you two could be together," suggested Toque.

"That was a one-off. And only because you were there!"

"I'll say the same!" exclaimed Lynn.

"Well, all I can say is that I need to be alone," repeated Toque.

Joe scowled, got up, and as he reached the door, said, with his volume too loud, "Take all the time you want. But I'm not waiting. I get offers every day. I don't need you two crazies."

"Don't take it so hard. It's me. I need to work it out. Please," cried Toque.

"How couldn't I?" questioned Joe.

"I just can't believe that you want me out, as well," cried Lynn.

"I'm afraid so."

"No. It just can't be. We were perfect together."

Joe, stinging from rejection, grimaced and let out an abandoned whelp-like moan.

Toque hung her head. "I'm so sorry, but I have to say that I wasn't sure about it all along and …"

"So, it's over then," realized Lynn, feeling the impact of rejection.

"It is."

Lynn felt the sinking feeling that had become all too familiar. First, Carla telling her that she wanted a divorce. Complete devastation.

Then the judge giving Carla sole custody of their child, Nikki. Total emptiness. Her life a void. The child that had given so much joy – then torn from her. Then, when Lynn tried to see her beloved daughter with one of her impromptu visits that didn't coincide with any legally-granted visitation rights, one bitch at the daycare called the police. If only that other daycare worker had been there. The one who'd let her spend time with Nikki. That daycare worker – what was her name? Petra?

But since the break-up, all nights were long … and alone. Days alone. One running into the other. No work. No contacts. Absolute loneliness. But then … Toque came along, like a beautiful sunrise. Finally, the days had become worth getting up for; in fact, worth rushing into. There was an amazing hiatus of joy. But now … rejection. Again. A murky gloom filled Lynn's entire being and she felt as if she was carrying lead weights and as if she was moving through something much denser than air, just getting to the door. Her whole sense of worth and vitality were gone.

"Come on, then, we might as well leave together," mumbled Joe, so low that one might have missed the emotional break in his voice.

With that, the three climbing buddies ceased to be, as two of the three trudged their way from the suite and into the hallway, with only a tiny dissolving remnant of toffee left in each of their mouths.

Tears ran down Toque's face and she further tightened the belt on her robe, so that it
almost restricted her breathing, then got up to double-lock her door.

From far off in the distance, she could hear the muffled wail of a passing train.

Chapter 75

Once again, Brock and Toque pulled up to the home owned by Alik and Yana Vasiliev. When it was built, it was considered to be somewhat of a monster house because it over-sized all the houses in the neighbourhood. But almost thirty years later, it was one of many huge homes, in fact, it was one of the smaller ones. Except for the institutional grey marble tiled front, it was attractive enough in appearance: it was a traditional-styled house with generous peaks, textured stucco, and clever use of contrast in the colour scheme, with the stucco a soft green hue accented by bright ivory-white trim and detail.

As they approached, a very pregnant Yana had one of the teak-coloured double-doors open and greeted them with a smile.

"I am so glad to see you, constables."

"You're pretty open-minded, considering that we had to confiscate your aquariums."

"I know you're just doing your job. But what I need now is the little help."

Brock raised his eyebrow, then asked, "Help? Is there something wrong?"

"Oh, not really. I just need a help. You remember that I'm volunteering at the aquarium and helping with handicapped children?"

"Yeah?" responded Toque, confused as to where this was going.

"Well, I have five of my handicapped childrens visiting for tea and the medovik. Plus, my youngest, Vanna, stays home from daycare so that she can do visit with her friends."

"That's great that she's made new friends. But what is medovik?"

Yana smiled. "Yes, it is the favourite dessert from when I was the girl – made with honey, butter cream, and layered cakes, and topped with the nuts and icing sugar."

"Sounds yummy," remarked Toque, though still bewildered as to where this was going.

"Anayana," called a young voice from the living room behind Yana, "I need to go to the washroom!"

"Anayana?" questioned Brock.

"Oh, that, it is the shortened version of Aunt Yana."

"Sounds good to me," smiled Toque.

"Actually, a few friends have heard it, and are using its name as well. In fact, if you want, call me Anayana."

"Maybe when we're not here on police business."

"Oh, no. Is there something else?"

"Not to worry: we just want to go over a few things. But first, how did volunteering at the aquarium lead to you having these children visit?" asked Toque, eyeing up the five wheel-chair bound children seated by the same coffee table where also sat Yana's youngest, little Vanna.

Yana smiled. "The kids and their parents are member of the aquarium. Over time, we have become friends. They know me; they trusts me. For the kids, it is quite special to be invited to a home of the volunteer care-giver-guide – for them, it is like the field trip."

As Toque and Brock surveyed the kids, little Vanna poked one of their small guests in the ribs who then started to cry.

"Anayana, please. I can't wait …" cried another: the one who needed to visit the washroom.

Yana was over-whelmed. "I know this is a lot to ask, but I thought that we are friend, and like I said, I need you to …"

The child who couldn't wait started to wail. Yana glanced at the child, then at Toque and Brock. "Gosh, I don't know what to do or say first. But to further answer your question, at the aquarium while the children and I were having a snack, we started talking about desserts and when I told the children about my favorite, they wanted to try it. Then, in thinkings about it, I thought they'd might appreciates a little field trip to my home so they could see a little more of what life is like for a Russian new Canadian."

"I'm impressed," remarked Toque.

Another child started to wail, seemingly for no reason.

"Only thing is," continued Yana, "I think I have taken on more than I can handle. I've been trying to tell you that I need someone to pick up my boy, Matvey, at the daycare. They are closing soon and there is no ways I can get all of these kids in the vehicle and I cannot leave them here unsupervised."

"Anayana, I gotta go!" again interrupted a now panicky young voice, squirming in her chair.

Yana was totally flustered. Tears were starting to form in her eyes. She continued, "My Mom is off, volunteering as a cashier at a Salvation Army. I thought I'd be okay because Alik was supposed to be here but there was the big problem in one of his sites."

"What happened?" asked Brock.

"Anayana! I need you now to help me! Wa-h-h- h-h-h- h-h-h-h-h-h-h-h!"

"Oh, crap! Do I ever need the extra pair of hands!"

Or a gaggle of nannies, thought Toque.

Yana continued, "But Alik's issues are not to concern you. You remember the torrentials rain last night?" asked Yana.

"Yeah, they're now saying it was the worst rain on record! We seem to be breaking more and more records. I don't know what is going to be next!"

"Exactly. I worry about the flooding. It has happened but it seems like the potentials have been worse now. We didn't sleep at all well the night last, and I am beside myselves!" moaned Yana.

The child who had to go to the washroom changed her screaming to intermittent sniveling and sobbing, then screamed, "Now!"

Yana lost it. "Oh no! Alik should have been here and if at the other night, Borya hadn't …"

Yana stopped mid-phrase. An hour-long pause seemed to occur over the next few seconds while she madly thought about how she could continue to cover-up for her brother. "If Borya had not disappeared … he could be here helping." Yana was so overwhelmed with her slip-up and her needy situation that she started crying.

Both Brock and Toque kept their faces expressionless but both could spot the cover-up.

Brock spoke first, "You do the bathroom break, and we'll try to make peace with the children here."

Yana flushed, though the tears still ran down her face as she picked up the washroom-desperate child.

Toque knew it was not her job but sympathized with Yana. "And after the washroom break, we'll pick up Matvey. It will be a thrill for the daycare kids to see some real live constables."

When Yana left the room, Brock and Toque exchanged knowing looks. But to hide their suspicions, they calmed the children, then returned to the weather topic.

"Unfortunately Yana might be right. With all that snow from November, this series of Pineapple Express storms is melting that ton of snow," remarked Toque.

"I know what you mean. On the way to work, I heard that the avalanche rating is at extreme."

"Jeez. I'm glad I don't live down on the flats."

"You and me, both," agreed Brock, "Who'd ever think that we'd be hoping for cold weather."

Once Yana came back, Brock spoke first. "As you know, since we found the aquariums, we have been forced to look into your life here. You should know that your boss spoke very highly of you and your work with DNA modifications."

"I love the work. It is just so bad that we are setbacks by the robbery."

"But another question – about Borya."

Yana blushed.

"There have been sightings of him here in greater Vancouver."

Yana's face turned a deeper shade of red.

"Have you had any contact with him at all in the last few months?"

Yana paused. Her entire up-bringing was being challenged. Should she give up her brother? Give up her family? Yet she was relatively certain that it was Borya who was behind the robbery of the university. The aquariums and insect remains in the garage pretty much proved it. She spoke, in a low voice. "You have to realize that he is family."

"But surely you haven't forgotten your oath of citizenship?" asked Brock.

"Anayana, Anayana, does the policeman have any candy?" asked the youngest visitor.

"I do not think so, dear."

Again tears formed in Yana's eyes and she felt completely torn. But then seeing the young faces all staring at her expectantly, answered, "Yes. He was stayed here. But I have no idea where now he is. He has left again, full of anger. I do not think he would come back."

Then unabridged fear encompassed her face. "At least not for me."

"What are you afraid of?" asked Brock.

"You must tell us if anyone is threatening you: if anything is not right."

Though she still looked frightened, Yana tried to focus. As she gently rubbed her rounded stomach, she said, "Please, just a picking up of Matvey before they close."

"Of course. We'll be back in minutes," responded Toque.

Yana looked relieved, smiled, then asked her small guests, "Anyone want to have another pieces of medovik?"

"I do! I do! I do!" chorused the children.

Later, in the cruiser, Toque could hardly wait until the door was closed so that she could speak. "I wonder if Borya could have stolen the eggs and larvae from the university and turned them into various plagues."

"Sounds possible, but only in part. The blood and frogs didn't come from the university. And the staph bacteria, like the virus that causes equine colic, could have come from any number of sources. Plus, I don't get why Borya would be working from the Bible."

"Don't know. Maybe Russian Orthodox has the same things?"

"Whether it does or not, there are a number of religions that are based on the Old Testament. The perp could be following any of them," observed Brock.

"Maybe."

"And there is still the problem that the leaky rig has not been at every site. There was
nothing near the shelter. And Borya's helpers, Egor and Ras, didn't even get day-passes until after the first episode at Rockwater."

Both were perplexed.

Toque considered the possible perpetrators. "Peanut, or for that matter, Lynn, have more motive than Borya and company."

"Or Delila," added Brock.

"Right. But I just feel that our ... um ... girlfriends are a long shot."

Brock blanched at the thought of Delila being called a girlfriend, but continued the conversation. "Sure. Lynn and Delila just don't seem to be ... plus, there is increasingly damning evidence about Borya and company: Yana has just admitted that he's been around; he was probably in the garage and there were definitely bugs in there. Plus, the Scheveningen guys are Borya's old buddies."

The conversation paused for a few moments before Toque spoke again. "And what else is scaring Yana? She couldn't be that worried about Matvey being picked up!"

Chapter 76

The rain continued to pelt down as Toque and Brock rode down the dismal grey streets. It was like a tropical downpour. As Toque drove, she leaned a little closer to the windshield, struggling for better visibility.

"Thank goodness there's no one around. I can hardly see through this stuff."

Toque drove through a puddle that was the width of several bath tubs lying end-to-end, causing the water to surge above the bottom of the door on the passenger's side.

"I'm just glad these doors are well sealed or I'd have wet socks."

"No kidding. It doesn't help that all the drains are plugged with leaves."

"Let's hope it doesn't get so bad that we end up filling sandbags."

"Who knows? This is crazy!"

"But have you thought any more about Borya?" asked Brock.

"I do wonder about him, and others."

"Like Peanut?"

"Yeah, good old Peanut, but his alibies seem good for most of the plagues … but also … even though we don't like to consider those close to us personally …"

Brock whitened. "Delila …"

"Her, yes, but I've also been wondering about Lynn."

Brock almost jumped with surprise, had he not been strapped into the shot-gun seat of the cruiser. He asked, "What?"

"Well, I hate to make a graph with just a few points, but Lynn is really intense on this Christian group she belongs to … and she is really full of hate towards her ex-wife."

"I'm confused. And how does this all connect to the plague stuff?"

"Most, if not all of the targets are connected with her ex."

"You've got me interested now."

"Her ex taught at Rockwater, she's now at Cap U, she's a member of the symphony that played at Centennial, and was the keynote speaker at the economic forum."

"You're kidding. And how does the federal leadership conference tie in?"

"As you know, I was there with Joe, and she is jealous because …"

Brock covered his eyes in a gesture of exaggerated horror. "Don't tell me the details, please."

Toque sighed and rolled her eyes at Brock's theatrics. He continued, "But then, what about the boils?"

"Her ex wanted to help the homeless – considered their needs a cause. She had her students handing out sandwiches down near the shelter."

"I heard about that, but am surprised that Lynn's ex was involved. I gotta say that I'm impressed with her. But how could Lynn be tied to the hail?"

"What?"

"You know: crack."

"Oh. Right. Lynn's pissed off that you're my partner."

Brock sighed, thought, *I wish*, but instead said, "Shit. And we barely like each other."

Both blushed.

Brock continued, "It seems we'd better have a look at her alibis."

"Believe it or not, I did."

"And?"

"She has just the one alibi – and it was for the university lab robbery: Lynn could not have done it because she was doing an all-nighter with her religious group."

"Plus, I don't' think she could have done all that stuff on her own, anyway," observed Brock.

Toque thought for a moment. "But she is in tight with the Christian Assemblage. Those who weren't at the all-nighter could have helped her – including by doing the robbery or by just giving her a fake alibi."

"So-called *good* Christians!"

"The whole thing is probably a stretch, though."

"I'm sure I could argue that Delila is just as much a suspect."

Toque smiled, then tried to cover up her facial expression with that of innocent questioning, and said, "Oh? Let's hear it!"

CHAPTER 77

Brock and Toque's cruiser pulled up in front of All Faiths Family Daycare and turned on their emergency lights, just for the sake of amusing the children who were waiting by the window, watching for their parents. Less than seconds passed when about fifteen of the small faces glued themselves to the window, fascinated by the roof-mounted lights. All found their own, individual peep-hole amidst the painted-on illustrations of holy, six-pointed stars, angels, snowmen, candy-canes and the star and crescent symbol. And as Brock and Toque exited their cruiser, all the small faces turned to stares of amazement as they saw the real, live police constables.

"Are they married?" asked one.

"Nah. They're not holding hands," observed a second child.

"But look, he's watching her closely," remarked a third.

"And she was looking at him when they pulled up!" observed the first.

"I think they were kissing before they got here!" rumoured the third.

Then, no sooner had Brock and Toque entered the daycare when one of the children hurried over to them, faced up, then placing one hand on Brock's slacks and the other on Toque's, asked, "Do you have any candy?"

"Sorry kids, maybe we'll bring something next time," responded Brock, apologetically.

"Can you bring candy-canes?" persisted the child.

"Let's see what your caregivers have to say about that. But where are they?"

Brock and Toque sized up the large room they'd entered. Encircling the entire space was a generous display of blinking multi-coloured miniature Christmas lights. Running alongside the lights were pine garlands decorated with red berries, cones, and red bobbles, all attached with matching ribbons. Cheery carols were being piped in through over-head speakers. Most of the children had been waiting near the window, and the communal play-or-reading area-rug that featured a life-size cartoon of Noah's ark. The colours of this carpet, like every wall and piece of furniture were crayon-bright. Beyond the kid-height tables, stools, play-kitchen, play-house and fake-sand box was a book case that covered most of the back wall. This wall was stepped forward, evidently flanking another room that was out of the line of vision. Almost every inch of the book case was filled with toys, art-and-craft plastic bins, and books. More than in the average daycare, there was a ton of them. For the most part, all of the books were not arranged in an orderly manner: in fact, some were on their sides, upside down, or even facing backwards. On the lower shelves, some seemed to have been forgotten and placed behind others.

Only a few minutes passed when a narrow, though well-built woman with brown curly hair and blue eyes, probably in her late twenties, entered from the room behind the book case. She was tucking her T-shirt into her jeans. The children rushed her and surrounded her. She gently pushed past them, and smiled at Toque and Brock over the flock of pre-schoolers that then turned their eyes back to Brock and Toque and became motionless.

"Hi there, constables: welcome!" The woman glanced around, seemingly bewildered, as she asked, "But where is Mandy?" Then looking confused, and with some remorse, added, "Cripes, she must have slipped out while I was indisposed. Heck! Thank goodness nothing happened to these children! But it's all good now. Whew! I'll have to find out tomorrow what happened to her. Crossed wires probably. But nevertheless, this is something that should never happen!

But I must say that I'm surprised to have you stop by. And delighted! You can see that the children are thrilled to meet you."

Smiling back, Brock and Toque introduced themselves.

"Call me Petra."

"Sure, but hey, the kids are wondering if we'll bring them candy."

"Unfortunately, we do have to be careful of allergies but I think that we might be able to work something out if you call me," said Petra, eyeing up Brock alone – as if Toque wasn't present.

A question mark formed on Toque's face, wondering if this was meant to be a come-on for Brock. And as she considered this possibility, another person lumbered out from the back room: it was Peanut. He was flushed pink, his shirt was buttoned unevenly, and his fly was half down.

Petra's face was unreadable, as she moved over to Peanut, put her hand on his arm in a gesture of experienced familiarity and he flushed further. Then she whispered something to him and he quickly turned and disappeared into the room in the back. Moments later, Peanut again joined them, then with his fly up and his shirt properly buttoned, although his face was still flushed.

"So, what brings you here?" asked Petra, as she put her hand on Brock's shoulder and smiled at Toque.

Peanut scowled as he looked at Petra's hand on Brock's shoulder.

"We've come to pick up Matvey Vasiliev."

Peanut moved closer to Toque, and after a second glance at Petra, placed his hand on Toque's arm, and asked, "How are you doing?"

It was as if Toque had been hit by lightning. She sprung sideways, leaving Peanut's hand dangling.

Brock, on the other hand, happily dealt with his surprise at being touched by the attractive daycare worker.

And as Petra looked at Brock in the eyes, she joked, "Oh, has Matvey committed a crime?"

And she again smiled a congenial grin at Toque, but kept her hand on Brock's shoulder, moving it down his arm ever so slightly, and then stepped so close that his libido suddenly activated – but then Brock thought that he could smell ... *Was that the smell of sex? Or was it ear wax?*

"No crimes to report," kidded Brock in response, then explained, "But Yana's tied up and we're helping out."

"No problem. We can get little Matvey packed up in no time. Pearce, I love it when you pitch in! Can you get Matvey's coat and pack?" She smiled at Peanut in such a way that most men would have lain down on the train tracks in front of an approaching train, just to get her approval.

Ten minutes later, Matvey was back at home, curtesy of Brock and Toque.

But as soon as they pulled from the Vasiliev's driveway, Toque spoke her mind. "What was all that! They reeked! Peanut's in high school, for crying out loud! Not only that, but I'm sure she's been around the block a few times!"

"I don't know about that. You're over-thinking their relationship. I thought that she was quite nice. She could very well be an international nanny and perhaps totally naïve: away from her homeland for the first time. You could have read her gestures all wrong. You never know!"

"Come on! She's got to be almost thirty!"

"Well, he's likely seventeen, and of the age of consent. But you do have a bit of a point. Although he's clearly really bright, he's a really young seventeen. But even so, the two of them having sex is legal … unless it's exploitation, but I'm not sure how that could be the case. That his parents make donations to the daycare doesn't at all put Petra in a position of power over Pearce, more the other way around," reasoned Brock.

"Whatever. But she should have been keeping an eye on the pre-schoolers and not fucking in the back room."

"You're a bit harsh. In her defence, it did sound like she thought that there was still another daycare worker present."

"Or so she said. I'm just glad I wasn't a fly on the wall in that back room. Yuk!"

"You and me both," but with a smile added, "Unless it was just watching her."

Toque grimaced a caustic smile and gave Brock the punch of reprimand.

CHAPTER 78

The rain continued to pound down as Toque and Brock pulled up to Muriel's Coffee Shop. In spite of the misery of heavy rain, for the most part, it was an appreciated breather from fighting the record-breaking series of extreme snow storms. Even as they pulled up, they could see the warm glow of the imitation Murano-glass hanging lamps. No one sat at the window stools: no one in their right mind would be looking out into that weather.

Brock stepped out, right into an icy puddle that rose up and beyond the height of his shoe and he cursed to himself. Toque didn't notice and ran through the rain to the door of the coffee shop where she immediately noticed Singh, Matthews, Scott and Brown sharing a table. All were laughing at some joke.

Brown saw Toque enter, with Brock just behind, and grabbed the adjacent table and pulled it nearer calling out, "Hey! Over here!"

Brock and Toque smiled a greeting, as they went to the cashier to order their usual snack: Toque a carrot muffin and rose hip tea, Brock a Boston cream donut and coffee – no milk, no sugar and Cheesesnacks on the side.

"Hey, you guys got a joke worth hearing?" asked Brock as he took one of the seats on which hung one of cop's jackets: it was still dripping from the run through the rain to the door of the coffee shop.

"We were just comparing notes," said Brown.

"Yeah. Would you believe that half a dozen invincibles drove through the barrier to Manning Park's ski hill?" asked Singh.

"Yeah, I might have heard something about that. Do you know the whole story?" asked Brock.

"They thought they'd have a jolly time of it skiing down, then hiking back up. But first they decided to start in on a two-gallon jug of hot buttered rum. They then proceeded to leave their lunches in pack-sacks at the start of the ski run, alongside the oversize insulated jug," said Brown, shaking his head.

"But when they got there, the snow was so sticky that their skis wouldn't move, so they trundled around, half pissed, to see if a hill further up would be better," continued Singh.

"Then after trying to make a go of it, they decided to at least eat their lunches," said Matthews.

"By the time they got back, their pack-sacs were torn to rat-shit, food wrappings were everywhere, the insulated jug was emptied, and lying alongside was a huge sleeping grizzly," laughed Singh.

"The invincibles then felt a little threatened so made their way on foot back to the highway to get help."

"And who should come by but the local RCMP, who proceeded to ticket the drunken would-be skiers for trespassing in a restricted and closed area and ... get this ..." explained Brown.

"This is good," noted Scott.

"They were ticketed for feeding and endangering the local wild-life," concluded Singh.

Brock smiled. "That's good. What happened to the bear?"

"That was good, too. He stuck around just long enough for the officers to figure out what happened. Then the bear staggered off, still drunk," chuckled Brown.

Toque looked a little concerned but then smiled and said, "I can't believe that there is a
bear that's not hibernating right now."

"Yeah, all sorts of weird things are going on with these tropical downpours and super warm temperatures. The bear probably thinks that summer is on its way."

As the constables paused at this thought, the coffee shop owner – Muriel – an intelligent but jolly woman who clearly enjoyed being at the donut shop, stepped forward, saying, "Glad to see you guys are having a good time." She smiled as she spoke, with a big grin and her large blue eyes twinkled under her wire-frame glasses that were under generous eyebrows and a mop of thin but curly brown hair. Muriel was always happy to have them spend time in the shop. In return, everyone loved her.

"Why not join us?"

"Why not?" replied Muriel, "There is something I want to mention to you guys anyway."

"Which is ...?" questioned Toque.

Muriel's face became serious. "If you peer outside over there, on the pavement in the glow of the light, you see where the rain runs off an oil leak."

Brock and Toque straightened and were definitely interested. The other officers tried to pay attention but couldn't resist another donut-hole and gulp of coffee.

"Well, over the past few weeks, the same rig parks there: an old green motor-home. More recently, there's been three guys in it. Except that it was beat-up, I'd say that it is vintage."

"Do you know the make?"

"No, but I think that it said, 'Chaser.'"

"Maybe it was one of those box-shaped units from the seventies?" asked Brock.

"And still running?" added Brown.

Muriel shrugged but then nodded.

"I'm impressed," laughed Brock, "I thought I had the oldest wreck still moving."

Toque added, "Some of those were hardly used. Then in around 2020 people were so hard-up for places to live that a lot of those old vehicles were reworked enough to keep them on the road – though just enough to move from one curbside to another so that they had no problems with time-restricted parking zones."

Brock regarded Muriel. "But what is your concern?"

Muriel seemed a little uncomfortable, as if she were a doctor having to give out confidential information on a patient. "When I first noticed the rig, it was just one guy that arrived on his own. He always kept to himself, kept his head down, so to speak. But lately he's been coming with two who look a lot like convicts out on parole. They are always whispering in another language … eastern Europe or maybe Russian. And they seem to get really worked up about whatever they are discussing."

"You think they might be illegals?" asked Scott.

"Could be," answered Muriel, adding, "But I'm more worried about what they seem to be planning."

"It's probably nothing," smiled Brock, "But we'll check it out, maybe starting with taking an oil sample."

"Good idea," added Toque, "But Muriel, do you have any surveillance cameras?"

"Of course. Any self-respecting 24-hour stop does, these days."

"Someone should take a look at the recordings," remarked Brown.

"This coffee shop is near the Cashdiscount store that was tied to the receipt found in a locker at Rockwater."

"For the blood balloons?"

"Maybe," replied Toque.

"Seems that we've got a few things to look into," remarked Brock has he finished his coffee and got up, still holding a half-eaten bag of Cheesesnacks.

Chapter 79

Toque paused as she reached for a toffee in the bowl on her coffee table and listened for footsteps. She'd heard the elevator door open, just down the hall from her suite. She sat motionless to create not an iota of sound, but heard nothing more. But then, as if struck, there was a knock on her door.

Dread.

Who could it be? Brock? Lynn? Joe? A salesperson? Should she pretend to be out?

But then she heard Lynn's voice. "Come-on Toque, I know you're in there. I saw your car parked in the lot outside."

Toque paused and thought to herself, *I could be out for a walk.*

"Come-on babe, I just need to speak to you. We've been through a bit too much to not even talk," pleaded the voice that was Lynn's on the other side of the door.

Toque sighed. "Just a minute," and begrudgingly rose from her couch and then, as if weighted down by concrete sneakers, moved with that feeling that one suffers when coming across a spurned lover.

Toque opened the door and there stood Lynn, as expected, though clearly had dressed in her most attractive outfit. The longer part of her hair had been bleached platinum which formed an almost boyish but striking contrast to a planned display of roots and the dark close-cropped hair on the sides of her head. She'd added eyeliner and her light brown eyes became compelling, though not as provocative as her lips that had a subtle but enticing shade of pink mixed with a warm golden sunset. Under the white fluffy-collared pink leather bomber jacket, she had on a white, generously collared TURTLE-NECK that suggested she'd dropped at least ten pounds. Visible on her jacket sleeve, were a few dark marks, that were like reminders of an early morning's rain on the petals of an out-of-season but full-bloomed rose, though those on her sleeve were caused by errant drops of rain, that managed to eke around the white and pink polka-dot umbrella. Below the ribbed turtle-neck, Lynn wore a pair of tailored viscose black slacks and matching ankle-high boots with a wedge heal, looking brand-new. Her clear pink cheeks were a little flushed, caused by the hope of spending even a few minutes with Toque.

Toque's interest piqued, though she internally fought with allowing any emotional connection. "Why are you here? You know it's over."

"Oh come-on. Can't we at least be friends?"

The loneliness that was Toque's usual company tapped on her shoulder as a cruel reminder of what was the defining characteristic of her life.

"I don't know."

"Come-on ... please ... aren't you going to let me in?"

Toque managed a hesitant smile and stepped aside so that Lynn moved in, walking without pretense, but carrying herself in such a way that an aura of sexuality surrounded her.

When the two were seated in the two love-seats, Lynn was aware of the scent of Toque's fresh mint breath.

Weirdly and coincidently, Toque also thought that she sensed a familiar scent; that of Cedar Forest shower soap. Her senses became alert, her blue-grey eyes brightened as she remembered seeing Brock with his shirt off at the blanket charity. As her face flushed and her nipples hardened at the memory, Lynn misread the cause of Toque's signs of arousal and put her hand on Toque's knee. Toque's flush paled then, though she tried to hold onto the diminishing fantasy of Cedar Forest scent as she grasped at the memory of Brock naked on his vessel ... his warm amber form, his wide shoulders, his flat stomach, his bulging six-pack, his ... but then she remembered ... there in the *Angel* with Brock was Delila – dressed in nothing but a size-too-small black lace open-nipple bra and hot pink split-crotch panties.

"Just tell me, Toque, don't you think that we have a chance?" Lynn's hand moved further up Toque's leg.

Toque closed her eyes as she thought of Brock's face.

Then their lips met, just after Toque had answered with a brief, "Perhaps ..."

Lynn moved over, beside Toque, so that their thighs were touching, pressed against each other, and Lynn wrapped her arms around this fantasy woman, who was more than anything Lynn had ever imagined.

Chapter 80

The rain continued to pour down as Toque and Brock drove up Lonsdale, eyeing the traffic for potential trouble. There was an occasional person walking the street, brave enough to be out.

Toque could sense Brock's Cedar Forest scent and fought with her memory of Lynn and the previous day when the two of them made up. For Toque, it was a commitment of which she was uncertain, yet when Lynn was so warm, so kind … so soft, yet so strong. So encompassing. It was hard to resist the offer of a solid relationship … and none of that other business … her Uncle Kane … that still haunted her nightmares. Plus, how could she ignore and not admire Lynn's commitment – of which she often spoke: the dire need for extreme actions before the planet becomes entirely uninhabitable. One could not help but agree that governments had failed the human race for decades: the planet earth was on a landslide path of environmental destruction.

Yet as she sat beside Brock she sensed his aura: the pulse of his sexuality, his strength, his warm amber complexion, his eyes the colour of a deep but warm blue ocean. Her breathing increased while Brock, oblivious, and enrapt in his own thoughts, let out an almost silent moan as he straightened in his seat.

But then, wondering about Toque's thoughts on the issue that was on almost everyone's mind, asked, "Did you hear about the tornados in Yellowknife?"

"In the sub-arctic? In December?"

"I know. It's crazy. While we're having an unseasonably warm snap, it's gotten down-right hot up there. They've got conditions similar to that in the southern states in the late spring or early summer."

"Insane. Any damage?"

"Crazy damage. Like us, they had heaps of snow in November which is super-unusual for a really cold climate, but it wasn't the typical well-below freezing temperatures there – it was like here. And the tornados – there was five of them, two of them in particular, touched town, pulled up a whack of snow, and later dumped it – one pile has trapped a bunch of people inside. And what is just as bad, if not worse, is that just after the dump at the entrance, the other exits got blocked by super-drifts caused by the tornado cluster stirring up a ton of ground snow."

"Shit!"

"Yeah! They can't get out! But now that the tornadoes have gone, the weather has turned to rain, which is another crazy thing for this time of year up there. They're trying to dig out the ones that are trapped!" explained Brock, "It's insane! Like a Sci-Fi movie!"

"I guess we can't complain. It seems that whoever is doing the plague thing is nothing compared to the crazy weather."

"Considering that global warming is the cause, it's all on us." Brock paused.

Toque, sensing that Brock had more to say, looked his way, again sensing his Cedar Forest aura. *He must have just showered.*

Brock continued, "But with regard to the plague thing, you know you were talking about Lynn …"

"I think I've changed my mind on that …"

"Should never put aside any suspicion …"

"I guess …"

"But I am suspicious of …" Brock floundered, wondering what word would describe his relationship with Delila.

"Not Delila?" If the suspicions weren't so serious, Toque would have smiled as she said, "You did say something about …"

"Yes, like Lynn …"

"Let's forget her for now," interrupted Toque, feeling guilty of betrayal.

"Whatever, I have a bad feeling about Delila … and what she's up to."

"Acting on her own?"

"Unlikely."

"She might have had friends helping her?"

Brock thought for a moment, then said, "No one I know of, but she has a number of contacts in her therapy group."

"What could be her motive?"

"There are a number of things. But I gotta say that I'm not totally comfortable telling you what she told me …"

Toque's eyes widened with the look of someone who is about to hear some good gossip. "But if she is a suspect …"

"Okay. I'll try to spare the weird details."

Details? I might want to hear the details! Thought Toque, though she said, "Go ahead. Tell me."

"Well, Delila has reason to have real gripes with anything related to Rockwater and Cap U."

Toque's face became serious, as she prodded, "Oh?"

"She was criminally assaulted by staff."

"At both places?"

"Believe it or not, yes. One teacher, then a coach."

Toque's face reddened with anger. "How teachers or those in similar roles can justify getting it on with students is beyond me. What an incredibly looser thing to do."

"No kidding. Both led Delila to believe that they were serious."

"So that could tie her in to the events at Rockwater and Cap U."

"Yeah, that includes the blood, the frogs, and the black flies venue owned by the university."

"But I'm guessing that Delila isn't the only one with ties to Rockwater and Cap U."

"True, but she had bad times at both."

"But lots of students bare some grudge or another."

"Possibly, but the horse poisoning also can tie to her …"

"Because …?" asked Toque.

"One of the guys who took her for a ride was the equestrian coach!"

"Is that a sick joke?"

"What's sick is his treatment of Delila. While he was seeing her, he was screwing some jockey behind her back. I believe the resulting child is in the same daycare as Yana and Alik's little ones, along with Lacey White's kid."

"Crazy! You know Lynn?"

Brock frowned, then tried to cover the pressing expression of intolerance with that of curiosity, as he said, "And …"

"Her daughter is also in All Faiths daycare!"

"Strange coincidence, for sure."

But Toque, oblivious to any jealousy on Brock's part, continued, "So what about the other plagues? The lice at Centennial, the crack on your boat, and the locusts, and the bacteria at the homeless shelter?"

"Strangely, those can also be tied in, though to a lesser extent. First off, Delila has a real issue with power figures. That could tie in with the locusts at the federal leadership selection, and also the premier's conference."

"And Centennial Theater's lice?"

"It was filled with the Vancouver elite."

"Okay. A bit of a stretch, but what about the crack on the *Angel* and at the school, to say nothing of the bacteria at the homeless shelter?" questioned Toque.

"I think that could have tied to her relationship with me."

"Because you're a power figure? I'm not sure about that. I'll bet that you're just a neighbour in her eyes. Plus, if she hates you that much, it's pretty weird that she bedded down with you." Toque blushed at raising the topic of seeing Delila and the stark-naked Brock on the *Angel*.

Brock wanted to moan, and thought that he'd rather have this conversation with anyone other than Toque. He tried to explain. "From the beginning – with Delila, I've been up front about not wanting to get serious."

Toque tried to hide her smile as she responded, "Funny way of showing it."

"Anyway, it's never been serious. But she seemed very put off … just before the planting of the crack."

"If it was her, where did she get it?"

"Don't know, but I think I saw some on her the other day."

"For crying out loud, Brock, can't you do better than a crack head?" Toque paused, momentarily uncertain, as a new thought formed in her mind. Brock a free man? But what of Lynn? Kind, caring, Lynn. But in seconds Toque snapped out of it. "Shit! So Delila might have been behind some of it!"

"Although the leaks of engine oil are a problem. Delila doesn't have a car and Lynn drives an electric, if I remember correctly."

"She does; but unfortunately anyone can have a friend with a leaky vehicle."

"Of course. In that case, either of them could have …"

CHAPTER 81

Mrs. Bean, with a hair-do that was spiked and white, except for the half-dozen lime-green high-lights, wore neon-pink framed glasses, and entered Grant's office. She wore high-top pink and lime green running shoes and a yellow track suit that was jazzed up by ten or more strands of pink, yellow and lime green beads that matched the clusters of bead drops hanging from her ears.

Grant was maggoty coloured from fatigue and the dark shadows under his eyes gave him the look of an ailing racoon. However, he almost reached for his sunglasses and had to squint when he saw Mrs. Bean and decided to think about having a dress code for volunteer police workers who moved into paying positions, especially top-end positions. But putting this thought temporarily to the side, he asked, as he had before, "The conference call set up, Mrs. Bean?"

"Captain Abraham and Director Graham are both on the line."

Grant picked up the phone and jumped right in, saying, "I suspect it's too soon to hope that the flooding was only an idle threat."

Abraham rubbed her eyes as if she could erase the mounting horror and fatigue. "I've got another email."

"And?" interrupted Grant.

"The sender reminds us, 'That we must release the same three …'"

Butting in again, Grant completed the wording of the email with the names they already knew: "Voronin, Kuznetsov, and Oblonsky in Scheveningen."

"Right. As before. And if we don't …"

Graham took his turn at interrupting as he audibly drummed his fingers, asking, "What now?"

Abraham gazed out her window, focussing on the boats in English Bay, as if to dispel the threats. "The sender says that darkness and death will accompany the arc of Noah."

Grant paused, momentarily stumped, then asked, "Is that all about flooding? And still nothing more on the fire threat? But darkness and death? What does that mean, anyway? And who *are* these people?"

"I wish I knew," sighed Abraham.

Grant cursed to himself, then spoke, "What the hell do they mean by darkness and death? These guys sound like Bible nuts."

Graham was the first to answer. "Let me remind you that the last two plagues of Egypt are darkness and the death of the firstborn."

Both Abraham and Grant moaned and looked exceedingly worried.

Like the others, Graham realized that more manpower was needed. "It's time to bring in some negotiators. Captain Abraham, email the perps that we want to talk."

The clicking of Abraham's keyboard momentarily filled the phone lines and in seconds she said, "Done!"

Graham continued, "Okay. But back to the threat of floods. Assuming it's still out there, and is part of this new ultimatum, I've found that the most vulnerable area in the lower mainland is the dyke area off Garry Point in Steveston."

Grant furrowed his brow. "What about other areas, like the North Shore?"

Graham explained, "In terms of damage, no place in the Lower Mainland really compares to an area in Steveston where a whole sub-division is protected by a dike. They're already vulnerable in a big storm. And with the extreme snow melt now, the Fraser River's waters will be crazy high. Add that to a king tide, if that dike goes, the devastation will be widespread. I've already contacted the armed forces and they are preparing their deployment."

Abraham cringed, then exclaimed, "Crap!" Then asked, "When's the next king tide?"

"December 24th."

Grant and Abraham responded almost simultaneously. "No-o-o-o-o. Why does it have to be then?"

Then Abraham began to iterate their shared fear, "Surely this sick group isn't waiting for …"

"Might very well be, though the saboteur has no control of the snow melt. It could turn cold … but then if that happens, it could cause avalanches … and then the situation might be even worse, if that is possible," projected Graham.

Chapter 82

An hour and a half before her shift started, Toque took shelter from her perplexing relationships and the endless deluge of rain by sitting alone, under one of the imitation Murano-glass lampshades at one of the golden oak tables in a booth in Muriel's. The walls were newly decorated with Santa images, there was a tree in the corner with multi-coloured lights, and the railings were covered with garlands which held blinking miniature red LEDs. But all of this Christmas décor provided no comfort for the unsettled Toque.

Her chosen booth was right beside the donut machine and Toque absently watched the donuts as they circled round the cooking loop until they slipped out and onto a pile in a cooling metal mesh tray. The air was filled with the scent of rising donut dough as the shop prepared for its after-dinner rush. Because of the recently discovered miraculous rejuvenating effect of donuts on the human body, the shop's popularity had made the owner, Muriel, consider opening yet another location. But this and its sister store on Denman, near the marina where Brock moored the *Angel*, was meant to be a cozy home-away-from-home, and not a starting-block for yet another world-conquering franchise.

Toque thought of Lynn, of their naked bodies together, smooth soft skin on skin, like silk on silk: Lynn in behind, pressed against Toque's back and butt, legs wrapped around legs, caressing Toque into wakefulness as the sunlight flowed softly through the narrow openings of the bedroom venetians. There was a brief moment of contentment as she reached wakefulness but for just a second, Brock's image appeared in her mind: his unclothed six-pack when he loaded the blankets, and – she swallowed uncomfortably as a tingling sensation permeated her whole body as she thought of Brock's complete nakedness. But then Toque flinched at the memory of Delila in her tart-porno ensemble, inviting Toque to join them. She rubbed her eyes and ever so slightly shook her head, as if trying to shake off the memory.

"Hey, Toque, you killing time before work?" asked a woman's voice.

There stood Lily Sun and Nat Boucher, smiling. Like Toque,

both were in civilian clothing as they were in the habit of changing into their uniforms at their detachment. While Sun and Boucher still had to remove their dripping-wet rain slickers, all three wore blue jeans and T-shirts.

"Yeah, I'm early," responded Toque, "You two in the same boat?"

After hanging their jackets on the hooks at the end of the booths, Lily took the opposite seat, while Boucher sat down alongside Toque. "Right. Lily drives right past my place every day and until my wife and I get a car, I'm taking advantage of Lily's ride in."

"And you're here early because …" asked Toque.

"Lily just finished an appointment for physio and I was checking out a maternity shop because my wife, Ricki, is getting a bit too big for all of her clothing. I thought I'd scout out some new tops for her."

"Nice. When is she due?" asked Toque.

"A couple of months, so she's probably going to get quite a bit bigger."

"Exciting times!" said Toque.

"You have no idea! We're thrilled! I have to tell you that the kid will have some of the same genetic make-up as I do!"

Toque's eyes widened with some confusion. "You mean Ricki is carrying a fetus supplied by yourself?"

Boucher laughed. "No, I have three brothers who donated sperm at the fertility clinic.
And the clinic harvested a number of eggs from Ricki. We wanted all three of my brothers to be donators so that the actual biological father would always be in question; so, none of my brothers would feel that the babe is his child and that he is responsible. So, they don't even have to think about contributing financially or in some ways taking on a father role!"

"And your brothers are okay on that?"

"Absolutely," smiled Boucher, "We're a really close family and why not bring a child into the world if that child is going to be loved entirely? Not only that, but my brothers will be uncles that are more special than ever-before imagined."

"Sounds like some really good birthday gifts will be coming from all three," smiled Toque. Then looking at Lily Sun, asked, "Are you hooked up with anyone?"

"More than I can cope with, actually. I have three boyfriends, four if you count the one who is stationed in Halifax and comes home every now and then."

"No wonder you need physio," chuckled Boucher.

"It can get awkward," admitted Lily, but with a smile.

"Three? I thought I had problems," laughed Toque.

"I'm surprised you're not onto your hunk-of-a-partner – like tree-sap on the butt of a new pair of linen slacks," joked Lily, "Personally, I'd go for it."

Toque shuffled uncomfortably, and Lily regretted her remark, though just a little.

Touching Toque's arm in support, Boucher felt an unplanned immediate rush of hormones, as her heartbeat increased and her nipples hardened, and were quite noticeable under her smooth T-shirt.

Noticing Boucher's reaction, Toque momentarily re-boarded the emotional roller-coaster.

Then, as she removed her hand from Toque's arm, Boucher asked, "Perhaps you enjoy the fairer sex?"

Though on her arm she felt a slight chill as Boucher's hand moved away, Toque's cheeks warmed, as she answered, "Not sure."

Boucher momentarily gazed upwards as she said, "If I wasn't married …"

Toque sighed, and tried to focus on the donuts going round and round in their metal cooker.

Lily's eyebrows raised and for the first time wondered about her choice of having gaggle of boyfriends. But sensing awkwardness, pulled out a law-protector's agenda. "Say, Toque, I believe you were involved in the Pearce Cudmore interview."

Toque's brain un-hazed as she remembered Peanut, then sighed. "Yep. There are a number of reasons why he could be considered a suspect. But he seems clean, for the most part."

"That's what we've been thinking," remarked Boucher.

"Exactly," said Sun. "His parents and brother were involved in a number of targets: the basketball game, the theatre, and the Premier's Forum."

"Yeah," added Boucher, "His parents were both at Centennial Theatre and his dad was the one who was supposed to introduce the keynote speaker at the forum."

Her face confirming Boucher's remark, Sun then thought for a moment, and said, "I've noticed that Pearce seems to really dislike his family: it could be some kind of revenge. Plus, he might be wanting to screw things up for his brother at Cap U."

"You're right on all of that, but Pearce does have alibis for some of the stuff," said Toque, "And yet, I also wonder about him. He's in a group that is very involved in protests about bitumen spills. They seem pretty driven by hate."

"I know. He has been very verbal about that," added Sun, "But his home security cameras show him at home when the towels were infected."

"Plus, with the oil leaks, Pearce drives an electric car," pointed out Boucher.

"Yeah, we know all that. But Pearce does, nevertheless, seem suspicious. Plus, he seems to have a really cruel streak to him," pointed out Toque, "He invented a water-bound gargoyle contraption that bites live beetles in half. And it looked like he was going to try it out on caged chicks."

"Gross!" moaned Sun.

Toque continued, "We called animal control but they couldn't find anything by the time they got there. But another thing, Pearce called the grade eights who ate the crack 'little nit-wits' who, according to Pearce, 'got what they deserved.'"

"You do wonder if he had some part with all the crack," commented Boucher.

"Yeah, but a school kid: not likely to get that quantity," noted Sun.

"It has been known though. Do you know if that grade eight kid who went into a coma is any better?" asked Toque.

"Oh? Didn't you hear? He's been discharged," explained Sun.

"That's something. So, he's back to normal?"

Sun's face saddened. "They're not sure. He has brain-fog. Don't know if he'll ever be right."

Toque's looked troubled, then angered. "Jeez, we've got to catch these assholes."

Boucher nodded, and said, "Now that the feds are involved, maybe there is more hope,"

"Yeah, especially since CSIS is sending in some manpower."

Toque thought of Brock, and his incredible performance just a few years earlier on Lions Gate Bridge. His image formed clearly in her mind. Again. She sighed.

Chapter 83

In the once-controversial co-ed change room, several constables were gearing up for their graveyard shift. On the monitor mounted near the ceiling, a news-cast covered the appalling number of avalanches that had been triggered by the massive warm rainfalls following November's snow.

Singh watched with anxiety mixed with concern. "Shit! Can you believe it? First responders out there must be up to their necks!"

"They are. No time off. Eighteen-hour shifts. It's gotta be brutal!" said Brown.

"I hope the local mountains manage to hold onto their snow."

Brock joined in, adding, "I might head up to the interior on my days off to help out."

Singh briefly considered Brock's plan, then said, "Good call. I'll do the same. Maybe we can ride together."

"Sounds like a plan," responded Brock.

Brown frowned. "Shit, I need some relief from this slop! But count me in! I'll be there too!"

Down the space of four lockers Scott, first chuckled, then called out, "Hey sailor-guy! I heard you were with a half-dressed gorgeous woman, down at your marina!"

Brock, with a white towel around his torso, tried not to think about the sexual encounter with Delila … or for that matter, Toque. He looked down to see the red brick-coloured asphalt tiled floor. "Not sure. Can't remember."

Brown couldn't resist. "Can't remember, my ass!"

Singh's dark eyes brightened and without pause, warmed to the idea of a date set-up. "Come on, Brock, we could do with a little help. Smith up in ticketing saw you at the marina with a real knock out. And Toque said that you might go out on a double date: Toque with someone … what was the name … I think that it was Lynn."

Toque. Again. Brock tried to focus. He didn't want to go there: double-dating, or Toque's sexual preferences.

"Your new lady must have a few friends," prodded Matthews, "It's not easy being a cop. Every woman thinks you're going to charge them with something."

"Don't think about it," chuckled Brown.

But Brock thought for a moment, wondering about Delila. It was odd ... Delila seemed to have no friends at all – unless you counted her therapy group. But then, he didn't have a ton of friends either – unless you counted Toque.

"Cat got your tongue, Romeo?" chuckled Scott.

Brock frowned. "The problem with you guys is not that you're cops, it's that you're way too keen for a poke-in-the-hole."

"Very funny, Getzlaff. I'm thinking that you're hiding something. Like maybe she's an illegal – or possibly someone who thought she'd found a dandy hiding place to store her crack!" joked Scott.

"Good one! Like maybe she's a spy ... how about a Russian spy?" laughed Brown.

"Right!" added Matthews, "Maybe she's connected with the Scheveningen guys?"

"This is funny stuff," groaned Brock, wishing he could change the topic.

"Brock's right. A Russian link is no laughing matter," sympathized Singh.

"You've got that right. Has there been anything new about the Bogdanov brothers and
what they do when they're out on their day passes?" asked Brock, grimacing as if he'd
tasted something bad.

"Nothing's come up. Plus, the word that's out is that the brothers were still locked up when the school was splattered," replied Scott.

Brown added, "All the other attacks would require more local knowledge than they have. Also, the Bogdanovs had limited time available on a day-pass."

"Good point," noted Brock, "But still, with the demands to spring their buddies in Scheveningen ..."

"It's hard to believe that the brothers aren't somehow involved ..."

"They could have managed setting up some of it on their ten-hour day-passes ..."

"And work around schedules of custodians and the like."

"I'm guessing that Borya Morozov is still in the wind as far as the Feds are concerned?" asked Brock.

Two of the others nodded.

"H-m-m-m-m. Do any of you know if video of the green motor home has shown up in the recordings from Muriel's? She tagged the wreck as being a leaky vehicle. And when I was on desk duty, I found that a green motor home had been at all five sites, up to that point. I wonder if Borya was the driver," mused Brock.

"*The* green motorhome?" asked Matthews.

"Right, the one that the West Van Police have on video near Rockwater."

Matthews added, "Ah, yeah, but it wasn't seen at the robbery down at the Vancouver station – where the frogs were taken."

"I know, and that throws water on our hunches. A bit, anyway," commented Brock, "But again, does anyone know if anything has shown up from the video from Muriel's?"

"Hey, give me a minute; I'll go and check upstairs," volunteered Matthews.

Seconds later, the door to the changing room opened and they all looked up expectantly. But it was Toque who was pre-occupied and seemed to scan past them, then focussed her eyes on the back area of the room where a bulletin board was attached to the wall. She checked the posted notices, looking to see if anything new had been placed there, then fixed her line of vision in the direction of the four watching her. But she saw only Brock. She paused. Then looked again at her surroundings, and as if seeing all five cops for the first time, and said, "Oh, hey, you guys. Time to get a move-on; don't you think? I've got an excuse for running a little late. But what's slowing down you four?"

With that, they all started rummaging through their lockers. But before even one shoe lace was untied, Matthews walked in.

"Hey, they've examined Muriel's tapes. They finished just seconds ago with the computer ID work."

"And?"

"The faces of two of the three guys in the motor home aren't visible."

"Great," said Brock, sarcastically. But continued, "And the third?"

370

Matthews resumed. "Even though he was wearing a hoody, with some computer enhancement and projections, the driver of the motor home is a dead ringer for Borya Morozov."

Chapter 84

Even though it was just four in the afternoon, it might as well have been midnight, as the heavy rain and dense cloud cover blocked all light. Rex sighed as he lolled about on the rusty-red carpet in the main cabin of the *Angel*. The sound of the rain pounding on the roof was as if every minute there was a million gigantic drops hammering the thick steel hull. But Brock was engaged. He had a shiny new winch on the table and was transfixed by the operating manual.

After fiddling with this new toy, reading a page or two, then tinkering some more for the better part of an hour, Brock glanced around the empty galley for something else to occupy his mind. He picked up, unlocked, then studied his cell phone and read a few old messages. Then, after several minutes passed, he relocked the cell and placed it in his back pocket and focused on his faithful companion, and was soon engaged in a serious effort of scratching Rex under the chin, one of Rex's favorite scratch zones. But after a quarter of an hour passed, both master and pet had had enough so Brock again pulled his cell from his pocket while Rex gave his master's free hand an appreciative lick, then moved over to his food dish and enjoyed a few kibbles that had escaped his last feeding frenzy. Brock again unlocked the cell, searched through his contacts, then pressed on the icon marking Toque's name. The icon was a picture of Toque.

But then, a rap on the hull: the sound of someone who was very anxious. "Brock! I need your help! Please be home!"

Brock re-iterated Rex's sigh, though for quite a different reason, got up from the galley table, and flung open the hatch. Even though he had a tarp over the cock-pit, the rain flew into his face as if he was in his shower. A freezing cold shower.

As his hair blew back, he stared at his visitor: Delila. Her blond hair was down, and soaking, as if she had been in the ocean. But her make-up stayed put: her captivating dark eyes were outlined and shadowed. Her mouth was bright red with lip-stick but, underneath … underneath … he tried to avert his eyes but couldn't. Although the weather was warm for that time of year, it was much too cold for even a light jacket but what she wore was unbelievably skimpy. She had on a man's black dress shirt, tied loosely, too loosely – so that it showed her black lace open-nipple bra. With the way the shirt was tied, he could immediately see one of her nipples, and soon both. The shirt was tied well above her hips, where she had wrapped something like a black scarf, tied in a knot on her left, exposing at least part of the Brazilian.

Brock's member started to swell. "But Delila, remember that I…"

Delila leaned over the side of the *Angel,* her lacey chest resting on the toe-rail. "Come-on. I really need you to check something on my boat. Please! After what we've done, you do know me. I just need you to have a little look at something. It will just be a few minutes. Please …"

"Oh, well wait a …" He couldn't help but focus on the nipples, though he tried in vain to keep his eyes on her face.

"Just leave Rex … no need to lock up. We'll only be a sec."

Brock grabbed his cell and in no time was on Delila's vessel, and was facing the open hatch and had just placed his foot on the top step of the entrance ladder … when all went black.

***

When his eyes opened, from what he could make out, he'd become like an obscene figurehead: he was naked and duct-taped to the prow of an old green motor home in a garage that strongly resembled that belonging to Yana and Alik Vasiliev. Brock could smell oil from the continuous leak. He could see a few dead insects in a corner … what seemed to be corpses of black flies and locusts.

Beside Brock's clothing thrown onto the floor, was the top of his cell phone – just protruding from a pocket. Next to that, on a grubby mattress, lay Delila, unconscious … or perhaps doped … he could see the white powder on her nostrils … her breasts and legs spread. Her scanty clothing on the floor along-side. He looked again at her face. Around the hair line he could see a couple of red swellings from insect bites. A fluorescent green louse moved quickly from the hair behind her ear and then back into the bleached strands. *Lice – like the ones at Centennial Theatre,* he thought.

Then ... a voice. "You'll have your fun with her soon enough. She'll come to before we're done with our big hero here."

Brock forced the tape holding his head to budge ever so slightly so that he could see the owner of the voice, standing at the far end of the mattress. It was Borya Morozov. Beside him were Egor and Ras who both looked as if they'd entered a candy store. They were fixated on Delila.

"We can do anything with her?" asked Ras, his lips so wet they were almost drooling.

"But we have to make curfew!" reminded Egor.

"Fuck. I don't care about curfew. They won't do anything anyway. They're wimps!"

Egor paused, thinking, then smiled. "For a change, you are dead right. We need to make the most of this ..."

"Let's just have a taste to begin with," drooled Ras as he salivated, bent over, and roughly fondled Delila's nearest breast. He hurried to kneel down beside her, put one hand on her crotch, finger in, and his mouth on a breast. He bit a nipple, leaving teeth marks, then laughed at the sight of the mark.

"Let me see what I can do," grinned Egor, unzipping his pants. "Hey, I'd like to ram ..."

As Egor reached into his fly, he was knocked in the head by Borya who cursed. "Shit, you guys. We've got bigger fish to fry – first." And with that remark, Borya, pulled out the famous fantasy knife.

Brock felt bile rise in his throat and wondered, *How the hell did these losers get ahold of that knife?*

"Let me do it first," urged Ras, moving to a standing position and reaching for the knife.

"Not going to happen ... at least not yet. We'll decide who goes first, later. But now it's going to be movie night!" Borya laughed the laugh of a crazy. "I want him erect when we make the first cut! You know where that cut will be."

Borya set the knife on the corner of the mattress, then moved over to a projection unit, turned it on, and Brock then saw that he'd been taped to the front of the vehicle so that he could see the movie screen propped up on a tri-pod not far from him.

"Ha. Ha. Great! Entertainment!" said Ras, as he unfolded one of several lawn chairs that were hanging on the wall of the side of the garage.

Before long, all three were seated and the film rolled. It had one star: Delila – if you don't count the dildo that played a large supporting role. Her hips moved rhythmically. The camera invaded. Her lips parted. Her eyes rolled back, as if in ecstasy. And the performance continued, and repeated, with a picture so crisp it gave new meaning to the term 'super-high def.'

"Once we get the asshole cop here aroused, we'll have some real fun ... we'll be creative as to where and how we can use the knife. But one saying I've always liked is 'the death of a thousand cuts.' Let's get a bit of sound enhancement going with this." With that, Borya found on his cell phone a recording he'd stored and set in on play: it was the sounds of two people engaged in sex – it was mainly panting and moaning, with a little guitar instrumental background.

Because of the sound effects, no one heard Delila moan for real, as she wakened and cringed as she looked at the bite mark around her nipple. Her eyes widened as she saw the film, the three men in lawn chairs, and Brock – taped to the front of the motor home.

"I'd rather have a go at her. Now. I don't need the movie," grumbled Ras.

"Later. But she'll be yours. Egor, too. But later. My use for the dumb cunt is over, now. I promise you, once we're done with Monsieur Limp, you can do whatever you want with her. Enjoy. But later."

Delila's face reddened in anger and her thoughts raged as she considered what kind of revenge she might take. She saw the knife on the corner of the mattress and reached for it. Handled it.

Brock watched Delila. The other three men were too engaged with the video to notice her actions. In his mind, Brock willed Delila to act; to do anything that might set the two of them free.

Delila thought about her options. She noticed the incised message running on the topside of the knife. Weird. No spaces between the words. She read it, quietly, to herself – struggling with the wording. "After *h* meets the sky I'll see one person die and when *m* meets the sea, total chaos will be, unless after babe I am thrown, to narrows dark and unknown, and from a bridge on the lee where in depths I'll be free."

There was an inexplicable flash of light. In response, the three seated twitched ever so slightly, and almost glanced sideways but they were just too mesmerized with the video to allow any kind of minor distraction.

But Delila did refocus and found herself staring at Brock's phone.

Brock followed her line of vision. *Yes,* he thought. *Dial someone: anyone. Or better still, press the emergency button.* She placed the knife down. Coyly, though hardly necessary, as the three captors were still mesmerized by the screen, Delila reached for the cell. She looked at the phone's screen with surprise and for the first time in a long while, thought she might be lucky. The phone wasn't locked. In fact, on it, was Toque's face by her phone number.

Delila reached and pressed the icon. Then just as she heard a faint, "Hello," Ras glanced her way.

"Hey, look, Sweetie is awake!" yelled Ras, "I can do her now!"

Delila pulled her hand back as if struck, but before she did, slipped the phone back under Brock's clothing.

"No. Later. We'll need her if the video doesn't get copper-boy going. I've got some pretty creative ideas on what we can do with her to harden him up."

"Fuck. Okay. But nothing is happening to Mister Limp so far."

"We'll get her to work on it if we need to … this guy is going to really regret what he did to …"

Toque had answered the cell and had heard enough. She could see Brock's location on
the phone. It was just a couple of blocks from where she was having a romantic dinner in the popular suspension bridge restaurant. In no time Toque, with her date, Lynn, were on their way to the location of Brock's phone.

"I'm sorry to drag you along, Lynn, but I can't lose any time. And we're right here."

"Always a pleasure, to be with you, no matter what."

But as they tore along the few blocks on Capilano, the road was like a river of rain and snow melt. And suddenly, as they moved, all the street lights went out, as did the lighting of all shops. And all apartments, townhouses, and houses went black, as did their Christmas lighting and the huge air-filled cartoonish inflatables deflated.

Likewise, there was no electricity in the garage set for torture: so the video stopped – leaving only the panting sound effects to continue in the darkness, curtesy of the battery-operated cell phone.

"Shit! What the hell? Those fuckers weren't supposed to take out the power yet! Can't they get anything right? But especially not now: I need this projector working!" cursed Borya.

But then the emergency generator of the attached house sprung to life, providing power to parts of the residence, including the back-up garage light which then illuminated with a dull glow.

The three captors waited in anticipation, motionless, staring at the projector, hoping for it to spring to life. But there was nothing, except for the sound of the panting from the cell phone's speaker.

Then, only seconds later, Toque and Lynn came crashing through the door.

Delila, though still a little hazed by the dope, sensed an overwhelming warmth in her very core and felt as if dual suns had arrived on the darkest of days. In spite of her own situation, Delila smiled at the sight of these two dream rescuers. Inspired by Toque and Lynn, Delila joined their quest and grabbed the knife, then threw it with all her might and it hurled through the air, soon skimming the top of Borya's skull, causing a deep wound, deep enough that his blood spurted freely, changing his fair hair to a bloody mess. The knife then clattered to the floor.

Ras rose from his chair but as he stood, Toque tackled, sending him crashing down and onto the concrete floor. Lynn assisted, sitting on the struggling convict to keep him from causing any more harm.

Egor, now off his chair, grabbed Toque from behind, but she raised her arms and threw him across the garage, knocking over the projector that fell to the floor with a crash.

Delila staggered forward, but still drugged, stumbled and fell. Then leaving Ras free to get up, Lynn ran to Delila's aide, and with a gentle strength wrapped her arms around the stark – naked beauty.

The sound of nearing sirens filled the air.

Toque ran to Brock, and then Lynn joined her, releasing Delilah. Toque and Lynn then struggled at removing the duct tape, which stuck much surer than any bandage ever invented. Delila, after scrambling to pull on her scanty clothing, hurried to help but ended up with the tape in her hands that was around his upper thighs, alongside his genitalia, and probably because of the dope, she found the process worth at least one giggle as he cringed.

Borya grabbed the knife and jumped into the motor home, followed by Ras and Egor as they stampeded inside.

Then, with only half of the entrapping duct tape removed, the engine to the motor home roared to life. Panicked, Lynn, Toque, and Delila grabbed Brock's limbs and tore him from the front of the motor home, just as it powered up, driving right through the closed garage door, and narrowly missing Brock and his three rescuers.

***

An hour or so later, Brock, Delila, Toque, and Lynn were exiting the detachment hall lit entirely with emergency lighting.

"How the hell could the power in the main North Vancouver terminal have been sabotaged?" asked Lynn.

"We'll find out. I guarantee it," responded Brock.

"This must be the ninth plague!" said Toque, thinking out loud.

"It seems that Borya, Ras and Egor have me for an alibi this time," said Brock, dryly.

Toque and Brock looked at their 'dates' uncomfortably, both thinking, *It seems to have provided you two with alibis as well.*

Lynn eyed up Delilah, and subconsciously licked her lips as her pupils dilated. She thought to herself, *Wow, luscious lady! If it wasn't for Toque ...* Lynn reined herself in, then spoke, asking, "Are you the one that Brock's been seeing?"

Delilah paused, not too sure as to what to say, it being obvious by then that she had been in cahoots with Borya when Brock was chloroformed and captured. For that reason, she responded with an understatement, "We've been together a few times."

"Yes, we have. But I gotta say that I've been on more enjoyable dates than the one we were on tonight," added Brock, caustically. But then, thinking about Delilah throwing the knife at

Borya and having been the one to contact Toque, looked at Delilah, and added, "But there's definitely been moments that were memorable."

While Toque thought of Brock and Delilah, on the *Angel*, clearly having just had sex, Toque would have harrumphed if she could have deemed that she herself, had a slate that was clean. But she didn't. She, too, had been involved in at least one relationship that probably had gone further than it should have. She was then even more uncertain. Maybe a bit confused.

Delilah was unsure of herself, and couldn't think of what to say.

"Well, why not make up for this nightmare by having a meal out together?" suggested Lynn, "We could go on that double-date sometime over the next few days!"

Delila, still emotionally numb from the night's events, and tormented by guilt, with a half whisper agreed, while Brock was distinctly uncomfortable but after a pause, thought again about being saved by Delila. And he thought about how Borya was clearly a misogynist who was using her for anything and everything. And, what made Delila even more pathetic, was the reason why she was an easy pawn for Borya: she was already diminished by lying and cheating lowlifes who took what they could. *In fact*, Brock continued to reason, *It is very likely that Delila is not even sure of what kind of life she now actually wants.* He inwardly sighed, reflecting on the unjust trials she'd suffered.

All three women were looking at Brock, waiting for his answer.

Though reluctant, he agreed.

CHAPTER 85

Grant glanced up from his desk as Mrs. Bean entered the room. She was back to her ball of white hair, but this time her dress was surprisingly conservative: she wore a navy-blue skirt-suit with a freshly ironed white tailored blouse. On her feet were shiny black pumps. It seemed as if she was in uniform. Her only jewelry was that of extremely small gold ear studs and a simple gold chain with a small heart-shaped pendant.

"Captain Abraham and Director Sandford Graham are both the line."

Grant picked up immediately, saying, "It seems that mother nature might do the flooding for these jerks."

Graham sighed. "You said it! This is the first time we've had to evacuate everyone living by the dike in Steveston."

Abraham summed up: "It's like the perfect storm: giant snow falls in November, huge melts in December, the king tide, and now another massive storm."

"The Fraser River flooding at this time of year has never happened! At least nothing like this! But, as we speak, more troops are on the way," reported Graham.

Grant moaned. "It is likely too late for that subdivision below the dike. All those homes will be toast!"

"It's worse than ever before: there used to be the odd log lost from a logging operation tossed over the dike when there was a storm ... but this!" exclaimed Abraham.

"Captain, you got anything back from our offer to talk to the plague lowlifes?" asked Grant, focussing on issue that had dogged them for weeks.

Abraham rubbed her eyes. "It's not good ..."

"What?" asked Graham.

"They said, 'Too little, too late' and they're taking credit for the sabotaging of the power station: they hacked into the system there."

"Shit! Who are these people? Computer hacking to deliver the threat of darkness! And now there's a new threat?" asked Grant, with fear in his tone.

"Now they've done the darkness, it's a modified version of the last email, that we must release Voronin, Kuznetsov and Oblonsky or there will be flooding and death."

"We feared it would be the death of the firstborn."

Abraham's voice trembled. "It is … and they said after that, perhaps they'll consider talk but after … and if we're lucky, before the fire of their wrath."

"The fire threat … again. What the hell are they thinking?"

"Shit! What do we do now?" moaned Grant.

"Track down that green motor home, bring in Pearce Cudmore, and bring in anyone else who is even in the least way suspicious! And find that bloody Borya Morozov," demanded Graham.

"Agreed."

"We bring in everyone who could know anything!" said Grant, determined.

"Let's do it!"

"That means we have to round them up in the next couple of days: the worst weather will be Christmas Eve!"

CHAPTER 86

It was just as the sun was rising behind the white-capped Mount Baker when Brock returned to the *Angel*. It was right after the horrid night when he was duct-taped to the green motor-home. From the marina gate, Brock could see an anxious Rex in the cockpit. Somehow Rex knew that his master had finally returned, and was restlessly moving back and forth, waiting for a sighting to match his hunch that his master was near. And then, when Brock reached the base of the ramp from the gate, he was in sight, and Rex jumped from the deck. In no time, Rex was upon him, licking every square inch of both of Brock's hands.

Brock beamed as he bent down and gave Rex's back a long stroke. "There, there, boy, I'm back. I'm okay."

And while Brock was bent over, Rex affectionately administered one big lick across his master's face. Brock laughed the laugh of a man who had returned to his home after battle, and found that his family was still there and were forever unmoving in their love for him.

Rex walked by Brock's side so close that his fur was touching Brock's pant-leg, as if somehow he knew that his master had just faced some terrible ordeal. When at the *Angel*, Brock reached his hand onto a stanchion to board, and he glanced sideways at a pile at the end of the pier: that had to be Rex's work. Rex had dutifully deposited his waste at the furthest corner of the pier, having no master apparent to take him for walks. Seeing the direction of Brock's line of vision, Rex looked worried, and whimpered, remembering his previous owner who would not have tolerated this. Rex cringed at the memory, but Brock patted Rex on the head, saying, "Good boy. You did the best you could when I wasn't here."

Though heart-warmed to be home with Rex at his side, Brock's whole body was one big ache; skin here and there all over his torso and limbs had been damaged by the duct tape or was left feeling itchy, bearing the remnants of duct tape glue. When his feet touched the floor of the cock-pit, he immediately sat on one of the seats, exhausted physically and emotionally. As soon as he sat, Rex cuddled close, placed his head on Brock's lap, and looked up sympathetically, somehow knowing that his best friend was in pain.

"Well, ol' boy. I'll have to collect the gift you left at the end of the pier. Then we can relax and have dinner."

"Woof," replied Rex, recognizing the word, dinner.

Rex clambered into the galley after Brock and as he opened a drawer of miscellaneous items, almost simultaneously Rex stuck in his nose to help. Also, there was no way Rex was going to get separate again from his master, if he had any say in the matter. Then, somehow knowing what was on Brock's mind, Rex nosed the roll of dog-waste bags towards his master's hand and while he did, licked the attached fingers.

Once the clean-up was complete, and they were back on board, the first thing Brock did was to tear open a bag of Cheesesnacks, eat a fistful, gulp down half a beer, then pour out an extra generous serving of kibbles. Trying to be good, Rex glanced at his food, then stared at Brock, who paused for a few seconds then smiled as he said, "Go for it, Bud," and Rex dug in, as if he hadn't eaten for over twelve hours, which in fact, he hadn't.

After Brock had taken Rex for a brief walk along the waterfront under skies darkened by the earie onslaught of dark grey clouds, Brock showered and removed the duct-tape glue, then pulled on an old grey track suit, soft against skin scrubbed pinkish in places where the glue would not release. He'd gone to town with dinner: a full can of pork and beans and three bags of Cheesesnacks. A second beer sat ready on the table. But before he could take even a sip, Brock leaned back on one of the bench seats of his galley settee, and fell dead asleep, with Rex on the galley floor, with one of his paws on one of Brock's feet, and his head on the other, as if a pillow.

But as Brock slept, he had an appalling nightmare: he was with Rex, his ever-helpful companion, and they could see Toque trapped on a narrow ledge of a cliff face, with the ocean crashing below. She called out for help, but there was no way of reaching her. His mind wondered wildly, *Where are Lynn and Joe?* Brock's neck ached from staring up at Toque. There was no way he could reach her: he felt totally useless. He looked and looked and called and called but she couldn't hear him and couldn't see him. He searched all around her precarious ledge, wishing to see some foot-holds and hand-holds: but it was a sheer cliff face, shining wet in the cruel sun.

He then desperately perused the sky, wishing for help from beyond. And then, as if a miracle, the supernatural occurred, with the strange and misty formation of the image of his beautiful wife, April. And with kindness in her voice, she spoke, "I said before when you were in trouble, our love will always be a splendid summer, but for you, a brand-new life should now begin. You must move on: a brand new spring is just around the corner."

Then, as her image faded, Brock woke himself by yelling, "I don't know if ..."

He jolted awake: his heart pounding and his body aching from the real world. And Rex, at his side, was waylaid with sleepiness, though in just a minute or two snapped awake. His long pink tongue reached out, and again he gently licked his master's hand.

Brock smiled, then struggled to his feet. With his body stiff, patted Rex on the head, and peered out the galley window into the wall of rain and skies that, because of dense clouds, were practically black even though it was day. Aside from the pounding rain, there was no sound – except that of a distant train whistle, from across the waters and from the tracks passing through the North Vancouver ship yards.

Chapter 87

It was mid-morning on December 24th. The West Coast was experiencing a brief hiatus from the storm, though horrific rain and wind were expected within hours. Already every single creek was in full flood. Many were running over their banks, including upper Capilano's McKay Creek that for centuries had gradually taken more than a couple of dog-legs in its path.

As strongly suggested by Director Graham, most of the suspects had again been questioned. Even Lynn and Delila had been held, but there was no evidence. So they had to be released. Only Peanut remained.

It was Lily Sun and Nat Boucher who went again to question Pearce Cudmore at his home. The house seemed empty: only Pearce's car was visible in the parking area.

After the two officers reached the top step at the front door, just before they knocked, they could hear noise in the adjacent pool. Then a loud moan. Then another moan. Then a male voice cracking as if going through the change of puberty. Then another voice demanding, "More! More!"

Before Sun and Boucher considered the source of the noise, they ran in its direction. They were on the pool deck in no time, almost skidding to a full stop, as they then stared in astonishment at Peanut's gargoyle swimming around, snapping at nothing, over and over again. But then they saw them: the backs of the naked Petra and Peanut.

Sun and Boucher had no way of knowing that it was Petra from the daycare: the young woman that Cudmore's mom seemed to hate. But she was the one that the kids loved. And they could see that she was liked even more by the young Peanut.

Peanut and Petra: the same couple that had been in the daycare's back room when Toque and Brock went to pick up little Matvey.

Sun and Boucher gaped at Petra and Peanut, both in the steamy pool, though it was nothing like the steam that was rising from Peanut as he rammed Petra from behind, over and over, as she supported herself on the side of the shallow end of the pool. The mechanical gargoyle maneuvered towards the pounding sex frenzy. They could see that Petra's modest breasts above the water level had turned a kind of a pinkish-blue from the cold with nipples harder than shelled walnuts.

Peanut's face was euphoric with glee while Petra's face was locked in a stony stare. "You're great," she murmured, though she was looking sideways at the view of the distant city, but maintained her position, resolved to get the job done.

The gargoyle arrived at Peanut's hip, just as he turned his face to see Sun and Boucher almost upon them. "Get me a towel," he demanded, regarding the officers as if they were paid servants.

Sun smiled the smile of seeing a bank robber who'd just tripped over the curb by the get-away car as she said, "I'm sorry, Master Cudmore. That's not in my job description."

But Boucher's face turned to a most angelic smile, as she picked up a couple of towels, and leaned over to hand them to the age-mis-matched couple. "Hey, I'll bend the rules this time. Here you go." But Boucher, with her trained morality of modest behavior, stood a little too far away for either Peanut or Petra to reach the towels. Peanut, wanting to play the male-protector role, reached up, as he boosted himself with one arm, and reached for the towels with the other. His shoulders cleared the deck level, while most of his slender whiter-than-white anatomy remained in the pool. At that instant, the gargoyle arrived, at first snapping its mechanical jaws, but then it paused as it nudged against Peanut's butt. And then the jaws opened wide and chomped down, cutting into the tender flesh of the seventeen-year-old buttocks.

"Fuck!" Peanut yelled, and if the sight of the visiting officers hadn't caused enough shrinkage, his penis then went into full retreat and soon resembled the head of a turtle when threatened. Flustered and hurting, he grabbed the gargoyle and smashed it down onto the tiled pool deck.

"Peanut's legal," was the first thing Petra uttered, seemingly not caring about her lack of clothing and climbing full-frontal from the pool, and planting her hands on her hips as if she was normally nude when she conversed with officers.

Then, just as Sun opened her mouth to speak, and Boucher, dumfounded, still held the towels in mid-air, Mrs. Cudmore stormed in, screaming, "What the hell is going on?" Glaring at Boucher, she voiced a full-volume, "I'll have my lawyer after you for this!" And then, focusing on Petra, shock preceded a sneer, as she regarded the young woman as being something akin to a giant slug that had risen to human height on the pool deck. "You! Another whore after my boy? Why aren't you at work? I donate wads to that hole, just to keep it going, and this is the thanks I get? And what in heaven's name have you been doing to my son? This is rape!" Then, as she eyed the nuts and bolts that once were part of the gargoyle added, "You've wrecked his toy ... er ... his invention! I'll see to it that you are sent back to whatever piss-pot country you've come from! After a full trial for rape!"

"Mother, will you let me explain ..." interjected Peanut, the last to climb from the pool. He stumbled out, trying to hand-cover his genitals, though he also tried flexing to look older. But it was his mother that was there. Right there. Just a few feet away from his naked penis. The last time she saw him unclothed was when he was in diapers, though that was not so long ago. But enough. Only seconds passed when he could feel the icy chill of his mother's stare, which was far worse than the cold of the December air. Then without a thank-you, he grabbed the towels from Boucher. Though to his credit, without pause, he by-passed his mother and moved to Petra, and helped her wrap herself in one of the towels. But then his hands hung – impotently at the end of his thin arms, at his sides.

Mrs. Cudmore harrumphed.

***

Shortly thereafter Peanut was apprehended, and again questioned. But as no new information could be gleaned and because he'd tampered with only some of the home surveillance recordings, many were unaltered, and some of those included the time periods of the crack planting – at both the *Angel* and Rockwater. No matter how one looked at it: Pearce had to be let go.

Ras and Egor Bogdanov had been be identified by Brock as two of his captors. An all-points-bulletin had been issued on the two of them.

Unfortunately, the police forces were no further ahead with Borya Morozov. He was still at large. He and the motor home's location were a mystery, though the tapes had found proof of where he *had* been. Borya had been spotted on CCTV at the gas station near Muriel's. The monitors clearly showed him staying in his motor home for the nights of the bloodying of Rockwater and also the night that the frogs were unleased at Capilano University. Also, the motor home had been recorded staying in the parking lot of a big-box store near the homeless shelter during the early morning hours of the week. That had to be the time-frame of the boils. But that was all history and only showed that he had been there in the past.

When they really wanted him, he and his motor-home had disappeared.

In fact, Grant, after forty-eight hours of a wide-scale search, stormed from his office, yelling, "How can a motor-home simply disappear?"

Chapter 88

While driving along in a cruiser mid-afternoon on December 24th, Toque and Brock were peering through the windshield. Everything was blurred by the pouring rain even though the wipers were on full speed.

What they already knew was being reported on the police radio: "Huge dumps of snow in November coupled with the current mass of Pineapple Express storms have caused an unprecedented snow melt, and never-before-seen flooding. More neighbourhoods may have to be evacuated." But then the radio crackled with a message from dispatch. "Please be on stand-by." Both Brock and Toque stared at the radio, as if they could see the words.

But nothing … yet … so they continued on, glumly taking in the news, while Christmas lights barely glimmered through the pounding rain.

"Shit! On my way here the radio said waves are starting to break over the Steveston dike!" reported Brock.

"I know! On the news yesterday it showed the cows mooing as they were being herded back over the dike. I felt so bad for them … and the farmers!"

"Were they the black ones that look like there's a white blanket around them?"

"Yup. They're called Dutch Belted." Toque hoped she wasn't sounding like a know-it-all.

"All part of this crazy weather!"

"Huge snow, now tropical rain."

"Welcome to global warming!"

"Unfortunately, that's the real key to this nightmare," agreed Toque.

"I have a real uneasy feeling that something is going to go down today."

"Me, too."

"I hate to think of it. Seems ripe for a man-made flood!"

"Something's brewing," ruminated Toque.

"But what do they have to gain if they go ahead with everything they've threatened? There goes the leverage for the release of their Scheveningen friends."

"There's still the fire thing."

"Crap! Of course!"

"But what can we do? I just can't believe that some sicko will be doing this on Christmas Eve!" moaned Toque.

"Unless …wait a minute. If Christmas is the day, which it might be, there is more than one faith that celebrates later …"

"Such as?"

"The Ukrainian Greek Catholic Church, and a number of others – like the Russian Orthodox. They all celebrate Christmas on … let me look it up on my cell: it's the seventh of January. If Borya is in the mix, the Russian Orthodox date would give him more time. And after the death of the firstborn – there will be an increased chance of them forcing us into freeing the three prisoners."

"And unfortunately, he is still out there."

"But after the episode in the garage, we do know that he is probably still in the Lower Mainland. The other thing is, he might justify in his sick mind that his sex-slave business was okay in the eyes of the church and that his buddies should have never been imprisoned."

Toque moaned. "The Bible justifying the sex-slave market! You're joking! You gotta be joking."

"Nope. I remember reading segments years ago. There are some things there that could be read the wrong way."

"Like using the Bible as a validation of slavery. A real twisted translation. Like the devil's rendition."

"If you believe in the devil. But no question about it being twisted. But remember when we wondered why Yana was so worried?"

Toque put her hands on her forehead, as if this thought was more than she could consider. "Oh, no, surely Morozov wouldn't target his own nephew!"

"She was *really* worried. Plus, some time ago, before you were attacked in the park …"

Toque cringed.

But Brock continued, "We wondered if it was Borya carrying the Bible. He could be using it for his own warped view of the world."

"I hope to hell ... but let's check out the daycare! Edgemont Village. Right?"

Brock cranked up the speed to full.

As they tore towards the village, Toque flicked on the siren.

Like the vehicle, their talk became rapid as thoughts cascaded.

"Another thing, with that daycare, I'm sure you remember Petra?" asked Toque.

"She didn't seem to be ... well, you've got a point – she is from Russia. Can you check on the computer and see if there are photos of the staff at All Faiths daycare?"

"You're wanting a picture of her?" asked Toque, feeling a sharp sliver of jealousy.

"Get the pic, then do a facial recognition on the web."

Toque shifted uncomfortably, agreeing, "Good point." Seconds passed. "Got the daycare staff pic. Doing a search. Images turning up. Let me see ... OH FUCK!"

Brock pulled over and looked at the images on the screen as Toque cut the siren.

Brock scowled at the half dozen photos displayed. One was a group shot with Petra, arm-in-arm with Kliment Voronin, Lev Kuznetsov, and Gleb Oblonsky. And there were a couple of pictures of Petra – on what looked like a date with Voronin. Then there was a side view of Petra with a frontal view of Borya Morozov. He had his hand on her butt, his thumb down the inside of the back of her jeans. And then another, of Petra in a revealing backless night-club dress with a lace front. Brock stared at the picture, stared some more, then focused on the content other than what was under the transparent lace. It was Ras that was holding onto her, a hand placed almost on her left breast. And, in yet another picture, was Petra in really short cut-offs and a halter top. In that shot, the arm around her belonged to Egor, his body pressed hard against her side.

"I don't know what Petra does to get these guys interested, but we'd better crank it up and get there ASAP."

As Toque was about to flick on the siren, the intercom came on: "All units in the Edgemont Village area, go direct. What was McKay Creek has turned into a river that has re-routed. Edgemont

Village in its direct path. The flood waters will be there momentarily! All units direct! Exercise extreme caution!"

"Oh my God!" cried Toque, "The daycare!"

Chapter 89

Just a couple of minutes later, on pavement already submerged, Brock slammed on the brakes at the entrance to All Faiths Family Daycare.

They had no way of knowing that on a road not far above the village, the green motor-home had crashed into a foot-bridge where McKay Creek veered west, at the beginning of a road called Emerald Drive. The motor-home rammed itself onto the bridge, taking out the fenced pedestrian railings. The wheels on driver's side, were on the bridge, but the other two hung in mid-air. Then, under the skewed vehicle's weight, the bridge crashed downwards, blocking the flooding creek's path enough so that the hurling waters backed-up, in a torrent-filled backwards surge. The churning waters found a new course, and flooded onto an ancient creek-bed seen from above as a narrow green belt a hundred feet to the east. McKay Creek-turned-raging-river again roared downwards, taking its new direction, and hungrily sucking into its currents any debris that wasn't grounded to bed-rock.

The driver of the motor-home, unobserved in the hurling storm, stumbled from the tail-gate and ran off towards Edgemont Village.

Toque and Brock were parking in front of the daycare. As they climbed out, Toque was shocked to see Lynn, with a wrapped Christmas gift in hand, standing on a raised planter area, attempting to keep her feet out of the water that was beginning to flood the sidewalk.

"Lynn, what are you doing here?" asked Toque, "You know this isn't your visitation day."

Although more than happy to see Toque, Lynn was experiencing the turmoil of the parent deprived of being with her own child. Lynn stammered, her eyes wet. "Yeah, but it's Christmas Eve, for crying out loud. I just wanted to drop off a gift for Nikki."

"But ..." interjected Toque.

"I know I'm not supposed to be here. I thought that if I could just see her leave with Carla, I could just give her ..." Lynn's voice cracked as she trailed off, her head hanging down.

"Look, how about if Brock and I see if Carla is inside, or maybe see when Nikki is going to be picked up," offered Toque, "You don't want to make things worse than they already are. I'll find out, and be back in a minute."

Lynn gave a downhearted nod, though her features showed a slight glimmer of hope.

As soon as Toque and Brock took a step into the daycare, they could see a crazy scene of children laughing or screaming with joy as they played in the waters that were moving in. But what was truly terrifying was that they could see Borya, with the bloody gash still oozing from above his eyes. He laughed as he grabbed Yana's son, Matvey, then spoke in a crazed tone mixed with fervour, "I have a special magic knife trick I want to show you."

Toque and Brock paused for only a few seconds. Seeing Matvey, they rushed forward. Outside their peripheral vision on the left of the doorway, Petra had been anxiously looking out the window. Behind her, two of three toddlers sat on the sopping area carpet, splashing their chubby hands in the rising water. The image on the carpet, the life-size cartoon of Noah's ark, seemed to mock the emerging crisis. The third toddler, a girl named Elsie, had a pink rubber elephant in her hands and was trying to get the toy to have a drink from the water. As Toque and Brock skirted around the three and were just about to grab Borya, Petra lunged towards them.

Exactly when Brock reached for Borya, Petra grabbed Brock from behind, before he
could react.

At just about the same instant, Toque grabbed Borya. Matvey fell with a splash, onto the flooding floor. He laughed, thinking that the drop was part of a pretty good game. But Borya, with all his strength, back-flipped Toque against a stool, where she cracked her head and passed out. She crashed to the floor and ended up lying at a skewed angle, with her head tilted up on the pink rubber elephant that hissed air as she crushed down on it.

"Here, Elpan," cried Elsie, as she tugged at the toy that was under the unconscious Toque.

Borya grabbed Brock's arm just as he was about to break free of Petra's grip but as soon as Borya pitched in, Brock was overpowered. Borya lost no time in doing a foot-sweep so that Brock crashed to the submerged concrete floor, bashing his head. But still conscious, he was alert enough to know that Borya had the fantasy knife held at his throat.

Borya laughed. "This should get my Scheveningen friends out!"

"But why the plagues? Why do the first born have to …" protested Petra.

"Nanny Petra, Nanny Petra. That lady's sleeping on Elpan!" complained Elsie as she continued to pull at her toy.

Borya ignored the child and looked at Petra. "Don't you remember: it was the peanut-brain's idea."

"No!" screamed Petra, standing up, ignoring the complaining child.

"Yes! What I do and what my partners do, is Biblical. We are like priests! Priests of the sex biz!"

"Devil priests," moaned Brock, struggling with consciousness.

The two toddlers on the area carpet continued to happily splash their hands and Elsie, seeing their fun, gave up on retrieving her toy, and joined in on the splashing.

"Women are just cunts," snarled Borya, "I am entitled to do what I want."

Brock continued the fight to retain consciousness.

With insanity in his eyes, Borya continued his rant, sounding like a crazed evangelist: "I almost hope that I will be able to enact the great plan I have: fire and brimstone – the fire of my wrath. The deaths will be nothing compared to what will come! The losers cops will wish they'd never been born!"

Brock attempted to move and Borya pushed the knife into Brock's throat. Blood was soon running down towards the nape of his neck.

"What are you doing with the magic knife? Are you going to show me the trick soon?" asked Matvey.

Petra screamed, "Borya, please, we don't want a dead cop. We're going to get married! I love you! Not this! Please!"

Peanut arrived and as soon as he entered the daycare, became stunned with indecision as he took in the chaos in front of him.

"Married to me! Ha!" snarled Borya, "You'll be Kliment's girl once he's free! You stupid cunt!"

Peanut looked from Petra to Borya, but then barely glanced at the pinned-down Brock when he saw the downed Toque and rushed to her, and started to undo her top collar.

Borya glanced over and laughed. "Ha! That's my boy! Take off her clothes! Let's see everything! Don't stop at the shirt!"

"That wasn't my ..." stammered Peanut.

But Lynn, who'd tired of waiting, entered the daycare, heard what Borya said, and
bellowed, "That's not going to happen." She rushed over and clobbered Peanut. He crashed to the submerged floor and then, to immobilize him, Lynn sat on him.

"Magic knife, magic knife!" chanted Matvey as he ran over to the three toddlers still splashing their hands while sitting on the area carpet.

"Magic knife?" asked one of the toddlers, "I want the magic knife!"

"Magic knife, magic knife," chanted the other two as they got up and ran over to a group of kids at the table who were taking an art break from running around splashing. One of the children at the table smiled and said, "Watch me! I'll draw a magic knife!"

With tears forming in her eyes, Petra looked at Borya. "But Kliment is an animal! You know what he does with women! I did as you said – time after time with him. Now you can go back to bringing in – fresh blood, you say. But I'd be there – with only you."

Peanut struggled, but couldn't break free. "Wait a minute ..."

Borya ignored Peanut and continued, "Okay, I'll keep you around. If you're not going to be with just Kliment, you'll do all four of us. You'll be with whoever I say. You've got to remember: you're a huge asset – but only as a team player!"

"I don't want to be a team player!" screamed Petra.

"Ah, relax! You'll have a smaller work load, or should I say fuck load? Egor or Ras are gone. I was going to put them down but they turned out to be of use. That is, along with Peanut's school pals, by doing most of the messy stuff. But now the two gofers are on their way to where-ever: they're stowaways on some freighter. Gone."

"I don't give a shit about those two. I don't want to be a team player! I want to be your wife," sobbed Petra.

"Wife!" roared Peanut, struggling to free himself, "You and Borya promised that you'd be with me! What you've done before is just that: done! That's over! It's you and me now!"

Two pre-schoolers, chasing one another, ran past the trapped Peanut, splashing water in his face. He blinked, twisting his head, trying to get the water from blurring his eyes.

"Shut up Peir...Peanut, and wait till I can get that lard-ass off you. We can talk this out later – man-to-man," yelled Borya.

Brock struggled in and out of consciousness and the vague sensation of something cutting his throat. There was a warm wetness there.

"Fuck you!" yelled Pearce, squirming under the hold of Lynn, "I helped you with all your plans. I even came up with the plague idea!"

"That *was* a great idea. And soon the fire! I have some fantastic plans; my Scheveningen friends will be freed by the time we get to the real Christmas. It will mark the birth of a second coming! Ha! But Pearce, man to man, help me with this fucking cop! Get away from that dough-mound! Come-on! You are part of my team. Look at Petra. Waiting for you. Tonight. Just look at those tits and ass. You can have her – all night, once we're done here. Tonight, is the night you can do anything you want! Just get up, and help me."

Peanut struggled but remained pinned down. "We're not a one-night stand! It was and will be – but what's this shit about being *your* wife?" Impotently, he floundered under Lynn's weight. Then he eyed the downed Brock being held by Borya.

Petra placed her hands on her hips and demanded, "Borya, I tell you. I'm finished being part of your team! I want you. Only you!"

Borya strained as he kept the knife to Brock's throat: determining the best moment for the final cut. "Petra, we can talk later. You know I love you. Don't forget that. You know I need you. And I need you to be part of this. As we agreed," uttered Borya, gritting his teeth. "Now get the kids and move them into the back room. Matvey will be first. And get that lard-ass off Peanut."

"Do I get to see the knife's magic? First? Oh boy!" exclaimed Matvey.

Meanwhile, three girls were happily playing tea time in the play kitchen. "Knife?" asked Matvey's sister, Vanna.

"We could use them for our tea. My mom can have some when she's not playing with those other people," suggested a second girl, Nikki, glancing at Lynn, just before she proceeded to find a pink rubber knife in the doll tea-set.

Danielle, the third girl, dipped cups into the water on the floor, singing, "Magic knife, magic knife. Stir it with a magic knife. Then we'll all have tea with the magic knife!"

The kids might as well have been invisible. Borya looked over to Peanut and tried to gush praise. "Pearce, you have been a real trooper. We need you as part of the team! I want you helping Petra. Now!"

Peanut eyed Borya, uncertain.

Borya continued, "You and your cronies have done a lot but I need you now! You are a real man! You know what I mean. And I know Petra would agree! You're a soldier! But now ... it's time for the first-born!"

Borya then laughed like a man deranged as he yelled, "It's slaughterhouse time!"

Chapter 90

The door to the street flung open as the floodwaters rose to several inches deep. In stepped Delila who surveyed the scenario.

"What the hell are you doing here?" cursed Borya.

"I tracked you on the cell phone. I thought that maybe I misunderstood and got it all wrong and that you and I …"

Brock inwardly squirmed, his consciousness tentative, at best. But aware of the knife … at his throat. Delila's words seemed so distant. He wondered if she was really present or if he was imagining her being there.

Petra ignored Delila, and continued her fight with Borya. "No! I'll only do what you want if you again agree to marry me! I am not like those other women: those sluts you controlled!"

Delila's eyes widened with the shock of extreme betrayal. She looked at Brock, the knife at his throat, and cursed. "What the fuck …"

Borya held down Brock, who was just semi-conscious, with the knife at his throat and blood oozing out around its blade. "Oh fuck! Okay, Petra, you and I can get married as soon as we've done the kids!" conceded Borya as he glanced in the opposite direction, making the face of someone who has just deliberately lied.

Lynn, still holding down Peanut, was weakening, and kept glancing sideways at the unconscious Toque.

Looking at Petra, Peanut yelled, "No-o-o-o-o. You are my girlfriend now! I did everything the two of you said! You both promised!"

"Where's Elpan?" asked the toddler, Elsie, as she wandered here and there with a revisiting concern, remembering her favorite toy.

"Not in here," called a pre-schooler peering out the window of the playhouse while two others took turns making splashes by jumping from the playhouse door-step and into the water.

Petra glanced at Peanut, then steadied her gaze on Borya. She paused, then seemed to feel that perhaps things were going to be alright. "Okay, but we'll be married like you said, right after – the business in the back room. But Peanut doesn't need to be part of this. He has to get out. I'll see to it and once he's gone, I'll do my part. Give me the knife."

With that, she took the knife from Borya, then grabbed one of the step-jumpers by the hand and moved determinately towards Lynn who was still holding down Peanut.

The other step-jumper looked miffed: although he no longer had to wait a turn, found that half the fun was lost if he was on his own. He called to the boy in the playhouse window, "Hey, you want to take turns?"

Before Petra reached Lynn and Peanut, Brock was gaining consciousness and almost tossed Borya who then panicked and yelled, "Oh fuck! Come back, you stupid cunt. Come back with that knife. Our first victim has to be this fucking cop! He's really starting to piss me off."

Petra paused, the knife hanging from her hand, the child held by the other.

Peanut's eyes turned to angry slits, though he returned his focus to Toque who was lying in the rising waters. Still unconscious, she fought for breath, sputtering, choking, gagging as the water moved in ripples over her helpless form.

Peanut then pleaded with Lynn, "I was only trying to help her breathe by undoing her collar button. Let's help her before it's too late."

Lynn paused momentarily, uncertain, but wanted to believe Peanut. Her feelings for Toque were so strong that in no time she was helping Peanut lift Toque's face from the flood waters that soon would have drowned her.

In a few minutes, Toque was coming to full consciousness. As she opened her eyes, it was with horror that she saw her partner, with blood oozing from his throat, as he thrashed in an attempt to break free of Borya. But as Brock flailed, Borya formed a full fist and plowed him in the side of the head. Brock's world turned black.

Paying no attention to the interchange between Peanut and Toque, Delila, hearing Petra's rant, screamed, "Marry her? You said I was the only one!"

"Fuck off, Delila. You're done. Go get yourself some crack!"

"But you forced me … and you promised!"

"That was a come-one, you moron! I have always known that you are totally useless except as a coke vacuum ... except for what's between your legs."

Delila's face reddened. "You drugged and used me as if I was nothing but a sex-slave. And now that I find you've got another woman you're stringing along ... I'm glad that I've finally woken up. I hope your new girl-friend wakes up and sees you for the asshole you are!" Tears were streaming down her face. She looked at the downed Brock, having blinked out that he was even there, but then saw him clearly and became overwhelmed with not knowing what she could do. He had tried to help her. The only one.

"Ha! A druggie slut like you! Interested in you! What a joke! Anyone with eyes will see what a useless whore you are!" snarled Borya.

"I hate you!" cursed Delila.

Seconds later, Borya, his eyes narrowed, laughed the laugh of scorn, then sneered, "The door is right behind you. See if you can manage an exit. As for me, I've got important work to do. Petra, you've got my word, now get your ass in gear, bring me the knife, and as soon as you get it to me, get all the first-born brats together! We have no time to lose!"

But before Petra responded, Matvey splashed close, hugged Borya from behind, while he was still holding down the semi-conscious Brock. Matvey persisted. "Unkabora, Unkabora! Can I go first? I want to see you do magic with the knife! Please! I love magic! What will it do? Please-e-e-e-e? Please show me first!"

Petra was unsure. There was Peanut with that other woman helping the female cop. Pearce: he was helping. She didn't know what to do. She moved towards the back room, the pre-schooler still in her hand, the knife still in the other. She looked at the child who held her hand. He was so young, so helpless, and so clear of any evil. And there was little Matvey, thinking this was only a game.

Toque saw her chance.

Borya glanced sideways into the pre-schooler's eyes that were like his own eyes, into the face that was so much like his own. He paused.

"Why does Nanny Petra have the knife? Is this part of the magic trick?" asked Matvey.

The flood waters were pouring in with vengeance, and most of the children were splashing and screaming with naïve joy. But the promise of a magic knife was spreading like a virus and their curiosity was stirred while they enjoyed the daycare-turned waterpark.

"We-e-e-e-e-e-e-e! Let's see the magic knife! What can it do? What can it do?"

Toque, then upright, brushed Matvey to the side. Then, as she grabbed Borya's nearest arm, the toddler Elsie rushed over, and cried, "Elpan, there you are!" and from the submerged floor picked up her toy elephant, then hurried off.

With the reflexes of a cornered cougar, Borya stomped on the oozing wound on Brock's neck, then kicked Brock in the head. Swinging around, he smashed Toque in the face so that a bruise was forming almost before his fist retracted. Brock reeled. And before Toque had time to react, Borya swung a monster punch to her chest, causing her breath to be completely taken. Then, for a second time, that day, Toque crashed to the floor, this time with face down in the water. Borya laughed, then lifted his free leg and placed one knee onto Toque's head so that her face was under water. His other knee, pressed into the wound on Brock's neck.

Toque struggled to free herself, but was weakened by the blows and in seconds her movements slowed, then ceased. But then, just as her movements stopped, Brock forced himself to overcome his pain and spinning head, to break free of Borya's hold, and heave him to the side.

Matvey again scrambled to Borya's side, wrapping his small arms around his uncle's neck, crying, "Unkabora, Unkabora, don't you love me anymore? Why are you playing with the police and not me?"

Brock scrambled over to the unconscious Toque, then brought his lips to her mouth as he expertly applied CPR.

Before Borya could remove Matvey and stop Brock, Delila ran forwards, nudged Matvey to the side, then face-to-face screamed at Borya, as she gripped his shoulders, digging her fingernails into the skin. She screamed, "I tell, you, I am not going to let you toss me off like I'm garbage. I thought I'd got it all wrong. I should have known after the garage. But now it's crystal clear. I was fucking wrong ... but not in the way I thought. Now I know. I'll be the last one who will have anything to do with scum like you."

Save for letting go of the one child, Petra just watched, the knife hanging from her hand, and her mouth open with indecision. She moved, ever so slightly: nudging the child at her side, saying, "Go to the play-house. I'll be there in a minute."

"Let me go, you stupid cunt!" cursed Borya.

But Delila's hands and nails held, though just for an instant. He pulled free, grabbed her, then body-slammed her into the rising waters snarling, "Good riddance, drug-slut."

"Unkabora, Unkabora! I want to play, too!" called Matvey. He grabbed his uncle, wrapped his arms around a leg, but Borya snarled, lifted Matvey by the collar, tearing the shirt as he tossed his nephew to the side, as if the child was nothing.

Lynn bolted over, wrapped her arms around Delila, and brought her face up, as Delila sputtered for air. Then, as Delila's breathing became steady, Lynn caressed her back. Delila, paused her hand on Lynn's shoulder.

But in an instant, angry venom again bubbled over, and Delila scrambled to her feet. She was not finished with Borya.

Then, for a second time, Toque reached full consciousness but this time, as she struggled, she felt Brock's lips on hers. The image of his face formed above her as if a dream. His lips on hers. For Brock, with his spinning head, it seemed the whole connection was an unreality. Like a touch in a haze. Toque almost responded to the lips on hers, but instead looked at her partner with the same kind of expression one might have if rescued by the Crown Prince of England. On a good day.

Two small faces watched from the window of the play-house.

Brock gained more and more awareness as he gazed into her eyes. With mixed emotions, he saw Toque become fully alert, and he moved back from her. He clambered to his feet.

As he stood, Brock was horrified to see Borya, his foot poised to kick Matvey in the head
but was momentarily paused by the crazed flailing and screaming of Delila. Matvey was helpless on the floor, his back exposed by his

403

shirt ripped wide open. Brock leaped up, and tackled Borya, just as his foot touched the pre-schooler's skull, but before any impact.

Then Brock and Borya both were crashing through the rising waters, making a bit of a bow wave as they barged across the flooded floor. As they careened forward, three children ran to make way, laughing at this new game.

Soon the two were wrestling past one of the play tables with stools all around, and then came crashing into the sand-box.

Then at full stop, Brock was on top; Borya was stunned.

Delila stepped back, ready to again pounce.

Two toddlers in the sandbox paused in their play of transporting water into a trench they had formed in the artificial sand, their shovels in mid-air, and gaped at the men who had crashed alongside.

Toque staggered over and with one huge effort, slapped hand-cuffs on Borya and held him secure.

One of the small children at the adjacent table jumped from his seat, entranced at the sight of the hand-cuffs. Ogling them, he placed his small hand on Toque's back while he asked, "Are they real cuffs? Do you have a key? Can I try it?"

"Can I try them on?" asked one of the two in the sandbox.

"Me too," added the second.

As Toque answered, "Another time," the children looked disappointed, then hopeful, and then went back to their stations of play.

But as the hand-cuffs clicked shut, cold, cruel reality cascaded into Petra's consciousness. Realization, shock, then hatred, affixed themselves to her features. "Borya, you piece of slime! You were engaged to her as well?" Her face reddened in anger. "You fucking asshole! And your piece of junk knife!"

With that, she raised the knife, and aimed it at Borya.

One of the watching children opened both eyes and mouth wide: amazed and impressed with the flailing of the weapon. He jubilantly shouted, "Let's see the magic knife work! But me first!"

"No, me first," yelled another daycare charge.

Deafening herself to the children, Petra paused, thought briefly, looked at the print etched on the knife and softly, to herself, read its text, unwittingly adding, "The evil here by good is taken."

She hurled the knife in Borya's direction. There was an inexplicable millisecond flash of light. Then, like a boomerang, the knife redirected itself and moved like a curve ball. As the knife flew, it seemed to lose momentum just as it reached a middle bookshelf where an ancient copy of the Bible lay on its side. The front end of the knife entered the book, then stopped suddenly and the lights in the room flickered, them seemed to become brighter.

When he saw the knife aimed at him, Borya broke free of Toque, and although his hands were cuffed, just seconds after the knife left Petra's hand, tackled her, sending her flying into the water.

Several children started crying, then realizing that this show was not meant as entertainment. The cold waters were getting more and more frigid. They were beginning to shiver. Matvey lay on the floor, crying, while the others ran – as fast as their little legs could carry them. They ran to the play-kitchen and the play-house, joining those already there.

As Petra crashed face down into the water, Toque and Peanut jumped in to help. Petra gasped for air. Peanut flushed: one of his arms had rubbed against Toque's left breast while he gripped Petra's arm, and also pressed into one of her breasts. It was almost too much for him.

As soon as Petra was upright and safe, Toque splashed after Borya.

As Borya staggered to the doorway, Delila raced to him, hooking a hand under his cuffed arm as she cursed. "Just wait a minute! You're not going to …" But Borya snarled, and with cuffed hands, bashed Delila hard. Her head whipped back as she flopped down. She was face down in the rising waters and not moving.

Lynn watched this, sprung in, and grabbed Delila around her torso. For just an instant, Lynn's arms and hands tingled as she gripped the soft body. Delila gasped for air but as her breathing steadied, she focussed on Lynn. Everything was in slow motion. It was just her and Lynn. They locked into a tight embrace. Their lips almost touched. Tears ran down their faces.

Twenty-seven little faces peered out, some from their crouched positions behind the play-kitchen counters, and others from the playhouse windows. All mouths were open wide.

Chapter 91

The door was heaved open, by someone desperate to enter, sending small waves across the daycare. In panic, Yana screamed, "Matvey, Vanna! Where you are?"

Borya had just reached the door and with handcuffed wrists, swung at Yana. "Get out of my way, you fucking traitor."

She spun sideways to the floor. Before she could raise her pregnant form, Matvey called out from where he'd been tossed by his hate-fuelled uncle. A few seconds later, Vanna ran out from the play-kitchen. Then crying for their mom, the two splashed their way over to Yana. And as they formed a huddle of three, tears spilled from Yana's eyes.

With one foot on the flooding street, Borya was just clearing the threshold when Brock threw himself over the huddle of Yana and her kids, making a perfect tackle.

Toque was practically there before it happened with some quick moves, the two constables had Borya pinned down.

Toque half-whispered to Brock, "Good work, Do-Right."

Brock grimaced a smile.

In seconds, more cops arrived, took Borya by the arms, and dragged him towards a waiting cruiser, one with bars separating the back seat from the front.

Yana's kids were more concerned about their own condition than the fact that their uncle had just been arrested. They were quick to be tattle-tales, with Matvey reporting, "Mommy, Mommy! Unkabora didn't show me the knife doing magic! And he said I would be the first! I was first!"

"And Unkabora's been fighting! With Nanny Petra and another lady! He hit them! And the police lady … and he hurt the police man!" added Vanna.

As the two pre-schoolers revelled in the close hug of Yana's arms, she held onto them as if she would never let go, and hurried them from the building as more officers pushed past them and into the flooding daycare.

Soon outside, Yana was tugging her children across the flooding street, heading for higher ground.

"Unkabora, Unkabora!" called Matvey as he recognized Borya being dragged towards the cruiser.

"What's he saying?" asked one of the officers as they struggled with the uncooperative Borya.

"Gibberish," replied a second officer.

"Stop!" yelled Borya, "I am their uncle! Don't you hear he's calling my name?"

The officers paused, skeptical.

"I am that woman's brother!"

The cop escorts kept their hands on the cuffed Borya.

"How will you two cops feel when you take me in, and find out that I am innocent! My sister right there can vouch for me!"

"Well?" asked one of the officers, looking at Yana.

"Not understand. We Russian."

The policeman thought, briefly. "But what about this guy? Is he your brother?"

"He not brother. No recognize," answered Yana as tears formed in her eyes while she hauled the kids across the street.

"Wait!" yelled Borya but Yana paid no heed.

In minutes, Borya was pushed into the police cruiser, and was on his way.

Before long, the daycare was filled with familiar police: Scott, Brown, Singh and Matthews from North Vancouver and from West Vancouver – Karimi, Trembley, Boucher, and Sun, all splashing towards the crying and frightened children.

The child named Nikki ran to her mother, Lynn, who hugged and soothed her terrified daughter.

Brock ran to retrieve the knife but as he reached it, had an unexplainable inclination to pause, and with great care, remove the weapon from the book in which it rested. Slowly, he opened the Bible and saw that the knife had intersected the book of Psalms and its tip was pointing at the compact text on the onion-skin paper which read, "Depart from evil and do good; seek peace, and pursue it."

The glimmer of a smile formed on his face, as he thought, *This intersection is one of most key messages of all time.*

As he picked up the knife, with some surprise, sensed that the knife was much smaller, yet inexplicably heavier than it had ever been, and rather than having a shiny gleam, was lackluster at best, like a coin that has been lost for years and the blade was as dull as a knife from the pre-schooler's tea set: it was as if the contact with the Bible had changed the knife's very chemistry.

The river waters continued to pour in everywhere. More police arrived, and were soon moving the toddlers and pre-schoolers up Highland Boulevard. There, inside the lobby of a retirement community, the children would wait for the arrival of their parents.

All traffic going towards Edgemont Village was being diverted.

Wanting to help, Petra lost no time in giving family contact numbers to the police. She finally understood what had almost happened.

But before the phone calls were made, some parents were already arriving. One was an extremely petit woman: it was the jockey that had run off with Delila's almost-fiancée.

Delila splashed towards her, snarling, "Do you remember me?"

The woman looked blank, then exclaimed, "Shit! How could I forget? You were hooked up with that looser I used to be married to!"

"You're no longer together?" stuttered Delila.

"How could I be? He'll run off and screw anything!"

Delila's jaw dropped open.

And then the petit woman called to the child being comforted by Singh, shouting, "Elsie! Mommy's here!" And in response, Elsie turned her head and smiled the smile of joy as she dropped her pink rubber elephant and ran to her mother's arms.

No sooner had the children's parent phone numbers been dispensed, when in the continued chaos of the huge river surge, the water gage in the daycare was at well over a foot, and Petra and Peanut, unnoticed, together waded out the back door.

The retirement community that became a rescue shelter for the children was aglow with seasonal lights, a huge Christmas tree, and carols were being softly played on built-in speakers. In the large welcoming lobby, on the mantle of a great stone fireplace was a menorah flanked on either side by a lighted angel. A huge banner in red and green with gold glitters read, "Glory to God in the highest, and on earth peace, good will toward men."

As the police arrived, with children in hand, other babes were arriving in cruisers. Lily Sun had a child on each hip while Boucher had child named Danielle, riding on her back, laughing at living through such an exciting day, and best of all, becoming friends with a police woman. Danielle's mother, Lacey White, arrived before Danielle was even set down. Lacey's cheeks were stained with tears, but when she saw Danielle riding on an officer's back, she couldn't help but laugh as she almost sang, "Sweetie, Mommy's here. It's time to go home and hang up your stocking! Santa's coming tonight!"

Toque was carrying a child over to a soft rug by a huge stuffed toy that resembled a cartoon Bernese Mountain Dog, just beside two ladies sipping hot apple cider and waving for Toque to bring the child over to the extra space on the sofa on which they were seated.

The resident seniors, having their pre-dinner appetiser and drink, were all smiles at seeing the arrival of the children: so young, so naive, and so endearing, especially considering that the hour marked the beginning of Christmas Eve.

Parents started arriving and like the others, an extremely worried Carla Rivers appeared. Lynn was still there with Nikki on her knee. Carla grimaced, seeing Lynn, but then paused, seeing their child truly happy. Carla heard the carols and her chest rose and fell with a sigh of relief. Her daughter was happy, and safe, and sound … and just as important, loved.

CHAPTER 92

It was at a popular restaurant where seafood, steaks, pasta, and vegan dishes were all proclaimed to be exceptional. It was the best waterfront restaurant in West Vancouver. The lights were dimmed and shed a soft golden glow throughout the dining room. Outside, Vancouver's sparkling lights were multiplied a hundred-fold by generous seasonal displays. The city seemed to be a fairyland. The storms had abated and clear skies were filled with brilliant stars twinkling on the black velvet back-drop.

Toque and Brock were side-by-side, with their dates across from them: Lynn and Delila. The table was small and very close. From the clash with Borya, stretching from Toque's cheek-bone to her jaw was a dark bruise, although it was very much muted by the soft dining-room light. Her other injury from the fighting at the daycare, the concussion, like that suffered by Brock, hung on, but only as a residual head-ache.

Lynn raised a glass. "Let's toast the solving of the plague mysteries!"

Brock and Delila glanced at each other uncomfortably. As promised, Brock had shown up.

Toque looked at Lynn, with an uncertain nervousness in her stomach, that was eased just a little, by the fact that Brock was beside her, almost like family ... except for that body of his ... except for his warm, deep, ocean blue eyes and ... except for the scent of Cedar Forest.

Then, just as they raised their glasses, Lynn smiled at Toque, placed her hand on Toque's hand that rested on the table, and asked, "You feeling better?"

Toque pulled back, Lynn cringed unhappily, but then became thoughtful as she perused the face of her semi-hesitant date.

Toque answered, "Sort of. But can't complain."

As she watched Toque speak, Lynn grasped onto something that no one else at the table understood.

Brock sipped at his drink, feeling ill-at-ease. "That was unbelievable how much water was in that village."

"No kidding. And the flooding in Steveston was horrific!" ruminated Lynn, "It was especially sad that it happened on Christmas Eve."

"Tragic," agreed Delila, "I've already signed up to help at the shelters."

"Me, too," added Toque.

"I guess we'll all be doing what we can," acknowledged Brock.

Lynn considered the others' words, and pointed out, "But in the bigger picture, we all have to get a better grip on what we've done to the planet."

"You got that right," observed Brock, "Borya's plagues were small potatoes compared to how we've screwed up the planet."

"Too true," commented Delila, "Now that the New Year is almost here, I've decided that
I'm going to get serious about doing something about it."

"Really?" asked Lynn, her eyebrows rising with new respect.

Toque affirmed the group's feelings. "We definitely all need to do something ... serious." Then turning to face Brock, paused a little too long, then asked, "But how are you feeling after the bashing we took from Borya?"

"Good as new," understated Brock, though as he took another sip of tonic water, he wished his head was clear enough to have a local beer. And his throat stung from the knife slash. "It's crazy that we were both knocked out by the same guy! I've got to say that Borya really is a force to be reckoned with!"

"You're telling me!" cursed Delila, "I'm telling you now, this is the last time any guy is going to take me in!"

"How about me?" said Brock, with a guarded chuckle.

Lynn and Toque sized up the exchange, more than interested.

Delila gazed at Brock. She paused, uncertain. "I have to say, that you've been really kind to me ... in every way ... but ..."

"But what?" asked Brock.

Before she could answer, a tall, heavily-built but well-dressed gentleman approached their table, followed by three other men who were also well-dressed in black fitted vested suits and were also tall; but unlike the first to approach, these three were model-like lean. And handsome. The best-looking men on the block, so to speak, not counting Brock.

Toque's mouth opened in surprise. "Joe!"

"Hey, Toque; Lynn: good to see you. Let me introduce you to my friends: Troy, Stefan, and Jimmy."

"Likewise – good to see you Joe, and glad to meet you – Troy, Stefan, and Jimmy. I'm Lynn, and this is Delila and there we have Brock."

Joe's three friends paused with a smile for Brock, gave him the once-over, then gave him the once-over a second time. They glanced at Lynn, nodded, scanned Delila, nodded, then turned what was initially a glance into a stare at Toque. An awkward moment.

"You're dining here?" asked Lynn.

Joe put his hand on Lynn's shoulder, a little too far down the front. "You're not the only one with divine taste, sweetie."

Joe's three friends chuckled at this joke. No one else did.

"I see you're starting the new year a little early with a fine dinner with friends," observed Joe.

"Good friends," replied Lynn as she smiled at Toque. Toque turned away, her eyes focussing on her wine-glass on the table, then looked up at Joe and his friends.

Joe grinned. "Likewise. Really good friends. The four of us are living it up before I have to again throw myself into the leadership race."

"I heard it's postponed to next month," commented Brock.

"Exactly right," replied Joe.

Then tentatively, Joe glanced at Delila, paused, stared, then managed to break away his locked focus but then his eyes met Toque's, and he could not turn away.

But for Toque, the eye contact was fleeting and she soon again gazed at only her wine glass.

No such focus for Joe, though. Between Toque's cleavage and Delila's almost exposed nipples, he almost got a hard-on on the spot. But then he returned his attention to his handsome companions, rallied himself together, and said, "Well, do have a good one, and while I'm here, I hope you'll all have a great New Year."

Lynn, Delila, and Brock, almost simultaneously smiled acknowledgment while Toque sat, motionless, trying to get over

412

being the victim of lustful staring. But as the four men headed off to their table, almost under her breath, she allowed a brief, "You, too."

Lynn regarded Delila. Wondered about the three bites at her hairline but as they were clearly healing, she put that thought on pause as she breathed in the beauty of this woman beside her. Yet three of the four men had barely glanced at this unbelievably stunning woman. As for Toque – no one could resist a prolonged gaze. Gay ... straight ... didn't matter: unabridged beauty was unabridged beauty. But they'd certainly taken more than a moment to size-up Brock. Not really confusing: as she thought briefly about Joe and his three friends. She and Joe were in some ways quite similar. Lynn further considered her table companions: but then focussed on Delila – sitting right beside her. This brown–skinned, dark eyed, red lipped, platinum blond was this night wearing a low-cut fluorescent blue body-hugging dress. She was beyond enticing, with her bust bursting outwards, above the flat stomach, even though she was sitting. In seconds, Lynn felt immersed in Delila's scent of Always Amorous, a fragrance that was like that of a tropical garden all in bloom.

Delila seemed almost dazed, and glanced at the ceiling, then at Lynn sitting beside her. Thinking that the gesture would not be an issue or even noticed by Toque or Brock, Lynn tried to be supportive of the over-looked blond-haired beauty, so reached her hand over and onto Delila's thigh, though unintentionally, a little too high and more on the inside than not. As she reached that area, the fold in Delila's wrap-around skirt slipped open and Lynn's hand touched the bare skin waiting there. Lynn paused her gesture, stunned at the touch of bare skin. Surprized at where her hand was pausing, she tried not to think about what lay so close to the exposed and unsheathed area. But Lynn could feel the smoothness, a softness, the curved shape over which her hand could easily slide further.

Delila's eyes seemed to waken to a world unknown. A glimmer of a smile touched her features as she looked at Lynn in the eyes, at first uncertain. But then, without resistance. Their eyes locked, rational thought was suspended, and some unexplainable subliminal permission was granted.

Lynn briefly got a grip on herself and thought, *I cannot do this; I must not do this. Toque is everything.* An urge stronger than her moral restraints took control. The result was that, rather than resting her hand as an intended gesture of support, Lynn's contact metamorphized into a subtle massage.

Toque noticed, and a glimmer of a smile surfaced. Inexplicably to the casual observer, Toque pretended she'd seen nothing, and reopened the topic of the nightmare at the daycare. "Well, at least Borya is locked up now ... and will likely be so for a long time."

Brock agreed. "Very likely. But we'll see: as you know, he's now talking. Along with his ranting at the daycare, we are now getting a serious amount of evidence from his crashed motor home that was towed out of McKay Creek."

"Right," added Toque, "We'll have a lot on him ... and the others ... from the combination of the oil leak locations, the fingerprinting, and the other lab work."

"Exactly," continued Brock, "With this mounting evidence, Borya knows that it is time to start trying to plea-bargain for any form of leniency – hoping for a break. But what amuses me, are those who are really talking now."

"Who?" asked Lynn, her voice cracking – betraying her aroused state.

Brock didn't seem to notice. "Borya's buddies, Egor and Ras, are now telling all from their prison cells. As soon as they found out that Borya was also caught and was implicating them, they're telling everything, hoping to cut a shorter sentence."

"But wait a minute, at the daycare ... didn't Borya say that ... you said the names were ... Egor and Ras ... had left the country ... stowaways on a freighter?" asked Lynn.

"He did," agreed Delila, looking at Lynn in the eyes as Lynn continued to move her hand along Delila's thigh.

"Unfortunately, Toque and I were barely conscious when Borya mentioned it. But we now know that the two fools thought that they were getting into a container for the shipping line Cosco. Unfortunately for them, they got into a Costco container of popcorn machines bound for Seattle. When the ship left English Bay, the two losers thought they were on their way to some distant land. But when the container arrived in Seattle, the Americans were really happy to send them back on the first non-stop bound for Canada.

"They're such disgusting, perverted creeps," scowled Toque.

"For myself, I'm glad they're back in prison. One can only hope that for Borya, a deportation to Siberia will be in the mix," remarked Delila frowning, though she flushed at the feeling of Lynn's hand running along her thigh. She glanced again at Lynn: her light brown eyes were inviting; her lips were a subtle but enticing shade of pink mixed with a warm golden sunset; and her short bleached-platinum hair with striking dark roots and sides was both mystifying yet exciting.

Lynn paused the stroking of Delila's leg and took off her fluffy-white-collared pink leather bomber jacket, revealing a silky black blouse under which one could anticipate a full-figure voluptuous torso just waiting to be caressed, just above a pair of tailored dark grey linen slacks, and matching slip-on shoes over sparkly socks. Her clear pink cheeks were a little flushed, and she seemed to carry with her the scent of clothing hung in the clean mountain air. Her moist lips parted, ever so slightly, as she turned to speak.

"It's unbelievable what evil he concocted from the Bible," remarked Brock.

"Yeah, exactly. But you know, I think that the plagues were like points of intersection: between our world and his evil mis-translations," said Toque.

"For sure: they were. But also, the flooding at the same time as the plan for the first born. Horrific. The worst intersection. Only a perverted mind like his could have come up with that," said Brock.

Lynn, mindful of Brock's words, remarked, "I get your point. Borya's actions were based on a total mis-translation. He twisted Bible stories into a hellish plan."

"No argument from us on that one," agreed Brock.

"It makes me think I'm ready for big change. More care for the planet, for sure, but also a change for myself," mused Delila.

"You're welcome to visit my Christian group, if you want," offered Lynn. Then, attempting to joke about it, added, "I haven't had any luck getting Toque interested."

Delila looked from Lynn to Toque. "If you don't mind, I'd really like that."

"Not a problem with me," smiled Toque and Lynn seemed particularly pleased.

But then the gravity of what had happened visited all four of them. And for a few minutes they sat in silence, thinking about how a faith tied intrinsically to good had been so misdirected. But then their minds wandered, to considering how they had survived Borya's ill intentions and how lucky they were to be sitting there together, as friends. And lovers. Lynn's hand returned to Delila's thigh.

"But," added Toque, "Another intersection we didn't think of was that it was likely Peanut who used Borya's vehicle to block the creek that caused the flooding. Although it was really climate change that got the whole thing moving. Another intersection."

"You're right," said Brock, "And I'm thinking that it's going to take a lot more than a few cops to go up against what's in store for us now."

The four returned to silence, considering the horror they'd all experienced.

Lynn thought about removing her hand. But didn't.

But then, thinking about how Lynn had saved her again, then again, Delila placed her hand on top of Lynn's who remembered as well: saving Delila. Lynn's whole core tingled again – in the memory of when she'd wrapped both hands, both arms, around Delila's amazing torso. Then with Delila's hand on top, but unseen under the table, Lynn's hand warmed and again returned to the gentle massage of Delila's inner thigh, her thumb accidently brushing that soft area that lay between her legs. Lynn smiled, tried not to beam, and to maintain a civilized conversation, asked, "But what happened to Petra?"

Toque raised an eyebrow, relatively certain that something was going on under the table on the other side. But she continued with the conversation, in any case. "Believe it or not, US Customs has a record of her and Peanut crossing the border in his car shortly before midnight on the 24th."

"Practically on Christmas Day! You're kidding! Those two? Together?" questioned Lynn, astounded.

Brock rolled his eyes in a gesture of I-can't-believe-it but added, "It seems that Borya demanded that Petra keep Peanut reined in on a free sexual favour tab to get his cooperation. They had him on a string! They could get him to do almost anything."

"But Petra said that she believed she was going to be Borya's wife!" exclaimed Delila, with a scowl, removing her hand from Lynn's.

"That's clearly over now, given that Borya's locked up. Now she's run off with Peanut. I guess what they had together wasn't all that bad, after all," observed Lynn as she moved her hand along Delila's upper leg.

Delila's lips parted in a subtle smile and with thoughts that seemed distant, sighed as she observed, "Right. It could be that she woke up and realized that Borya was past history and best forgotten, and that Peanut was like a breath of fresh air and was worth holding onto."

Lynn's hand continued to stroke Delila's leg, hoping that again there would be an accidental contact with that soft area that lay between Delila's legs. But then Lynn wondered if she needed to wait. Maybe she could move her thumb, again, and this time deliberately. Delila breathed deeper, focussing on Lynn targeting the zone.

There was a pause in the conversation.

Brock and Toque seemed as if they were about to speak but Delila cleared her throat and though a little hoarse, forced an observation. "Being truly loved may be all Petra really wanted: like everyone."

Delila turned to Lynn and their eyes locked. The two women then mentally looped out and entered the world of intense sexual attraction. They were as good as crash-test dummies sitting at the table. Oblivious to their intensity of emotion, Toque and Brock blithered on about the two that had escaped across the border.

"I agree with Lynn and Delila. Possibly Petra figured that Peanut was truly hers. Not shared or cheating or making horrible demands, like Borya. Although Peanut is just a kid and was involved in some questionable and gruesome stuff, he has potential. He is incredibly bright," surmised Toque.

"I guess," conceded Brock, "He did head up that group, To Advance Global Species."

"Yeah, and being young, and relatively inexperienced, he's certainly a much better catch than that corrupt piece-of-work, Borya. But it does seem incredible that he'd leave home and his last year of high school and probable scholarships for an uncertain future," mused Toque.

Brock glanced at the ceiling, but just couldn't resist the spelling out of the obvious answer. "He's male, seventeen and she's not bad looking and is willing. End of story."

"Oh!" Toque's eyes finally showed total understanding.

Brock's cell buzzed. He glanced at the screen, and then picked up. He listened to a few brief remarks and responded, "Crazy! Does his mother know?" More information from the other end of the phone line. And Brock continued, "Got it! No kidding! Okay. I'll talk to Toque about it. Thanks."

Lynn and Delila mentally returned to the table of four and all three women looked expectantly at Brock, though Toque noticed that Delila's hand was mysteriously missing under the table, as was Lynn's. It seemed that Delila and Lynn were breathing a little heavier, though trying to not let it show. They were zoned out.

"I need to talk to Toque outside about something that has come up. But I can tell all of you about what is soon to be public knowledge: Peanut and Petra just got married in Vegas!"

The jaws of all three women dropped.

Toque was the first to respond. "I can't believe it! They must have caught a short-hop flight as soon as they reached Bellingham after clearing the border!"

Then Lynn spoke. "But isn't he a minor?"

Toque shook her head. "He's seventeen, so he's legal although I'm not sure about Vegas but probably the marriage will stick one way or another up here in Canada."

"Boy, I'll bet that his parents are unimpressed!" exclaimed Lynn.

"You got that right! Mrs. Cudmore is on the rampage. She never liked Petra to begin with. But Toque, we need to talk for a bit – let's go into the foyer. Delila and Lynn, do you mind if we leave for … uh … say… twenty minutes – on cop business?"

Lynn smiled the smile of a cat that had just caught a mouse while Delila seemed as if she'd just been given a very special gift.

"Not a problem," the two dates replied, almost in unison.

"Take your time," added Lynn, while Delila just grinned.

Toque and Brock exited the dining area, grabbed their coats from the coat-check, soon to find Karimi and Sun waiting for them.

Karimi was abrupt. "You've got to come with us: it won't be long. Mrs. Cudmore is at the station demanding to talk to you two."

"Why us?"

"Mostly because on the 24th you were at the daycare for most of the incident," explained Sun.

"It can't wait," said Karimi as he moved closer to Toque.

"We're hoping you'll help get her off our backs. She's going berserk. Boucher and Trembley have Boxing Day off, so it was up to Karimi and I to make a run for you two," explained Sun as she squeezed herself between Karimi and Toque.

Karimi frowned, was about to say something, but then saw Sun's face beaming a quiet, but slightly mischievous smile. His frown changed immediately, as he suddenly recognised what was going on.

Toque looked at Brock; he at her. Inwardly, they chuckled at the moves being made between Karimi and Sun. But suddenly they, too, came to an awareness. They finally saw each other for what they were: extremely attractive members of the opposite sex. Together they smiled, but briefly, then gained the serious expression of going back to business as Toque said, "Okay. We'll go, but fifteen minutes. Max."

***

Forty minutes later, Brock and Toque re-entered the restaurant where they'd left their dates.

They had left the crazed Mrs. Cudmore, having settled her somewhat. They also gleaned the fact that Pearce had emptied his entire education savings account and moved it to an untraceable location. After all, the money was legally his to do with as he pleased, and he knew exactly what would please.

On their way into the waterfront restaurant, Toque and Brock dropped off their gear at the coat-check. Both were feeling better: their head-aches had cleared. The view from the restaurant was still spectacular: though a couple of wisps of clouds had wandered into the sky, the stars and the city lights were still gleaming.

But then, they entered the dining room, and were startled to see that their table was empty and set for two.

Brock paused at the restaurant host, and asked, "Did the two ladies at our table leave us a message?"

"No. Not really."

"Did they seem angry? We were away a little longer than we'd said."

"Not at all. They just said that you two would be back. Other than that, all I noticed was that they seemed extremely keen to be alone ... to make their dinner date truly memorable, if you know what I mean," responded the host with a wink.

Brock was astounded. "But they weren't ..."

But before he could complete his sentence, the host added, "Whatever, they're gone. They took their coats."

Toque and Brock looked at each other with a touch of bewilderment which was mixed with a tinge of relief that the double-date was over. But then they both emotionally prepared themselves for another night ... probably like the previous night: Christmas night – alone.

While Brock wasn't entirely on his own, as Rex was always a good companion, often Toque was most comfortable by herself where there was no threat of someone letting her down ... or worse. The result was that they were generally unbothered with the prospect of being on their own. But this night seemed different – possibly because of the strange reality of their dates running off with each other.

On other occasions, he chose to dodge the reality of Toque's appearance, but this night, with over-whelming clarity, he focused on Toque's amazing Botticelli's Birth-of-Venus-like body. No toque hiding her hair. This night her auburn locks were draping over her shoulders like that of an angel. And Toque ... Carol ... was dressed in a sleek red Christmas dress, and on a gold chain a small droplet of a pearl that was just an inch or so above her not-showy-yet-enticing cleavage ... her pale soft pink skin, her form so incredibly perfect. And those eyes: those soft blue-grey eyes with long dark eyelashes and perfectly arched eyebrows.

"You want to eat here, then, just the two of us?" asked Brock, hesitantly.

Carol looked at Brock: his warm amber skin; his thick wavy coal black hair and glanced down beneath ... at the sleek well-fitted vested black suit that she knew covered an amazing bod. She looked up and into his eyes that were the colour of a warm blue ocean. She hesitated as an over-whelming stirring – a kind of tingling sensation – grew in her very core.

It was then that, for Toque, Lynn became no more than a distant remembrance: their romance nothing more than a soft and misty memory.

Every person in the dining room was stealing glances or was outright staring at the two of
them. Had Toque and Brock been a couple, they would win an award for the best-looking twosome on the planet.

It seemed that Carol paused for several minutes or perhaps hours, as it seemed to Brock, and the question hung in the air like the subdued seasonal background music.

But then she answered with just a hint of a smile, saying, "Why not?" as she put her arm through Brock's, "But only if I later get to visit with Rex."

Brock smiled. "In that dress?"

Toque grinned back. "Absolutely."

And the two of them, arm in arm, drifted off, towards their waiting table.

Outside, illuminated by the light from the window, a couple of lacey snowflakes gracefully floated down, in front of the sparkling city on the other side of the bay.

Primary Characters

- Borya Morozov: criminal-at-large
- Brock Edwards: male protagonist, previous CSIS agent, RCMP constable, Toque's work partner
- Carol Burdon: female protagonist, nick-named Toque, RCMP constable, Brock's work partner
- Delila: Brock's live-aboard neighbour
- Egor and Ras Bogdanov: Borya's henchmen
- Joe: Toque's friend, from rock climbing
- Lynn Ashton: Toque's friend, from rock climbing
- Peanut (Pearce Cudmore): student at Rockwater Christian Secondary
- Petra: daycare worker at All Faiths Family Daycare
- Rex: Brock's dog
- Toque: see Carol Burdon (above)

ALL CHARACTERS

- Abraham (Captain): West Vancouver Police Chief
- Angela: Brock's infant child
- Alex Vasiliev: husband of Yana
- April: Brock's wife
- Blanchard, David: Professor and Yana's boss
- Borya Morozov: criminal-at-large
- Bothe (Principal): of Rockwater school
- Brock Edwards: male protagonist, previous CSIS agent, RCMP constable, Toque's work partner
- Brown: RCMP constable
- Boucher, Natalie: West Vancouver cop
- Carla Rivers: ex-wife of Lynn Ashton
- Carol Burdon: female protagonist, nick-named Toque, RCMP constable, Brock's work partner
- Elsie: child in daycare
- Grant (CO Grant): RCMP Commanding Officer
- Cudmore (Mrs.): Peanut's mom
- Delila: Brock's sexy live-aboard neighbour
- Egor Bogdanov: Borya's henchman, brother to Ras
- Gleb Oblonsky: Scheveningen inmate
- Joe: Toque's friend from rock climbing
- Karimi, Erv: West Vancouver cop
- Kliment Veronin: Scheveningen inmate
- Lakewood (Dr. Bella): lawyer
- Lev Kuznetsov: Scheveningen inmate
- Lynn Ashton: Toque's friend from rock climbing
- Marol Carrier: RCMP lab tech assistant manager
- Matthews: RCMP constable
- Matvey: son of Alex and Yana Vasiliev
- Muriel: owns the coffee shop frequented by cops
- Nikki: Lynn & Carla's daughter
- Peanut (Pearce Cudmore): student at Rockwater school
- Petra: daycare worker at All Faiths Family Daycare
- Ras Bogdanov: Borya's henchman, brother to Egor

- Rex: Brock's dog
- Rita: one of Brock's live-aboard neighbours
- Sandford Graham: CSIS director
- Scott: RCMP constable
- Singh: RCMP constable
- Sun, Lily: West Vancouver cop
- Toque: Carol Burdon (see above)
- Tremblay, Marcel: West Vancouver cop
- Vanna: daughter of Alex and Yana Vasiliev
- Yana Vasiliev: sister of Borya Morozov; husband named Alex, pre-school children named Matvey and Vanna

Another Toque and Brock Story:

AT LIONS GATE

Set in 2035, a United Nations-mandated task force struggles with assassinations of international cyber-intelligence workers. Meanwhile, in North Vancouver, Canada, a petty thief faces a related and unimaginable threat while attempting a robbery on the beat of constables Brock and Toque. The two cops soon discover a deeply troubling connection between the unsubstantiated confession by an eccentric woman, the elusive existence of a violent knife that seems to have otherworldly powers, and an emerging horrific terrorist threat. Adding to Brock and Toque's difficulties, is that their lives and recently assigned partnership is stilted by the fact that they were both profoundly wounded by horrible and cruel pasts.

Also titled **Valentine's Day At Lions Gate**.

Published at Amazon.ca
Copyright © 2020 JB Wall
ISBN: 9798648888593